ost Boys trilogy.

...it over the world, but for

...as and places that her mind can

HERTFO...

...works with illustration as well as the next

...e _Lost Boys_ series.

520 293 82 9

Also by Lilian Carmine:

The Lost Boys

THE
LOST GIRL

LILIAN CARMINE

EBURY
PRESS

1 3 5 7 9 10 8 6 4 2

Published in the UK in 2014 by Ebury Press, an imprint of Ebury Publishing
A Random House Group Company

Copyright © 2014 Lilian Carmine

Lilian Carmine has asserted her right to be identified as the author of
this Work in accordance with the Copyright, Designs and Patents Act 1988

This novel is a work of fiction. Names and characters are the product of the
author's imagination and any resemblance to actual persons,
living or dead, is entirely coincidental

All rights reserved. No part of this publication may be reproduced, stored in
a retrieval system, or transmitted in any form or by any means, electronic,
mechanical, photocopying, recording or otherwise, without the prior permission
of the copyright owner

The Random House Group Limited Reg. No. 954009

Addresses for companies within the Random House Group can be found at:
www.randomhouse.co.uk

A CIP catalogue record for this book is
available from the British Library

The Random House Group Limited supports The Forest Stewardship
Council® (FSC®), the leading international forest-certification organisation.
Our books carrying the FSC label are printed on FSC®-certified paper.
FSC is the only forest-certification scheme supported by the leading
environmental organisations, including Greenpeace.
Our paper procurement policy can be found at:
www.randomhouse.co.uk/environment

Printed and bound by CPI Group (UK) Ltd, Croydon, CR0 4YY

ISBN 9780091953423

To buy books by your favourite authors and register for offers visit:
www.randomhouse.co.uk

Chapter One

Ending with a Bang!

I walked backstage with my ears ringing and heart thumping hard in my chest. It was always like this after every show we did; the rush of blood to my head made me feel like I was having a wild hallucination. I never understood why so many of our musician friends needed drugs to get through a concert. I got all the rush I needed just by playing; hearing the crowd cheering and singing our songs at the top of their voices was enough. By the end of each of our shows, I felt as high as I could get. And I knew all my band felt the same way. Especially Harry and Sam – it took them a long time to calm down after our concerts.

I could still hear the crowd screaming as I walked backstage. Harry was tagging right behind me, jumping around and being as wild as usual.

"That was pretty outrageous, eh? This last show was raging!" he said loudly. Even this far backstage we could still hear Josh coming to the end of his drum solo, and Seth starting to say his goodbyes to the crowd.

"Yeah, it was insane!" I yelled back, but Harry couldn't

hear me over all the noise. He wrapped his sweaty arms around me and landed a smacky kiss on my cheek, and then let go of me as suddenly as he had grabbed me, whirling away like my own private hurricane.

Tonight had definitely been special. It was our last show of the tour and it had ended with an epic bang! And the crowd had been amazing. I had mixed feelings about the tour ending: even though life on the road could be very exciting, we'd been away from home for a long time.

Three years ago, my band, The Lost Boys, and I had been graduating school and our only worry was finding a way to keep Tristan with us. I had met Tristan, the love of my life, in a cemetery, one fine winter's day in December the previous year, and had fallen in love with him the second he'd flashed me his incredible smile. It had been love at first sight for both of us. He had the most stunning gray eyes I'd ever seen in my life. They shone with a silver edge around the corners, reflecting the sunlight in a mesmerizing mercury pool.

To begin with, I didn't know he was a ghost; he kept that a secret and I only discovered the truth during a New Year's celebration when we accidentally performed a spell that brought him back to life. But Tristan's ghostly past brought us many complications, and we found ourselves fighting for his very existence. We had a year – our last year of high school – to find a way to keep Tristan in the land of the living. For a boy who was originally alive during the 1950s, he actually adjusted remarkably well to twenty-first-century living. However, nothing could have prepared any of us for how successful our band became after we finished school. We landed a record deal soon after graduation and launched our first album by the end of that year. The Lost

Boys grew bigger and bigger in our home country with each passing year, and the release of our second album even looked likely to take the band to an international level of fame. That was what we were hoping for.

Tristan was living the dream with his second chance at life, cherishing every single moment. Our first year together had been an intense, scary rollercoaster, what with magic spells, the supernatural bond between us and the struggle to keep him alive. In the end, I struck a deal with Death – or, as I liked to call her, "Sky" – to get him back, and now he was safely in my arms. I not only had the most incredible, beautiful boyfriend – albeit an ex-ghost – by my side, but also the best band-mates of all time as well! My beloved geeky singer, Seth Fletcher; my goofy guitarist, Sam Hunt; my warrior drummer boy, Josh Hart; and my lovely bassist, Harry Ledger. Life couldn't get any better than this!

All these memories flashed through my mind as I followed Harry through a dark corridor towards the back security door that would take us outside to our tour bus. The walls around us shook a little with the vibration of all the stomping and shouting the crowd was still doing at the front of the stage.

Harry started talking excitedly to our personal security guards, Johnson and Jarvis, while we waited for the rest of the band to join us. It was sort of a tradition for us to leave the stage one by one, rather than en masse. Normally we'd then hang around to give the fans a little attention, sign some autographs, or allow them to take a few pictures, but today the crowd outside the venue was so dense, Johnson had insisted we head straight off after the concert.

"It's just a precaution, Miss Gray," he'd said reassuringly, after noticing my worried expression earlier.

Big Johnson, as we called our giant, muscled head of security, still insisted on calling me "Miss Gray", no matter how many times I had told him to call me Joey. He'd been with us for over two years now, and his cousin Jarvis had joined his team a year ago. Jarvis wasn't as tall or as impressively built as his cousin, but he was still big enough, with a habitual steely expression that most sane people would take as a warning not to get in his way.

I pulled my orange hoodie over my head, trying to prepare myself for the short but difficult walk to the bus. I could already hear the noise of overexcited fans waiting outside the exit door; it sounded insane!

As we continued to hover anxiously by the back door, Josh and Sam caught up with us, but Tristan and Seth were still finishing up onstage, delivering their final, parting words of the show. Jarvis opened the security door and rushed out, with Harry tagging closely by his side. As soon as the crowd realized one of The Lost Boys was in close range, the noise doubled in intensity. I hesitated for a second, but Big Johnson's towering presence reassured me that everything would be all right. I smiled up at him before running outside, where a voracious sea of screaming faces and bright flashes engulfed me in a blazing explosion of sound and light.

Chapter Two

Life on the Road

I watched as Josh and Sam climbed up into the bus a few minutes after me, their eyes wide with excitement after all the commotion outside. Harry hadn't moved from the window; he had his face glued to the glass, making funny squashed faces at the fans outside, even though they couldn't see him because of the tinted dark glass of the tour bus.

This year's tour had been crazy. We'd never had so many shows booked and had completely sold out during the final week. Our record label couldn't be more happy to be hitting the jackpot with The Lost Boys. The band was becoming a huge success considering we'd only been around for three or so years and had worked our way up from the bottom rather than being launched off the back of any reality TV show.

"Did you guys see all that?" Sam asked, his deep blue eyes wide in awe. "We almost couldn't get through the crowd!"

Tristan joined us a few minutes later, followed shortly after by Seth, our blond boy wonder; the whole band was now on board.

Our tour bus was a luxurious double-decker. The bottom deck was for bunk beds, bathroom and an area for a few of the crew to hang out. The top deck was just for us, the band, and it was kitted out with a long couch, TV and some video games for entertainment.

Harry finally gave up pulling funny faces at the fans and was now jumping onto Seth's back, making him stumble forwards a little, and Sammy was cracking up laughing at them.

Tristan peered out through the bus window, before turning towards me. He slumped, exhausted, on the couch, pulling me towards him and wrapping his big arms around me.

"You look beat," he murmured in my ear.

"You're one to talk." I laughed. "You look as beat as I do!"

He only smiled in reply, a weak, tired smile. Long concerts like today's always drained him. He was going to sleep like a log tonight. I lay my head on his chest, closed my eyes and sighed. All I wanted now was to go to our hotel, hit the shower and dive into bed. The prospect of a few hours' sleep sounded like utter bliss for my tired bones.

Jamie arrived a few minutes later, clutching the video camera that seemed to be permanently attached to his hands. Jamie was Josh's old friend from high school, a short, brown-haired, shy boy, who had been taken on as our media guy. He'd been hired to record our shows during tours, plus a few events and interviews we had to attend from time to time. Jamie was always around, always with his camera. He was also spookily quiet and sometimes we even forgot he was there at all.

Only a small group of people, just our closest friends, knew about me and Tristan being together, and Jamie was one of the chosen few. Our manager, Becca; my best friend, Tiffany, and our producer, Mr. Silver, also knew about us.

In our first year of the recording contract, Mr. Silver had asked the whole band to keep our relationship statuses a secret. His orders were to inform the media and press that we were all single, so our records would sell better. It was the first time we'd had a glimpse of how "ugly" this music business could get. It wasn't just about the music, Mr. Silver said; it was about being a good product to sell, for our record deal to be profitable.

At first we thought it was kind of wrong for him to ask that of us. Who could be that superficial? Wasn't our music enough for the fans to decide whether they liked us or not? What did being single or not have to do with selling our records? We wanted to make it as a band because of our music, not because of our looks or our supposed "availability".

But apparently we were very young and very naive. We didn't know how this business really worked, so Mr. Silver told us to let him take care of everything and we would do just fine. And since the boys – except Seth – weren't dating back then, they didn't seem to mind much. It was only Tristan who'd been really bummed about it. It seemed to him we were back at square one, trying to hiding our relationship all over again.

When we'd first met, Tristan and I had to pretend to be siblings so that he could get his application accepted at Sagan, the prestigious boarding school that I attended. With the birth certificate and other important documents that my mother had secretely arranged for him, with the help of some people in her law firm, Tristan was passed off as her own so that the school would take him. We didn't just lie to the school, though; we didn't think my mom would approve of us dating while living together under the same roof, so Tristan and I pretended to be just good friends for the whole of that year.

But then I managed to get Tristan back from the dead (again) and everything was brought out into the open. Mom found out the truth about our relationship and she was fine with it. We were finally free to be a couple. Then we started our first tour, only to be told by Mr. Silver to continue the lie about being "just friends" – just for a little while, until we had launched our careers.

Around that time, before the band's official debut concert, Tiffany helped Tristan to get all of his papers, legal documents and IDs bullet-proofed with the help of her family's name, power and influence. After the Worthingtons' lawyers were through with everything, there were absolutely no holes that any nosy reporter could find. Money could truly buy anything, we learned back then: even bringing the dead back into legal existence.

The heavy lifting had already been done, Tiffany used to say, when we'd made a ghost come back to life. Mere paperwork was an easy feat after that.

Three years have passed since then. Three years of smiling to reporters and lying through our teeth, and still it wasn't enough for Mr. Silver. After so many times repeating The Lie, I was now a master at this pretending game.

Tristan didn't like lying, though, and so had become skilled at deflecting The Question.

But for the past year or so, the rest of the band had started rebelling against these conditions. Seth was tired of sneaking out with Tiffany, a particularly hard feat since Tiff was also famous in her own right as she came from a wealthy family and was easily recognized everywhere she went. We managed to cover it up because as my best friend she was always around Seth anyway; sometimes I even had to hang out with them during their dates, so nobody would suspect anything. It sucked being the third wheel, and they hated it as much as I did.

But one day, at the beginning of this year, Tiffany decided she had had enough, and grabbed hold of Seth in front of a dozen paparazzi, kissing the living daylights out of him. Mr. Silver didn't say anything. He was no fool – Tiffany was a Worthington and it was not a clever move to have a public fight with the aristocracy.

Sammy was dating a beauty queen, Miss Amanda Summers. She was real pretty, sweet and looked like a doll. I didn't know much about her but Sammy liked her a lot and he was getting pretty grumpy about having to sneak out with her too.

Josh was always in and out of relationships, but never "in" for long enough to bother about having to lie to hide it. Still, he supported our rebellion because he was on our side, no matter what.

But it was Harry who was the second to break the deal with Mr. Silver. One sunny day, without a single warning, there he was in public, making out with Jackie Sunford, the lead singer of a rising pop rock band. Jackie was the complete opposite of Amanda: she had a truckload of bad manners in her arsenal.

For me, covering up my relationship with Tristan was fairly simple because he was also my band-mate and we were *supposed* to spend a lot of time together; we only needed to be careful not to be too intimate while we were out in public.

The crowd around the bus was still cheering when Becca, our super manager and all-round lifesaver, arrived announcing we were leaving for the hotel. Rebecca had been with us from the start of our first tour, keeping everything organized with her impeccable and efficient scheduling skills. Without her, we'd be completely lost.

I had a feeling our cameraman, Jamie, might have a little crush on her. Or maybe not. Jamie was hard to read. His eyes were usually blank, like his camera lens, recording everything he saw without thinking much about it.

The crowd continued screaming as the bus pulled away, and I could hear them chanting my name now. I was always surprised when they started doing that. I mean, I could understand that reaction to the boys in the band; they were all really handsome, young, fit guys. It was normal for teenage girls to go wild about hunks like that. But for them to do that for me? I couldn't undersand it.

I put the blame on Paul Brady. His talk show was one of the most important interviews we did in our first year. Mr. Brady was notorious for his teasing way of dealing with his guests, and that night he kept directing all his questions towards me. He was the first to start the joke about me being the only lost "boy" with "lady parts", and also about how I even had a boy's name to complete the act. The fact that I was kind of dressed like a boy at the time didn't help my case, either. Things started to escalate pretty quickly after Paul Brady's show. I was the headline in every gossip mag, the star of every chat show. "The only Lost 'Boy' that was a 'girl'." People thought it was amusing, and the line had a certain ring to it, so they kept repeating it everywhere. After that interview, I couldn't stand at the back of the band any more. People demanded that I was up front in the spotlight. Girls loved my tomboy attitude – they shouted "Lost Boy Power!" and "Joe Gray rocks!" everywhere I went.

Tristan laughed at my shock, saying I should stop trying to swim against the tide; it was a battle I was sure going to lose. It was "impossible not to fall in love with me", he would say.

The bus pulled up when we reached the front of the hotel Becca had booked for us, but there was no way we'd be able to go inside right away because another horde of fans was already waiting at the doors, blocking the path to the lobby.

"Man! How could all these people know we're staying here?" I cried in dismay, sensing that it would take us hours to get past all those groupies. I glanced sideways and spotted Seth looking shifty. When he noticed my scolding glare he shuffled on the spot and sagged his shoulders guiltily.

"Sorry, Joe. I may have been tweeting and … it kinda slipped out … Sorry!"

I groaned half-heartedly and took a deep breath, trying to accept our inevitable fate. Tomorrow we were going to be heading back home, so I supposed we could spend a few more hours with our fans.

"All right, then. Let's give them some love," I said, motioning everyone out of the bus.

We were in the middle of signing autographs, taking photos and giving hugs, when I grabbed Tristan as inconspicuously as I could and pushed him to one side.

"Tris, I'm going to sneak away and head into the lobby to get my room key. Becca just waved a signal that she's finished with the check-in," I whispered, glancing around to see if anyone was eavesdropping. "Boy, at times like this I bet you wished you still had your fading thing, eh?"

Tristan used to have this fading power for the first year after our New Year's spell – a sort of ex-ghost ability he brought back from the "deadland". He could fade into the background and be invisible to the human eye. Except to me: I could still spot him, even if it was just in a blurry, shifty kind of way. But after my deal with Death, when Tristan had earned another chance at living, he stopped being able to work his fading ability.

Tristan gave me a funny look at this comment and glanced away, but I couldn't quite decipher it. He was probably just as tired as I was. I was so intent on getting my room key, I immediately forgot about it.

"Okay, Joe. I'll make a diversion and you get inside. I'll be right with you," he said, looking away.

He sometimes sneaked out of his room during the night and crashed in mine when we were on tour.

"Okay. So, I'm going in. Cover me!" I said, hunching down and making a signal, as if I were in a war movie. He chuckled and nodded, walking away and preparing to create a diversion.

A few minutes later I was letting myself into my room, bags in hand and a relieved expression on my face.

"Hello, Joe," came a voice from somewhere inside the room.

I flinched, feeling my wrist start to throb, and clenched my hands into fists, glancing around quickly to see who it was but half guessing that I'd find the familiar face staring back at me.

"Hey, you almost gave me a heart attack!" I said.

"You know, we've talked about this. Don't just show up unannounced like that!"

"Sorry. I had forgotten," he replied.

"Tristan is coming up any second now. He won't like seeing you here."

"He does not like to see me anywhere," he pointed out in a logical, calm tone of voice.

I sighed loudly, too tired to have this conversation all over again. "Listen, now is actually not a good time to talk; I just got out of a really long show. Can we do this some other time?"

"I have important advice I need to ask of you, and since I am already here, maybe you can help me?"

I watched as he stared at me with intense, unblinking eyes, and sighed in defeat.

"Okay. We can talk *a little*," I said, putting emphasis on the "little". "But not here. Wait for me downstairs in the hotel bar. I'll come down as soon as I finish my shower. I don't want Tristan catching you here."

I walked to the bathroom without waiting for a reply, heading straight for my well-deserved shower.

This was going to be a long night …

Chapter Three

Hotel Bar

When I was out of the shower and dressed, I heard the door slam shut and Tristan's voice calling out to me. I glanced at my reflection in the bathroom mirror. A tired-looking girl stared back at me. I really wasn't in the mood to argue with Tristan right now, but I knew he was going to be upset about this. I just knew it.

He was lying on the bed when I came out of the bathroom, his bag by the foot of the bed and an exhausted look on his face. He was flipping through the channels on the TV, the sound on mute. Turning the TV on was always the first thing Tristan did when he got inside a room. He liked the flickering of the lights in the room and was always amazed by modern TV shows and special effects in movies, a technological novelty that never wore thin for his Fifties mindset.

"Hey. You're all dressed up to go out. Why?" he asked, raising one inquisitive eyebrow. "I thought you'd be in your PJs by now."

"I, um … I need to go out for a little bit. I'll be back real soon," I said, trying to avoid giving him too much information but at the same time answering his question honestly.

"Where are you going, then?" he asked, not satisfied with my answer.

"I've got to meet Vigil. He's waiting for me downstairs. I think it's something urgent, I don't know ..." I mumbled hurriedly, fiddling with my bag instead of looking directly at him.

"Vigil? He's here? And you're seeing him *now*? Why? It's really late, Joey," he protested, just like I knew he would.

Vigil had been our enemy for a whole year, the year after I first met Tristan, but then we became linked by the powerful spell that had brought Tristan back to life. Vigil was an unearthly being whose job was to restore order in the world, which effectively meant he had to return Tristan back to his ghostly state. He succeeded in this by the end of the year, as he was supposed to, but then, as my eighteenth birthday present, he helped me bring Tristan back again, by helping me to make a deal with Sky. I owed him for ever for that.

The awkward thing that became apparent at that time, though, was that Vigil had confessed to loving me, as much as a creature of his kind could: emotions did not come easily to him. We'd settled for being just friends, but it was something that still bothered Tristan. He never liked it when I went to meet Vigil. He was grateful for his help, but struggled to control his jealousy when Vigil was around me.

"Listen, Tris, it's just for a few minutes. I'll be right back," I insisted.

"You always say that. And you always end up spending

hours away, talking to him. What is it that you two need to talk so much about, anyway?" He huffed, exasperated, a disgruntled frown shadowing his face.

"He needs my help, Tris. I owe him; you know that. *We* owe him. And it's not only because of that. He's my friend. I'll help if he needs my help," I explained.

"But you don't have to go running like this every time he snaps his fingers. Like you're at his beck and call. That makes you more like a doormat than a friend." He muttered the last part to himself, but I still heard him.

That stung a bit. But I knew I shouldn't bite back now. It would only make him more angry.

I breathed in, trying to control my temper. "Tris, don't be like this. Listen, I already told him I would meet him. He's waiting downstairs. I'll be back in a minute, I promise."

"Yeah, right. Go, then. We don't want to leave him waiting, do we?" he jeered acidly. "And here, let me make this real easy for you, so you won't need to sneak guiltily back into the room tonight," he spat out, grabbing his bag. "I'm crashing in my own room. Have fun with your pal. Stay out as long as you want, I won't be in your way." Jealousy burned fiercely in his gray eyes and he stormed out of the room.

Tristan wasn't usually very jealous. He handled the male attention directed at me in a reasonably fair way. I knew he'd been brought up at a time of really conservative and old-fashioned standards, when men decided everything for women, but now he needed to get used to a modern way of life filled with independent, brave women, such as myself. But when the subject was Vigil, he always took a few steps back in his progressive development. At first he'd pretended he was okay with it, but as Vigil and I continued meeting, he grew restless. He knew Vigil "liked" me and he thought Vigil was only biding his time, he said – that he was just waiting for the perfect moment to steal me away.

At that point, I would always ask Tristan if he didn't trust me. Vigil could "try to steal me" all he wanted, but I still had to agree to it. How could he possibly think I would ever betray him like that?

But jealousy wasn't about logic or reasoning. It could take you over and make you say horrible things, do horrible acts. As the Bard would say, "Trifles light as air are to the jealous confirmations strong." And everything I ever said about Vigil, even the way I said it, became a confirmation of Tristan's suspicions. Sometimes he wouldn't even say a word, but I could see the look in his eyes: the fear and anger of losing me growing inside. I could see it taking root, gnawing at his heart, like a viciously wicked worm.

But I couldn't let Tristan's jealousy control me. He needed to understand that he must trust me and that Vigil was only my friend.

I followed him out of the room but Tristan had already disappeared. Riding the elevator to the ground floor, I stepped out into a grand hallway, which I wandered along until I reached a more intimate, dimly lit room. Tables were spread around and a small bar was nestled in the farthest corner. As soon as I stepped into the room, I recognized the never-failing pain throbbing in my wrist – just like it had done back upstairs in my room. I fisted my hand again, trying to make the pain lessen. It was always this way when Vigil was around and it was how I knew he was nearby.

The pain was a side effect from some high-level magic I had accidentally performed while trying to protect Tristan – without having any practical experience or knowledge of what I was actually doing. The end result was a black marking tattooed on my wrist and, whenever Vigil was in my proximity, the constant pain. The only way to make it stop was skin-to-skin contact from Vigil – something Tristan particularly hated seeing.

Whenever Vigil realized I was suffering he would always try to hold my hand or lean over me, trying to touch me any way he could so the pain would stop. He didn't mean anything by it; there was no covert intention in his touch, but that didn't stop Tristan from being royally pissed about it.

The room was practically deserted: only a middle-aged man was drinking alone at one of the tables next to the bar. And then I spotted Vigil's slim silhouette, sitting at the other side of the room. His hands were crossed and resting on the table in front of him, and he gave the impression of waiting patiently. As I approached him, and before he noticed me, I could see that his eyes were glazed over, as if he was focused on something far, far away from this reality. With Vigil, that might well have been the case. Who knew what kinds of realities Vigil was capable of seeing?

I sat down at the other side of his table, which made him jump a little, startled by my sudden appearance. Vigil was normally very alert to his surroundings, but today he seemed distracted.

He was wearing his usual clothes: an impeccable dark-gray suit. His stern and formal dress sense seemed at a disconnect with the softness of his delicate features.

Vigil could control his physical appearance and, given this ability, he had tried to match his age to mine. As I grew older, so did he. The changes were subtle, though; he still looked very much like the boy I remembered from when we first met. His black hair still fell over an angelic, pale face, and the steely glint of his black eyes still pierced my own. His stare was cold and sharp, always vigilant and analytical. That stare alone made everybody approach him with a certain caution and a small sense of fear.

Vigil was still trying to understand human behavior, and his physical movements and verbal phrasing were slightly affected by what he had so far learned from us. The ways of humanity offered a difficult puzzle for him to solve and it was one of the topics we usually discussed.

"Hello, Joe." He smiled faintly, watching me as I sat across from him.

"Hey," I greeted him back. "So, Vigil, wassup?"

"Excuse me?" His expression was puzzled at my question. I usually avoided using slang whenever speaking with Vigil. He was very literal-minded.

"I mean, what is going on? What do you want to talk about?"

"Oh, yes," he said, unfrowning his face. "You see, I have this new job …" he began.

Ah. *The job*. Vigil's job. That was another regular topic of our long meetings. Vigil liked to discuss his various assignments with me. He said I was good at understanding chaotic things, and how they would turn out. His race had a very strict and narrow-minded way of seeing things, so I provided a more flexible reasoning and a human perspective, and somehow it helped him fix whatever needed to be fixed.

I was his "Consultant on Chaotic Affairs". His "Expert on Unstable Matter".

The thing was, after Vigil started "consulting" with me, he also started getting better at his job. Like, a lot better. His levels of efficiency rocketed sky high and he was now becoming renowned for it among his "colleagues". Now he was *The Guy* you called when you needed help.

"… and it is giving me some grievance," he continued. "I can't manage to get a grip on this one; it is a sneaky little thing. Maybe you can find something I'm overlooking?" he said, putting his hands on top of mine in a gentle, familiar gesture. The throbbing pain in my arm stopped immediately.

"Okay. First I need to ask you: Is this new job dangerous, Vigil?"

"I don't know what you mean by that," he said. After I rolled my eyes impatiently, he added, "You mean, dangerous for me?"

I sighed and glared at him.

"No. Hardly anything is dangerous for me," he continued. "Now, for you, I have to say yes. But *everything* is dangerous for you humans. Staying in the sun for too long is dangerous for you. Not drinking water is dangerous for you. Bleeding for more than a minute is also very dangerous—"

"Okay, okay. I get it! Everything is dangerous for us. We are a very weak species," I snapped, annoyed. "So, it is not dangerous *for you*, then?" I stated, watching him as he nodded an affirmative. "Is it urgent? Like, it needs to be solved in a few hours tops, urgent? Or do you have some time to work on this?"

He thought for a minute, probably contemplating the differences in the time lapse between his reality and Earth's reality, so that he could figure out what I meant by a "few hours". Sometimes talking with Vigil was very complicated. It could get so philosophical and metaphysical that it would give me a heavy migraine.

"I have 'some time' to deal with it," he answered cautiously.

"Some time, as in …?" I asked.

"Well, now, that is a tricky question, you see, because time is a very relative concept when you consider—"

"OKAY! All right! I know where this is going, and I'm so *not* going there right now!"

He gave me a baffled look.

"What I meant to say is, if this new job is neither dangerous or urgent, can we please discuss it some other time? I am exhausted right now. Us 'weak humans' need to rest, remember? If we don't sleep, our brains don't operate properly, and I can't really help you when I'm tired like this …" I hunched over in my seat and rubbed my eyes.

"Oh. I see. Okay, Joe, I understand. We can talk later."

I smiled weakly. "I'm sorry I'm not in the best place to help you right now," I apologized, standing up.

"That's perfectly understandable," he said, standing too. "We will talk about it later and you can help me then, right?"

I nodded and gave him a quick goodbye hug. As usual he tensed a little, but I had already let go before he could do anything about it. He was never a fan of people invading his personal space.

"Goodbye, Joe," he said, taking a step back.

"Night, Vigil." I yawned and waved one last goodbye before walking away.

I stepped inside the elevator in a gloomy mood, the fight with Tristan back in my mind.

When I reached my door, my attention was drawn to something that had been placed in front of it, on the floor.

I crouched down and picked it up. It was a white lily, my favorite flower. A black ribbon was tied around its stalk with a little note attached to the ribbon. It read:

> *A beautiful white to a beautiful Gray.*
> *From your devoted and most loyal*
> *Secret Admirer.*

I glanced around, but there was no one in the deserted corridor. It was probably from a fan, I thought to myself. They sometimes managed to get past hotel Security and left gifts at our doors: stuffed bears, boxes of chocolate. We also received piles of letters, and sometimes we were sent flowers, like this lily.

I walked inside my room and could hear the TV blaring out, accompanied by Harry's laughter. He was lying on the bed, shirtless and wearing only his loose jeans, watching some cartoon.

I crossed the room to lay my flower on the nightstand before slumping down next to Harry.

"So, I guess he really is staying in his room tonight, then," I mumbled.

"Yeah, I saw him storming past and thought I should check on you and see what had happened."

"How angry was he?" I asked in a small voice.

Harry eyed me with sympathetic green eyes. "He just needs some time to chill. He'll be back to his normal self soon."

"I only said I was going out to talk to Vigil for ten minutes and he blew a gasket," I muttered, upset.

"He does have a point, though, Joe. You *do* go running every time that dude calls you."

I leaned away from him and crossed my arms, affronted. "So, you're taking his side, is that it?"

Harry raised his hands in an appeasing gesture. "Hey! I'm not taking any sides. But if the big man is feeling a little 'uncertain', you should put him at ease, you know, let him know he's the number one guy in your life."

In other words, set your priorities straight, Joe Gray. Boyfriend comes first. Unearthly-being friend, second.

"I have to confess to you, I'm not much a fan of the little dude myself," Harry said, biting his bottom lip.

I rolled my eyes. "He's not *little*. He's about the same height as you and Seth."

"Pssht! He wishes. He's way smaller than me, and thinner. And weaker," he teased, flexing his biceps at me. "Oh, and uglier too!"

I grabbed a pillow and stuffed it over his face, straddling his lap at the same time. He laughed then pretended he was suffocating. Then I felt his body go limp beneath me and I heard a muffled "You killed me!" from underneath the pillow.

I tossed the pillow away and poked him in the chest. "Stop. Picking. On. Vigil."

He grunted. "All right. Gosh, you're such a bully!" he complained and prepared to get up from the bed. "Now that I see that you're okay, I'll be going ..."

"No! Please, don't leave! Can't you stay with me for a little while? You can at least finish watching your cartoon," I urged, giving him a pleading look. I didn't want to be alone in the room after my fight with Tristan. I knew I would just keep thinking about it and feel awful, and Harry's company would help me feel a little bit better. He sat back and settled next to me, making himself comfortable on the bed.

I curled up around his arm and rested my head on his chest as we watched the TV show together in silence. Harry was always there for me whenever I had a fight with Tristan; just his reassuring presence was enough to help me.

Tristan was still on my mind as I fell asleep by Harry's side.

Chapter Four

Home, Sweet Home

I woke up in a panic, startled by a series of loud bangs. I blinked, confused, and sat up in bed quickly, trying to work out what was going on. Where was I? What time was it? Who was banging on the door like that, for crying out loud?

I swept a look around the hotel room. Ah, okay. Hotel room. That was one question answered already. Harry was still sleeping peacefully beside me, his green and red tattoo snaking over his chest and shoulder. What I finally recognized as Becca's muffled voice and continuous banging finally made me snap out of my sleepy daze.

I leapt up and ran to the door before she could break the damned thing, and threw it wide open. Becca was indeed on the other side, her fist raised ready to pound again, while Jamie stood right behind her, holding two cups of coffee.

"About time, Joe Gray! I've been calling you on the phone and banging on this door *for ever*," she shouted, exasperatedly. "Everybody is anxious to get back home, you know. Only you and Harry aren't ready to go. Jamie, give her the coffee. We're leaving in ten minutes. Hurry up and get Harry ready!" she exclaimed and turned around, speedwalking to the elevator.

I nodded, even though Becca wasn't even there any more, and then rubbed my eyes, trying to wipe the sleep away. I still felt so tired. Jamie cleared his throat, a small smirk twitching at the corner of his mouth.

"Here, for you and Harry," he said, handing me the two cups, and then added smartly, "You look hot waking up."

I snorted loudly and in a very unladylike way, thinking that no way in hell would I look good waking up with my bird's nest hair and the morning breath of doom.

Jamie shrugged, like he had been enjoying the view very much, no matter what I thought of it, and then gave me a short nod before retreating back into the hallway.

I closed the door, holding the two cups of coffee, and then it hit me properly that Harry had fallen asleep beside me last night and had never left the room. He was still sleeping right there on the bed, even after Becca's thunderous knocking a minute ago. I shuffled towards him and put the coffees on the nightstand, watching him sleep. Harry could sleep through a hurricane and not be disturbed by it.

I passed my hand softly over his face, brushing aside some of his long blond bangs. He blinked and looked at me through half-open eyes.

"Hey, Harry Bear," I said quietly. "We need to get ready and leave. Everybody is waiting for us. We overslept."

He nodded but made no effort to move, merely blinking lazily at me. Harry was never much of a morning person. He usually woke up in "quiet mode" and needed to gulp down copious amounts of food and coffee before he was ready to talk.

"Here, some coffee for you, sweetie," I said, handing him one of the cups. He leaned on his elbows to sip at the coffee and I ran to the bathroom to get myself ready.

When I came out dressed in fresh clothes, Harry had already left for his room to get ready as well. We met in the lobby a few minutes later, ran together to the bus and climbed up to the second floor to find everybody spread around the couch, waiting patiently for us.

"Finally!" Sam greeted us, clapping his hands in celebration. "We were considering leaving without you two," he exclaimed, ruffling his brown curls. And then he teased, "I mean, who needs a bass player really? And Joey ... what is it that you do in this band again?"

"Shut up, numbnuts," I grumbled, swatting at him and then slumping down on the couch next to Josh. Harry did the same on the other side and we both rested our heads on Josh's shoulders.

"How can you two still be tired? You've had more sleep than everybody else in here!" Josh mused with a chuckle.

"Hrumphrgh," Harry and I grunted in unison.

I peeked in Tristan's direction. He was staring at the TV, watching some program intently. My gloomy mood increased considerably. He was avoiding looking at me and I could tell he was thinking that I was still tired because I had been out with Vigil all night long. He didn't know I'd been back in the room *ten freaking minutes later*. I couldn't even tell him to ask Harry for confirmation, because then I would have to explain about Harry sleeping in my room, in the same bed as me, as well. He was not going to be very pleased about that, either. I huffed to myself. I didn't want to make things worse than they already were.

The bus's engine started running and Harry stood up,

announcing he was going to crash in his bunk on the bottom deck for a while. Shortly after, Tristan followed. I rolled my eyes as I watched him leave, still avoiding eye contact with me. I could tell he was still mad about Vigil. For how much longer was he going to give me the cold shoulder?

I stared at the TV until I couldn't any longer, becoming drowsy with the rumbling of the bus lulling me into sleep. I headed downstairs and as I reached the last step I could hear Tristan's voice drifting through from where he and Harry were talking by the bunk beds; instinctively, I stopped to listen.

"I'm telling you, man, she was really upset last night. She said you flipped pretty bad on her," came Harry's voice.

I heard Tristan huff loudly. "I know. I was in a bad mood. She said she was so tired but then the next minute she was scampering away all happy to meet him."

He had a point. Maybe it was time to listen to Tristan. I made a promise to myself that as of today, I would stop running off to meet Vigil the second he called. And I would stop "touching" him, too, even if it meant being in constant pain around him. If it made Tristan that upset, I would stop it. I could endure some pain for the sake of our relationship.

"And something happens to me when I hear his name," Tristan continued. "I just lose it. I just stop thinking – I don't know why! You know I'm not usually like that. I woke up today feeling really bad about everything I said last night ..."

"Look, man, just apologize, all right? And you'll be fine. Joey never holds a grudge. She's got a good heart."

"I know. I will," Tristan conceded quietly.

I left them talking and climbed back up the stairs quietly. I didn't need to hear anything further; my heart already felt lighter.

Back on the couch, I sat beside Sam. But again, after a few minutes spent looking at the screen, my eyes were so heavy that I gave up trying to keep them open and let myself drift off to sleep. I could hear the boys muttering about something on the TV, and a breeze blowing in from an open window brushed my face. My whole body felt as heavy as lead.

And then I felt someone holding my head softly. Sam shifted away and someone else took his place on the couch. I didn't need to open my eyes to know who it was; I knew his scent from miles away. Tristan started running his fingers through my hair, which was his favorite habit. I loved when he did it too.

I snuggled comfortably in his lap as he hummed a song.

In that moment, just like that, everything was forgiven.

I drifted back into a deep sleep, all voices and feelings fading away into oblivion. I didn't know how long I was out but when I woke up, Tristan was nudging me softly. My eyelids fluttered open and I looked up at his handsome face. He, in turn, smiled back at me.

"We've stopped to grab some lunch. Everybody is outside," he said, quietly.

"Oh. Okay. It's past noon already?" I mumbled, rubbing my eyes.

"Yeah."

I hauled myself upright, trying to shake the grogginess away. I felt stiff and my body was aching all over. That couch was really no good to sleep on; my back was going to hurt like a bitch tonight.

"Listen, Joe," Tristan began hesitantly, trying to find the right words. "About last night … I'm sorry. I was out of line. I shouldn't have said the things I said—"

"Tristan, it's all right," I said, cutting him off. "Seriously, it's okay. I shouldn't have gone to meet him yesterday. You were right, I act like a doormat sometimes."

"No, Joe. I was upset, I didn't mean …" He passed a hand over his black hair in frustation. "Listen, you're not a doormat. You have a good heart and you were just trying to help. You always try to help people. You're a good person, I should never have turned it into a bad thing. It was wrong of me, I'm sorry. Can you forgive me?"

I hugged him tight. "I'm glad you're not mad at me any more," I whispered. He shifted so he was facing me, our noses touching.

"Love you," I whispered, giving him a light peck on the lips.

"I love you too, Buttons." And he came back for a longer, deeper kiss.

Tristan and I had been together for three years, give or take, but his kisses still made me melt under his lips. I'd thought it was something that only happened at the beginning of relationships, that this euphoric feeling would eventually pass when we got used to each other, and we'd settle down and sail into calmer waters, but he still managed to cause havoc inside of me.

"Now, come on. Let's get you lunch. If we don't hurry, we'll miss it, and you've already missed breakfast. At this rate you'll end up a skeleton," he said, standing up and extending his hand to me.

"Why eat if we can survive on luuuurve?" I teased, pinching his side.

"Yeah, yeah. You can love *and* gobble down some food at the same time, buttercup. Let's go," he said, tugging me downstairs.

"Got her to wake up, then?" Jarvis asked as we passed him on our way to the store.

"Hey, Jarvis. Yeah, it's really hard to wake Sleeping Beauty here," Tristan joked, interlacing his fingers with mine and pulling me along.

The drive home was quick afterwards and we soon arrived at the house's front lawn. I dropped my bags loudly on the floor as soon as I stepped inside.

"Honey! I'm home!" I shouted to the air.

Tristan came up behind me, wrapped his arms around my waist and rested his chin on my shoulder. His warm breath tickled the side of my face.

"I'm right here, you don't need to shout!" He chuckled and gave me a kiss behind my ear. "Good to be home," he murmured, surveying the living room.

Here we were: home sweet home.

Or as we liked to call it: "The Lost Boys Headquarters".

The Lost Boys Headquarters was a big, comfortable, two-storey house with six bedrooms – one for each Lost Boy – two guest rooms for visitors, a small but comfortable kitchen, a big, airy living room, music room – plus our private studio – and a small gym.

Mr. Silver had arranged the living situation for us. Putting us all under the same roof kept things a lot easier and also saved time; things were a lot faster to organize with everybody in the same house. It sure made Becca's life a lot easier, too.

We'd been sharing the house for three years and I loved

having the boys as room-mates. I was already used to sharing living quarters with Seth and Tristan from our last year of school; the only difference now was that we had Sam, Harry and Josh along with us. Living with them was amazing and the most fun I had ever had! We all respected each other's space and moods, so if someone was a little cranky, we tried to leave them alone; if someone was sad, we tried cheering them up; and if someone was happy, we all celebrated together. We took care of each other.

Also, we weren't in Esperanza any more. We lived in the same city as the base for our record label.

But the best part of living here? It was miles away from all our moms!

I mean, *really* far away. Don't get me wrong, I love my mom, as well as the boys' parents, but they could be a bit overbearing sometimes. We were on our own and loving every *second* of it!

I walked up the stairs and headed to my room so I could dump my stuff.

My room was more like a gigantic personal closet. I mostly used it to pick up clothes rather than sleeping in there. The room was also everybody else's storage room: Josh's old practice pads were in there, with a few pieces of his drum kits lying around; Sam and Seth's old guitars were laid in a corner, and a bunch of other junk was spread haphazardly over the carpet.

"Hey, you people!" I could hear Seth shout from downstairs. "Just got a call from Becca saying she'll be over here soon to go through our schedule for tomorrow. She will be here after she sorts out some things."

The tour was officially over, but we still had a few promo events to attend before we were officially free for our much-dreamed-of summer vacation.

"Oh, and just so you know, I'm not cooking tonight!" he added.

The doorbell rang, shortly followed by a high-pitched shriek. It vaguely resembled my name being called out, but in an inhumanly shrill way. I swear a few dogs even started barking in response.

Before I'd even made it to the top of the stairs, a towering blonde hurricane tackled me like a professional wrestler. I could feel my bones being crushed under her arms.

"Joooeeeyyyyyy!" she squealed at the top of her voice.

"Tiffany!" I screamed back, and laughed.

Tiffany Worthington the Third. Multi-millionaire. Fabulously blonde, beautiful, fierce and smart. Also, my best friend in the whole wide world.

"I can't believe you guys are already here," she said, squeezing me one more time. "I missed you soooo much, Jo-Jo!"

"I missed you too, Tiff," I said, pinching her cheeks.

"Hey! What about *me*? I'm the boyfriend, you know," Seth whined.

"I missed you … more or less," she said, and then ran and tackled him with a bearlike, crushing hug, subjecting him to a flurry of kisses all over his face.

"OKAY! OKAY! Broken rib here," he squeaked, grinning.

Tiffany sometimes tagged along with us for a few shows, but she was too busy working on her own fashion line to be with us all the time. "Where's Dad?" she asked me, as we made our way back downstairs. She meant Tristan. "Dad" was due to the fact that every time there was a major rumpus, Tristan was always the one to restore order to the room.

"Right here, Miss Worthington," he said, walking over to Tiffany and giving her a big hug.

Sam, Harry and Josh joined us in the living room, where we all sat on the couch, chatting excitedly about our last days of touring. We were interrupted when Sam's girlfriend, Amanda, arrived. She let out a girly squeak when she saw Sammy, and hugged him for what seemed like fifteen minutes.

Harry went to the kitchen to answer the phone. I watched as he leaned against the wall with his back to us. I knew who he was speaking to.

Jackie Sunford. They had been together for a year now. My lips pursed involuntarily just at the thought of her. It wasn't that I didn't like her per se, it was just that I didn't like what she did to Harry. For a start he was more serious when she was around. He stopped doing the silly things he did when he was just with us; he stopped being *himself*. I could see his posture shifting already, just by talking to her on the phone.

Tristan chuckled and shook his head at me, telling me I was just being jealous – that I was very possessive of Harry.

Jealous. Pfft. Maybe I just didn't like what Harry became when he was with her. He changed, and not for the better.

Jackie never wanted to hang out at our house. She knew I would be here and I don't think she liked me that much, either. I could always see the animosity flickering in her eyes, the resentment. Especially after some rumors that Harry and I had had "a fling" started to circulate. She hated it when I was near him, and that turned out to be a major issue since Harry and I were room-mates, co-workers, best friends and spent all our time together traveling. This meant "us" living together, sharing bunk beds and hotel rooms, working and playing together, and hanging out in our free time.

Harry struggled to keep his both love life and our friendship intact. He really liked her, and he was trying to make things work. But it was difficult, and after a year together it was beginning to take its toll.

I was always walking on eggshells around Jackie because I didn't want to hurt Harry's feelings. It was like trying to relax with a ticking time bomb by your side. *Tick tock.* No sudden movements. *Tick.* Keep a neutral face. *Tock.* Stay away from Harry. *Tick.* You don't want to piss her off. *Tock.*

It was only a matter of time before the explosion ...

After a few minutes of hushed conversation, he hung up and went to his room. Minutes later he was dressed up all handsome and ready to leave.

"I'm going out to meet Jackie. Talk to you later," he said in a hurry, waving goodbye and closing the front door after himself.

The rest of us stayed home, chatting and chilling. Becca came over to discuss our schedule, telling us about the autograph signing we were scheduled for tomorrow in a famous bookstore downtown. When evening came, we ordered some food for dinner. It was a peaceful and uneventful night.

After dinner, we all said our goodbyes and I went straight to the bathroom to take a hot shower. Tristan relaxed in the bed, watching TV.

As I turned off the shower I caught a glimpse of a shadow outside the bathroom.

"Tris?" I called out, watching as the foggy shadow advanced towards the bathroom door. I peeked out of the cubicle, sweeping my wet hair out of my eyes. There was no one there. "Tristan? Is that you?"

No reply. Maybe Tristan had gone to the kitchen to grab a glass of water or something. I stepped out of the shower, dried myself and then put on my comfy PJs. When I walked into the bedroom, all the lights were out and Tristan was fast asleep in the bed, the TV lights flickering softly over his face.

As I looked around the room I noticed that the door was open. I was sure I'd closed it before going in the shower, but maybe I just thought I had. I walked into the hall and leaned over the landing banister, surveying the living room downstairs. The lights were out: the house was quiet and peaceful. I squinted my eyes. Nothing moved; from up here, the room didn't look any different than normal. I shrugged and went back to my bedroom. Maybe I was too tired and my mind was playing tricks. It was nothing …

So why I couldn't shake off this eerie feeling?

I shut the door behind me and locked it. We had a pretty good security system in the house, but it was better to be safe than sorry.

I scuttled under the covers and took the remote out of Tristan's hands. I turned off the TV, leaving the room in near-darkness, the only light coming from a small beam which slippled through a slit in the blinds. My eyes were just adjusting to the dark when I saw a shadow moving by the wall on the other side of the room.

The floorboard gave a tiny squeak. I started to freak out.

Shadows weren't supposed to make any noise, right?

I reached out for the lamp on my nightstand, almost knocking it over in my urgency to switch it on. The light flickered and then bathed the room in its soft, reassuring glow. I glanced urgently around the room.

There was nothing there. I bit my lip, contemplating waking Tristan up. But then I just felt stupid, like those useless wimpy girls in horror movies that can't do anything by themselves. I didn't need to call Tristan. What was he going to do, anyway? Look around and find nothing, like I just had? It was just shadows playing in the room, I told myself; totally normal shadow behavior. And houses always made odd noises. I sat on the bed and huffed, annoyed at myself for being such a wimp. I'd never been scared of the dark before. I was Joe Gray. I wasn't scared of *anything*. So why I was still freaking out about this? This was just plain stupid.

"This is seriously pissing me off," I mumbled under my breath.

And suddenly, as if by magic, the eerie feeling left me and I felt a whole lot calmer. The room was just ... a room. No evil shadows lurking in the dark, no wicked things going bump in the night. I smiled contentedly and pulled the covers up to my neck, getting myself comfortable at Tristan's side.

He shifted and turned over, wrapping one arm around my waist. I snuggled into him, and a part of me was a little ashamed for feeling much safer now that he was holding me in his arms.

I breathed deeply, relaxing myself. If there were more evil shadows or mysterious noises in the room, I wasn't aware of them, because within seconds I had drifted into a deep sleep, safe and sound in Tristan's arms.

Chapter Five

Kitchen Love

I tried to move but I wasn't fast enough. He grabbed a hold of my collar with a tight, vicious grip, and I knew I was doomed.

There was a reason why you never let Josh get a hold of you. Because if you did, there was no way you could weasel your way out of his steel-like grip. I tried anyway, but lost my balance, landing on my back on the mattress with a loud bump.

"*Whooof!* Ouch, Josh! Take it easy, will ya?" I yelled at him.

I was mostly annoyed at myself for being this out of practice. But it was hard to train during tours, so we always resumed our martial arts practice when we were back at home. Josh and I both had black belts so we never got too rusty.

I woke up really early, leaving Tristan sleeping comfortably in my bed, to go looking for Josh because I knew he would be up too. Josh was always an early riser.

I was beginning to regret the idea, though. My moves were so slow. We had only been training for a few hours and I was already sweating buckets and feeling pretty out of breath. Josh was going to kick my butt all day long at this rate.

"Come on, Joey. You can do better than this," he taunted me.

Huffing, I grabbed his hand and he helped pull me up. He had tossed me on the mattress, like, a hundred times already and I hadn't managed to take him down one single time yet! *Damn him.*

As he made sure I was back to standing position, I took advantage of this momentary distraction and swiftly moved to his side, grabbing his elbow while pushing my entire arm against his neck, making him stumble back and lose his balance. Now, it was his turn to fall back on the mattress.

"YES!" I shouted smugly. "I win! I'm the man!" I laughed, raising both my arms in the air and doing a quick wriggling victory dance.

The celebration didn't last long, though, because Josh swept his legs at my feet. I tried to jump over them, but only one foot was fast enough; I was on my butt in the blink of an eye. He landed on top of me, pinning me down, and leaned close to my face with a wicked grin.

"Who's the man, *now*?" He reveled in his moment of triumph. Served me right for gloating in his face and doing a silly victory dance just because he fell once.

"Oh, *puh-lease*. Who says being 'the man' is a better thing anyway? Being a girl is just as good," I scoffed, and pushed him away from me. I was officially done with training for today.

"What? Quitting already?" He laughed. "Don't be a baby, Gray. Just because I'm epic at all martial arts doesn't mean you can't be some day, too! And hey, there's always second place on the podium."

Josh was the most competitive boy I knew. "Good, you can have that spot. I'm just rusty now, but you wait until I'm back on form and climbing to that epic first place, drummer boy!" I huffed before storming out of the gym room.

Losing non-stop tended to put a dampener on my mood. Josh's relentless banter wasn't helping improve matters, either. I headed into the kitchen with a thunder cloud above my head. I found Tristan sitting on a kitchen stool at the table, twisting his spoon over a big cup of tea. He was wearing his usual black sweatpants and white singlet shirt, hair all roughened up and a thin stubble darkening his jaw. He looked sexy. Even when he'd just got up in the morning, Tristan looked annoyingly good. And it wasn't just me who thought it. An article once ran photos of him and discussed: "Does Lost Boy Tristan always look this good?" It was published in a teen magazine and afterwards the boys kept teasing him with "Wonderboy" and "Looking good". But the fact remained that he did indeed always look this good. You could get him exhausted, sweaty, soaking wet, hungover, and he still managed to look effortlessly well put together. Everybody in the band had occasional unflattering moments caught on camera, but Tristan … Tristan was in the Greek Pantheon of Gods department. It was very irritating.

"Hey, good morning, sunshine," he greeted cheerfully. His face fell after taking a good look at my face, and he corrected himself: "I mean, good morning, thunderous black clouds of doom and gloom."

"Oh, ha ha. Hilarious," I snapped.

"You and Josh done training? I could hear a lot of noise

coming from there. Sounded like an exciting training session."

"Yeah. If by 'exciting' you mean getting my ass repeatedly kicked, then yes, sure," I mumbled, slouching on to the stool next to him.

"I can try to make this morning a little more exciting for you, then," Tristan said, pushing his tea away. He grabbed me from my seat and lifted me on to the table, facing him.

"Is that so? How are you planning to do that, then?" I asked, trying to hold back my smile. I locked my legs around his waist and wrapped my arms around his neck, pulling him closer.

"It's not something I can say. I need to show you," he murmured in a husky tone, his eyes darkening dangerously as he stared at me.

"Show me," I whispered in his ear, grazing his earlobe with my teeth. It made him shiver. Suddenly I was feeling up for some "excitement", my bad mood forgotten.

He took a sharp intake of breath and pulled me even closer, hungrily claiming my lips.

We usually didn't have much alone time when we were on tour. Most nights we spent in our bunk beds on the bus, and there wasn't much space for privacy there. After shows we crashed in hotels, but we were always too tired for anything more than sleep. So I'd been missing these kinds of intimate moments with Tristan. And by the way he was touching me now, I reckon he'd been missing them just as much.

I grabbed him by the neck as he leaned me down on to the table, and kissed him back, hard. Hmm … Tristan's kisses. They were electrifying. They made me melt. He was almost lying on top of me when I heard Harry's freaked-out voice from the kitchen door.

"Eeew! Oh my God! I can't believe you guys. We *eat* at that table, you know that?" He covered his eyes with his hands. "Becca messaged me saying to be home early in the morning and *this* is what I find in my kitchen?"

"Erm, sorry, we got a bit carried away," Tristan mumbled, embarrassed. He leaned away from me and liftly me gently back to the floor.

"And I had to sit through Tristan's torturing lecture, listening to how we 'all' had to behave decently around here. That was such bull," he complained. "I would say that 'practically having sex on the kitchen table' does not qualify as 'decent behavior', mister!" he said, pointing an accusing finger at a flustered Tristan.

"I'm sorry, man. It won't happen again. Plus, she started it!" he said, pointing at me. "You know how it is. You kinda stop thinking when they wrap their legs around you, whispering in your ear and biting your—"

"Tristan!" I blushed fiercely.

Tristan faked innocence by my side.

Harry snickered.

"Harry, I'm serious. I did not!" The more I denied it, the more they snickered. Then Tiffany and Seth entered the kitchen, looking curiously at the three of us.

"What's going on in here?" Seth yawned. "Why is Joey's face all purple?"

"TristanandJoey … werehavingsex … onthekitchen table," Harry spilled out between laughs before I could stop him.

"We were not! It was *just* a kiss, Harry!" I was getting seriously vexed at the situation.

"Oooh! Sex on the kitchen table?" Seth high-fived Tristan.

THE LOST GIRL   43

"This table is actually quite nice," Tiffany mused. "Do you remember, Seth, when we were here, and you—"

Seth slapped his hand over her mouth, a panicked look in his eyes but a weak smile on his lips.

"Er … nothing happened here … Nor on the counter," he added hurriedly, giving a sideways glance to Tristan.

"Okay, that's it! This kitchen officially needs an exorcism now. And a sanitizing crew. *Urgently*," Harry shouted as he left the kitchen, his arms in the air. "I'm not eating in here *ever again*!"

"Well, look what you did, Joey," Tristan teased. "Now Harry is having a fit because you can't keep your hands off me!" Tristan immensely enjoyed seeing me blush. He said I looked cute when I was embarrassed.

"Yeah? Okay, mister, let's see how long I can keep my hands off you, then. Prepare to wait a long time!" I stomped out of the kitchen.

Tristan ran after me. "No, wait! Let's not be hasty here. I take it all back," he said, still laughing. "I'm the one who can't take my hands off you. I swear. I really can't! I can't control myself! I will shout for anyone to hear if you want to!" He grabbed me by the waist, locking me in his arms tightly and burying his face in my neck, showering me with tickling kisses.

That's when we both heard Becca clearing her throat by the front door.

Tristan was the one blushing now. He coughed, a little embarrassed, and released me quickly, straightening his clothes and self-consciously patting down his ruffled hair.

Becca was only a couple of years older than us, but she looked a lot older because of how extremely serious she was. She always had this slightly disapproving parental stare. It always made us feel as if we were little kids who'd been caught doing something wrong.

"So, we need to be leaving in a couple of hours," she said, adjusting her glasses over her freckled button nose and checking her notebook. "Also, Joey, your mother rang me last night. Said you never call her and she only knows how you're doing through magazines and TV shows." She lifted her head for a second to look at me.

I hunched my shoulders and sighed quietly. Oh, poop, I forgot to call my mother again. I used to call her every time we got back home from a tour, but it had completely slipped my mind.

"She also wanted me to inquire" – Becca addressed both Tristan and me now – "about your plans for giving her that grandson she was promised. I think we can all fairly state that you are dutifully trying on that one ..." she said, giving us a pointed look.

"It was just a kiss," I mumbled, shuffling my feet, embarrassed and glancing quickly at Tristan. He looked dejected now. He always did when the "grandchildren subject" was mentioned. We didn't know if he could even father any children, due to his backstory as a supernatural glitch and because of his ex-ghost status. This lingering doubt was something that bothered him a lot, because he wanted to have a big family – which meant having lots of kids – to make up for the siblings he hadn't had growing up, and his small family of one he had left behind in his past life.

"So, which Lost Boys are still not up?" Becca asked while checking her notes. "We'll be leaving soon, so I suggest you hurry up, and shake a leg."

That made us snap to attention and scurry away to our rooms. We had to get ready for a full day of promo events.

Before we left the house, I wondered how many people there would be showing up at the signing at the bookstore ...

Chapter Six

Book Signing

We arrived at the bookstore in time, thanks to Becca keeping everybody on schedule. The store was in a prestigious, four-storey high Victorian building, situated in the busiest part of the city. All high-profile events were done in this building nowadays. It held signings, meet-and-greets for all kinds of celebrities, and also hosted artists' exhibitions and cultural events.

As to how many people would be attending, my question was quickly answered as I glanced at the massive crowd huddling outside the front doors, waiting for a chance to get in. The place looked packed!

Our record label's experienced driver cannily bypassed the crowds in our SUV and parked at the back of the building, and we hurried inside, Jarvis and Johnson by our sides, plus a few extra security guards from the bookstore helping as an added precaution. We were led to a room with restricted access on the third floor, where offices were located.

"Sorry about the mess outside; word got out that Miss Worthington and Miss Sunford were coming to the event, and the volume of people doubled," a flustered middle-aged man explained as we stepped out of the elevator.

He signaled for us to follow him inside the private room, where we found Tiffany and Jackie already waiting for us. Tiffany was becoming a major celebrity in the city, and Jackie's fame had risen considerably after she had started dating Harry.

"Hey, you came!" Harry greeted her happily, giving her a quick kiss.

"I thought I should drop by and support my man." Jackie smiled. She was wearing black shorts, heeled boots and a sparkly purple top which complemented her vibrant pink lipstick. Her black hair was in her usual asymmetrical cut with a long side-bang sweeping over her eyes. She wrapped one arm around Harry's waist and with the other waved a greeting to everybody else in the room. I forced a smile in her direction.

Despite the building being impressively big, the crowd today was still almost overwhelming. The security crew and event coordinators had a lot to organize before we could head downstairs to the signing room. As usual I tried to avoid being around Harry, because of Jackie. I could feel her distrustful glares at me while we waited.

And all the while I couldn't shake a weird feeling I was having. Maybe it was the tension of having to deal with Jackie that was making me nervous, but something deep inside told me that, actually, it had nothing to do with her. I kept glancing around all the time, searching for something, although I didn't even know what I was looking for. I just had this sinking feeling in the pit of my stomach, telling me to be alert, warning me that something bad was about to happen.

"Are you all right?" Tristan asked, noticing my tense demeanor.

I shook my head, dismissing how irrational I was being. "Yeah, everything's fine."

He didn't have the chance to press the matter because the store's supervisor announced they were ready for us downstairs.

"Wow!" Sammy exclaimed when we walked into the signing room.

A million camera flashes exploded in our direction; paparazzi, reporters and fans fought each other for a better spot to take their pictures. The room was completely overloaded; even the air felt stuffy and suffocating because the air conditioner couldn't handle the extra heat generated by so many people in the room. Several tables had been placed side by side in a long row, for us to sit at, and a security line was secured a few feet in front, blocking any advance of fans towards us. And as usual, Jarvis and Johnson were at our backs to ensure our safety.

I sat down at a table between Tristan and Josh, looking around. There was a square glass table behind us, presumably where we could put any gifts we were handed, and a display of our albums had also been arranged. I smiled and turned my attention back to the crowd, preparing myself to meet the fans. From the looks of the throng, this was going to be a long day.

Five hours had passed and I was beginning to get tired, but I tried to cover it up as best I could. All those people had waited in line for such a long time, just for a chance to see us, even if it was for a brief moment. There were also a lot of fans who pleaded to meet Tiffany or Jackie too, and obligingly they stepped forward to give a handshake and a quick hello.

The girl now in front of me was talking at the fastest tempo possible. I mentally nicknamed her "Flash Girl".

"… and ohmygosh, you look sooo much prettier in person, I can't believe I'm, like, actually talking to you!"

I glanced fleetingly to my right to see Tristan talking to another fan, who giggled and blushed all over. I could see he was beginning to become weary as well. Big crowds like this drained Tristan the most out of all of us.

I smiled and gave Flash Girl my autograph and she stepped out of the line while I prepared to talk with the next fan. A tall teenage boy stepped in front of me and handed me a poster to sign. He was wearing a long, heavy jacket and one hand was stuffed inside the pocket.

"I waited a long time to see you today," he murmured.

"Yeah, I know! Thanks for coming. It's crazy in here today, huh?" I said, scribbling quickly on the poster.

"I'm glad I got to meet you. I have something important to talk to you about." I glanced up for the first time to have a look at the boy. He was very burly, with big strong arms and a taut, nervous face. The thing that drew most of my attention, though, was his eyes. I tensed up, reacting to them immediately.

Today was one of those days when I was really grateful for having my special ability. I'd had this skill since I was really young, but I hadn't known then that I was one of a very few people in the world who could do it. At least, so far I hadn't met any other person that was like me. Just by looking in someone's eyes I could tell what a person is feeling; I could tell if they were nervous, sad or happy.

I couldn't see exactly what they were "thinking". I could guess many things, though. It's called "empathy-sight", as Miss Violet, my senior occult teacher, had explained to me. It could be real handy sometimes, but a real pain at other times. People needed to have their private feelings, and I couldn't control my powers, couldn't turn them off. When you are in a relationship, finding out what your significant other is feeling *all the time* can become a problem.

But today I was glad that I could read these things in other people, because otherwise I would have been completely unaware of what was going on inside this boy's head. What I saw when I looked directly into his eyes scared the hell out of me.

Madness.

It was the best word to describe it.

"You should quit the band, *Joe*," the boy said, his tone becoming urgent.

A jumble of confused emotions swirled around inside his mind in a chaotic blur. It made me slightly dizzy; the intensity of his feelings was too much; the agitation in his mind warned me that he was a second away from snapping.

I was so immersed in trying to decipher his scrambling thoughts that I wasn't thinking straight. I should have said something, but nothing came out of my mouth. The eerie feeling I'd been having rushed back to my mind.

Something bad is going to happen today ...

The boy snaked his hand out and grabbed my wrist, his eyes manic. "You have to stay away from these guys. *All of them.* They are no good for you!"

No one was paying attention to what was happening. I glanced over to Jarvis and Johnson but they weren't looking my way.

The boy tightened his grip on my wrist. "I am serious, *Joe*!" He seemed angry at my silence. His emotions crashed around in his head, making mine hurt. He thought I was mocking him.

"Don't you believe me?" he growled, tugging at my arm and making me lurch into the table. My sudden fear at last made me snap out of my daze and react normally to the situation.

"Stop it! Let go of me!" I shouted, standing up and pushing him away.

"No! You *have* to believe me!" he shouted back, and tried to pull my arm again, but I twisted it, making him lose his grip.

Thanks, martial arts training, I thought to myself.

He leaned over the table, desperate to have a hold of me again, but he only managed to grab my necklace; he pulled it with a sharp tug. The necklace gave way and snapped; black beads scattered everywhere and I stumbled back as I escaped his hold on me.

Everything happened so fast then. In a second Tristan was leaping over the table and tackling the lunatic boy. Josh tried to catch me as I fell backwards, but we both ended up losing our balance and crashing through the glass table behind us. The sound of breaking glass was so loud that the entire room burst into a panicked commotion, as frightened cries and confused shouts exploded everywhere.

I lay crumpled on the floor with Josh, shards of glass all around us. My mind was still a chaotic mess, reeling from my foray into that lunatic boy's mind. The room was in turmoil. The security line was broken and everybody was running over to us.

Where were Jarvis and Johnson?

Josh had glass all over him, too, his eyes wide and scared as he gazed at the uproar around us. I felt something warm and wet trickling down my face and I tried to stand up, but the crowd was so huge that we kept being pushed back to the floor. Josh wrapped his arms around me, trying to protect me, but when he saw his hand he stopped and stared at it with a puzzled expression, his eyes flashing with fear at what he saw. I glanced down; it was bathed in crimson red. There was blood all over him. That's when I put two and two together.

My blood.

The crowd's fear slipped through me, making me feel even more helpless. I looked at Josh, fear and panic engulfing me. I couldn't think straight; I couldn't move!

Josh decided it was time to take action and scooped me up in his arms and carried me quickly to the elevator, pushing through the crowd like he was freaking Moses parting the waves. I tried to catch a glimpse of Tristan or any of the boys, but they were lost in the chaos. In a flash Big Johnson and Jarvis were at our side, helping to open the way. Well, better late than never, I supposed … Where the hell were they when that lunatic boy was going for my neck?

Jarvis used his usual threatening stare that caused people to get out of his way pretty fast, while Big Johnson shouted for people to move. Then we were inside the elevator and the doors were closing, leaving us huddling inside in shock.

I risked a glance at Big Johnson; his eyes were fixed on the doors, like he was expecting them to open at any moment to reveal a horde of invading monsters. His jaw was clenched tight and his forehead beaded with sweat. He noticed me staring and flicked his eyes to me for a moment. Guilt poured out of him like punch.

"I'm so sorry, Miss Gray!" he blurted out. "I didn't notice what that guy was doing until it was too late. I should have been more attentive. It won't ever happen again, Miss Gray, you have my word."

"That's okay, Big J," I said, my voice trembling a little.

Jarvis was looking intensely at his cousin and me, his eyes also full of guilt.

The elevator pinged loudly into the eerie silence that followed, and the doors opened at the third floor. Josh darted out, still carrying me, and checked the empty hallway.

Holding the doors open with his bulk, Big Johnson boomed over his shoulder at his cousin: "Jarvis, you go back downstairs, check if everything is all right, find the others." He issued his instructions in a hard, clipped tone; he was Chief of Security after all. "I'll be here with Gray. Keep me posted on events."

Although a part of me was really grateful that Big Johnson was going to stay with me, a bigger part was worried about Tristan and the boys still in the mess downstairs. They'd be needing all the help they could get. And the last time I had seen Tristan he was launching himself at that crazy boy. What if something happened to him?

"Johnson! Please … go with Jarvis, too. Help the boys, please. I'll be fine."

Josh turned and we both watched the two guards standing by the elevator doors, waiting to see what they'd do.

Big Johnson stepped out and signaled for Jarvis to follow his orders. "I won't leave her side," he said decisively. "Go now. Bring them all back here," he ordered, with finality in his voice.

I hunched down in Josh's arms, too shaken to argue any more. Big Johnson must know what he was doing.

Josh carried me inside the private room we'd used earlier, towards a big couch in one corner. As soon as he sat down, he lifted me gently onto the couch and started checking me to find out where the blood was coming from.

"Where does it hurt?" he asked urgently.

Big Johnson was surveying the room, barking orders into his radio and positioning himself close to the door to block anyone who tried to enter without his permission. I shook my head while Josh tended to me. I let out a deep breath which I didn't realize until now that I'd been holding in. "My head stings a bit."

"It looks like a superficial cut, but we might need to take you to a hospital, just to be sure it's nothing serious," Josh said, probing lightly at my head. Then he took off his shirt and wrapped it into a bundle. "Press this on your head to stop the bleeding. Don't worry, you're going to be fine," he said calmly, trying to reassure me.

He pulled me close and wrapped his arms around me, causing me to lean my head on his big chest. His skin felt so warm, and the beat of his heart made me feel a lot calmer. My insides still churned in nervousness, though. I was so worried for Tristan, the boys and Tiffany; they were still down there in that pandemonium. I hoped they were okay.

The door burst open and I jumped, startled, my heart pounding in my chest in fright. Big Johnson was already blocking the path of whoever had barged in, but as swiftly as he had stepped forward, he moved away even faster to let a stricken-faced Tristan pass by. His intense gray gaze swept the room until he spotted the couch, and his eyes widened in fear when he saw me. Until now, he hadn't seen all the blood. He ran to me and knelt in front of the couch. "Joe! Are you all right?" he asked, his voice deep with concern.

"I'm all right, Tris. Is everybody else okay?"

I looked behind him and saw Seth and Tiffany coming into the room, Harry and Jackie right behind them and a wide-eyed Sammy at their heels. I couldn't see any sign of Jamie; come to think of it, I hadn't noticed him in the signing room, either. But maybe he was still downstairs, trying to capture footage of the affray, as legal evidence rather than for souvenir purposes, I'd imagine. I hoped he was all right.

Jarvis and Becca were the last ones to arrive. She took a quick glance at me on the couch and was already dialing on her phone, calling downstairs for a paramedic to come up here as well.

Tristan was broadcasting so many emotions, it made me wince from the intensity of them. Fear, worry, nervousness, one flooding after the other in an emotional tidal wave.

"Why is there so much blood?" he asked Josh quietly while he helped put pressure on the shirt against my head.

I wasn't sure if I could handle any more feelings today. I'd had enough. My body couldn't take anything else and my head was pounding so hard, I thought it would split open any second now.

Tristan was holding my hand, trying to reassure me that everything was really all right.

"Don't worry, I'll be fine," I told him with a weak smile.

He laughed lightly, his voice still coming out a little tense. "Only you, Joey, would try to calm me down when *you're* the one injured here. That's my job, you know," he scoffed playfully, making everybody laugh.

The mood in the room relaxed considerably after that. Tiffany, Seth and Sammy huddled closer to get a look at me, while Jackie and Harry remained a little behind.

I closed my eyes and sighed, focusing on the feeling of Tristan's fingers on the palm of my hand. His touch always made me feel better, like an instant balsam of relief.

Jarvis was quietly reporting back to Big Johnson at the back of the room. "It's a hell of a mess downstairs. There were a few people hurt in the crush, but paramedics are already taking care of it. Tristan had the guy firmly secured by the time I got to him. The police have taken him off for questioning."

"He didn't hurt you, right?" I asked Tristan, checking to see if he was injured.

"I'm fine. The guy struggled a little at first, but he stopped when the bookstore security guards arrived and took him off my hands," Tristan said softly, but then his eyes took on a dangerous glint. "If I'd known he had done *this* to you, though ..."

"Actually ... he didn't quite do this to me. It was an accident. I tripped and fell on that damned glass table," I confessed, embarrassed by my clumsiness.

"All I saw was the guy going for you, and I leapt at him," Tristan continued. "Then all hell broke loose!"

I glanced around the room and caught a glimpse of Jackie, at Harry's side, staring at me. Her eyes flashed with disapproval at the way I was still leaning into Josh.

What the hell was that girl's problem? Why couldn't she give me a freaking break, for once in my life? Was she jealous of Josh now too? I couldn't go near any of the boys, was that it?

A paramedic entered the room, which distracted me from my silent rage. He gave a quick look around and walked straight towards the couch. I guess the sight of a girl covered in blood did flash "emergency" signals.

"Okay. Let's get a look at you, love," he said, putting his medical bag on the floor and opening it up. "You can let her go now," he told Josh, as he pulled on surgical gloves.

I nodded and Josh reluctantly let go of me, and scuttled to the other side of the couch. Tristan took the seat next to me, his hand still securely clutched around mine.

"It's quite common for cuts to the head to bleed a lot, but it seems yours is not too deep," the paramedic said, inspecting the laceration on my head. "I just need to clean this up and you won't even need stitches."

Tristan let out a sigh of relief. He squeezed my hand lightly for support while the paramedic expertly patted bandages and antiseptics over my wound. After a little while the man finished working on me, gave me a painkiller for my headache and hurried off to help other people in need downstairs.

The building was swarming with paparazzi by the time we got out. Becca stayed behind to announce we were all okay and unharmed, and the boys and I, along with Tiff and Jackie, slumped in the back of the chauffered SUV as we were driven quietly home.

I went straight to Tristan's room when we got back, after reassuring everybody *for the hundredth time* that I really was all right. I didn't want to be around Jackie a second longer than was necessary or I would be the one blowing up this time.

Harry had been acting really weird since we left the bookstore, and I wasn't sure why. But I wasn't in any condition to analyze anything at the moment; I just wanted to go to bed and rest for a little bit.

A soft, yellow light drifted through the window blinds,

giving a cozy warmth to the room. I heard Tristan coming into the bedroom to check up on me. He pulled a warm blanket over my shoulders, kissing me tenderly on the forehead before silently walking away to let me sleep in peace.

I woke up with a start when I heard the door open and someone walk inside. I blinked sleepily at a dark shape sitting next to me, and felt a hand resting lightly on my shoulder. For a second I started to panic, fear climbing up my chest because of this strange shadow looming over me, but at the sound of Tristan's voice, washing over me soothingly, all of my fears disappeared as quickly as they came.

"Hey, sorry to wake you, Buttons. How are you feeling?" he asked. The room was dark. Was it night-time already?

"I'm fine. Hmm … How long I have been sleeping?" I asked groggily.

"A few hours." He cupped my face in his hands and gave me a soft kiss. "I'm waking you up because Becca just arrived with some news about what happened at the bookstore. I thought you might like to hear it."

"Yeah, I want to know. Thanks," I said grabbing his hand, letting him help me stand up.

Everybody was waiting in the living room. Becca was instructing Big Johnson and his cousin to put the gifts they'd managed to recover from the signing on the dinner table. Tiffany was also there, but Jackie was nowhere to be found, which meant she had already left, *thank the gods*.

"Hey, Joey," Becca greeted me with a concerned expression. She checked me from head to toe, to certify that I was really okay before speaking again. "You can go through the gift pile when you feel like it; I know how much it cheers you up, reading the fan letters," she said with a comforting smile.

I sat at the end of the couch; Tristan hunched down on the floor, sitting between my legs, and Becca started telling us the news.

"So, the kid that attacked Joey today has a mental health problem and had been without medication for a while," she began. "The kid was in a catatonic state so his mom was brought to the police station to answer some questions. She said he sometimes fakes taking his pills, which aggravates his condition.

"Usually when he's not on his medication, he starts to harbour some crazy conspiracy theories, and she said that he had been fixated on the band for a while now, listening to your albums all the time. But she thought he just enjoyed the music; she never imagined he had something like this planned. The kid was diagnosed with early-onset schizophrenia when he was just twelve. It's very sad.

"He's back on his medication now," Becca said to calm everybody down. "He won't be bothering you guys again." Then she smiled a big smile. "On the bright side, all your fans are all right; no one was seriously hurt in the commotion."

"Yeah, the TV has been broadcasting the incident non-stop today," Seth said.

Apparently, someone had recorded the exact moment when Josh had picked me up, bridal style, and rushed to the elevators with me in his arms, and now the scene was being replayed all over the internet with *The Bodyguard* theme song in the background. Funny.

Sam started to sing "I Will Always Love You" to Josh,

with a hand over his heart; at his side, Seth tried to French kiss him.

"And, Joey, call your mother," Becca shouted over the ruckus of the boys. "She's been freaking out all afternoon trying to reach you."

Later, as I made my way to the phone, I walked past the pile of gifts on the dining-room table. A white flower amongst the wrappings caught my eye. I walked closer, curiosity getting the best of me.

It was a white lily. With the same black ribbon as before, and another little note tied to it.

Chapter Seven

Perfect Day to be Okay

I spent that night tossing and turning, thinking about that damned note on the flower. I hadn't told anyone about it, especially not my mother earlier on the phone. She was already worrying enough over the news coverage of the bookstore incident. But I knew the boys would say I was overreacting or being silly, so I kept it to myself, at least for a while.

The message was like the first; another creepy love declaration:

Lovely Gray,
I hope you liked my other token of affection.
I wonder what it would feel like to have you all to
* myself.*
You're always surrounded by your boys. It is hard
* not to feel jealous.*
It pains me so much having to share you ...
So many people stand between us.
But I will prevail over them all,
And I'll never give up on you.

From your true and faithful
Secret Admirer.

I'd always received fan letters; sometimes they were a bit on the kinky side, but this was different. Too personal for my taste, and with a creepy edge.

Could these lilies have been sent by the crazy boy from the bookstore? The two notes had a romantic slant to them, whereas the boy had no romantic feelings in his head – at least, not at the time I was looking.

After a turbulent night, I got up early the next day because I felt too jittery to stay in bed any longer.

The sun was shining brightly in the living room, and just for a moment it made me completely forget about creepy notes and Crazy Boy; my head didn't even hurt any more. I sat on the couch and rested my head carefully on the cushions, appreciating how the morning light was bathing me in its warmth.

The boys were soon up and bustling around the house, preparing things for the barbecue we had planned to cook in the back garden, to kick off our official summer break. Every now and then one of the boys would again whistle *The Bodyguard* theme song to Josh, enjoying teasing him. Tiffany made an appearance in the garden wearing a lovely pair of light-blue shorts and a yellow, flowery, short-sleeved shirt that complemented her blonde curls perfectly. Later, Amanda also arrived, dressed in a colorful summer dress, quickly followed by Jamie with a couple of his friends. The day was especially warm and sunny, and it was nice to have everyone there. I spent time laughing and chatting with the boys, the memory of broken glass and eerie omens left completely behind.

As I left the group to get another drink, Harry approached, eyeing me cautiously. He was still acting a little weird. It seemed as if he was debating what to say; he bit his lower lip on the spot where his lip-ring used to be, which is something he always did when he was anxious. It was his nervous tick. The silence stretched out for a few seconds before he finally spoke.

"Hey, how are you doing?" he asked, watching me, worried. "Your head okay?"

"Yeah, I'm fine. Stop worrying, I'm really okay, dude." I tried to put on a brave face to reassure him, make him stop worrying about me.

"I'm so sorry, Joey," he murmured quietly, gazing at me.

"What for, Harry? It was not your fault."

"No, I mean, yesterday ... after you got hurt."

"Sorry about yesterday? Why?"

He glanced down quickly, like he was ashamed. "After they brought us upstairs, and you were hurt ... I kept away from you. I didn't want to upset Jackie, because she gets so jealous. I didn't want her to make a scene; you had already been through so much. So I stayed at the back," he explained. "But I shouldn't have done that. I should've been there for you, by your side. No matter what Jackie thought. I'm really sorry."

"Harry, come on. You don't need to be sorry, I understand."

"But ... am I forgiven? For being a crappy friend yesterday?" he asked, his emerald eyes brimming a little.

"There's nothing to forgive, Harry." I squeezed him in a tight hug. "You know I love you, Harry Bear."

I felt a hundred times better after clarifying things with Harry. I knew then that it was going to be a good day.

We had no work, no crowds of eager fans, no worries, no thinking about creepy letters – or at least I was going to try not to think about them – and Harry and I were okay again. Nothing could put a dampener on my spirits today.

Tristan was in charge of grilling the steaks while Seth and Sam were in charge of eating as many ribs as they possibly could. Seth vowed to only stop eating after he exploded.

Amanda, beautiful as always, chatted amiably with Tiffany while holding firmly on to her plate of salad. Her long, slim, beauty queen silhouette got plenty of admiring looks as she ambled around the garden.

"Hey, Joey. Having fun?" Tiffany stopped to chat, smiling as she saw how much I was enjoying the free day out with friends. She had been pampering me all day long, still worried about my head and making sure I was feeling all right whenever she bumped into me in the garden. The sight of all the blood yesterday had scared her half to death.

"Yeah, loads. Today is such a perfect day," I declared, beaming widely.

"Yeah, you look really happy today," she mused.

"I'm just relieved that everything turned out okay, and you guys weren't hurt. I was so worried in that room while I was waiting for Jarvis to get you guys upstairs!" I confessed.

"I'm glad everybody is okay," she told me, giving my arm a reassuring squeeze. "I was pretty nervous too. But that's in the past. What matters is that you're happy now. We can all see it, it's like you have a bright halo around you. It makes everyone drift towards you, like moths to a flame," she confessed with a smile.

"Come on, Tiff. You're joking, right? I don't have any halo or whatever. I'm just *me*!" I laughed at her.

"You don't see how all the boys chase after you all the

time? It's like they can't stand being away from you for too long!" she said, amused. "Don't be embarrassed. It's. your thing. You're a *charmer*. And the best thing is that you don't even know you're doing it, which makes it even more special."

I shuffled my feet self-consciously. "Am not," I protested. "I was never good at charming anyone, you know that. How many times did you have to help me with my seduction skills back at school? If it wasn't for your lessons I would have never gotten together with Tristan, remember? Remember when I only wore boys' clothes? I was hopeless. You saved me!" I said, throwing my arms up in the air.

She laughed at my theatrics. "Yes, you *were* hopeless back then. But look at you now! My baby girl is all grown up!" She pinched my cheeks proudly and we ended up reminiscing about the old days at our boarding school.

The afternoon passed by in a cheerful mood, with everybody joking, laughing, playing around and relaxing in the sun. By the end of the day, the boys were all excited about the raging party that was supposedly happening later at some trendy club downtown. Amanda and Tiffany were already discussing what clothes to wear, and everybody began drifting off to start getting ready for the night out.

I watched Tristan as he walked up the stairs with a spring in his step to take his bath, excited to be going out tonight. I hunched down on the living-room couch and sulked: I *really* didn't want to go out tonight. I didn't want to deal with people in another crowded and stuffy room. I wasn't in the mood to dance, or drink, or tell people over and over again about what happened in that bookstore. I just wanted to relax in my own home, drink some tea and go to bed.

"Hey, what's the matter, Joey?" Harry asked as he walked by the couch and noticed me sulking by myself.

"Do you think there's any way I could weasel out of going to this thing?" I mumbled, staring at my feet.

"You don't wanna go?" he asked curiously, and then chuckled as I pulled a face. "If you don't wanna go, don't go."

"Yeah, but … everybody's going …"

"So?" he said, and then he paused, like he was just realizing something. "Stay here with me," he proposed. "I'm not in the mood to go out, either. I think I'll stay home tonight. You can stay with me."

"Harry. You don't need to do that. I know you want to go …"

"Please, Joe. I need to make it up to you. Let me do this?" He smiled and wrapped an arm around me.

"Okay," I agreed, after seeing his pleading eyes. I was so relieved that I wouldn't be on my own anymore.

"Great, then," he said, slapping my back lightly, giving me a quick kiss on the cheek and standing up.

"Harry …?" I called after him, making him stop and turn to look at me. "Thank you."

His smile was big and he shot me a quick nod before leaving.

I walked upstairs to talk to Tristan about my last-minute night-out cancelation.

He was leaning over the bathroom sink with a white towel wrapped low around his waist, smearing shaving cream over his jaw.

"Hey, I'm about to hit the shower. I'll be ready in a minute," he said, glancing quickly at me. "You don't look too excited."

"Yeah, I'm not really in the mood for this, Tris."

He stopped mid-shave. "You don't wanna go?"

"Sorry, no."

He furrowed his brow, clearly disappointed at the news. "Are you sure? We never go to these kinds of parties with the boys … It might be fun. Plus, it's a very selective guest list. All our close friends are going to be there." He looked at me for a few seconds and then sighed in resignation. "Well … I guess you are right. It will be a loud night and probably bad for your head; we should stay home and get some rest."

"What? No, you don't need to stay with me," I protested. "You can go with the boys. I'll be fine here."

"What are you talking about, Joe? I'm not going without you." He turned to look at me, clearly annoyed.

"Why not? You're not glued to me. Just because I'm not going it doesn't mean you can't go, either. We have been to lots of events before without each other!" I felt bad; I could see in his eyes how much he wanted to go out tonight.

"That's different. Those were job-related events," he stated, leaning his hip against the sink and crossing his arms over his chest with a stubborn scowl. "If you're not going, I'm not going. I'm not leaving you here all alone, especially after what happened yesterday."

"That's very sweet of you, Tris, but you don't have to worry. Harry is going to stay with me. He's not in the mood for going out, either," I reasoned.

He pursed his lips, not really sure what he was going to do.

"Come on, Tris. Please say you'll go? I'll feel like crap if you have to stay here because of me, and then you'll resent me later for having missed all the fun. I'll feel obligated to go, just so I won't ruin the night for you," I exclaimed, moving closer to him and wrapping my arms around his waist. "Please, Tris. Say you'll go? This way I'll be happy about staying and you'll be happy about going, so we'll both be happy. What do you say?" I gave him my best puppy-dog eyes.

He chuckled and, after a moment, conceded defeat. "All right, Buttons. I'll go."

"Yay!" I exclaimed and stood on my tiptoes, giving him a small peck on the lips, getting shaving cream all over my face. He laughed and wiped the cream off my nose before going back to his shaving.

When everybody was ready to leave, Tiffany whined a little about me and Harry not going, but she dropped it when she saw how adamant I was about staying home.

It was just me and Harry tonight.

"So, are you ready to kick some zombie ass?" he asked, waving our favorite video game in his hands, after everybody had left.

"Hell, yeah!" I shouted happily.

Chapter Eight

Bumps in the Night

After a few hours spent contentedly killing zombies, Harry and I decided to call it a night, and I went for a quick shower before hitting the sack. I had the water running and was feeling quite happy and relaxed when a shiver ran up my spine, making the hair on the back of my neck stand up: that eerie feeling was back, putting me uncomfortably on edge again.

I shook my head and tried to get back to enjoying my steamy shower. Then I caught a shadow moving by the bathroom door. It was so subtle and fast, I could almost swear it was only a trick of the light.

I quickly turned off the shower and stepped into the middle of the bathroom, wrapping a towel around me in a protective gesture. I was about to shout to see if there was anybody outside in my room when I realized that would be the most dumb thing in the world to do. *What was I? Stupid?* This wasn't a horror movie! And if it was, I sure as hell wasn't going to be one of those bimbo girls that always got themselves killed off doing idiotic things in the few first minutes. If there really was a psycho in my room, he wasn't going to reply, "Sure, I'm right here, watching TV and waiting for you to get out of that freaking long shower. By the way, be a doll and toss me that knife there on the nightstand, will ya? I wanna hurry up with the atrocious murder; my favorite show is about to start!"

Maybe I really was losing my mind here, seeing shadows lurking in the dark, waiting to get me. But what if that boy from the bookstore had broken into the house and was here now, waiting for me, in that dark room? I looked around urgently, searching for something I could use as a weapon.

As it turned out, bathroom facilities aren't particularly great at doubling as weapon storage. Unless I wanted to soap the killer to death, or tie him up with toilet paper, there was nothing I could use to protect myself. Curses!

Well, I guess I did have my martial arts training to put to use. But then again, martial arts were all fine and dandy until the murderous bastard appeared with a gun in his hands. No amount of karate chops can counter a bullet to the head ...

I stepped out of the bathroom into the darkness of my room, and turned on the lights. There wasn't anyone there.

Yeah, that's what the murderous dude wants me to think, right? To relax and let my guard down. Then he'll be inside the closet or under the bed, waiting to murder me ... with that knife he left on the nightstand while he was watching TV!

I searched under the bed, and then inside the closets. If this had been a horror movie, a scary soundtrack would have been playing in the background this entire time.

It had just been a tricky play of lights and shadows again. There was nothing to worry about. Maybe if I repeated this to myself a dozen times, over and over, I could convince my jittery nerves …

After I was done inspecting my room, I quickly got dressed and left my bedroom to inspect the dark living room downstairs. Silhouettes and smudges of light danced around the quiet room, branches and leaves on the trees outside creating shadows that played over the walls and floorboards. Suddenly I could see things moving everywhere, and hear suspicious, creaky noises teased out from all around the room, with unseen threats lurking in the corners of my eyes.

Panic started to rise up in my chest and my heart pounded. My body's instincts screamed for me to run. *Run. Run! You need to get out of here! Now!*

I was completely taken over by fear as I bolted upstairs for Harry's room, yanking the door open and running inside without thinking twice. His room was completely dark, so I turned on his lights, shouting his name at the top of my voice.

Harry shot upright in his bed, momentarily blinded by the bright lights bursting unexpectedly through the room.

"WHAT? What? Is it a fire?" he asked groggily, trying to understand what the hell was going on. I glanced around his room, searching for lurking shadows or any murderous strangers holding big scary knives, but found nothing out of place. Only Harry staring back at me with a stunned expression.

Boy. Talk about being embarrassed now!

"Erm … Sorry about barging in like that. I-I just wanted to know … if I could stay with you until Tristan comes back?" I mumbled, all red in the face. No way in hell was I going to stay in my room all alone tonight.

Maybe I hadn't left the bookstore incident so far behind me after all. I'd thought I was over it, but this embarrassing meltdown was proof that maybe that wasn't the case.

I was glad when Harry agreed to stay with me. I would have been scared out of my mind if I'd been all alone in this house. Harry sighed, relieved that the house wasn't in fact on fire, and patted a place by his side on the bed. I switched the lights off and hurried to sneak under his covers. Somehow being in the dark with Harry by my side didn't seem so scary now. I pulled the covers up to my neck and rested my head comfortably over his chest. Harry always slept with no shirt on, with his tattoo of green waves crashing endlessly over red licking flames. After I had finished counting the waves on his chest, I started to count how many times his chest would rise and fall, and I guess I fell asleep in the middle of counting.

I woke up to the sound of voices and laughter coming from downstairs, and after a couple of seconds I drifted back to sleep again. It was probably Tristan and the boys getting back from the club, I thought, in my slurred, cotton-candy hazy head. The bed was too warm and too comfortable; I snuggled back against my pillow, giving in to sleep once again. Tristan should be coming back to sleep with me in a minute.

A few more minutes must have passed before someone turned the lights on. I squinted my eyes as a harsh, angry, female voice shouted across the room, making me wake with a start.

"Harry! *What the hell?*"

And only then did I remember I wasn't in my room.

Recollections of the night drifted through my blurry

head as I remembered how I had fallen asleep in Harry's bed. *With Harry*. Who was now sitting by my side, with the same stunned expression on his sleepy face.

"J-Jackie?" he asked, confused.

Holy Moses. It was his girlfriend. This was *soooo* not good.

"Yeah, damn right it's Jackie!" she shouted again. "I came back from the club with your friends because I missed you, and this is what I find? This is beyond fucked up, Harry!"

"Wait, Jackie, it's not what you're thinking ..." I started to say, but stopped when I realized how lame it sounded. That was so the typical reply people came up with when they were caught cheating. Even though it *was* the truth; this was not what she thought it was!

She snapped her angry eyes back to me, jealousy and anger pounding like a sledge hammer, making me flinch under the intensity of her fury.

"Tell her to get the fuck out!" she spat.

"Jackie, please ..." Harry said, but she turned her outraged glare on him, and he stopped whatever it was he'd been about to say. "Joe, could you please leave us alone for a second?" he said, his eyes fixed on Jackie the whole time.

I nodded and walked out in a hurry. As soon I stepped out of Harry's room, Jackie slammed the door behind me, making me flinch again. Everybody was standing in the living room and turned their heads to stare at me as I emerged downstairs.

"Joey, what happened?" Tristan asked, coming up to me, all worried.

"Oh, God! What should I do?" I repeated to myself in

panic, wringing my hands anxiously. "It's all my fault. I-I was scared to be alone in my room, so I asked if I could stay with Harry until you came back from the party."

"Jackie walked in and saw you guys sleeping together." Tristan connected the dots. "God. I'm sorry, I didn't think … We met her in the club, and she wanted to see Harry," Tristan explained. "I should have thought …"

"No, it's all my fault. If I had stayed in my own room, like I was supposed to—"

"No, Joe. It's my fault. I should've stayed with you. I knew you would be scared being alone after what happened yesterday. I'm sorry …" Tristan cut in.

We could all hear shouting coming from Harry's room.

"So? What's the big deal? You were hanging with Harry in his room, waiting for Tristan to get back, so what?" Amanda asked, standing at Sam's side. "Do you remember, Sam, when you were watching that chick flick in your room with Joey? And you two fell asleep and I walked in and caught you two drooling over each other," she said, chuckling lightly. "It was so funny!"

"Yeah, very funny! And for the record, it was *not* a chick flick. It was a thriller, a very *scary* movie!" Sam corrected, embarrassed.

"Right. So, anyway, what's the big deal? You guys crash in each others' room all the time," she said with a shrug.

The shouting intensified in Harry's room, making everyone in the living room shuffle awkwardly. The fight was getting intense up there. It was to be expected, since they both had fiery personalities.

"Should we just … go to our rooms? To give them privacy?" Josh asked uncomfortably, but it was already too late, because the bedroom door burst open and Jackie barged out with fury in her step.

We all froze as she stormed down the stairs to the front door.

"Jackie! Wait, let me explain, this is all a big misunderstanding!" I said, pulling my arm free from Tristan's grasp and hurrying towards her. I had to try to say something, to explain myself. This was all my fault; I had to do something!

Jackie stopped by the door and stood with her back to us for a few seconds, as if she was holding her breath, waiting for a big explosion to come. The ticking time bomb was down to its last seconds. Tick. Tock. But she just turned slowly to look at me, her eyes fixed on me in a furious, cold stare.

"Save it. I don't wanna hear your lies, *Gray*." Her voice dripped with contempt. "My friends were right all along. They kept telling me this was happening and I just didn't want to believe it. I should've listened to them."

Harry was running downstairs, trying to catch up with her.

"I'm not lyin—" I tried to say, but she raised her palm, making me stop mid-sentence.

"You know what? Don't. You win, okay? I'm done with it," she said, looking coldly at me. "You can have him. He's all yours. I won't put up with this crap any more. You pull his strings and play with him like he's your damned puppet.

"I don't know how you stand it," she said, turning to Tristan. "How do you stand it, Tristan? Watching her rub against all your friends in front of your very own eyes, all day long, every day? It's like she's bewitched you. You're all like her lapdogs, obeying every snap of her fingers."

She turned back to me again without waiting for Tristan

to reply. "All you do is manipulate them. All of them! 'Your boys'. You seduce and spin them around in your web of lies. I'm done with this," she said, with hurt in her eyes, looking directly at Harry. "*We* are done."

And she turned and left the house.

Everybody stood there in shocked silence, staring at the open door.

Sam was the first to snap out of it. "Whoa. What a bit—"

"*Sam!*" I cut in sharply. Harry was still there, right behind us. Whatever Sam had been going to say, it would only hurt his feelings. Sam shut his mouth and pursed his lips, understanding my warning glare.

Harry snapped out of his daze and ran outside after Jackie.

I hunched down on the couch, burying my face in my hands in despair. What had I done? Had I ruined Harry's relationship just because I couldn't handle being alone for a few hours in my own room? How pathetic was that? How was Harry ever going to forgive me for this?

Tristan sat by my side and wrapped an arm around my shoulder. "Joey, come on. Don't be like that. Jackie was upset. People can say awful things when they're angry," he said, trying to console me.

"I just ... feel so bad. This is all my fault. Harry is going to hate me now," I mumbled through my clasped hands.

Harry walked back into the house then; his hair was disheveled and messy and his eyes sad and tired. "She didn't want to hear anything I had to say. Maybe it's for the best ..." he muttered, visibly upset. "I'm not sure I even want to carry it on anyway. If she can't get past this, if she can't accept that Joey is my friend ... I'm tired of fighting over this."

"I'm so sorry, Harry. I can talk to Jackie and explain what happened and … I'll apologize to her," I offered.

"Apologize for what, Joe? None of this is your fault. You didn't do anything wrong. *We* didn't do anything wrong," he said. "Listen, it's all right. I'll be fine."

I was almost in tears hearing how brokenhearted Harry sounded. I looked pleadingly at Tristan and he squeezed my shoulder, trying to reassure me that everything was going to be all right.

"Listen, everybody, we all need to get some rest now, okay?" he commanded to our gathered group in the living room. "Things will feel better in the light of a new day."

I went to sleep with a heavy heart and woke up feeling weary and tired. The light of a new day turned out to be bleary, gloomy and full of bad news.

After storming out of our house, Jackie had gone and "let slip" the news about her break-up to a few paparazzi. By the next day, a "few" paparazzi escalated to the whole press, all TV channels, blogs and gossip sites, radio stations, everyone.

Harry sat in front of the TV, his eyes shining with a mixture of sadness and anger as he watched people discussing his personal life on the flatscreen for all the world to see. After a while he shook his head, turned the TV off and stood up, his jaw clenched in rage.

"Well, I guess that makes it official, then."

The boys tried to cheer him up, talking about other things to take his mind off the blasted news. Fortunately, we had a big, important meeting scheduled with Mr. Silver at his main office that afternoon, so the appointment took everybody's mind off the unwelcome topic for a while.

We were told at the meeting that we still had one last event to attend before our vacation finally kicked in: A National Music Awards ceremony that The Lost Boys would be attending as musical guests as well as nominees for the Best Album of the Year Award.

We were going to play one song live between award acceptances, and one of us had to present the Outstanding Artist Award as well. We drew straws to decide which one of us would be the lucky one to go up onstage to deliver it, and to my upmost joy – note the sarcasm – I picked the short straw. I wasn't very fond of public speaking, as it always made me nervous. Singing was one thing, but to be a host (even if it was just to present one award) was a whole different tune to dance to. But the straw contest had been a tradition since the band's first official engagements and I had no choice but to abide by its rules. Being a wimp last night had already caused me enough trouble as it was.

Then, to close the meeting, Mr. Silver discussed the upgrade to our security system. He had been really worried after hearing about what happened at the bookstore. He asked me a dozen times if I was really all right, assuring us that serious measures were being taken so that incidents like this wouldn't happen again.

Harry was still feeling pretty bummed, so the boys arranged to take him out to forget about his problems with a boys' night out. They were trying anything to make him feel a little less depressed.

I wasn't even going to mention the fact that I'd be alone in the house again. I was done with being a wuss. I could die of fright in my room but I wouldn't say another word about this subject ever again.

The evening started out quite uneventfully, but when

it was time for my shower, I was careful to take some precautions. This time I made sure all the lights were on in the whole house so there wouldn't be any haunting shadows lurking around.

Then I went to Josh's room to retrieve a heavy baseball bat he had stored in his wardrobe, and put it against the tiled bathroom wall for my protection. That should serve as a fine weapon if I needed to smash some lurking murderer's head in.

After ten minutes in a steamy hot shower, all my worries were washed away. The tension in my neck slowly melted, leaving me completely relaxed. I whistled along to a song I had been working on inside my head for some time now. It could be our next single for the new album, who knew? It had a catchy rhythm … I needed to work on the lyrics with Seth later.

When I was done with my shower, I stretched out my hand to open the cubicle and found a dark silhouette standing right outside.

Someone was standing next to the marble sink.

Chapter Nine

Plan of Action

I clasped my hand to my chest, more surprised than scared. I already knew who was outside the cubicle. The stabbing pain in my wrist was all the sign I needed.

"Vigil!" I grunted, opening the cubicle door and peeking only my head out.

He was leaning against the sink, arms crossed over his chest. His habitual gray pants and long-sleeved shirt were impeccable as always. He raised both eyebrows, confused by my reaction.

"What did I tell you about *never, ever* appearing in bathroom facilities? Isn't this, like, our most important rule ever made?" I asked him.

"Oh. Right. I had completely forgotten. My apologies," he said, genuinely concerned. "I searched before and Tristan was not in the house, so I thought it was okay to show up with him not present," he explained.

"No, no, no. This has got nothing to do with Tristan. The bathroom rule stands, *no matter what*, you hear?" I said, exasperated.

Could you imagine if I was doing something else and

he just appeared out of thin air? Oh, God! I would die of embarrassment.

"And when I say, *no matter what*, Vigil, it means that even if the universe is ending, you do not enter while I am in the bathroom, do you understand?" I said one more time.

He uncrossed his arms and leaned backwards in a defensive stance. "Yes, I understand. I apologize again. I thought you only worried over Tristan's ... But I am aware now. Never at bathroom facilities. Duly noted," he stated, slightly annoyed.

"It is a place where we *humans* need some privacy, okay?" I explained in a calmer tone, while I grabbed my towel and wrapped it around me. "It's not very nice making me jump out of my skin with these pop-ins you do – not to mention the threat of heart attacks ..."

"Do not be silly; it is quite impossible for you to jump out of your own skin. And you are in both perfect form and condition; the likelihood of cardiac problems is minimal and improbable."

I rolled my eyes, remembering Vigil was never very good with figures of speech.

"Speaking of pop-ins, have you been around lately, Vigil?" I asked. "I mean, popping up unannounced in the house?" I was thinking about all the weird shadows and the bumping sounds. Could it have been Vigil all along causing all the rumpus and making me worry over nothing?

He frowned, not quite understanding the question. "No. This is the first time since the hotel bar meeting. Why do you ask?"

"It's nothing ... I suppose it's just me going nuts, then: seeing weird shadows and imagining things," I mumbled, disconcerted.

Vigil shifted his stance by the sink, suddenly uncomfortable. "Are you seeing weird shadows around the house?" he asked in a cautious tone.

I glanced up curiously. "Yeah. Don't tell me you know something about that?"

"Hmm," he said hesitantly. I could tell he was trying to hide something as I caught the undercurrent of emotion: worry with a mix of guilt.

Vigil was really hard to read. The fact that he wasn't human and that his unearthly race was exceptionally good at concealing emotions made him a master of disguising his true feelings. I had learned through years of being friends with Vigil the right way to understand him and the trick to catch his emotions. Plus, Vigil had been spending a lot of his personal time learning "human things". The more he learned, the more human he became, the easier it was for me to read him.

"So, Vigil, what is it that you're hiding from me?" I said, deadpan, watching him flinch at being caught.

"Yes, well, about that," he began, shifting his feet nervously. "Did the weird shadows start after my last visit?" he asked, still being vague.

I paused, thinking about it. It seemed about right. "Yeah, I guess so. I haven't thought about it, but it all started soon after your last visit. Shadows and bumps and noises in the dark. And my body seems to react in overdrive for no reason at all. It is driving me nuts here. I thought I was seriously going insane over the past couple of days …"

He glanced at the floor, deep in thought. "Well, you are certainly not insane. You should trust your instincts; they are giving you the correct reactions, perceiving danger instinctively. It is not just your imagination playing tricks on you," he stated seriously, looking straight at me now.

He had a weird look in his eyes, like he'd been caught doing something wrong. That was a major deal for Vigil and his kind. They were sticklers for rules; doing something wrong was a serious cause of shame to them.

"There is a great possibility that my work may have followed me here somehow," he confessed. "I always take extreme caution that I am not followed, but this latest job is particularly devious. A sneaky little thing, it is," he said, pursing his lips. "I am deeply sorry for the inconvenience. But it seems it has tagged on to you and your house."

"Tagged on to me? Why?" I asked, startled.

"I do not know. It has a confusing way of thinking. I do not understand its behavior, which is why I am struggling to capture it."

"Capture what? What is this thing?"

"This creature has been disrupting things in many worlds, breaking in and stealing priceless items of special uniqueness. I can't disclose the importance of these items to you, but their absence is causing serious disturbances in many realities. It is my job to put these items back where they belong and prevent the being from continuing its activities. It needs to be caught at all costs: these are the orders I have received so far."

"So, is this thing dangerous? I mean, for me? How worried should I be right now?" I asked, getting slightly agitated.

On the one hand, I was actually kind of relieved. I wasn't crazy after all. I wasn't imagining things; there were indeed monsters lurking in the shadows. But on the other hand, there was some "thing" in the house. But hey, at least now I was aware of it and could properly protect myself.

"This creature can be very dangerous when cornered," Vigil replied. "It will fight back fiercely and sometimes nastily to avoid being captured. Which is what I have been trying to do for a long time now: capture the damned thing. It is quite ingenious at escaping. It is sleek and misleading, a dishonest, deceitful being, causing many problems wherever it goes. I have had it in my grasp a few times, but it always manages to slither away. It is most vexing," Vigil said in a strained voice. "That is why I came to talk to you the last time. I sought advice from you about a new way to trap it."

"Okay, let me think ... You said you've been following it. Can you track this thing, then? What's its weakness?"

"It is a very vague tracking I do, but it has slipped off my radar for a while now ... to be precise, after our hotel meeting." He looked guilt-stricken then. "I cannot sense its presence around the house at the moment. It is probably far away from here. But eventually it could try to come back, for whatever reasons it has."

"So, what happens if this thing shows up again?"

"The easiest way for you to find it is to follow the sound. Do not trust your eyes; it has a mimesis mechanism. Trust your ears, then you will not be misled."

"Mimesis?" I asked, confused.

"It can shift, copy and blend in with the environment; mimic light, colors and textures. It becomes almost invisible to the human eye. You will not be able to see it, no matter how hard you look. Darkness is its best cover, the perfect environment in which to blend in."

"It's like Tristan's fading?" I asked, remembering Tristan's special ability during his first year as a living boy.

"Not quite. It has the same results but the mechanism is different. Tristan's trick worked more by the way of stepping partially out of your reality, and this being basically copies patterns, like your chameleon does. I do know it frightens easily with light." Vigil pondered. "If you need to defend yourself, find something that produces light. It should scare it away from you. If you are positively certain you have found it, use the marking on your wrist and call me. I am the best option to seize this being."

"Oh. Okay, got it," I muttered grudgingly, not at all appreciating his patronizing tone.

"I am serious, Joe. I am best equipped for this. Do not try to do it by yourself. Call for me," he repeated. "It is a dangerous magical being with a lot of tricks up its sleeve. Believe me on this; I have been constantly reminded of that."

"OKAY, fine. You don't need to say it again, I'm not stupid."

"I was not in any way insinuating your absence of intelligence. I merely pointed out the known stubborn streak in your personality."

"Yeah, yeah." I waved a hand at him, annoyed. "So, to sum it up, I'll be here serving as human bait so when this thing comes back, I call you, you zap in and grab the sneaky little bugger and problem solved?"

"Correct." He straightened his clothes with a satisfied smile. "Well, that was a very productive talk," he exclaimed, sounding as close as he got to happiness. "We have a plan of action in process, and soon this nuisance will be all over. You always come to the rescue, Joe Gray. I am very grateful for your help, as always." He bowed lightly.

"No problem, V."

He stopped mid-bow and raised an eyebrow at me. "You and your habits of nick-naming," he said, slightly amused.

"You know you love it," I teased him.

He had a mocking smirk on his lips, but he didn't contradict me.

"Well, I shall be going now. Take care, Joe. Call me if anything strange happens," he said, and gave me a curt nod before blinking out of the room.

I went to bed in a much brighter mood. Now I knew what I was dealing with, the true nature of this furtive shadow thing. I had a plan in action and I also knew the sneaky little bugger's weakness.

But, just to be on the safe side, I grabbed the baseball bat and placed it by the side of my bed, put a flashlight on my nightstand and left the bathroom light on.

I woke up late in the evening as Harry burst into the room.

"No, no, Harry! This is not your room, dude," Josh said in a hushed voice, pulling him back into the hallway as I sat up in bed, startled.

"Sorry, go back to sleep. Harry ran ahead of us and we couldn't stop him in time," Tristan apologized from the doorway.

"He had a little too much to drink tonight," Sam explained, while trying to hold Harry up with Josh's help.

"Harry, it's time to go to your room now, okay?" Tristan ordered, pulling Harry firmly into his own room. Wide awake now, I followed them.

"What? Nooo! I'm not tired! Let's go out again. I'll bet we can meet some chicks. I'm single now, it's time to celebrate!" he said, trying to walk right back out of his room, but Josh pulled him easily towards the bed again.

"No, you've had enough for one night. It's time to get some sleep, buddy," Tristan said.

Harry slumped onto his bed and scowled at us all.

I sat down on Harry's bed, smiling at him.

"Joeyyy. You're here! You're the best! You know I love you so much, right?" he said in a slurred voice. Excitement masked his grief, but I could see past it. His eyes were shifting and blurry with too much agitation. I hugged him and passed my hand through the locks of his blond hair. I felt him relax instantly under my fingertips.

"Shhhh. I know. I love you too, Harry Bear," I whispered into his ear.

His agitation washed away with every stroke of my fingers. After a while I let go and laid him back on the bed. His eyes were closing in exhaustion.

"You go to sleep now, okay, sweetie?" I said, sweeping his bangs gently off his face.

"M'okay," he mumbled, already half-conscious.

I took his shoes off, pulled up his blanket and covered him, before walking out of the room.

The boys watched the scene in amusement. "Wow, I don't know how you do it; it's like you cast a spell on him or something!" Josh exclaimed in a low voice, really impressed.

"It takes hours to make him go to bed when he's like that," Seth added "You're the only one who's able to calm him down easily, you know."

I signaled for them to step out of Harry's room and talk outside. "Yes, Josh. I am quite the 'witch', remember? And getting a really drunk boy to sleep is a hard spell to cast," I mocked him. "Now, you boys better go to sleep right now as well, before I magic some warts on to you, you hear?" I joked.

The look on their faces? Priceless.

Just because I had a history of dealing with the supernatural – bringing Tristan back from the dead, casting spells against Vigil, and also having a close relationship with Death – the boys all freaked out over any little thing I said about magic.

I grabbed Tristan's hand and pulled him along with me to his room. I needed all the rest I could get tonight, because tomorrow I was going to have a busy day presenting awards, playing live and having to wear blasted heels.

For a moment, I wished I could stay at home to fight magical, dangerous creatures rather than face that stage all by myself in high heels …

Chapter Ten

Beanie Boy

But the high heels did beckon, and I found myself wobbling around in a pair of *really* high ones somewhere backstage at the National Music Awards.

The black heels and the dress were Tiffany's treat for the night. She was, after all, an incredible clothes designer as well as my official fashion advisor.

She'd had made for me a classy custom-made gown which resembled the one Grace Kelly wore in Hitchcock's *Rear Window* movie. It had a tight black top with a deep V which showed my cleavage and gave me a "Y" silhouette, and an embroidered round white skirt which flowed gracefully as I walked, all cinched together at the waist with a thin black belt.

The black heels were forced upon me. I could not escape that painful doom.

I liked dresses inspired by the Fifties. Firstly because it was the period of time in which Tristan had grown up and it was an era that moved him dearly. Secondly because I genuinely loved the Fifties style; it was elegant, reserved and sophisticated.

The way Tristan looked at me as I walked down the stairs in my dress had rendered me speechless. The expression on his face had been frozen in awe, but from his eyes I could see that inside he flared with a blinding admiration. He didn't say a word; he just stared in reverent silence.

And now I was roaming the maze of corridors in this iconic building on my own, desperately trying to move without tripping over and twisting my ankle in the process. The award I was presenting was coming up, and I was hopelessly lost in the labyrinth they called backstage of the most prestigious concert hall theater in the country.

My eyes were focused on my feet and the floor when I crashed into someone. I staggered back and looked up, startled to see a guy shooting daggers at me.

"Hey! Watch where you're going," the guy barked. "Why is everyone in here running around like headless chickens, for crying out loud?"

I squinted my eyes angrily, profoundly offended by his excessive rudeness.

Even though he kind of had a point there, since I had actually seen a handful of people running round all flustered and – quite frankly – a bit like headless chickens. But there was no need for him to bite my head off like that.

He looked older than me, maybe in his thirties, and he was wearing a gray beanie which covered most of his dirty-blond hair. I poked him hard in the chest, my nostrils flaring; the force I'd put through my finger made him stagger back.

"Hey, pal. *You* watch where you're going," I barked right back at him.

His light-blue eyes flashed with surprise, but he recovered from the shock fast enough, a conceited smirk already plastered on his face.

"Did you just poke me?" he asked cynically.

"What do you think, Captain Obvious?"

"You shouldn't poke people twice your size, doll face," he said in a threatening tone. "I could easily poke you back." He stepped forward to add weight to his warning.

He didn't know I wasn't easily intimidated, and would never back down from a bully. He also didn't know I had a wealth of martial arts training, and could probably knock him down twice before he could say "doll face" again.

"I can watch you try, mister. And then you can watch me kick your ass."

He looked down at me incredulously, taking in my outfit. His eyes lingering way too long over my cleavage.

"Are you serious?" he said, his eyes glinting in amusement. I'm sure he couldn't believe a petite, delicate girl had just threatened to kick his ass.

"Are *you* serious?" I replied, irritated. What I really meant though was, *are you seriously this much of an ass?*

He quickly caught on to the subtext beneath my tone.

We both stood there, locked in our staring contest, until I decided I'd had enough of this chauvinistic caveman. I didn't have time for this nonsense right now. I was late and lost and had a freaking award to present.

"You know what, I don't have time for this. I have better things to do than teach you good manners." I waved a hand over his face and walked away, leaving him with yet another shocked expression.

Unfortunately, my storming off was less than impressive due to my slow, staggering step. I cursed the gods of high heels under my breath but persevered with my dramatic exit.

"Why don't you have time to teach me now? Do you

have somewhere to go?" Beanie dude had caught up with
me with his long strides. I frowned, but continued walking
all the same.

"Yes, I do have somewhere to go, if you must know," I
stated plainly. I could rub it in his face that I was a special
guest hostess for the evening, but that would mean acting
like a conceited snob, and that was beneath me.

"Where?" he asked.

"It's none of your business,"

"Ooh, spunky. I like it!" he teased. "Do you even know
where you're going?"

"I know *exactly* where I'm going," I lied.

"Are you sure? You look kinda lost."

"I'm not lost!"

"You don't even know where you are right now, do
you?"

"Yes, I do! I'm backstage. Happy?"

"Well, that was kind of vague …" he mused, that
irritating side-smirk back on his face.

"Listen, I know where I am, and where I'm going. The
question is, why are you *following* me?" I was getting more
irritated by the second.

"Oh, I'm not lost. You amuse me. It's fun following
you around," he said, beaming radiantly. "And you're the
prettiest girl I have ever seen. And I've seen quite a lot in
my life. So that's a plus."

"Don't you have other people to annoy and be rude to?
I don't want to keep you from shouting at someone else."

He laughed loudly. "You're funny with all your
snapping."

A small usher girl turned a sharp corner in front of
us and almost crashed into us both. She stumbled back,

looking baffled, and then blushed, apologized and scurried off in a hurry.

"Headless chickens everywhere," he pointed out.

"Seriously, can't you go somewhere else and leave me alone?" I half asked, half whined.

"I *could* ..." he began. "But I won't! You're too much fun, doll face."

"Stop calling me that," I snapped.

If he called me doll face one more time I was going to blow a gasket here.

"What should I call you then? What's your name?"

Like hell was I going to tell him my name. He'd tease me mercilessly with the "you have a boy's name" response I always got.

"I *could* tell you ... but I won't," I said, echoing his taunt to me.

That only made him laugh at me again. "Would you like to know *my* name?" he asked teasingly.

"You know what? I really wouldn't," I said in a bored voice, turning the corner.

He turned right alongside me.

He chuckled. "I'm starting to grow fond of you and your snapping ways."

"Funny, cos I'm starting to seriously dislike you and your annoying ways."

"Aw, come on, Snappy! You don't like me even a little bit?" he said, nudging me in the side. "I'm calling you Snappy from now on, since you're not telling me your name. I enjoy giving people nicknames; it's my 'thing'."

I was about to say "No way? Me too!" but then I remembered I couldn't stand him and just glared instead.

"Okay, Snappy, I apologize for biting your head off. I

only want us to be friends," he said with a sincere, honest smile.

I eyed him cautiously, agreeing to a truce. I took a good look at him. He was kind of cute, in an annoying sort of way. He was wearing a rock band T-shirt, dark jeans and black boots, and he reminded me somewhat of Tristan: tall, broad-shouldered. Even his eyes were like Tristan's, a blue hue so soft and faded, it nearly looked like gray. But instead of Tristan's sweet charm, Beanie Boy oozed cynicism with an irritating bad boy aura.

The important thing, though, was what I saw when I looked into Beanie Boy's eyes. He was playing me. I could see how much he was enjoying this, and thinking he was winning me over. I was no more than an entertaining and amusing target to chase.

That was quite enough of a read for me. *Only wants to be friends, my ass!*

"You know this nicknaming quirk you say you have?" I asked, taking a step back and away from him. "I have a quirk too, you know. It's *my* 'thing'. I always know when people are lying to me."

Before he could reply, another guy popped his head round the end of the corridor and shouted, "Hey, man! There you are. I've been looking all over for you. What the hell do you think you're doing? We gotta go."

I took the opportunity to quietly slip away round a corner, disappearing out of sight.

I walked as fast I could, until I finally bumped into the event coordinator. He was freaking out at me, grabbing my hand and pulling me through the hallways like they were on fire. One minute we were walking through corridors, the next I was being pushed into an antechamber at the side of the stage, a trophy being shoved in my hands, and all the while he was shouting instructions at me at the rate of machine-gun fire. He stopped and looked at me expectantly, as if waiting for a reply to a question I hadn't even heard him ask.

"So, did you get everything I just said?" he asked.

"Yeah, sure," I lied. I hadn't got anything. *At all.*

"Fabulous! So, go present the award now and call for Cale, okay?" he instructed me one last time.

"Okay. Wait. So, this is the award fooor ..." I rambled, trying to fish for the name of the damned title I was suppose to introduce.

He stared at me, looking baffled, and then rolled his eyes. "Here," he said, pointing to the engraved inscription on the trophy and reading it aloud, very slowly. "Outstanding. Artist. Award. Hand it over to Caleb Jones, will ya?" he said, clearly exasperated.

"Caleb Jones?" I gasped. I didn't know this award was for Caleb frigging Jones! He was the lead singer of The Accidentals. That band was incredible! And he was the most outstanding musician ever – oh, I got the award title now – but, but, seriously, he was amazing. A genuine prodigy; a genius musician. He'd probably played instruments since he was, what? One year old? He was probably composing songs in the womb, that was how outstanding he was. And his music? Just incredible.

And I was going to meet him. And give him an award! But I didn't have time to freak out or even have my fan-girl moment because my name was called on the speakers and then I was being shooed on to the stage. I hadn't had the chance to process what was happening.

I clutched the trophy and stumbled forward, while the

show host finished up introducing me: "... and please welcome to the stage, my favorite, and – let's be honest, folks – the prettiest of The Lost Boys. Joe Gray!"

I was greeted with a wave of applause as I walked slowly to the center of the stage. Inside, I was repeating to myself, "Please, God, don't let me trip over." The spotlights were blinding and stung my eyes. I stopped in front of the microphone and smiled back at the host, who had stepped a few feet behind me.

I took a deep breath and leaned close to the mic.

"So, it is time for me to present the next award." I cleared my suddenly incredibly dry throat. "It is a great honor for me to be here, delivering this special award for the Outstanding Artist of the Year. And the winner is ... Mr. Caleb Jones! So, Mr. Jones, this is for you. Come and get your award."

I held out the trophy towards the audience and then turned to look at my side, where Caleb Jones was already walking across the stage. Everybody in the whole auditorium was clapping and cheering hard for him. My eyes widened as I watched him approach where I standing – stock still.

Caleb Jones, leader of The Accidentals rock band. Caleb, award winner, Grammy collector, living legend and, in my opinion, the most talented and ingenious musician of his time. Always number one on the radio; endlessly on the "hot list". Woman seducer extraordinaire and internationally renowned rock star.

Caleb Jones, also known – to me – as Beanie Boy.

Chapter Eleven

Afterparty

He wasn't wearing his gray beanie any more; his long, dark-blond locks fell sexily over his eyes now. He stopped by my side, smiling, and gave a short wave to the audience, who applauded him even more.

But ... but ... How could that be? I knew Caleb Jones. I mean, I'd seen him on TV shows, interviews, music store posters – and he did not look like this! Caleb Jones had a thick beard and really short hair. He had vivid blue eyes. And he did not act like a chauvinistic caveman! This Caleb standing right here by my side had long hair falling over his face, no beard at all, almost-gray eyes, and he was certainly very chauvinistic!

He stopped waving at the audience and focused for the first time on my surprised face. He frowned ever so slightly, a hint of recognition drifting across his face, and then it hit him too. He grinned wickedly at me, that irritating smirk back in place. I was still too shocked to react.

And then he did the unthinkable: he took a step closer and held me in a *very* tight hug as if we were long-lost friends. For a second, I almost thought he was going to squeeze my bum, but he contained himself – only just, I might add – and his hands slid dangerously towards the small of my back.

He noticed that I was about to protest and quickly whispered into my ear, "Hey, Snappy. Nice seeing you again." And he stepped back, a victorious glint bright in his gray-blue eyes.

He turned from me to the microphone. He was about to give his acknowledgement speech. That was my cue to step back and walk inconspicuously offstage. As he began making his speech I couldn't help cursing him under my breath.

I stayed at our table with the boys for the rest of the evening. Our performance had gone smoothly and afterwards we'd been surprised to win Best Album of the Year. We'd been rushed onstage to collect the award and give our acknowledgment speeches. Tristan and Seth had done most of the talking, while Sam and Harry did their funny gimmicks and made jokes. Like me, Josh wasn't very fond of public speaking so we stayed at the back.

Most people were already drifting off to the afterparty, so we followed the crowd. The boys went ahead, all excited and looking handsome in their fancy black suits, while Tristan and I tagged along behind. Tristan looked stunning in his tailored black suit, with a long-sleeved black shirt and silk black tie. As we walked, his hand rested protectively on the small of my back.

"I'm glad you're with me now to clear the way. I'm one bump away from falling to the floor in these blasted heels," I said to him. Tristan had such an awe-inspiring presence, he could part any crowd.

"What are you talking about, Joe?" Tristan asked with

a tender smile. "They are parting to let *you* pass, not me. You look like a princess." He turned to look at me, a mesmerizing glint in his eyes. "It's really endearing how clueless you are about it."

I laughed and waved my hand at him, not quite believing his flattering words.

We were surrounded by people as soon as we walked inside the oval room where the party was being held in the ceremonial chamber at the concert hall. I tried to stick by Tristan's side, but people kept calling me over to them. Tristan went to the other side of the room to congratulate a fellow musician on their award, so we ended up drifting apart in the swarm of people which buzzed relentlessly around us.

Every time I caught a glimpse of Tristan he was surrounded by women. It was kind of annoying how any female in a room always managed to make a beeline for him. Although I guessed Tristan also had to deal with the male attention that was directed towards me too, so I tried to not let it bother me. I was not going to be that girl who threw jealous fits, like Miss Jackie Sunford.

That said, my cool demeanor was blown into thin air when I saw the woman who was leaning over Tristan. *Jessica.* Or, as I liked to call her, Jessica Red, because she always wore red wherever she went.

Jessica was the kind of woman every man fantasized about, with her long chocolate hair falling daintily over plump red lips; long legs, thin waist and huge breasts. She was a femme fatale and also the queen of seduction. Jessica didn't walk, she swayed. She didn't talk, she purred. And she liked to toy with men like they were assorted candy. A man-eater if ever I saw one.

The most important name on her list of desired conquests was Tristan: he was her dream guy, and she made no secret of it. She treated him as if he were the ultimate prize. He was the guy who had dismissed her over and over again, and apparently she'd vowed to make him crawl at her feet at any cost. Every time I saw her, she was trying to make a move on Tristan. I hated her guts.

As I watched Jessica rubbing herself all over him, all my self-control went out the window. I marched over there, fists balled at my sides and my jaw clenched. I grabbed his hand hard and yanked him away from her.

"Hey, Tristan, sorry to interrupt" – *not sorry at all, dude* – "but I need to talk to you urgently." And by talk I mean *slap you senseless for letting her rub all over you like that.* "Come with me." *Or I swear to God someone will die very soon.*

I turned around and pulled him with me without waiting for a reply. We hurried to the other side of the room, and when we stopped Tristan looked at me with a relieved smile.

"Thanks. She had me cornered there and I couldn't escape no matter how hard I tried. I was trying to catch your eye for a while, you know, to see if you could intervene and rescue me." He chuckled.

"You were?" I asked, a little taken aback. I had so been preparing an angry speech. Lucky I had kept my mouth shut.

"Yeah … for about fifteen minutes."

"Oh, erm, sorry about that."

"That's okay," he said, smiling "You were very … *efficient* … bailing me out. Not very subtle, but very efficient."

"Sorry again," I apologized, embarrassed. "But I had to act; she was one second away from shoving her boobs in your face!"

He let out one of his sexy laughs just as Seth appeared out of the blue and grabbed our arms.

"Hey, guys. Quick, follow me! You won't believe who wants to talk to you!" he said, pulling us in a fluster. He hurtled us through the crowd and straight into a more secluded part of the room, where Sam, Josh and Tiffany were already waiting with three other people. One of the guys I'd never seen before, but another was the guy who had appeared backstage shouting at Caleb – and the third was Caleb Jones.

"Guys, found them!" Seth shouted, beckoning us over. "This is Tristan Halloway and Joe Gray. Guys, this is Caleb and The Accidentals, Neil and Lee. *Haha*." He laughed to himself. "Why am I telling you that? Of course you know them; who *doesn't* know The Accidentals, right?" Seth had clearly gone into fan-boy mode.

Tristan's eyes widened a little. I could see that he and all of the other boys were trying to act cool to impress Caleb and his band. Seth was still freaking out. I didn't know he was that much of a fan.

Tristan extended his hand and introduced himself. Trying to be inconspicuous, I shifted closer to Tiffany and Seth – they were standing the farthest away from Caleb in the circle – as the rest of the introductions were made.

Caleb kept taking sly peeks in my direction while he congratulated Tristan on our performance, and I noticed that slowly he continued manoeuvering himself around the circle to get closer to me.

I excused myself, saying I needed to find Harry – he was

going to be devastated to know he had missed meeting The Accidentals – and darted quickly away.

Nobody paid much attention except for Caleb. He watched me disappear into the crowd with a mixture of disappointment and surprise in his eyes. He couldn't understand why I wasn't interested in him, why I wasn't hovering around him like all the other girls did, and why, even after I had discovered who he truly was, after we had been formally introduced, I still ran from him.

He wasn't to know I had one of the most charming rock stars already in my arms.

Chapter Twelve

Baby and Doll

We didn't stay long at the afterparty.

Harry was beyond upset by the time we got him home. The harassment he had suffered at the party had been non-stop, with people endlessly asking about his break-up. He had drunk a lot, so Tristan and I decided to drag him home before people started talking. It took me quite some time to get him to cool down.

It seemed like I had only been sleeping a couple hours when Sam woke me up by knocking softly on the door. "Sorry to wake you, Joey," he whispered, evidently trying not to wake Tristan too. "But, erm, it's just that Harry isn't feeling well … huge hangover. Seth and Tiff aren't in good shape, either, and Amanda isn't here. There's too many sick people and I'm not so sure what to do …"

I leaned on my elbows and rubbed my eyes wearily. "Honey, the kids are crying again," I mumbled at Tristan, smiling.

"… went last time … your turn," he grunted in a muffled voice, his face buried deep in the pillow.

"Swell," I muttered under my breath, and tossed the sheets away from me, getting out of bed.

Becca arrived after lunch to collect a couple of Lost Boys for a quick meeting at Mr. Silver's office. We were needed for some poster approvals for the marketing department and a few press releases about the band. Tristan was the only one in any condition to deal with work, so he left with Becca. I stayed home to rest a little.

It was late in the afternoon when he arrived back from the record label's office to find me waiting for him with a little surprise.

"You all owe me big time for going out to work while you all stayed here lazing around and relaxing," he called out as he walked into the bedroom. From the en suite bathroom I could hear him slumping down on the bed and tossing his shoes away.

"I know, I've been waiting for you to come home so I can repay you," I said as I walked in wearing a pearly babydoll slip that Tiffany had made especially for me.

The main lights in the room were out; only the shimmering yellow glow from the bedside lamp illuminated the room.

"If you're planning to give me a free massage, I'm all—" he started to say, but then he stopped.

"I was thinking of something else, but if you want the massage—" I stopped too. "What's wrong? Are you okay?" I grazed my fingers lightly through his hair.

He looked down very slowly and placed both his hands around my waist. "You ..."

"Something's wrong with me?"

"No ... nothing's wrong. I just ... want to have a good look at you," he said, his eyes roaming over my body. "*Baby* and *doll* are indeed the first words that come to mind." He slipped the lace shoulder strings carefully down over my shoulders. "You ... look amazing."

I looked down at myself, feeling the heat of his stare on every inch of my skin, and smiled, pleased with his reaction. "I take it you like it, then? I thought this would be a good way to compensate you for going to that meeting alone."

"Oh, it compensates all right," he stated firmly, grabbing my waist and pulling me closer. "You can compensate me more, if you want to." He lay me down on the bed and leaned over me.

I was about to give a witty comeback when he crushed his lips against mine. All thoughts escaped my mind. He kissed me with so much hunger that it left me reeling in bliss. His hands roamed urgently over my body while mine grabbed fistfuls of his hair, my fingers sliding through dark locks in my haste to pull him closer. We rolled in bed as if a storm was engulfing us both, taking away all our restraint and leaving only need and longing. Our mouths crashed and merged into one. I dug my fingers into his back, feeling his muscles bulge and strain with every move. As I clung to him fiercely, fighting to breathe him in, taste him, feel him, the heat of his skin burned beneath my fingertips. He finally gave in and lost himself in me completely.

He pushed himself on top of me in wild abandon, his breathing uneven and labored as he let a throaty moan escape his lips in blissful release.

"That ... was ... amazing," he said between gasps a few moments later. "Sorry about ... the haste. Couldn't control ... myself." He dropped back onto the bed next to me.

"That's okay. You call it haste, I call it rampantly voracious." I smiled, slightly breathless as well.

He pulled me close and snuggled his face in the crook of my neck, his strong arms enveloping me firmly. "You know, I've missed being with you," he said.

"You're with me all the time, Tris." I chuckled, grazing my fingers through his hair.

"You know what I mean. I miss being with you, like right now," he said, trailing his fingers lightly over my hips. "I don't know ... I feel like we are always too busy these days, dealing with work all the time. Life keeps getting in the way. I hardly get to be with you. I mean, really with you. I don't know if I'm making any sense ... We are with each other, but we're not together."

"But I'm with you now," I said, laying my hand on top of his. "Can you feel it?"

"Yeah." He smiled, interlacing our fingers. Silence surrounded us like a comfortable blanket. After a while he said, "If you're really with me, let me tell the world you're my girlfriend. I get that you are not marrying me ... yet. But throw me a bone, at least."

That was absolutely true. Tristan had asked me to marry him many times since we'd started out as a band, three years ago. With respect to his Fifties mindset and old-fashioned upbringing, we should have married soon after graduation. If it had been up to him we would have tied the knot even before that. He didn't understand what was taking me so long to finally agree to marry him. The first time he'd proposed I had freaked out big time. We were still in our last year at school. The second time, we had just started our careers and there was so much work to do, and so many tours yet to play. We had all the time in the world, I thought, so why did he want to rush into it?

He had been very disappointed the first time I said no,

but he hadn't given up. He pressed the question year after year. After a while he got used to me declining. I kept telling him it was just not the right time. I liked the way things were. Why mess up something that was working just fine?

"I get it, Joe. You're not ready. I can wait for as long as you need," he would say.

But why was I so strongly resisting coming clean about my relationship with Tristan? Seth had done it. Harry and Sam – and even Josh – didn't care about announcing whichever girl they were seeing. Why were we still hiding our relationship? What was I so afraid of?

For a while I'd told myself it was because of our record label demanding we keep it a secret. But then again, there was always something getting in the way; every time I thought about coming clean, a problem appeared: a busy tour, accidents at bookstores, Harry's break-up, award ceremonies. There was always an excuse. As Tristan put it, there was always one more problem to deal with. What was my excuse now?

There was no good excuse. But I knew deep down the reason I avoided this so much. Because I knew the next step was going to be marriage. And once we'd publicly announced that we were together, I really would have to say yes to Tristan's proposals, no matter if I was ready or not. The whole world would be pressuring me then. And I wanted to accept him not out of fear, or pressure, but because of my heart.

So I kept stalling. And left Tristan in suspense all this time. That wasn't right, either. Maybe it was time to let this secret out. Once and for all. Maybe it was time to face my fears.

"You're right. I have been stalling for too long. We should tell everybody," I finally agreed.

"Are you serious?" he asked, stunned.

"Yes. I'm dead serious. Any time you want. You decide."

I closed our deal with a deep kiss.

Chapter Thirteen

Sneak Attack!

At the news of our "outing", the boys decided to throw Tristan a "bachelor party". They were treating it as if we were officially getting married now, which annoyed me greatly and also confirmed my deepest fears. My closest friends had already started with the pressure. I could well imagine how the rest of the world was going to behave after they got the news.

Tristan and the boys had gone to a club to celebrate his last day as a "single man". I'd rolled my eyes at their jesting, but let them get on with their party. Although I suspected that this was just an excuse for the guys to go out clubbing without the girlfriends.

Tiffany had cancelled on me – a job emergency was going to keep her busy all night in her studio – so I was left to celebrate my "last night as a single lady" on my own, which amounted to falling sleep on the couch while watching a stupid reality show.

Yeah. Wild party girl, that was me.

I woke up in the middle of the night to thunder rattling the window panes and with this eerie feeling rising inside my chest, making the hair on the back of my neck stand up and goosebumps rise all over my arms.

I blinked, quickly switching to full alertness. I knew what those shivers were all about now.

So, tonight was going to be *the night*.

I had wondered how long it would take the sneaky shadow creature to come back to haunt me again … It had certainly taken long enough.

Another rumble of thunder cracked loudly outside. The shadows in the living room danced around me, but this time I didn't panic, I didn't run.

I was prepared. I had mulled over this plan ever since after the award ceremony. I was going to catch that devious thing, and tonight was the night!

A floorboard creaked at the other side of the room. This thing could be anywhere! My body screamed for me to run, warning me of imminent danger, but I forced myself to keep still.

Lightning flashed outside like it was trying to scare me too. I looked at the windows and bit my lip. A few drops of rain were splattering over the windows, with the threat of more to come. A summer storm wasn't going to help me with my plan. But it was not like I could reschedule another meeting with this thing, for when the time was a little more convenient. It was here now, and I had to deal with it, with or without rain.

I needed to remain calm. It wouldn't do me any good to panic. Creaks and snaps sounded from everywhere in the room; from the corners of my eyes I could see shadows move in quickly, and I swore I could feel something brush lightly over my ankle. But I still didn't run. Or scream. Or even flinch. It took all my willpower to make me stay still.

Tonight was the perfect opportunity; I couldn't waste it.

I stood up slowly from the couch and walked to the middle of the room. "You know, you can stop it now," I called out, crossing my arms over my chest. "I'm not scared and this is getting really old, really fast."

I waited as the noises continued for a while, but I kept my face blank and stood my ground. After a few seconds the noise subdued and there was nothing but dead silence in the room. If it wasn't for my body telling me I was still in danger, I would have thought the thing had left. But I knew I still needed to be alert. Danger was still afoot.

"Good. Now, how about you show yourself? Obviously you want something from me. I can't help you if you keep your little spooky show going on. You need to talk to me," I explained slowly.

There was a soft thump right in front of me and a low, terrifying hiss. I flinched a little, and then cursed myself for reacting. My eyes squinted, trying to focus on the patch on the floor where the thing seemed to be, right in front of me. But I couldn't see anything.

What if this thing was big? What if it was huge and could eat me in just one bite? What if it had six arms, or claws, or talons? Vigil hadn't told me anything about its appearance. Focus on the noise; don't trust your eyes: I remembered his warning.

The hiss in front of me intensified, diverting my thoughts away from Vigil.

"Okay, so, hmm ... Can you talk? English, preferably. I don't understand hissing, sorry." Yeah, way to go, *smart ass* Joey.

"Yesss, I talks," it hissed menacingly.

I was really impressed with myself for not flinching

again at that scary voice. The growl that followed was hoarse and guttural, a threatening warning.

"W-what can I do for y-you?" I asked. I was trying desperately to sound brave, but my stammering betrayed me.

"You helpss him." It hissed out every word like a nervous rattlesnake. "The Grayss. He huntss me, for ever and ever. Never givesss up, never stopss. But he comess for you alwaysss. Whyss?" it asked again, moving closer.

I took a step back. I didn't want that thing too close. Vigil had said it was only dangerous if cornered, but I wasn't taking any chances.

"Ah. You mean Vigil. He is only … a friend," I replied.

"Hmm. You liess … you knowss when I'm near … alwaysss. No one elsess doess that. You iss a ssorceress, you hass powerss!"

"I am a type of sorcerer, yes. You could say that." I took another cautious step back, walking casually to the glass door that led to the garden outside. I needed to get him in the backyard somehow. That was a very important part of my plan.

"You liess, witch! You helps him; you're powerful. Liesss and liess, iss all you sssays!" it hissed, following my steps.

Good. Follow me, wicked little thing.

I opened the glass door, pulling the keychain out with me. I'd had this planned for a couple of days. The small control for the sprinklers was tied to the keychain and was now safely tucked in my hand.

"Youss can help me! Essscape him for good! I can givess you anythingss! Anythingss you wantss! I hasss many thingsss!" it proposed, following me.

For the first time since the creature had started talking to me, I could discern his shimmering form on the grass. It appeared that its cloaking mechanism failed when it came into contact with water, the raindrops apparently short-circuiting his camouflage, making me able to see it.

The thing wasn't big at all. In fact, it was quite small. I sighed in relief. At least I knew it couldn't eat me in one quick bite. I tilted my head to get a better look at it. It looked sort of like a cat ... a distorted, alien-like cat. It was also the size of a big cat, with a long tail which flipped sideways. The light flickered and I could make out some type of fur. I couldn't see its face clearly but it had two feral-looking, bright-yellow eyes which stared straight at me. Its black pupils were thin horizontal slits, freakishly scary. I could read its eyes: they were filled with malice, cunning, dishonesty and evil.

The rest of its face blended into the darkness, but I could discern a faint glint of sharp teeth. Scary teeth. A whole lot of them. I shivered just looking at them. Those could bite your hands off for sure.

It noticed I was staring and grinned wickedly. "Sssee this?" it asked, holding up a small leather pouch. "I has many treasuress, sspecial thingss. Magic thingss. I givess you one, you helpss me?" it offered, and then hissed in surprise as a few drops of rain fell on him. Just like a cat, it wasn't very pleased at getting wet.

"Listen, huh ... what's your name?" I asked.

It was glaring menacingly at the sky, but at my question it glanced back at me, frowning. "Namess? You cannot ssay it. Not in your language." I could tell it was reluctant to tell me.

"Oh, come on. How hard can it be?" I scoffed.

"Wells, it'ss something like thiss ..." and then it gave a sort of screech so horrible and loud that I had to put my hands over my ears to muffle it.

I gasped. It was like hearing nails over a chalkboard, razors cutting glass ... a cat dying a horrible death.

"Erm, I guess you were right about that. Please, don't ever say your name again," I moaned, feeling as if my skin wanted to crawl away in fear. "I'm calling you Nick from now on." Sneaky Nick. Sounded just like him. "Listen, Nick, I can't help you escape from Vigil, sorry."

The rain started to gain force, falling heavily on us. I needed to act fast. Sneaky Nick wasn't going to stay out here in the rain much longer. I walked to the middle of the lawn, the remote control still safe in my hand.

"Whysss not?" Nick growled, following me close behind. His fur was trying hard to cope with all the water, and sometimes he would blend with the grass so perfectly that if it hadn't been for his bright-yellow eyes, I would have missed him completely, lost in the rain and the dark.

"If you won't help me, maybe I should get rid of yous then. Yous can't help the Grayss if you are no more!" he threatened. "I can eatss you up, quickss, easy! No one will ever know ..." Nick growled, showing me all of his teeth and taking one more step in my direction. The one last step I needed.

I smirked and raised my sprinkler control, pressing one button, hard. This remote wasn't used just to control the sprinklers on our lawn; it also controlled the garden lights, and that was what I'd come out here for – the bright spotlights tucked neatly in the lawn.

A circle of spotlights flashed on, blasting all of their

bright, white lights to the center of the circle where Sneaky Nick was standing now.

According to my calculations, when all the lights were up, they would form a trap surrounding my furry, sneaky little friend. Light was his weakness, wasn't it? That's what Vigil had said.

Nick recoiled in the grass, fear crossing his sickly yellow eyes, and then he started writhing and thrashing about in pain. He folded himself into a tiny ball, hissing, crying and cursing, but unable to move away. I stepped behind the spotlights and watched him. His little leather pouch had been thrown down at his side and its contents were spreading out all over the grass. A glass ball the size of a baseball rolled out of the bag, glinting oddly sharp for a second.

Nick's camouflage fur stopped working entirely because of the overload of light and rain, and then I could see him fully. I didn't know what the hell he was, but he sure was no cat.

Well, maybe a cat that had been munched up, swallowed and spat out again. Not a pretty sight, I tell you. The fact that the rain was completely drenching him wasn't helping his look, either. Have you ever seen a cat soaking wet? That was what Nick vaguely resembled. Pissed, scared and quite hideous.

"Pleass, pleass, make itssstop! Make itsstop," he cried out, little paws covering his eyes protectively. The rain was pouring on our heads and we were both totally soaked.

I beamed proudly at a job well done. The trap was working fine. Sneaky Nick was completely in my hold. Time to call Vigil.

Nick yelled and cried but did not move, frozen by all the

lights surrounding him. I glanced at the little trembling ball of wet fur and felt a pang of guilt.

Focusing my mind on the tattoo on my wrist, I called for Vigil. A few minutes passed with only the sound of the rain pouring on us and the whimpering sobs of the poor creature shaking in the light. I was feeling really sorry for him now. I hoped Vigil would come quickly. I closed my hand over my wrist and concentrated harder, calling out his name in my head, over and over again.

"Havess mercy, haves mercy, witch!" Nick's loud wails were disconcerting and distracted me from my concentration. "It hurtsss, sso much!"

I bit my lip. Nick sounded in so much pain. His moans were just … awful.

"Vigil will be here any minute now. Then I'll turn off the lights, okay? It won't be long, just … hang in there just a little bit more," I said, trying to comfort him.

A sharp stabbing pain shot through my arm, making me drop the remote control on the grass. "Oh, thank God, Vigil," I mumbled, holding my throbbing wrist.

Vigil was standing on the other side of the circle of spotlights, watching the scene curiously. His eyes searched for me and when he found me he smiled softly. Then Nick's loud wailing caught his attention and he shifted his gaze to him.

"Joey, what did I tell you?" He frowned, upset. "You should not have done that by yourself …"

I was about to reply when one of the spotlights in front of me blinked and buzzed, then went out. The rain had short-circuited the lamp. Both mine and Vigil's eyes snapped urgently to the broken spotlight. A dark line of shadow now broke the circle.

"Oh, no," I whispered. Then everything went downhill, fast as lightning.

Vigil's hand shot upwards, trying to summon something to enclose sneaky Nick, but it was already too late. The small patch of darkness in the circle was more than enough for Nick to dart forward and escape his luminous trap.

He now stood in front of me; murder flared in his yellow, glowing eyes.

I dry-gulped and stepped back, and Nick let out the most scary sound I had ever heard in my life. He wasn't crying or begging any more. He was mighty angry and wanted revenge.

His body was now visible, and for the first time I wished it wasn't. I wished I could not see the evil in his stare, the wicked grin of his mouth as he licked his pointy sharp teeth and prepared to pounce, his eyes glued to my neck.

I knew I had to act fast to avoid having my throat ripped apart. I bolted towards Vigil, trying to cut through the center of the spotlights. I wasn't fast enough. A tearing sound and a pressure on my legs made me stumble and fall, face down on the grass. I heard Vigil shouting my name.

I flipped myself over and saw Nick bite ferociously on the end of my jeans leg, by my ankle. He had me and I couldn't get away. I wriggled and kicked him in the face with my other leg, then scrambled in the wet grass to try to crawl away from him, but Nick wouldn't let me go, gnawing and biting viciously.

Now I knew what Vigil meant by that thing being dangerous if cornered. It was frigging ragging on me!

A sharp pain shot up my leg and I yelled, watching blood drench the fabric of my jeans, but I continued trying to kick him the hell away from me. He was wickedly fast and so strong for such a small thing.

Then Vigil's hand broke into my line of vision and grabbed the little devil by its furry neck. Nick yelped in surprise and let go of me.

I grabbed my leg, trying not to cry, but the pain in my ankle was too intense.

The danger was far from over.

Nick twisted around Vigil's hand and bit down on it, hard, succeeding in his bid to escape.

Vigil grimaced, cradling his hand. Rain washed over the spluttering blood that gushed from his open wound. I stared, astonished, as the wound healed itself in a matter of seconds.

Nick landed on the grass with a soft thump, making me snap my eyes back to him. I watched, almost hypnotized, as he licked a set of glistening, bloody teeth and focused his full attention on me.

"Crap, crap, crap," I muttered, dragging myself over the grass in sheer panic.

Nick prepared to jump, eyes on my throat, and pounced fast. Vigil appeared right in front of me, tackling Nick at the last second. He lost his balance because of the impact and tumbled down, falling on top of me.

We landed in a tangled heap and for a fraction of a second both of our hands lay on top of the glass ball – the one that had rolled out of Nick's leather pouch when I first trapped him.

A beam of piercing light exploded from the ball, engulfing everything around us and blinding me completely. The light was so fierce that it burned through my eyelids.

Hell, it felt like it was scorching inside my skull. It was

like a small sun was being born right in the middle of my back garden!

I tried to cover my eyes with one hand – the other was still glued to the glass ball – but the light kept bursting, implacable and searing. Excruciating pain shot through me, bombarding every cell, every nerve, flesh, blood and bone. Everything hurt, like I was being incinerated. It was just too much for me to handle, so my brain took over and did what was best for me. It shut down and I blacked out completely.

Chapter Fourteen

Mismatch

"Joe! Joey!"

I thought I was sleeping. It felt so good; everything was so dark, and hazy. Someone was shaking me, calling my name over and over again in a worried tone. It sounded familiar ... yet so far away ... As the shaking grew stronger, the voice got louder.

"Joey! Joey! Wake up!"

I grunted and risked opening my eyes, slightly afraid of what I would see. I was lying in Tristan's arms as he stroked my cheek, sweeping the wet hair out of my face, his own face a mask of concern. I blinked again, trying to understand what was happening, my blurry vision slowly adjusting to the night sky.

"Hey. Thank God, she's waking up," Tristan said, relief pouring out of him. "What happened here, Joey? Are you all right?"

I sat on the grass and looked around, feeling completely bewildered. It wasn't raining any more. Flashes of what had happened drifted back into my head in a jumbled mess as I surveyed the garden.

"When we got back from the club you weren't anywhere in the house; then Harry noticed the back door was open: the floor was all wet from the rain. We found you and Vigil lying on the grass, unconscious and completely drenched. What the hell happened here? Are you sure you're all right?" he asked in a strained voice.

"I feel okay." As I said it, I realized it was true. In fact, I felt better than fine. I felt like I could run a marathon right now. Which was very odd.

Sam and Harry were looking at me all worried, while Seth and Josh were kneeling close to a body lying on the grass a few feet away from me.

"Vigil!" I gasped, remembering our last seconds together in that blinding explosion of light. "Oh, God! Is he all right?" I scrambled to my feet and ran to him.

"It looks like he's unconscious, but not harmed," Seth answered, checking Vigil's pulse and airway.

I remembered sneaky, evil Nick and looked around, alarmed. "Did you guys see anything else when you arrived?"

"No. There was nothing here, just you and Vigil. Why?" Tristan asked. "Joey, what *happened*?" His tone was urgent now, demanding.

"Uh, I'll explain everything in a minute," I said, looking suspiciously at all the shadows around us. "Let's get Vigil inside first, where there's lots of light."

I wasn't sure myself what had really happened. I mean, it was all a mess in my head. One thing I knew for sure, though: Tristan was going to be pissed when he heard what I had tried to do tonight.

Josh and Sam carried Vigil, still unconscious, inside and laid him carefully on the living-room couch. Seth handed me a towel and Tristan went to get me a cup of tea. I knelt by Vigil's side and laid the back of my hand on his forehead. He didn't have a fever, his breathing had leveled and his pulse seemed steady. He was fine – unconscious, but physically fine.

When I took my hand away from him I realized for the first time that despite being close to Vigil, my wrist didn't hurt. Even when I wasn't touching him. That was … extremely odd.

Tristan returned with a hot cup of tea for me. I wasn't feeling cold but I took the tea anyway.

We all sat on the couch, Tristan next to me and the boys perching on the back and arms to give Vigil some space, and I explained what had happened, with everyone listening intently. Tristan's lips were pursed the whole time, his eyes fixed on me, his brow furrowed in a deep frown. He was getting angrier by the minute.

When I got to the part where Nick was biting my leg off, all of them glanced quickly at the hem of my jeans. So did I. I had forgotten about being hurt. Why was I not in pain? I lifted the ragged, blood-stained leg of my jeans to see my injury.

There was nothing. I mean, of course there was my leg, and some dried blood, but my skin was smooth and unscathed, not a single scratch or cut on it.

Okay. Definitely one more odd thing to add to the list. I swore Nick had bitten into my leg; I remembered the pain, the blood, the sound of his teeth ripping through my skin. How could there be nothing wrong with my leg now?

They all looked up at me with baffled faces. I shrugged and continued my story to the point where the light had burst out of that freaking glass ball and I had blacked out.

Seth went outside to retrieve Nick's objects that were still scattered over the grass – including the glass ball. Apparently Sneaky Nick was in such a hurry he had left all his precious magical artifacts behind. Or maybe the light had killed him? Obliterated him completely from the face of the Earth? That was a cheering thought.

Seth placed the small weird things and the leather pouch on the coffee table. There were a few battered wooden boxes, some misshapen metal objects, and the glass ball. They looked nothing like anything I'd ever seen before; the whole collection looked like useless, worthless bits of junk.

The glass ball wasn't transparent any more, though. It had turned a deep inky black color. For a moment I thought about telling Seth how reckless he was being touching all the objects with his bare hands – God knew what those blasted things could do – but I refrained. I was in no position to warn him about doing stupid things.

The ball stood still in the middle of the table, ominous and foreboding, a dangerous edge to its dark orbit. I leaned in closer and squinted my eyes, focusing on its smooth black surface. Tiny specks of brilliant white floated inside, like little points of ether floating in the thick black ink. It was quite eerie, yet beautiful at the same time, little stars floating aimlessly in the dark.

I glanced up and saw Tristan staring hard at me. Before he could unleash all his anger on me I straightened up and raised my hands in surrender.

"I know what you're going to say, Tris. I'm sorry, okay? I had no idea this whole thing would end up like this."

"That's just the point, Joey! You never think before you go and do stupid things. You could have ended up really hurt, or worse, for God's sake! What made you think you could handle this all by yourself? And why didn't you tell me this was happening? Did Vigil ask you to keep it a secret?"

"No, I just thought I didn't need to say anything. I know how worked up you get when Vigil is involved, and you get so mad at him. And it was all going to be over soon anyway; there was no need to worry anyone about it."

Harry was shuffling uncomfortably on the couch; he hated fights. The boys looked like they were dying to get out of there too. Tristan and I could go on for hours arguing about Vigil and they knew better than anyone not to get involved. They usually stayed quiet to avoid taking sides.

"I knew one day Vigil's 'job' would put you in danger. I've told you to stay out of it, but you never listen! You think I say this out of jealousy, but it's not that. This is really dangerous, Joey. You could've gotten hurt."

"I said I was sorry. Come on!" I shouted, throwing my hands up in the air.

The sound of our shouting made Vigil stir on the couch; he groaned, finally waking up. We both stopped arguing and everybody turned simultaneously in Vigil's direction.

He blinked and winced, trying to stand up. He managed to drag himself upright after a lot of effort.

"Vigil, thank God you're awake," I said, moving closer to him.

"Huh … what happened?" he asked in a small voice.

"Are you all right?"

"I-I am … not sure. I feel … weird. What happened?" he asked again.

I told the whole story to him, even the part for which he'd been present and had witnessed himself. Tristan huffed the entire time.

"Okay, I remember now," Vigil mumbled, rubbing his temples and then glancing at me with a slight scowl. "I told you not to do anything by yourself! You never listen!"

"Damn right," Tristan muttered in a low voice. I rolled my eyes at the both of them.

"How is your leg? Is it hurt too badly?" Vigil asked, worried.

"I'm fine. Leg's totally fine," I said.

"Why do you have to be so stubborn? How hard was it to follow my *one* instruction? Just one thing: you feel that thing near your house, you call me. Was that too much to ask?" Vigil scolded.

"You mean you didn't tell her to do this?" Tristan asked, uncrossing his arms.

"Of course not! I specifically ordered her *not* to do anything. This is very dangerous; she could have been really hurt," Vigil exclaimed. "All I asked was for her: To. Just. Call. Me."

"I DID. I *did* call you!" I shouted, trying to defend myself. They were both ganging up on me now, with their glares and scolding faces.

"... to call me as soon you noticed it was in the house. Did you call me as soon you noticed it was in the house, Joey?" Vigil asked, quirking an angry eyebrow.

"Yeah," I lied. "Well ... like, just a few minutes after."

They both stared at me, their faces full of disbelief.

"Oh, *all right*. I waited until I had it trapped. I had a plan. And it worked to perfection! Until that blasted rain and that freaking spotlight short-circuited on me ..." I huffed.

Vigil sighed heavily and slumped back on the couch, really tired now. I had never seen him looking tired before.

"Something is wrong here ... Why do I feel like, I don't

know, my body is heavier than normal? Is there something wrong with your gravity?" he asked, looking around the room.

"Uh ... I don't think so," I said. "That glass ball must have done something to you. It got my leg healed too." I lifted my jeans and showed him the smooth skin, scratch-free.

He frowned and leaned forward to have a better look. "That is odd. I remember clearly ... you were hurt. There was ... a lot of blood," he mumbled.

"I got the ball and all his other things from the backyard," Seth said, trying to be helpful.

Vigil's eyes shifted to the glass ball on the coffee table. He sat forward and picked it up cautiously and turned it around in his fingers, focusing all his attention on it.

"It was transparent like glass before. Now it's all black," I offered, in case he hadn't remembered.

He tilted his head to the side and his frown deepened, his customary move when he was concentrating. "Strange. I feel ... nothing," he muttered.

"What do you mean?" Josh asked. "It's not dangerous any more?"

"No, I mean, I do not feel anything. It is a magical object; I am supposed to feel its magic, the amount and concentration of it inherent within. That is how I measure the level of power. But I cannot feel anything in this," Vigil stated, placing the glass ball back on the coffee table with a frown.

"Maybe it's a one-shot sort of thing ... Maybe it's empty now," Harry ventured.

"Even in that case, magic leaves a residue. Like gunpowder after a shot. I should be able to feel it, something ... anything ..." He grunted and rubbed his temple again.

"My head is … annoying me," he stated, as if it were a malfunction of some kind.

"I'll get you a glass of water and an aspirin, hang on," I said, and headed for the kitchen. When I returned I handed him the glass of water while I fumbled with the aspirin bottle. Vigil reached out to me, his hands trembling slightly, and the glass slipped from his grasp, crashed to the wood floor and shattered into many pieces. He looked baffled for a second, like that had never happened to him before.

"I-I am deeply sorry. I do not know what is happening to me today …" He knelt down, picking up a bigger shard of glass from the floor. The glass slashed through his skin and he sucked in a sharp intake of air. He stared at the cut on his finger, and so did I. We all stared at his finger. Nothing happened.

"Hmm. Why are you not doing your magic healing thing, Vigil? Like you did when Nick bit your hand before?" I asked, hastily tucking the aspirin jar into my jeans pocket and reaching out to take hold of his hand.

He seemed agitated now, pulling away from me. "I-I … I am trying. It is not working. Wait, Nick who?"

"You know, the invisible cat from hell; the thing you're trying to catch. His name is Nick," I said. It was, now. At least for me.

He opened his mouth to say something, looked into my eyes, thought better of it, closed it, and then opened it again. He looked like a freaking fish out of water, gaping at me and holding his bleeding finger.

"Okay, I'll get something for his cut. Be back in a minute," Tristan said, thoroughly confused, and left the room, shaking his head and muttering something under his breath.

Vigil still looked shocked, and was still holding his finger. "Huh, this is very aggravating. I think it is better that I leave now and discuss this with my colleagues. They will advise me on the best course of action I should follow, and maybe help me understand all these ... unusual occurrences." He was still glaring at his finger as if it were a piece of broken, useless equipment.

He stood up and stayed quiet for a second. Then his eyes widened in bewilderment. He looked panicky now, sweat beading over his forehead.

"Oh," he said, and slid down on to the couch in complete and utter shock.

"What? What's going on? Are you feeling all right, Vigil? What is it?" I asked in a panic too.

"I-I ... I can't," he whispered.

"What? You can't *what*?"

He flickered his eyes at me. Then back at his finger. Then back at me again and then at the glass ball on the table.

"How are you feeling, Joe?" he asked slowly.

"I feel fine, Vigil. Why?"

He looked deeply into my eyes. "You feel ... anxious. A little scared, and curious. A little excited. I can see it. Very clearly."

"Huh. Okay?"

"I think ... I know what is going on," he said, mostly to himself.

"What's going on, Vigil?"

"I cannot leave. It is not working. Nothing is working."

"You mean you can't beam out of here?"

"Yes. I mean no, I can't," he said, looking a little distressed, and stood up again, after first grabbing a piece of glass from the floor. He walked up to me and took my hand into his. "I am sorry, I need to be sure," he said, and pressed the glass against my palm, sliding it through my skin.

Everybody gasped in surprise. Tristan, who had just come back into the room with the first aid kit, looked alarmed and called out.

"Hey! What the hell?" He ran over to me. But before he could do anything, Vigil raised my hand aloft and we all watched as the cut healed itself perfectly, just like it was supposed to have done with Vigil.

"You see? What is happening is that I do not have my powers any more," Vigil said, letting go of my hand. "You do."

Chapter Fifteen

Fragile

"WHAT?" Tristan and I both shouted at the same time.

The boys looked at each other, wide-eyed and scared, but still didn't say a word.

Vigil shifted his feet uncomfortably and stared at the glass ball again. "I have heard of magic orbs like this one. Never seen one before, but I have heard about them. They hold the power to switch inherent properties of potential vessels."

"Say that again? In English this time, please," I asked, baffled.

He glanced up and frowned, trying to understand what I wanted. "This magic crystal ball here switched our powers," he stated more simply.

"Oh," was all I could manage.

"Do you mean she has *your* powers and you have *hers*?" Tristan asked.

"Yes, in a word," Vigil answered, getting a little irritated at having to repeat himself. "She is surprised, nervous and a little anxious," he stated, glancing quickly at me before turning to Tristan. "You are worried about her

safety, angry that I have somehow put her in this situation
– which, by the way, I cannot really be held accountable
for since it is not entirely my fault – and you are also
feeling a small amount of jealousy. I might add that this
is really not the time for those types of emotions, if I may
put it so bluntly, for there is a much more important matter at hand. But, yes, I can now see all your emotions by
looking into your eyes, just like Joey could. It is rather
disconcerting. Do you have a way to turn this off?" he
asked me, rubbing his eyes.

"Huh. I haven't figured out how to block it yet, sorry,"
I said.

He sighed and wearily sat back down on the couch,
while Tristan, obviously affronted, scowled but remained
silent.

Okay, that explained a lot, actually – such as why my leg
was all healed, and my wrist mark wasn't hurting: I was all
buffed up with Vigil's powers.

"So ... I can really do all the stuff you could do, like,
really?" I asked, struggling to take it all in.

"Yes. You already have. You instinctively healed yourself." He rubbed his head again. It looked like his headache
was getting worse by the second. "Maybe we can make
this thing switch us back," he said, picking up the glass
ball again. "Joey, can you touch it, just like we did at the
garden?"

I nodded and touched the ball at the same time as Vigil.
We all watched expectantly.

Nothing happened.

He let out a frustrated huff. "It's not working."

"Maybe if we did this outside. You know? Maybe the
location matters," I suggested.

"Yes. Good thinking. Come on," he said, grabbing my hand eagerly and pulling me outside.

Boy, was he in a hurry to get his powers back or what?

Tristan and the boys followed, observing us in silence. It was a bit unnerving, the way they just stared and said nothing. I suddenly realized it was because I couldn't read their feelings any more. It had never occurred to me how much I depended on my sight to know what I should do. Now I was left in the dark.

Vigil and I stood in the same spot in the garden, and reenacted what had happened earlier to see if that would make the magic ball work again.

Again, nothing happened.

"Come on!" I yelled, squeezing the ball hard between my fingers. "What if it is really a 'one-shot' deal?"

Vigil was staring at the ball, deep in concentration. "It is a possibility ... but I highly doubt it. Honestly, this sort of device usually works by switching things back and forth. It is their most known particularity," he said, thoughtfully. "It was used by your people in the old days, you know, as a teaching device, of sorts."

"Teaching device?"

"Yes, witches used it to teach a lesson, to make the other person feel what it is like to be the other – what is the saying again? 'To walk a mile in someone's shoes'? Something like that." He leaned his face closer to the ball, squinting his eyes. "It should have a trigger ... some key to make it work again," he mumbled to himself. "We need to find out what it is."

"Hey, maybe you could ask your gray-hooded pals to help us out," Josh suggested.

"Yeah, maybe they can put everything back in its place? It's their job, right, to fix things?" I asked as we went back inside and made our way to the couch again.

Vigil wouldn't look me in the eye. "Well, I do not think I will be able to—"

"What? You think they won't help us? They have to. It's their job!"

"No ... I ... There is no way to contact them. You have my powers now and you do not know how to call for them. Also, they have been ... strongly advised not to come near your planet," he confessed, looking embarrassed.

"Strongly advised?"

"I ... prohibited them. I did not like them getting involved in my business and following me here. I wanted them to stay away. Earth is now my territory; they are not allowed here. They cannot help us."

"Oh, fudgesicles," I groaned.

All of us sat in silence, deep in thought, trying to find a way out of this.

Vigil leaned forward and buried his head in his hands. "And now I am stuck in this human form. My eyelids feel heavy, my body aches everywhere, I can't think straight," he whispered in despair. "I never knew being human was this awful ..."

"You mean by switching powers you are human now?" Tristan asked, startled.

"Yes, I now have all of Joey's powers, in essence, and that means having her humanity as well. She, on the other hand, has mine, making her temporarily a Gray Hooded One. We need to figure out a way to switch this back quickly. It is imperative that she does not stay in this state for long. Things can become ... unstable." Vigil closed his eyes tiredly. "I am sorry, it is really hard to think with my head hurting like this ..."

"Okay. Let's take a break, guys," I suggested, standing up. "Come on, Vigil, we'll get you cleaned up," I said, grabbing the first aid kit Tristan had left on the table and pulling out antiseptic and Band-Aids. Then I dug into my pocket for the bottle of aspirin. "And take these; they'll make your head feel better." I handed him a couple of tablets and watched as he stared at them suspiciously before abruptly popping them into his mouth. I nodded in satisfaction. "Let's all get some rest and we can think about this tomorrow, okay?"

Everybody shuffled off to their rooms, looking worried and tired. I took Vigil to my bedroom so he could sleep there for the rest of the night, and then I went to Tristan's room. He was already lying in bed, deep in thought, by the time I wriggled underneath the sheets.

"I was thinking about what to do," he began, his voice low and cautious. "We have to go see Celeste tomorrow, Joe."

Oh, God! And I thought the night couldn't get any worse.

"She might be the only one who can help us," he continued. "So you have to suck it up and go see her. And be nice while we're there!"

"I am *always* nice. She's the one who always provokes me," I muttered under my breath.

"We need her help, Joey. In fact, you are in this mess right now *because* you didn't ask for help when you needed it."

"Fine," I huffed, and turned my back on him.

I hated to admit it, but Tristan was right. Celeste could get us out of this mess, so I really needed to do as he suggested: suck it up and ask for her help.

Just. Freaking. Great.

Celeste Harker. The eldest of the Harkers – Celeste, Arice and Luna Harker – the witchy sisters. They knew pretty much everything there was to know about magic, spells, curses and incantations, all sorts; if magic was involved, they knew all about it. Especially Celeste, Miss Smarty Pants.

God. This girl irritated the living hell out of me.

Tristan said we were both too stubborn, and that's why we fought so much all the bloody time. I liked to think it was because she was a bossy, wise-ass-know-it-all, always-had-to-have-her-own-way type of person.

I couldn't see any relation to me whatsoever.

Celeste was pale, blonde and petite, and looked like a delicate snow princess. But once you got to know her, you quickly realized she was not as fragile as she appeared. She was strong-minded, bad-tempered and old-mannered for her twenty-five years of age. Celeste studied all types of magic and was like a living human-encyclopedia of the occult.

Her younger sister Arice was the most outgoing and cheerful of the sisters. Arice was expert in Wiccan magic: white, healing spells for the mind, spirit and body. Whereas Luna was a bit on the odd side. Luna studied dark magic and wore heavy gothic make-up. I was always rather scared of her.

Together, the three Harker sisters commanded the three forms of magic: Arice the White, Luna the Black and Celeste the Gray.

Celeste had been my tutor the first year we arrived in the city, recommended by Miss Violet, my occult mentor, who had helped with Tristan's case after the New Year's spell. Back then, she had tried to help us find a magical way to keep Tristan alive, but she was too far away to guide me now.

Celeste was supposed to teach me the basics of magic after that: guide me along the supernatural path, so to speak, and help me hone and control my empathy-sight ability.

The fact that I didn't know how to switch off my sight was a constant source of aggravation between Celeste and me, which wasn't helped by the fact that I could read her so easily, even when she tried to block me. Every time I tried to turn off my sight, I ended up with the most intense headache, so after a while I just stopped trying.

Celeste also tried to boss me around, although I wouldn't let her. That made her extremely mad at me. She said I didn't have the correct discipline to be a real witch. So I stormed out of her house one day and never went back. That was a year ago. One entire year without contacting the Harkers. Tomorrow's reunion was going to be swell … I could hear the nagging already.

Next morning I woke up really early to find Tristan talking to Vigil in the kitchen. All the boys were still fast asleep in their rooms.

"Hey, Vigil, how are you feeling?" I asked, watching him from the other side of the counter. He looked a lot better today.

"I am feeling well, thank you. My head is not annoying me any more, which is a relief. But I woke up with a … void in my stomach. So very strange," he said.

"He was hungry," Tristan explained, trying to hide a chuckle.

I laughed, watching Vigil munching a piece of toast quite happily.

"Yes, Tristan helped me understand this 'hunger' thing. It was very uncomfortable. But I have found the eating occupation quite satisfying." At this he burped lightly. "Pardon me," he added.

"So, you were saying this thing that attacked you is probably going to be back soon?" Tristan continued the conversation they had been having before I came in.

"Yes, most likely," Vigil answered. "It has left all its possessions behind – some *very* precious magical artifacts. It will surely want them back."

"How do you know that? Maybe that light explosion killed him. You know, disintegrated his shadowy little ass," I said with relish, hoping that would be the case.

"Interchange magical orbs do not have the exterminating powers. It is certainly alive. The light of the glass ball must have scared him into hiding yesterday. But he will soon try to return to this house."

"So we need to get this mess sorted before he comes back," Tristan reasoned. "And that means ..."

"... I need to talk to Celeste," I finished for him. "I know. We're going, we're going."

"So, it's settled. Let's go see Celeste."

Tristan clapped his hands and stood up. He was cheerful; he'd never wanted me to stop seeing Celeste. He liked the idea of me being able to turn off my sight. Sometimes it became an issue, the lack of privacy for his intimate thoughts. He was probably hoping I would resume my witching training activities after this get-together today.

"Who is this Celeste person?" Vigil asked, confused.

"Celeste is a witch. We are going to ask if she can help switch us back," I explained.

"You don't seem very pleased," he pointed out.

"Oh, don't worry about it, she's thrilled!" Tristan answered for me, slapping my back playfully and walking away with a knowing smirk.

I followed him with dark, foreboding clouds over my head.

Chapter Sixteen

Witch & Crafts

Tristan closed the door of his car with a wide grin on his face.

"See? We even found a parking space right in front of her house. It's a sign we should be here!"

I looked around. The street was almost deserted; there were plenty of parking spaces.

"Maybe it's a sign that business at the Harkers' is going sour," I muttered.

Okay. I was majorly sulking. I hadn't wanted to come. We had left the house in such a hurry, only stopping to leave the boys a quick message about where we were. Tristan pretended he didn't notice my gloomy mood while he'd driven us to the Harkers'. Vigil had looked terrified throughout the whole ride. He hated cars; they were a far too primitive and dangerous way to locomote for his taste.

We walked to the front door, rang the bell and after a few moments someone answered.

"Hello?" Arice Harker greeted, opening the door. "Oh, my. Joey! Long time, no see."

Arice Harker was wearing a flowery summer dress; her auburn hair fell over her chubby shoulders.

"Hi, Arice," Tristan and I greeted her back.

"Ah, you brought Tristan with you, too. Hi, Tristan! And who's the cutie, behind you?" she asked, glancing around us.

"This is Vigil," I introduced him as he stepped forward and dipped his head in a formal bow.

Arice gave him a baffled look, before turning back to us with a warm smile. "I reckon y'all want to talk to Celeste? She predicted we'd have special guests today." She winked and motioned for us to follow.

The Harker residence was pretty much what you'd expect of a stereotypical witches' house. It was kind of dark and gloomy, and odd occult things were stacked everywhere you looked. Scented candles and incense were laid on every table, and colorful gemstones of all shapes and sizes, along with amulets and magical objects, filled the shelves on the walls.

We shuffled quickly to the back of the house, passing Arice's sister Luna on the way. She was sitting on the living-room couch, wearing a revealing black tank-top, tight black jeans and a lot of dark make-up.

"Well, hello, there, Joe Gray. Looking ... different," Luna said with a sneer. The Harkers' pet, Mr. Skittles, was lying lazily on her lap, looking as bored as Luna sounded.

Mr. Skittles was a big, feral-looking cat with black fur matted with scars. Its left ear was missing a huge chunk and it had yellow, intelligent eyes that followed you everywhere with suspicion. Yeah, taste the rainbow, Skittles. Right. More like a rainbow of deadly claws and lots of pain. Skittles took a few steps towards me, and the fur on his back rose immediately. He let out a loud hiss.

I retreated a step and cowered behind Tristan. The cat's behavior suddenly made me remember Sneaky Nick with his yellow eyes, sharp teeth and all the scary hissing.

"Don't mind him. He's probably reacting to Joey's weird aura," Luna said, trying to grab him and pull him back onto her lap.

"W-what?" I asked in surprise.

"Luna!" Arice admonished her sister, appalled. "You know it's not polite pointing out people's auras, weird or not. Don't mind her," Arice apologized, urging us to carry on down the hallway.

Flipping weird witches with crazy weird cats. Ugh.

Arice knocked on a door at the end of the hall, and Celeste's annoyed voice beckoned her to enter.

We walked inside her office to find her slim figure hunched over a desk covered in folders that lay open in front of her. Papers were scattered everywhere, along with manuscripts, piles of battered books and old scrolls.

She looked up with a start when she realized her sister wasn't alone, quickly adjusting her white blouse and patting her golden hair back in place, her eyes staring curiously at us. "Oh, sorry. Didn't know you had company, Arice," she said in a formal tone. "Hello, Miss Gray. Mr. Halloway."

"Hello, Miss Harker," I replied.

She picked up the undercurrent of sarcasm in my voice and clenched her jaw, her eyes narrowing ever so slightly in my direction.

Tristan nudged me sharply in the ribs and stepped in quickly, seizing Celeste's hand in a polite handshake and giving me quite the heated glare.

"Hello, Miss Harker," he greeted with a soft smile. He

gave her hand a gentle squeeze, and the way he said her name was soothing and respectful. "I know you must be busy, and we didn't call in advance to announce we were coming, but if you could spare us a minute of your time, we'd be so immensely grateful." He spoke in the nicest way he possibly could.

She eyed him warmly for a second before slowly withdrawing her hand and nodding, motioning for us to sit down.

She tidied up the mess on her desk while everybody found a seat, and then she swiveled her chair around to face us, leaned back and cleared her throat.

"So, what can I do for you?" she asked, her face calm and her hands crossed in front of her. "Is this about Joey's aura?" she said, hazarding a guess.

"What do you mean by that?" I exclaimed, annoyed by all the weird-aura comments. "Why do you guys keep saying my aura is wrong?"

"Well, usually your aura is wavy, like flowing water. Now it's all flaring red and bursting in bright lights, like the surface of a small sun. Never seen one like that before," Celeste mused.

"Oh. Right. That's because I'm buffed up on Vigil's unearthly superpowers now. Hmm, remember Vigil?" I said, pointing at him by my side. "I've told you about him before."

Her eyes bugged out of her sockets as she stared at Vigil.

"You mean he is *the* Vigil? The Gray One Vigil?" she asked.

"Yes. That's him. Vigil, this is Celeste Harker. Celeste, this is Vigil."

"Miss Harker, it is very nice meeting you. Thank you for helping us in this difficult moment." Vigil bowed his head and offered a kind smile.

"O-oh ... G-gosh, it's an honor having you in my home, sir," she said, blushing fiercely.

Huh. This was a first. I'd never seen Celeste blushing before.

"H-how can I be of assistance?" she stammered, trying to cover her embarrassment.

Vigil began telling her about our little power-switch situation, and when he'd finished explaining things, Celeste paused, a thoughtful look on her face. I wished so badly that I could read her right now. Did she know a way to help us? I had no clue whatsoever.

"I understand, Mr. Vigil," she said. "Thank you for explaining matters to me."

Then her eyes glazed a little and her voice softened, like she was in some sort of trance. *"There cannot be redemption without the virtue of humility. You cannot see clearly if you are filled with too much pride. The end of your journey lies within the moment of acceptance of your flaws and errors. It is what makes you human. You cannot forget this or you will forget your humanity as well."*

After a few seconds she blinked rapidly, like she was waking from a dream.

We all stared at her in silence while she blinked a couple more times. "Huh, what was I saying?" she asked, a little uncertainly.

"What was *that* all about?" I was the first to ask. "Why did you sound all weird like that?"

"Weird like what?" Celeste asked, obviously baffled.

"You were talking about the virtue of humility, and

about flaws and errors," Tristan offered, as if she couldn't remember.

"Okay, I know what this is all about. You can stop with the act." It finally dawned on me. "You won't help us unless I beg, am I right? Fine. Please, I need your help, Celeste. There, I said it. Are you happy now?"

I was really upset. She wanted to hear me plead, and rub in my face how much I needed her now. I had stormed out of her house a year ago, telling her I didn't need her for anything, and now here I was tail between my legs and knee-deep in a mess that I had caused.

"W-what? No, I was meaning to say I'll try to help. I don't know if I can do much, but I'll try my best," she said, seeming genuinely puzzled, turning to look at Vigil. "Do you have this glass ball with you, sir?"

"Yes. Here it is." Vigil took the dark glass ball out of his pocket and put it in the middle of the coffee table in front of us.

"Can you two touch the glass ball, please?" Celeste asked.

We touched the glass ball and waited a minute while Celeste sat in silence, deep in concentration. After a while she opened her eyes.

"I'm sorry, but it isn't working. Nothing I try works. There is a key. You have to find out what it is," she concluded, stating the already obvious fact.

"Oh, God! Really? Is that all you have to say? We already knew that! All this time wasted for nothing," I protested loudly. "Are you saying there is nothing you can do to help us? Not one thing? Aren't you supposed to be the top-notch witch in the area?"

She had made me beg for her help and now she was

saying there was nothing she could do? She'd gotta be kidding me!

"I don't know the key to make it work. Perhaps you can find out from the owner of the artifact, the creature you were trying to capture. It will know how to make this work again, I'm sure," she pointed out.

"And how do you suggest we ask him? I don't know where that damned evil cat is – and even if I did, how can I make him tell us? This is, like, the perfect thing that could have happened to him. He won't ever spill because this way he'll get Vigil off his back!"

"Joey, this is not Celeste's fault." Tristan intervened, seeing how upset I was getting.

"Oh, so it's all my bloody fault, then; is that what you're saying?" I snapped at him.

Something inside me was boiling, turning my thoughts into a red haze, growling, upset and frustrated. I wanted to slap Celeste round the face for making me go through all this for nothing. I reeled in, controlling my hands at the last second.

"Joe, you need to calm down," Vigil said in a quiet, controlled voice.

That made me even more upset. I mean, couldn't he see how screwed we were?

"Yelling won't solve anything, Joey," Celeste said. "That's why you'll never be a better witch; you don't know how to control your temper," she said, clearly making a point to remind us all about the way I had stormed out of her house a year ago. I knew she would rub that in my face!

"Who told you I want to be a better witch? Or a witch at all?"

"Joey—" Vigil tried to get my attention but I didn't respond.

"Here we are needing your help and you won't do a damned thing about it!" My blood was boiling, rushing through my head, clouding my thoughts.

"Joey, please—"

I heard myself growling, but I couldn't stop. I wanted so badly to break Celeste now.

"*Joey!*" Vigil shouted, grabbing me and shaking me with force.

"What?" I shouted back at him.

"Please … Look at me," he begged. "Look at me … and calm down."

I let out a deep breath and stared at him. His face was really close to mine and he looked so pale, his eyes searching frantically for something. I breathed slowly, feeling the blood rushing out of my head, leaving me dizzy. Vigil nodded slowly when he saw that I was calmer, his grip on me relaxing a little.

When I looked around I saw Tristan standing in the middle of the room, and Luna and Arice huddled by the door, everybody looking scared out of their minds. Celeste was up out of her seat as well, her hands tightly gripping the edge of her desk.

Only then did I notice the state of the room. Picture frames had fallen on the floor, the window was shattered and all the chairs and some ornaments had been tossed around. And a long crack had appeared in one of the walls. It looked as if a mini earthquake had hit us.

"Huh … what happened?" I asked, confused.

"You mean you didn't realize what you were doing?" Vigil asked.

"What was I doing?"

Vigil sighed and sat back down in his chair, while Celeste's sisters walked cautiously into the room.

"Joey, you were getting angry. The more angry you became, the more things got ... *bumpy*," he explained.

I put a hand over my chest in shock. "Oh, my God. I did this? How?"

"This is what I was afraid of; this is the reason it is so urgent I get my powers back," Vigil said, passing a hand through his black hair. "You see, Joey, emotions are a trigger to unleash my power. They are also its fuel. That is why my race is known for its lack of emotions: it is a safety mechanism of sorts. No emotion means better control," he explained, and sat forward, looking deeply into my eyes. "It is imperative that you start suppressing your emotions now. Once they are unleashed, your ... my power can get out of control really fast. The results could be ... disastrous. This is very important; you need to learn how to suppress emotion. Or it could end up taking over like wildfire."

I was really scared now. I hadn't known this could be so dangerous ... that I could end up hurting people. And heck, how could I stop feeling? I looked at the crack in the wall. I had done that, because I was angry, without even knowing it. I had this mighty gift inside of me, with no clue whatsoever how to control it.

"I-I don't know how," I said in a small voice.

Vigil stood up and took my hands in his. "I will teach you," he promised. "Everything will be all right. We will fix this."

I nodded at him in silence while he stepped to my side. I pulled my hands out of Vigil's when I realized Tristan was looking at us, though I couldn't read his blank face. But I didn't need my sight to know how much he disliked me having any close contact with Vigil.

"I'm sorry, Celeste. About … everything. I don't know what I was doing … I'll pay for all the damage. And I apologize for what I said to you, too. You were only trying to help and I lost my mind. I am truly sorry," I said.

"That's all right, Joey. I understand. I'm here to help you with this. I'm going to research more about this magic ball, and in the meantime you practice controlling these powers. We'll make a plan to trap this creature, to reveal the hidden key we need." She crossed her fingers again. "Try to avoid stressful situations if you can from now on. And come back with Mr. Vigil tomorrow; we can start working out a plan together."

"Okay. Thanks," I said. I felt like crap for having yelled at Celeste and she was being so nice and helpful now.

"Oh, and keep an eye on Mr. Vigil at all times. We never know when this creature may strike again, and Vigil is vulnerable at the moment in his human form. You need to be around to protect him," she added as an afterthought.

"B-but … I don't know how to protect him. And didn't he just tell me I'm *not* supposed to use this power? That it could get out of control?"

"Hmm, yes. I suppose you're right. Well, Mr. Vigil can stay here with us. Our house is well guarded with protective spells, and my sisters and I can help too, if push comes to shove," she offered.

"That's really kind of you to offer, Celeste," Tristan replied. "We're very thankful for your help …"

I eyed him suspiciously, wondering how much he was genuinely worried about Vigil's security and how much he just wanted Vigil away from me.

"O-oh, you mean you are leaving, Joey?" Vigil asked. A hint of panic laced his voice. "I mean, I need to be with you, to help you if you lose control again. I need to be close . . . to help you!" he repeated in distress.

He looked so lost. And scared. Like a little kid being abandoned by his mother. Even though I was pretty sure he was going to be safe with the Harker sisters, I didn't know that for certain. I didn't have the heart to just leave him like that. Not now, when he needed me the most.

"Okay, Vigil. I guess you're right. I'll just go home to pick up a change of clothes. I'll get some things for you too; you're going to need them. Then I'll come back to stay with you. If that's all right with Celeste, that is . . ."

"Yes, that's fine. You two can stay in the guest room," she agreed promptly.

"Okay. I'll be back as soon as I can, okay?" I told Vigil one last time before leaving.

I tried not to look at Tristan as we left.

Chapter Seventeen
Turning Tables

"I just don't get why you need to go, that's all," Tristan said for what seemed like the thousandth time. "He will be perfectly safe and protected with the Harkers. Why do you need to stay with him?"

"You know why, Tristan. I can't just leave him there. He doesn't know anyone, he's scared and he needs me. Listen, I don't have time to argue about this any more, I have to go. He's waiting for me," I said, picking up two backpacks, one holding my things and the other stuffed with a bunch of spare clothes I'd gathered from the boys for Vigil.

"So nothing really changes: he calls, and you rush off to him," he spat out.

Here we go again.

"Tristan, come on, please. Can we not do this?"

"Why can't you see my side of this, Joey? I mean, here you are, running to be stuck with him, in the same room and all … and this will be for what? Just tonight? The whole week? A month?"

"I don't know how long, Tristan. I guess until this mess is fixed."

"And that could take for ever! Do you plan on sleeping with him for ever?"

"Tris, I'm not *sleeping* with him ..."

"No? Do you even know if there are two beds in this guest room? What if they have only one bed in there? What are you going to do then?"

"I'm sure there are two. And even if there aren't, I can sleep on the couch or something. Stop making this into something it's not ..."

"What? What am I *making* this into, Joey?" he said, crossing his arms. "He doesn't think of you as a friend! He still loves you. And now he is all scared like a lost puppy and you are taking his bait. I know where this is going to end, Joey. You'll make it your mission to protect him, save him from whatever, and then you'll end up falling for him!"

"Are you crazy? Do you not trust me at all?" I was upset. The windows in the room started to rattle like mad.

"I know because that's what happened with me, with us." He was also shouting, oblivious to the rattling windows. "I was lost too, and scared, and needed your help, remember?"

Oh. My. God. Did he seriously just friggin' say that?

"Oh, so that's all you are to me, then, is it? You're just a charity case. Someone I took pity on, you poor lost soul. I decided to help you and like the silly brainless girl that I am, I ended up falling for you. And now, silly me, I'm bound to do it again with Vigil, because I just can't help myself. I'm *that* silly! That's what I do; I help lost causes and fall for them, one after another."

Tristan looked pained, as if I had just declared his inner fears out loud and made them all come true.

"Yes, it's the same thing, happening all over again," he said in a quiet voice.

"Yeah, Tristan, it's the same damned situation, only this time there's something really important missing from the equation," I said.

He looked at me, completely lost.

"YOU! You damned idiot. *You* are the thing that's missing. Vigil may be lost, and scared and helpless, just like you were a long time ago, but I won't fall for him. You want to know why? Because he is *not you*!" I softened my voice. "I didn't fall in love with you because you were lost and scared; I fell for you because of who you are!"

"But you still choose him over me any time of any day …"

"Are you freaking kidding me? I'm not—" I stopped and huffed, too tired to argue any more. "You can't honestly believe all this crap, Tristan. This is beyond stupid. You are just making this up to pick a fight with me now. Is that what you want? You want me to go to Celeste's mad at you, is that it?"

"No, I want you to *not* go! I want you to stay here with me. And I'm the one supposed to be mad, not the other way around. Stop turning the tables here. You are the one leaving to be with someone else. You are the one—"

"Stop it," I cut in before he could say anything else. I didn't want to know what he was going to say next. It wasn't going to be anything good. "I'd better leave now before you say something you'll regret. And I know you will. We can talk again when you cool down." I left the room without waiting for his reply.

It was best for me to leave before I started another mini earthquake. I needed to learn to control my feelings, and arguing with Tristan right now was not helping the situation. He was pissing the hell out of me.

I knew Tristan tended to lose his mind and act all crazy whenever the subject of Vigil came up. But I couldn't let his jealousy keep me from helping my friend. If I let him get his way, what kind of a person would I be? What kind of friend would I be?

I'd always sworn I would never be like those girls who let their boyfriends tell them what to do, who they could see or talk to, what they should wear, how they should act. It was absurd. And I was not going to let him do that to me – not now, not ever.

He was going to have to deal with his insecurities and learn to trust me, whether he wanted to or not.

I stomped my way to the front door, not bothering to call out to the boys. I bumped into Becca on my way out to the garage. She greeted me and told me she had news about something important coming up in a few days, but I excused myself and told her I was in a hurry. I had more important things to worry about right now. Work and gigs could wait.

All the way to the Harkers' I kept going over my argument with Tristan in my head, my anger slowly melting into regret and guilt. I felt really bad for having left him that way, but I was pretty certain that walking out had been the best thing to do. There was no reasoning with Tristan when he was like that.

The sun was setting when I got back to the Harkers'.

Luna opened the door for me and ushered me inside. There was a lot of rattling, fumbling and cursing inside the kitchen. Arice poked her round, rosy face around the kitchen door, beaming like her usual jolly self.

"Ah, hey, Joey. Welcome back! Celeste and I are making dinner here; it should be done in a few minutes ... if Celeste doesn't mess things up again." She mumbled the last part but then brightened up again. "Well, at least she's trying, right? She's not the best at cooking, but she made a point today of helping me out. You know how it is, special guest of honor and all," she said, wiggling her eyebrows.

"Hey, Arice. That's nice, you didn't need to go to all this trouble. Where is the special guest of honor, by the way?" I asked, looking around for Vigil.

"Oh, he's in Celeste's office. We had a little *bathroom incident* a while ago, but it's all sorted now," she said, giggling.

"Bathroom incident? Oh no, don't tell me ..."

"Yeah, you could have told us he didn't have ... bathroom experience ... before you left, you know? Poor thing, was fretting all over the place not knowing what the hell was going on!" She was trying hard not to laugh. "He's so adorable! 'Good heavens, there is something wrong with me, what should I do?' It took me a while to understand he only needed to go for a wee. Had to ask a lot of weird questions to find *that* out. Celeste didn't know where to look; she was as red as a tomato when she discovered what was really going on.

"But I've explained everything to him and showed him a 'Human Physiology' Wiki article," she continued. "He was astonished at all the information, and has now discovered the wonders of the internet. Can't seem to unglue himself from Celeste's laptop. He's been reading non-stop since then."

"Oh ... my. I'm so sorry, Arice. I completely forgot to tell you guys about Vigil's new human condition. Thank you so much for helping him out in this ... difficult time," I said, relieved that I had escaped the potty training session. I could relate to Celeste's tomato-red face.

"No prob, hun. I'm not one to be abashed about these things."

"Do you need help in the kitchen?" I asked, noticing a slight smell of smoke drifting through the doorway.

"Nah. We're good. Too many hands in here; you'd only get in the way. I wish Celeste could leave me alone so I can cook in peace, but she's set on helping tonight. Cos of the *special guest*," she said, with the wiggling brows again.

"I'm going to check on Vigil, then."

"'kay. Tell his honor that dinner will be done in a second. If you can pry him away from the laptop. Bring him to the dinner table, will you?" Arice winked and then froze, looking alarmed, and sniffed the air. "Celeste! Aren't ya checking the oven? Ugh! I gotta go before she sets the whole house on fire!" And she darted back inside the kitchen.

I found Vigil hunched in an old armchair in Celeste's office, looking unblinkingly at a laptop on his knee.

"Hi, V. I'm back!"

He glanced up and his face lit up so much when he saw me, I had to bite down the urge to pinch his cheeks. "Hello, Joey. I am glad you are back."

"How about we head to the dinner table to take care of the void in your stomach, what do you say?" I proposed with a smile.

He stopped and concentrated, putting a hand over his stomach, before nodding in agreement. We got to the living room and the table was all set and ready.

Celeste fretted nervously during the whole dinner. She was really trying to impress Vigil, who in turn was engrossed in his food, oblivious to his host's efforts.

The food looked really good, the table was nicely set; I could tell they all had put a lot of effort into this meal.

I tried to acknowledge their hard work, complimenting everything, while Vigil just sat there and ate like a starving man. The best he came up with was a small comment about how he had learned that "nutrition was important to ensure essential prerequisites for human life and to enable the human body to function properly". That earned a weak smile from Celeste, a blank stare from Luna and a puzzled glance from Arice.

After we'd finished dinner, Celeste showed us to the guest room. It was a small, cozy room with pale-blue walls and two single beds, one on each side.

In your face, Tristan.

Vigil lay down on his bed and was out as soon his head hit the pillow. He didn't even take his clothes off, leaving Seth's PJs untouched by the side of the bed. I guess being human made him truly exhausted.

I pulled on my old sweatpants under a large T-shirt, snuggled beneath the covers and decided to take a quick look at my phone. There were no missed calls or text messages from Tristan. I guessed he was still mad at me for leaving. I punched at the buttons, typing a quick message:

2 beds in guest room

I stared at the message for a while, wondering if I should send it. Would he be less upset knowing this? After a few minutes' consideration, I sighed and hit send. Maybe that would appease his temper. There was nothing more I could do about it, so I decided to go to sleep.

The next three days at Celeste's house were full of activities. I passed most of the time trying to learn how to block any emotion. The teaching technique they used was basically getting Celeste to irritate the hell out of me – which was quite an easy feat, I might add – with Vigil coaching me on how to block my anger, giving me tips on how to recognize the early traces of emotion building up inside.

The key was to cut things off right at the beginning, and not to let the emotion get too strong. The first day was quite unsuccessful, ending up with every glass surface in the house full of cracks. But by the third day, I was actually getting good at the blocking technique. Vigil was very proud of me.

Celeste had also starting searching for Nick's where-abouts. She had a magical ritual that helped her locate hidden things, and she was using it to track Nick down. After we got hold of him, we could interrogate his sneaky little ass and learn how to switch our powers back, and *voilá*, everything would go back to normal.

That was the plan, at least.

The most important thing we had to worry about was not letting Nick know about the power switch, so he wouldn't try to hurt Vigil while he was vulnerable. That and trying to prevent me from blowing everything up in the process.

During breaks, Celeste and Vigil would disappear some-where in the house, chatting amiably, and I would go to hang out with Arice. Vigil and Celeste talked a lot about magical stuff and metaphorical things. I also noticed Celeste had stopped calling him "Mr. Vigil" and they were now on first name terms. When Vigil wasn't talking with Celeste, I could always find him glued to her laptop, researching things, or deep in thought in her office, staring blankly at the glass ball in his hands. I had brought with me the leather pouch holding all of Nick's other magical gizmos, which were now securely locked away in Celeste's safe in her bedroom.

I kept rehearsing phone calls to Tristan during the three days I was there, but never got the courage to go through with the call. He still hadn't sent me any text messages or tried to call me, and I feared he might still be angry with me.

But I missed talking to him, a lot. I had so much news: the switching plan we'd conceived, my advances in magic, how I'd been making progress blocking my powers ... By the end of third day I decided to call the house instead of Tristan's cell phone. I could leave a voicemail message or talk with one of the boys, see how things were going back there. Seth picked up on the second ring.

"Y'ello?" He sounded cheerful. That was a good sign. Seth was always in a bad mood when someone else in the house was angry.

"Hey, Fletcher boy!"

"Hey, Joey! How things are going there at spooky manor?"

"It's good. Lots of work to do, but it's good. How about you?"

"I'm fine. Things are a bit boring without you around ..."

"Yeah. So ... how is he?" I finally asked. Seth probably knew all about our fight by now. Better get straight to the point.

"Who?" He faked ignorance.

"The frigging tooth fairy, Seth. Who do you think?"

He chuckled. "I don't know how he is. Why don't you ask him yourself. Wait up ..."

"Wait, no! I want to talk to you firs—" But Seth was already shouting for Tristan to pick up the phone.

Damn you, Seth Fletcher. I needed to fish for some information first, see if Tristan was still mad or not.

"Hello?" Tristan's voice came on the line.

Crap. So much for having rehearsed conversations in my head over the last three days; I was now being put on the spot without any time to think about what I was going to say. Seth had caught me completely off guard. "Hmm. Hey. It's ... me," I mumbled, while still mentally cursing Seth. "Hmm ... thank you for taking my call ..."

"When did I ever not take your calls, Joey?"

"Yeah. I didn't mean it like that, sorry. So ... I take it you're still mad at me?"

Tristan could be as stubborn as me sometimes. He paused and gave a big sigh. "I'm not mad, Joey. Is that why you haven't called until now?"

"I was giving you time to cool down. I don't want to fight with you any more ... Did you get my text message?"

"Yeah ... I did." There was a pause on the line and then he spoke again. "How are things going over there?"

"It's going good. We've made a lot of progress in the last couple days." And then I told him everything that had been happening to me at the Harkers', our plan, the lessons I'd been taking, how fast I was learning and that maybe we could have this mess all sorted out real soon. He listened to everything in silence without commenting, but I could tell he was attentive. "... so soon we can find the secret to make the glass ball work again and switch our powers back," I finished in a hopeful voice.

"That's good," he said.

"Yeah."

"I miss talking to you," he said.

That was out of the blue.

I smiled. "I miss you too, Tris."

"When do you think you'll be coming home?"

"Soon, I hope."

"Good. No, wait. You'll have to make it tomorrow. Becca told us we have an important meeting with Mr. Silver. It's mandatory. So you'll have to be back for the meeting, at least. It's going to be held at that small hotel next to the record label's main office; we've been there before, remember? She said she was going to talk to you about it, but I don't know if she did. I thought it was best to remind you …"

"Oh, no, thanks, I'm glad you did. I didn't know about this meeting tomorrow. I was supposed to call Becca but I forgot … I'll be back tomorrow, then. Do you know what it's about?"

"I have no idea. But it's important. Becca told us we couldn't miss it for anything, so we better be there. Five p.m."

"Yeah, okay. I'll be there."

"Okay. I'll see you tomorrow, then, Joey."

"See you tomorrow, Tris."

He hung up. I stared at the phone, my heart feeling lighter after having spoken to him.

Chapter Eighteen

Elevator Lockdown

I was late. I was seriously late. Do you want to know why I was *this* late?

Here's reason number one: Celeste Harker.

She'd kept nagging me the whole morning, about how I should prioritize things in my life, and how training to control Vigil's powers was more important then anything else in my life right now, certainly more important than my silly rock band get-togethers. Her words, not mine.

I had stared at her in silence, trying to conjure the control to not blow up her entire house. I promised her and Vigil that it was only going to be a quick thing and I'd be back immediately after that.

She only let me go after I promised solemnly that I'd stay away from trouble.

She was talking with Vigil in the living room when I left, an open bottle of wine in her hands. I guessed she was showing him the amazing human experience of getting wasted. I didn't want to be around when Vigil experienced the wonders of a hangover. Especially if he'd inherited my tolerance to alcohol.

So I was already very late when I left Celeste's house.

Want to know reason number two? Tiffany Worthington the Third.

She'd kept messaging me and calling me on the phone until I picked up, and she'd distracted me so much with this nonsense rumor about me and Harry having a secret affair that I didn't see the red light ahead of me and crashed my car into the back of a truck. I'd left the insurance company to deal with the mess and hailed a cab, mentally cursing Tiffany for creating the distraction.

Reason number three for being super, ultra late: Mr. Evil Traffic Jam.

My most feared arch enemy. There was nothing I could do about that. Another few precious minutes lost in the myriad of honking horns and angry scowls. At some point I gave up and decided to get out of my taxi and just run over to the hotel.

I have to say I was impressed with myself; I was pretty damned fast.

I was immediately ushered to a private conference room on the second floor where Mr. Silver held most of his important meetings. Everybody stopped talking and turned to look at me when I burst into the room, all breathless like a deranged maniac.

I started apologizing before anyone could bark at me for being super late – it was really not my fault, people; blame the nagging witch, my gossiping best friend and Mr. Evil Traffic Jam.

I hurried towards the seat closest to the door and only then did I have the time to look around the conference table. Tristan, a few seats away, acknowledged me with a small nod and a smile.

"Are you okay? I called your phone twice and got voicemail both times. I thought something bad had happened," he said, with a worried look.

"No, I'm fine. Tiffany was hogging me on the phone and then ... you know, stuff happened," I said, smiling weakly.

"Yes, it's awful when stuff 'happens'," Caleb intruded, a provocative smirk on his smug face.

That's when I realized that he was there, too, sitting at the head of the table. I froze.

"Hello there, Miss Gray," Caleb Jones – Mr. Rock Star – greeted in a casual manner. "I was thinking you were going to stand us up today. I'm glad you could make it," he remarked with that sarcastic sense of humor of his.

"Uh, yeah, hmm ... Sorry about that. There was a traffic jam and ... stuff."

Mr. Silver clapped his hands excitedly and I had to stop what I was saying to listen. "So, it is all settled, then, gentlemen? I'm really happy with this. I can't wait to see what you boys will come up with in this joint enterprise! What an exciting project – a collaboration between The Lost Boys and Mr. Jones. It's marvelous, marvelous news!" he said, beaming.

"Wait ... what?" I asked. What the hell was he talking about?

"Yes! You boys – and gal – working side by side with Mr. Jones here. Isn't it great?" he asked, his mind already figuring out how much money he could make from this joint venture.

"Yeah!" Seth exclaimed, excited for completely different reasons. Working with Caleb – his childhood idol – was like a dream coming true for him. "Caleb called this meeting to ask us if he could record a cover of one of our songs." He looked across the table, giving Caleb the brightest smile I'd ever seen on him. "So I suggested that we could maybe record a song together, because that's way better than doing an old one, and Caleb thought it was a great idea! So we're doing it!" he said, squirming with joy in his seat.

"It will be great, Joey, don't you think?"

I glanced around the table. Sam, Josh, Harry and Seth looked at me with expectant faces. Tristan remained silent, his expression mildly curious.

I could tell that everybody was thrilled with the news, so I smiled and nodded, trying to act thrilled as well. I wasn't much of a fan of Caleb Jones as a person, and after our bumpy first encounter it seemed that working with him would be a major pain in the ass. He was such an arrogant, egotistical, chauvinistic prick. But hey, to be fair, the guy was truly a genius musician, and if that was what everybody else wanted, who was I to say no?

"Yeah, it's going to be great," I said to a grinning Seth.

Everybody cheered and soon afterwards we all got up and headed downstairs to the hotel's bar to celebrate the deal.

The bar was packed with people. Somehow the news that we were meeting Caleb had already gotten around to a few paparazzi, which resulted in a solid mass of press and eager fans waiting for us. The place was buzzing with people and I began to feel edgier by the second. The room was teetering on the brink of becoming a rave.

I tried to find Tristan – we hadn't had a chance to talk properly yet – but I'd already lost all of the boys in the crowded room. Finally, after a long time searching, I spotted Josh at the corner of the bar. I fought my way over and grabbed him by the arm. "Hey, Josh! Have you seen Tristan?"

"I think he just walked through that door a minute ago," he said, pointing to a dark, wooden door behind him. Tristan always hated crowds, just like me. It was definitely his thing to try to escape to somewhere quieter.

I nodded and pushed my way through it, stepping into a dimly lit corridor that looked like a staff area of sorts.

It took me a few minutes to process what my eyes were seeing. At the end of the corridor was Tristan, leaning flat against the wall, with a red-haired girl pressing up against him.

Her arms were wrapped around his shoulders, her hands sinking into his hair and her lips only a fleeting whisper away from his.

I watched the scene unfold in a mesmerized stupor. I watched as he parted his lips ever so slightly. That little tell was what shattered me the most inside. He was about to kiss her. He wanted to kiss her.

Then I recognized *her. Jessica Red*.

The shock made my hand falter, and the door I was holding closed behind me with a loud bang. Tristan and Jessica snapped their heads in my direction, startled by the sudden noise.

Something inside me snarled viciously, an alien, animalistic growl that reverberated through my soul. This thing slashed forward, grinding and gnawing on its leash, rattling its chains loudly. It wanted release. It wanted to rip Jessica's insides out, tear her to pieces. It was angry. Very angry. It wanted freedom, wanted out of its chains. It watched her touching Tristan. It wanted to hurt him, too. Hurt him bad.

Tristan's eyes widened in surprise as he shoved Jessica away from him. She yelped and scowled at his rudeness, but he showed no signs of caring, already walking in my direction. "Joe, wait, please ..." he begged, a hand outstretched.

I closed my eyes for a second, trying to drown the angry snarls inside my head, trying to tame this furious alien thing that rattled madly in my core.

I realized I could really hurt them with a snap of my fingers. All I needed was to wish for it. I had my newfound powers and all I needed was to let this thing within me take over. I breathed out slowly, trying desperately to control it, to tame my emotions, block everything out.

I could hear Tristan calling my name and I opened my eyes. I didn't know what was worse: the look of guilt on his face or the pleading tone of his voice. Instinctively I raised my hand to protect myself from him.

"No," I whispered, trying to deny everything I had just seen. I didn't want Tristan near me.

"J-Joey, please ..." he whispered in agony, and when he tried to take another step forward I reacted and opened the palms of my hands.

"No!" I growled, and he staggered backwards, like something had just punched him forcibly in the chest. He was even more surprised when all the glass in the windows of the corridor cracked and burst, shattering to the floor.

"No, please, wait!" he cried out.

But I didn't wait.

I turned around, yanked the door open, and ran back into the crowded bar without looking back. I pushed through the crowd, trying to get away from that place, from Tristan. I could feel myself losing control, something inside threatening to get out. I chanted to myself over and over again to be calm, to block everything out, to stay in control.

So many thoughts crammed inside my head. *He was going to kiss her. Go back there and hurt her; hurt him the way he hurt you. You need to get away. Stay in control, hurry, forget about what happened back there, don't forget* ... I was slipping, losing my mind. I could barely see where I was going, or hear what people around me were saying. Everything was a blurry mess.

I continued to advance through the room, bumping into people as though I were drunk, the noise inside my head driving me insane. I pressed my hands over my ears, trying to block the snarls, but it only made it worst. The voices seemed like they were trapped inside now, banging in my skull in a hellish cacophony.

"Gray? Are you okay?" someone close to me asked, the question muffled amidst the noise inside my head. I pushed the person away and continued walking. I needed to get out of here, find a quiet place. I just needed a second to breathe, to work things out – then everything would be all right. I could control this. I could do this. I *knew* I could.

But he had almost kissed her, the thing inside snarled to me.

The lights in the room flickered violently above our heads, making everybody look up. The thing inside still wanted out, wanted its revenge.

I growled, looking up at the flickering lights. My voice was hoarse, out of key ... unnatural. The chandeliers trembled and a tremor passed through the room. Was I the one doing this?

"Joe, hey." The voice came from behind me again. "Is something wrong?"

I turned back to see Caleb staring at me with a heavy

frown. My eyes danced from his worried face to the people around him. The lights stopped blinking and people went back to their quiet chatter around the room. He looked so much like Tristan – the same angles in his face, the same squared jaw. The eerie resemblance refuelled my anger.

"Joey!" Tristan's shout reached us, making me jump. He had followed me into the bar, looking hopelessly around, trying to find me.

I didn't want Tristan to find me. If he got near, I was going to lose it completely. I was going to blow this whole place up.

Caleb grabbed my hand and pulled me with him into a corner of the room while Tristan shouted urgently in the background. I let myself be dragged like a rag doll, my mind a jumbled mess of manic thoughts.

What was Caleb doing? Where was he taking me?

We sneaked surreptitiously through a narrow, hidden entrance and into an even narrower hallway. Was it just chance or had he known about this secret passageway?

Caleb walked in silence, pulling me along as he turned at random intersections. We couldn't hear the chatter from the bar any more.

We ended up in a gloomy room, somewhere at the back of the hotel. He continued pulling me until we reached an old elevator door. He pushed the button, hard. The metal door opened with a loud bing and we quickly walked inside. As soon as we started going up, he let go of my hand and stared at me.

"There you go," he stated, like he had just accomplished a job well done. "I've done press conferences in this hotel for years. I know all the secret escape routes. It seemed like you were in serious need of a way out, so … there you go," he repeated.

I stared, baffled, at his intense, pale-blue eyes.

"So, now's the time when you thank me," he teased, crossing his muscled arms over his chest. "Or maybe start explaining what was going on back there?"

I took a defensive step back. This wasn't a subject I wanted to talk about, especially with him. My mind was still a scrambled mess as I tried to make sense of what he was saying.

"Come on, talk to me," he encouraged.

I hugged myself and stepped back again, leaning against the elevator wall, a grimace on my face. I wanted to be alone. I wanted him to leave me alone.

"Fine. I'll guess, then. I'm really good at guessing games," he said, faking cheer. "Let me see … Tristan, your boyfriend there, must have screwed up real bad for you to flip out the way you did."

I snapped my eyes upwards to his face in surprise and alarm. The wall behind me started vibrating softly.

"It probably has something to do with women," he continued. "I'll bet good money that this is about another girl, from the desperate way he was trying to find you in the bar, and the way you looked … So, maybe you caught him cheating on you?" he hazarded, watching intently to see my reaction.

"Stop it," I said quietly, a warning in my voice, the chains still rattling slightly inside my head.

"Hey, a guy like him, this was bound to happen," he continued, not paying any attention to me. "Relationships tend to end this way in this business; it's tough keeping all the groupies away all the time."

"Stop it."

"It can get pretty wild, this rock-and-roll lifestyle. It was really a matter of time before you caught—"

"STOP!" I yelled. The elevator shook violently, lights fizzing above us, making sparks fly through the air above our cowering heads.

Then the elevator gave a hard jolt, and we started freefalling …

The emergency breaks cut in the second after the elevator started plummeting, jerking it to a screeching halt. Caleb had both hands planted firmly against the walls and I had my legs in a wide stance for balance. Everything went really quiet and still for a moment, except for a few last sparks falling from the ceiling.

Caleb was still in shock, frozen, his eyes as wide as they could be. "Holy shit!" He exhaled a deep sigh of relief, breaking the long seconds of eerie, stunned silence. "Are you okay?"

"Huh … I guess so," I mumbled, also very scared. "W-what is happening? Are we stuck?" I asked, walking on shaky legs to the elevator control panel, punching buttons randomly; but nothing seemed to be working. The scare of our momentary freefall had temporarily banished all thoughts of rattling chains from my mind.

He swatted my hands away from the panel. "Stop doing that or you'll break the thing for good." He scowled.

A second later, he pushed the intercom button himself. Nothing happened. Then he pushed the emergency button. Yet again, no response.

"Fuck," he muttered under his breath. "I think we are really stuck. No, wait, maybe if I call someone …" he said, pulling his cell phone out and tapping a few keys. He cursed again. "It's not working, either ..."

I rubbed my temples and hummed to myself ... a "calm-down" mantra. This could not be happening! Stuck in an old, unused elevator for God knew how long with the obnoxious Caleb Jones? I wasn't going to make it. It was an impossible feat, to remain calm with Caleb in the same room. I would blow up the elevator for sure, and kill us both.

As my panic grew stronger, my humming intensified.

Calm down, Joey! Calm down, calmdowncalmdown-calmdown, calm the fuck down.

"Are you claustrophobic or something?" Caleb's voice drifted into my ears.

He was leaning against the wall, calm as a lamb now, looking at me curiously. I stomped to the elevator doors and started kicking them. I was going to open them even if I had to claw my way out. But the door wouldn't budge.

"I. Want. Out. Of. Here. You. Stupid. Broken. Piece of—"

"Chillax, Snappy. There is nothing we can do about it. We have to wait. Soon someone will get us out."

Oh, dear God. He was so calm: it was so friggin' irritating.

I huffed and puffed at the door for a long time, before letting my shoulders sag in defeat. I shuffled back to the corner and sank slowly against the wall.

Caleb sat down opposite me while I went back to humming softly to myself and rubbing my temples. He stared at me like I was a loony.

I probably was.

"Hey, is it so bad, to be stuck in here with me?" he asked softly.

I snorted loudly in a *hell yeah* kind of way.

"Aw, come on. What did I ever do to you?" he scoffed, mildly offended. "Why do you hate me so much, Snappy?" he asked again, his voice softer this time, almost a bit hurt. "Honestly, I'd like to know."

I shot him a look that said, *You really don't want to know, pal.*

"Snappy, come on. Just tell me."

"Fine. You want to know so badly? First: my name is not 'Snappy', so please stop calling me that. Second: the narcissistic personality, the annoying remarks, the arrogance, the patronizing things you do which you think are so damned amusing. There." I took a breath. "Happy?"

Then I mentally slapped myself, because all chances of working with The Accidentals were now as dead as could be. Seth was going to kick my ass. I could almost hear him crying.

Caleb looked at me with raised eyebrows. "Wow. That was a *lot*. Thanks for the vicious bluntness."

I buried my face in my hands and sighed. "I'm sorry." *I really was.* "But you asked for it." *He really had.*

Caleb just chuckled at me. "That's cool, Snappy. I'm glad you got it off your chest." He seemed completely unfazed by everything I had just thrown in his face. "I guess you have the right to think anything you want of me," he said, shrugging. "But just so you know, you're wrong, *Miss Gray.* You don't know me at all."

"I just call it as I see it," I retorted. "That's how you portray yourself."

"I guess that's fair to say. I've been in this business for a long time now; it's what happens: you start building masks to keep people from seeing the real you. But I'm not like that at all."

I stared at him, but couldn't see what he was feeling. I kept forgetting I had lost my sight ability and couldn't read anyone any more.

"Listen, how about you tell me what really happened back there and I'll try to help you?" he offered with an earnest smile.

I tensed up, fearing that if I started talking about it, my mental stability would shatter into tiny, deadly pieces. "I'm sorry," I whispered quietly.

"About what?"

"About everything I just said to you. I hardly know you and you don't deserve to be treated like that. Sorry … In my defense, I'm really messed up in the head right now … and this day has been really hard for me."

"Aw, now you just lost a lot of points, Snappy. I was really impressed with your speech. Nobody has ever talked to me like that before. And now you've just ruined it by apologizing. No fair," he joked playfully.

After a few minutes' appeasing silence he spoke again. "Seriously, Joey. You can talk to me if you want."

I played with my bracelets and looked down at the floor. "How did you know … about me and Tristan being together?"

He smiled, happy that I was finally letting him in. "You got me curious that day at the awards, so afterwards I looked up your band on the internet. I searched for videos and stuff about you guys and noticed how close you are to the boys," he said, looking at me with an intense stare. "You are always hugging and kissing them, like they are all your boyfriends," he continued. "Except for Tristan.

"I mean, with Tristan, you are always restrained, careful

with your moves. Why do you only act like that with him? I had to watch what you were *not* doing in order to see what you were trying to hide," he explained. "And also, there's the way he looks at you. That's a dead giveaway. Seriously. He's not very subtle."

"But how did you know about … the reason we're fighting now?" I asked.

"That scene downstairs had relationship crisis written all over it. Best logical guess, I suppose. I'm sorry. I know how it sucks."

I laughed bitterly. "Yeah, right. You? I don't think so." He was, after all, the one famous for always doing the cheating, not the other way around.

"Yeah. *Me*. I've been cheated on. Is that so hard to believe?" he asked with a shy laugh.

"Well, yeah, sorta."

Caleb definitely fell into the same Greek Pantheon of Gods category to which Tristan belonged. And he knew how to take advantage of it. No wonder he'd been called the sexiest rock star of all time.

"Trust me, Joey. I know how you feel," he stated seriously.

"Yeah, well. He could at least have had the decency to pick someone better to cheat on me with. I mean, Jessica is beyond bad taste," I said, disgusted.

"You mean Jessica Mirtles? 'Red Jessica'?" he asked, and then explained, "It's my nickname for her."

"Shut up! Mine too!"

He chuckled. "But you know, I think I have to play devil's advocate now," Caleb said, shifting a little on the floor. "If you know Jessica already, I'm sure you also know how … determined she can be."

I snorted loudly. Yeah, a 'sexual-harassment-lawsuit' kind of determined.

"Hell, my first time with Jessica, she practically raped me," he confessed. "You have to cut your man some slack here. Jessica can be crazily aggressive when she's after a dude. I hear she's been after Tristan Halloway for quite some time now."

My head felt heavy and my chest tight.

"Go home. Talk to him. Let him explain," Caleb said quietly. His soft, calm tone felt like a soothing balm to my jittery nerves.

But I still had a lot to think about before talking to Tristan.

Maybe I'd overreacted. I didn't have my empathy-sight any more so I couldn't tell what Tristan had really been feeling. Maybe his lips had been parted because he was trying to say something, not trying to kiss her? But maybe this was his way of telling me he was not happy with things. After all our fights about Vigil ... I had no way of knowing for sure.

"How long do you think we'll be stuck in here?" I asked, changing the subject.

Caleb smiled softly at me. "I dunno, maybe a few days, a week? You look skinny, so you'll probably die first. I'm letting you know I don't have any problems with cannibalism in order to survive. Your thighs look delicious," he teased.

I gave him a dirty look but he just sat there laughing his ass off.

Then someone rapped on the outside of the metal door and I scrambled up quick as lightning, shouting to get attention. "Hey! We're in here! We're stuck! Get us outta here!" I yelled, banging at the door.

Half an hour later, we were finally freed from the elevator.

I had to admit, my opinion of Caleb changed dramatically following the time we'd spent in there. He really did have a way with words and had known exactly what needed to be said to calm me down. If it hadn't been for his intervening in the hotel bar, his quick rescue of me, something really bad could have happened. Without even realising it, he had prevented a major catastrophe from happening today.

It was dark already when we walked out of the hotel. Caleb stood with me while I waited for the taxi he'd called. I'd resisted at first, but I did need some time to think, so a cab seemed like a better plan than phoning someone to come and pick me up. As we waited, Caleb took out a bit of notepaper from his pocket and quickly scribbled something on it.

"Here's my contact number. If you need to talk, call me. Any time."

I took the note and folded it into my pocket. "Thanks, Caleb."

He flashed a shy smile, tucking his hands back inside his jeans. He stood awkwardly, a little embarrassed at being caught in an honest, heartfelt moment. It didn't do any good for his bad-boy persona. I smiled as he swiftly tried to cover it up.

"Definitely call me if things don't work out with the boyfriend. I'll take you on the most amazing date you'll ever have!" He gave me a wolfy grin, back to the normal jokey Caleb.

The taxi arrived and I got in, Caleb closing the door

behind me and then stepping back to bang his hand on the hood of the car, signaling for the driver to move on.

"Where to, miss?" the taxi driver asked.

"Home," I said with a heavy heart.

Chapter Nineteen

Without a Word

The journey home was quick and quiet. I buzzed down the window and stared out at the dark, empty streets and my heart tightened in my chest. There was a knot inside me that wouldn't go away. It felt stuck in my throat, making it hard to swallow.

I closed my eyes and focused on the feel of the wind rushing past my face. The streetlights flashed their yellow glow while the cab sped past. The only sounds I could hear were the humming of the engine and the low buzz of the radio. Thankfully the cab driver was one of those rare ones that didn't like engaging in mindless conversation to pass the time.

I sighed and rested my head on the back seat, trying to gather my thoughts, bracing myself for what I needed to face. I knew Tristan would be waiting for me at home. This was going to be a hard conversation, but it needed to be had. I was going to trust my guts and do the best thing for us. Which also happened to be the hardest thing, but wasn't the right thing always the hardest? I needed to be brave enough for the both of us.

I visualized Vigil's lessons to better control my feelings and breathed deeply, counting my heartbeats, feeling the wind cool my skin. My agitation subsided and I felt myself slowly relaxing.

After the cab stopped in front of our house, I paid the man and walked up to the front door, accidentally stomping on something on the ground by the doorstep. It was a white lily with a black ribbon and a little note. I just kicked the flower out of my way and entered the house; there were more important things needing my attention.

There was no one in sight, so I headed straight for Tristan's room. I had a feeling he would already be there, waiting for me.

I felt so tired and, suddenly, so very old, like I had the weight of everything laid on my shoulders, and it was with leaden steps that I walked inside, with numbness swelling and pouring out of me.

Tristan was indeed sitting on his bed, his head bent low as he stared fixedly at the floor, his hands digging through his dark hair. As soon as I stepped into the room, he turned his head in my direction, the yellow glow of the lamp at his back softly bathing the side of his anguished face. He tensed and rose from the bed, leaving his hair a disheveled mess.

"Joey," his hushed voice called out to me in a strained whisper. "Please, you didn't give me a chance to explain," he began hesitantly. "I-I know this sounds like a cliché, but it really wasn't what you're thinking."

I crossed the room quietly and sat down on the bed. Tristan sank down next to me, looking at me with pleading eyes. I sighed. I felt so weary.

"Really, Tris? You know what I am thinking?" I asked, and found it so strange how distant and detached my voice sounded. It was like the numbness I was feeling inside was spreading through my vocal cords, too. He looked hesitant for a second; his lips parted slightly but no words were able to come out.

"Joey, please …" he managed quietly at last.

"Let me tell you what I think happened, Tristan," I said, calmly crossing my hands over my lap. "I think the bar was too loud, too crowded. You hate that; it makes you feel suffocated. So you sneaked through that door because you thought you'd get to a quiet space where you could be left in peace for a while. Jessica, of course, had her eyes on you the whole time and followed you there. You tried to turn her down politely, but she came on to you like a randy tigress. I bet she had something like a 'it's now or never' deal in her head. You didn't have anyone to get you out of that tight spot. That's when I came by and caught you two," I finished evenly, while he just watched me in surprise. "So, tell me, what really happened?"

"Hmm, no, that's … pretty much dead on what happened," he acknowledged in surprise. Then he knelt down in front of me and looked me straight in the eyes. "So … everything is fine, right, Joey? Because you looked so mad. I was scared you wouldn't believe me."

"I also believe that a very small part of you really did want to kiss her, though."

He flinched a little. "Joey. I didn't … I don't …"

"It's a very small part, really, in the back of your mind. But it was there, wasn't it?" I leaned closer, looking him deeply in the eyes. The amazing thing about human behavior is that you can always count on people falling into old steps, through force of habit. Tristan had conditioned himself to avoid eye contact whenever he wanted me out of his private feelings, because he knew that as soon as I glanced into his bright gray eyes I could see them as clear as daylight. And that was what he instinctively did. He glanced down instead of looking me in the eyes.

"You don't need to answer me. You just did, without saying the words," I said coolly. "I might be temporarily blind right now, but I can still get my answers from you."

He looked upset. "Joey, this isn't fair. That may even be true – this small part of me might exist – but it's way too small. It's not important. And it's not like I'm lying; I just don't want you to notice and misunderstand it, because it really doesn't matter to me. You are the only thing that matters to me," he said, exasperated.

"But I've seen this in your eyes before. When you go out alone with the boys, the curiosity is there. I pretend not to see it, but it's there."

"I'll never act on it, you know that, Joe." Then he stopped and passed his hand roughly through his hair. "I'm sure Seth has it as well, and Sammy. I'm sure you have it, too. It doesn't mean anything. It's just a silly fleeting second of curiosity. It's mindless and unimportant. If it wasn't for your sight, you wouldn't even know," he pleaded.

"I'm sorry, Tris. I know it's not fair to you. Everybody should be able to keep their private thoughts to themselves, without feeling guilty for hiding them."

He let out a deep breath. "That's not what I meant, Joey. I wasn't trying to blame it on you. I told you once, a long time ago, this is a gift and a special part of you. I'm only trying to explain to you that it is human to wonder about those things, but in the end, what really matters is the choices we make," he said, taking hold of my hand. "And you are my choice. Always."

I shook my head. "I think you have the right to be curious, Tristan. I'm not mad, honestly, I'm not. We have been together for so long." I tried to explain. "We met when we were, what? Seventeen? We were so young and you've only been with me all this time. It's normal to want to try something new.

"I can see your excitement when you go out with the guys, the thrill you can almost taste of being single and free. I know how much you are pestered out there. It must be tempting to reach out and just … take it."

He huffed loudly, frustration seeping through his breath. "I don't … Joey, come on! That's not what I want. You can't be serious."

"A part of you wants it," I said, and then paused a little, to gather my thoughts. "We keep having this fight all the time, this jealousy consuming us both. All these insecurities: it's Vigil, it's Jessica … Maybe we just need to take a break from each other, live a little outside of this relationship."

He stood up and started pacing back and forth, like a caged animal. "What are you trying to say, Joey? What are you trying to get at? Are you seriously trying to tell me that I need to just go out there, have a blast, and just fucking leave you?" he spat out.

"Yes," I finally let out on a regretful sigh.

The blunt force of such a small word halted him in shock.

"No." He turned to stare at me with crazed, despairing eyes. "How does leaving you make any sense? I'm not going to. I don't care about anyone else but you. I'm not leaving."

"Tris … please try to understand. We have to."

"No. Why? Why do we have to? You're not making any sense. Just because this stupid Jessic—"

"This isn't about her," I said, interrupting him. "It's not her fault, or yours … or anyone's fault, for that matter. There is no one to blame here, Tristan."

He walked back to me and knelt in front of me again. He was about to protest, beg me to listen, when I cut in. "This is about *us*. I think we need to do this. Please, try to understand that I'm not trying to punish you. I'm not trying to make you suffer. I'm doing this for *us*," I said, taking his hands in mine.

I blocked the grief that threatened to surface and forced the numbness to fill me completely. "You know why I almost lost it when I saw you and Jessica like that? It wasn't because I thought you were cheating on me. It was because, for a split second, I thought about what it meant to not have you in my life any more, to lose you again." I sighed. I remembered when I'd lost him the first time, in the first year he was alive. I remembered what it felt like. It was the most intense and unbearable pain I had ever felt in my life. I remembered how I drifted through life like a ghost myself. In pain, and hollow, living without a heart, like a crippled soul.

"And when I realized, Tristan, how much this single frail thought could destroy me, I ran. I couldn't face it. It was … too much for me. That's when I also realized how weak I am." I shook my head when I saw he was about to protest. He used to say all the time that I was the bravest person he'd ever known.

I was the biggest fraud.

"No, Tris. It's the truth. Just the mere idea of living without you terrifies me to death. And that is just so wrong.

Can't you see?" I asked, slipping down from the bed and kneeling in front of Tristan, facing him, on the floor, my hands never leaving his. "I know it terrifies you too. We are so mashed up together, mixed in to one another, that we can't tell where one ends and the other begins any more. We've stopped existing as individuals, that's why the thought of losing each other is so damned scary. We have crippled ourselves. And we can't keep doing this. That is why we need to leave each other for now. Do you understand?"

Do you? I silently asked. *Do you understand, my love?*

I put my hands over his heart, begging for him to understand. He shook his head, refusing to let go. His cheeks were wet with salty tears and he pulled me close and hugged me tight, his face buried in my neck.

"Don't leave me, Joey," he begged, his voice a frail whisper.

"Please, my love, don't cry," I whispered in his ear, cradling him in my arms. He pulled me closer to him so my legs were wrapped around his side, and we rocked silently in sorrow.

"I-I … can't do it. I can't do this without you, Joey."

"That's why you need to do it, Tris. We owe it to ourselves to be true and honest. Don't you think we need to find out who we really are, to stand on our own two feet, without each other to lean on all the time? Or would you rather stumble forward with crippled feet for the rest of your life? We need to find a way to be truly complete while alone. Only then would we be worthy of each other. There wouldn't be any more fights about guilt or jealousy. We could be together and strong," I said, stroking his dark locks. "Because, right now, we are together, but we are weak. We are together *because* we're weak. So we might as well not be together at all."

"I knew it … I knew in my gut something bad was going to happen today," he sobbed.

I hugged him for some time while he cried. I forced myself to remain numb. I had to be strong for the both of us. I couldn't allow myself to cry, to *feel*. After a while Tristan's sobbing subsided but he still had his face buried in the crook of my neck. I continued stroking my fingers through his hair, trying to sooth his grief, to give him strength for these next steps in our lives.

"Let us be brave, now, Tristan," I said, leaning slowly away from him when I noticed he was calmer.

"I can't … I'm not ready," he said, with so much sadness in his voice. "I'm sorry. I-I can't. I can't do this. I can't leave you, Joey."

I gazed at him with a soft smile and wiped the tears from his face. "Do you think I'm wrong?" I asked him softly. "Do you not agree with me?"

He blinked, pushing back the tears that kept coming, unable to answer my question. He knew I was right. He knew he had to agree with me. I nodded in silent agreement, and started to pull away, but he grabbed my hands and pulled me back into his arms.

"Please. Don't," he whispered, hugging me tightly. "Just … don't leave. At least, not tonight. Stay with me tonight?"

"I'll stay here tonight … if you prefer," I said, caressing his face while he looked at me with his piercing gray eyes. I was too tired; I had no strength left to fight him any more.

A final single tear escaped from the corner of his eye, despite him willing himself to remain strong. I leaned closer until our foreheads were resting against each other's.

"I love you." I cupped my hands around his face. "I will love you always. No matter what. You know that, don't you? That could never change."

He nodded in silence and stared down, unable to meet my eyes.

"Tris, don't be sad ... I-I'm doing this for us," I said, my voice faltering a little. Seeing him like this was breaking my heart, making me falter and doubt my decision.

He still didn't say a word, but he looked up, our foreheads still touching. He looked at me deeply for a long time in silence before kissing me softly on the lips. It was a delicate kiss at first, filled with so much emotion and so many unspoken things, but then he deepened it, and I was lost in the warmth of his lips. His body smashed against mine; his scent in his every pore intoxicated all my senses, and the hot flavor of his taste was in my mouth. He was like a drug and once again I was lost in my addiction to him. I was too tired to fight it.

I shouldn't have let him lift me up onto the bed, his hands tangled all over my body, our lips never leaving one another's. I shouldn't have let him undress me, with such urgency, need and longing, despair flowing from each of his fingertips, from every stroke of his hands over my skin, burning me with desire and pain and so much sorrow. I shouldn't have let him have me just out of fear of losing me.

I thought of so many things I shouldn't have. But I was too lost, and too tired.

And for tonight, I needed him as fiercely as he needed me. Tomorrow, I would have to start learning how to live without him, but for now all that mattered was that I was in his arms, and the pain of separation was dulled by the hunger of his kisses, and my lips were numb and swollen with my craving for him. I needed him like an addict, and tonight I would have my fix.

The whole time we were burning and melting into each other on that bed, gasping and moaning in pleasure and despair, I knew I should have been stronger. I should have stopped this from happening for it would only cause us more pain in the morning and fill us with more regret.

But I couldn't stop him. I couldn't stop myself, not while we both rolled in waves of pure ecstasy exploding deep inside our cores, in anguished release. In the end, I could only sigh a quiet plea for forgiveness, for not being as strong as I should have been.

For giving in when I should have walked out.

But I was just too weak, and so, so tired.

Chapter Twenty

Evil Is Going On …

I remembered not getting any sleep that night. At some point I watched as the sunlight broke through the window, casting its warm glow over the hardboard floor, stretching its rays over the bed, lingering over the sheets and then stroking Tristan's smooth skin with a soft, gentle touch.

I watched Tristan's chest rising and falling slowly, his face free of any sorrow and his whole body safely cocooned in the relief of sleep. His nose was slightly buried in the pillow and he faced the other side of the room; a few locks of hair covered part of his eyes. I wanted so badly to brush those locks out of the way so I could see him fully, so peaceful and perfect in the morning sunlight, but I was scared of touching him. He would certainly wake up if I touched him.

I snuck out of bed, dressed as silently as I could and walked out of the room holding my breath so I wouldn't wake him. If Tristan were up, if he looked at me with his blazing silver eyes, I knew I wouldn't have the strength to walk away from him. His eyes would always be my doom.

I only dared to let out the breath I'd been holding when I reached the front door. I stepped outside, locked the door and was about to turn towards the garage when I bumped into Jamie. He looked at me with his usual blank stare before greeting me with a quiet good morning.

I always had a hard time reading Jamie; he was very good at hiding his emotions. I think the fact that he was behind a camera most of the time made him build up an unintentional protective mental barrier. Looking in his eyes was like looking at blank lenses. Now that I didn't have my sight, it was near impossible to read him.

"Seth told me to come early today. We have plans … Is everything all right, Joe?" Jamie asked, frowning.

"Huh? No, yes, everything is fine."

"I mean, because you're never up this early. And you sound a little off …" He seemed anxious, like he wanted to ask something more but didn't know how to do it.

I fumbled with the car keys in my hand, trying to avoid eye contact. Jamie was a good observer; I didn't want him to see how troubled I was. "No, everything is okay, Jamie. Some friends are waiting for me, so … I have to go." I quickly excused myself and ran off to the garage before he could ask any more questions.

I sped out of the driveway in Josh's car and drove straight to Celeste's house. I arrived relatively fast since it was so early in the morning and there was no traffic yet.

The first strange thing I noticed when I arrived was that the front door had been left open. The Harker sisters weren't careless like that; something was definitely afoot in there. I walked inside the house with cautious steps. Then I knew for sure something was very wrong. Jars and vases lay broken and shattered everywhere: art canvases slashed in tattered frames, benches tossed and turned on the floor, claw marks on the walls. It looked like there had been a war in here.

I could feel my eyes widening and I kept silently praying that nobody had been hurt. I couldn't see any blood stains anywhere ... that was a relief ... of sorts.

"Vigil? Celeste?" I called out in a small voice. "Anyone?"

"Joey?" Arice's worried face peeped around the kitchen door. "Oh, thank God you're okay!" She ran in my direction, curly auburn hair bouncing all over her scared face. Luna, Celeste and Vigil walked out of the kitchen shortly after, all of them looking disheveled and ragged as well. Celeste was supported by Vigil, who was holding a bloody cloth to her forearm. Vigil looked like he was about to be sick, but was holding up the best he could.

"Oh, God, what happened here?" I gasped, seeing their faces.

"What the hell happened to you?" Celeste cut in, only just restraining herself from shouting. I could see the anger radiating from her in heated waves. "We've been calling your cell phone for hours! We left messages; we were worried sick," she snapped, waving her bandaged arm and wincing in pain. "You said you'd be back soon, and you were gone all night. You never called or answered your damned phone!"

"I-I'm s-sorry!" I stuttered. "My cell phone isn't working and I stayed home tonight because ... some stuff came up ... and then I got up really early and didn't remember to check for messages. Is everyone all right?" I asked, walking up to her. "Is Vigil okay?" My voice was coming out a little strangled.

"Yeah, yeah, we are all all right, *now*," Celeste grumbled, while rubbing her temple with her slender white fingers. It looked like she had a hell of a headache.

"What happened?" I asked again. "It's like the place has been blown up," I said as we made our way into the living room.

"Raided." Celeste sat down on the couch with a weary grunt. "The place has been raided. Your little friend 'Nick' turned the place upside down looking for his magical things last night."

"Did he take the glass ball?" I whispered, sitting down next to her, dreading the answer. If we didn't have the ball any more, all would be lost. The possibility was too terrible to fathom.

"No, the glass ball is safe," Celeste reassured me, taking the bloody cloth from her arm.

"Oh, my God! Did ... did he bite you?" I asked, worried.

"No, I slipped and cut myself. Too much broken glass on the floor."

Vigil sat down the other side of Celeste, dressed in black sweatpants and a crumpled white T-shirt. His glossy black hair was as messy as the girls'.

Only then did I notice how pale he was – even more pale than usual. His skin was so transparent I could almost see the outline of green veins beneath it. He looked kind of ill.

"Are you okay, Vigil? You don't look so good ..."

"I feel like my head is liquifying, my insides are agonizingly sick, and breathing either makes me want to throw up or makes me feel like hot needles are being stuck deep inside my brain. Other than that, I am fine," he said, sounding tired.

"He's *fine*. Just a little hangover, that's all," Celeste interjected, a little miffed.

"That's what too much wine can do for you, pal," Luna jeered.

"This hangover thing is awful! If I survive this, I will never drink wine again," he vowed, grimacing.

"Yeah, heard that one before ..." Arice said, trying hard not to chuckle.

"How did Nick get in the house in the first place? I thought you guys have protective spells and wards ..." I asked.

Celeste looked flustered, and was staring hard at the floor. "Erm ... yeah, well, you see, every night I cast new spells on every entrance, but yesterday I kinda ... forgot ... a few spots," she mumbled.

I glanced at Luna, who was looking at her sister and sniggering. Then she noticed me watching and made a drinking hand gesture.

"I guess she had *something else* on her mind last night," Luna explained, looking from her sister to Vigil in amusement.

"I woke up at the crack of dawn with Mr. Skittles scratching my face like a maniac, and soon after that a hell of a rumpus started in the living room," Arice began. "I walked in and that evil thing was here trashing the place, and when it saw me, it flipped. The thing was raging, hissing nonsense about his belongings, and setting jinxes and curses on our house. It was possessed by the devil, I swear to you!"

Luna began her part then. "I woke up to Arice's screams and we tried to toss that thing out of the house, but as she said, it was flipping mad! It only stopped clawing at things after Mr. and Miss Booze-head over there—"

"Arice!" Celeste blushed.

"Sorry. After *Celeste* and *Mr. Vigil* finally woke up. As

soon as this Nick saw Vigil, it hissed and vanished from sight. It was seriously scared. The last thing it said was that it was coming after you, Joey. That's why we've been calling you."

"But that was near the break of dawn. It must have given up because the sun was rising. Mr. Vigil says this thing hates sunlight, right?" Arice said.

"So you'd better watch out tonight," Luna remarked. "That thing is definitely coming for you."

"Oh ... God. Do you think he'll go back to my house?" I jolted upright on the couch.

"You bet your sweet ass."

"Luna! Language!" Celeste admonished, looking at Vigil with another light blush on her cheeks.

"Oh, he doesn't care, Celeste. He's too focused right now on trying not to throw up."

"Guys, I'm serious! What am I going to do? Should I be getting back home now? Are the boys safe at our place?" I asked.

"I think they are safe for now; at least, during daylight," Celeste said. "But at night ..."

"What am I going to do? I can't leave them alone to fend for themselves. I can't leave Vigil here alone, either. What am I going to do?"

Shards of glass that were scattered over the floor started shuddering as if they had been hit by a small quake. The thought of any of the boys getting hurt because of me – of Tristan getting hurt – made my heart fill with horror. And it was making my new powers have an effect on my surroundings.

"Everything is going to be all right." I heard Celeste trying to soothe me, but her voice sounded so far away.

"No, it's not! What if something happens to the boys?"

"Joey. You have to stay calm," Vigil said, leaning over and touching me lightly. "Remember, deep breaths, do not let your feelings overcome your thoughts. Do not let your fear rule you. You are stronger than that. You have to keep calm."

I stared at his deep black eyes. Once, a long time ago, they had been cold and emotionless, but not any more. Now they were filled with worry and concern. I knew I could trust them. I knew I could always count on him.

I closed my eyes and breathed slowly until I was calm again. The shards of glass stopped tinkling on the ground and the room fell silent.

"Good. That's good." Vigil breathed out in relief.

I opened my eyes and saw him smiling softly at me. Then he turned to the girls and crossed his hands over his lap. "Now, let us talk about a plan of action, ladies. I think perhaps now it is time to speed things up a little. We have been discussing a way of trapping this creature. Celeste, do you think it can be done tonight? Do you think you can set things in motion over at Joey's house?"

Over the last few days we had been discussing lightning spells that could trap Sneaky Nick when he showed up. Celeste would be responsible for the spell part. The interrogation would be done by Vigil, so we could find out how the damned glass ball worked, but he wouldn't – couldn't – let Nick suspect anything about the switch. That was the tricky part of the plan.

Celeste turned to look at him, a little pale and uncertain. "Yeah, I think so," she said quietly. "I need to prepare some things first, pack everything for the spell, and then we can go."

"Good," Vigil said, resting his head back on the couch. "Now, can we talk about how much medication I am going to need for this blasted aching in my skull?"

After Celeste and Vigil had taken a couple of aspirins for their headaches, we started getting things ready. Luna and Arice stayed behind to protect their house and the magical items in the leather pouch, while the three of us drove to my place. We arrived with spell books and protective amulets of all sorts and shapes, and made our way slowly up the drive, our arms laden with magical accessories.

"Oh, my God, I forgot Mr. Skittles!" Celeste shouted suddenly, turning back to look frantically inside the car.

We'd agreed to bring Mr. Skittles with us to help us locate Sneaky Nick. The cat was like a walking security system for supernatural activity. It was he who had woken Arice the night before, and we were betting he could do it again.

"I can't believe I forgot him," Celeste continued, her eyes filling up with tears.

I glanced at Vigil, who stared back at me, clearly at a loss. What was with Miss Snow Queen's waterworks? It was just a *cat*. Apparently, I wasn't the only one having problems controlling emotions around here …

"We have to get him back, Joey. How am I supposed to take care of this spell? I can't even remember the cat! I can't believe I left him behind. I'm messing things up for you, Vigil, I'm so sorry!"

"Celeste, it's okay! I'll go back and get him. Please, stop crying!" I said, trying to calm her down. "You start preparing the spells and I'll go fetch him, okay?"

She looked at me in relief. "Really?" she asked, sniffing

rather loudly. Watching an over-emotional Celeste was a bizarre experience. She was always so composed and collected. Vigil was really affecting her. I thought maybe Miss Snow Queen had a thing for our unearthly friend.

"Yes, really, Celeste. It's no problem. If you guys need anything, ask Seth or any of the boys. I'll be back before you know it," I said, handing my stuff to Celeste and opening the car door.

Vigil had his hand on Celeste's shoulder – his way of comforting her, I suppose. He wasn't overly fond of close contact, but he was trying his best with her.

It took me about ten minutes to drive back to the Harker house and find Mr. Skittles; then twenty minutes more to convince him to scramble inside the car. Mission accomplished, I sped through the streets, eager to get back home. The sun was just setting on the horizon, leaving a faint purple lingering in the night sky. I chose a slightly longer route home because I knew it was more likely to be clear of traffic, and I was right: it was just my car cruising along the street. By now it was properly dark, except for twinkling lights from the windows of the many houses nestled along the road.

I flicked the headlights on, and at the sudden movement Mr. Skittles, sitting next to me on the passenger seat, tensed up on full alert. The hair on his back stood on end and he hissed at some spot behind us.

"Hum. Mr. Skittles? What's wrong?" I asked, glancing in the rearview mirror. There was nothing there. Mr. Skittles continued hissing and attempting to claw the air. "Okay, calm down, kitty, we're almost there." But then I quickly glanced back again and caught a suspicious shadow heading for the hood of the car, a tiny glint of yellow eyes blinking for a split second before fading out of sight.

Crap. It was Nick. He was here!

I didn't pause to think; I just reacted and stepped on the brakes, hard, making the car skid to a halt with a loud screeching of burning tires. I was lucky this was a deserted street or I would have caused a major accident. I busted open the door and scrambled outside, Mr. Skittles following at my heels like a shadow.

There was a ripping sound and a sharp tug on my shoulder, but I didn't stop to look at it. I saw the two strong beams of the car's headlights and ran into them. Sneaky Nick hated light. I stopped in front of the lights, my heart thumping loudly in my chest. Mr. Skittles was right next to me. That cat had a good survival instinct, I gave him that.

I glanced quickly at my shoulder and saw that my shirt was ripped in the shape of claw marks and there were a few drops of blood, but when I peeked underneath, there was no wound. The skin was smooth and unscathed, healed by Vigil's powers.

A hiss from Mr. Skittles jolted me back to attention. Nick was still around. I turned in a full circle, searching for him. Nick could be anywhere, at my back, at my sides, even right in front of me.

I glanced down and saw Mr. Skittles staring directly at something; then he turned his head slowly, as if following something through the darkness. Best to follow the cat's lead. He really was the best Nick-detector.

After some time manoeuvering myself in pursuit of Mr. Skittles' concentrated glare, I started to grow impatient with this game of tagging shadows in the dark. My heart still pounded loudly in my chest, but I tried to keep my cool as best I could.

"Okay, Nick," I said to the dark street. "Let's stop this silly game. What do you want?"

Something stomped on the hood of the car. "What do I wantss?" Nick hissed, clawing at the car, making me flinch at the sound of scratching metal. "What do I wantsss, hag? You know what! I wantss my things. Give me back my thingss, witch."

"Okay. I don't have your things with me. I wouldn't be *that* stupid, walking around with them in my pocket, would I?" I scoffed. "They are safe – and protected with many spells and wards – in a very secret hidden place."

He screeched like a banshee and continued clawing viciously at the hood. It was clear he wasn't one bit happy, and the car was ruined.

"Give it back, hag! Give it back," Nick cried out. Major hissy fit.

"I can make you a deal," I proposed, stalling for time. I didn't know a light spell to cast at him – that was Celeste's area of expertise. But I needed to try something to make him tell me how that damned glass ball worked. It was now or never.

"Listen, how about ... how about I give you all your stuff back, but I get to keep one item? That seems fair, dontcha think?" I said, gambling my way out of this one.

"I just want one thing. You can keep the rest."

He seemed to be pondering this. "Which thing?" he asked, suspiciously.

That was the tricky part. I couldn't tell him I wanted the glass ball and then ask him how it worked. He would instantly work everything out and go straight for Vigil's neck. Then he would be free from his hunter.

"Hmm. How about you tell me how they all work, and I decide which one I want?"

"NO!" he hissed defiantly. "No! You just wantss to know how they workss sso you can keep them all for yoursself! You lying, cheating thief!"

"No, I won't! I give you my word I will only keep one thing!"

"Your word? Your word? Your word meanss nothing, hag," he spat out.

"Listen, Nick, I'm trying to be reasonable here. I promise you can trust me. I mean, what else can you do?

"And, by the way, the only reason Vigil is not coming after you right now is because I asked him not to," I continued, my brain still working at super-speed to come up with something that would convince Nick to hand over the secrets of the glass ball. "I wanted to make this trade with you, you know? This way I will get a powerful magical artifact and learn how to use it properly, and you get to leave with the rest of your things. Everybody wins!" I said, trying to give him a reassuring smile.

"But if we can't make a deal, then I suppose I can ask him to get back to his mission ... of hunting you down." I was bluffing, squinting my eyes in the dark.

Nick jumped off the hood and landed on a dark patch of road, making sure to stay clear of the headlights' beams. His deadly yellow gaze locked on me.

"You liesss," he hissed again. "A Gray Hooded One would never stop hiss duty for ssuch a thing." I could see him narrowing his eyes.

"He likes me very much," I pointed out. "He always does everything I ask. You saw how he chose to protect me in my garden. He could have gone for your neck back there, but he chose me. He would do anything I say." I suppose there was some truth in that.

"No, there iss sssomething elsse holding him back," Nick said, suddenly making himself visible to me. I could see his whole body: his flashing white teeth in that wicked, evil smile of his, the tainted yellow eyes searching mine with intensity. "And I can alwayss try sssomething new …" he said, grinning menacingly. "I can alwayss take ssomething of yourss, like you *took* miness. And THEN we can make a trade."

I uncrossed my arms. I had a bad feeling about this. "I have nothing valuable," I said, shrugging. Whatever he took, it would be only an unimportant material thing which could be replaced.

"Ah …" he said tsking me, teasing me with that wicked scary grin. "But you do." His eyes glinted with malice. "You sseem very … 'attached' to those young males in your housse. I thinkss perhapss I could ssnatch one or two … slice them up, huh? Trade their pieces for my things? I could do thiss, yess, yess … What do you think, hag?" He let himself blend into the dark street again, only his yellow, glinting eyes visible.

At this, it felt as if my heart had stopped beating. A fierce coldness ran down my spine, freezing my every move. Inside my head, chains started rattling and that alien voice boomed through all my thoughts.

He threatened your boys, the voice snarled; and I snarled too. *You must kill him. Tear him into pieces.* All I could hear was rattling and snarling. *Your boys. Your boys are in danger. You need to strike him. Destroy him. Destroy everything!*

"You stay away from them, you filthy thing," I growled, and my voice sounded alien, not my own. "You touch them, and I will destroy you." The air around us stirred and a fierce wind picked up speed, brushing leaves off the ground in a swirling hurricane. Thunder rolled in the night sky. I could feel energy building inside me. I was already losing control.

"But first ... you have to catch me, hag," he whispered with malice, then disappeared swiftly, completely out of sight.

"No! No!" I shouted, overwhelmed by a fury so strong it rattled my core and made my soul reverberate with violence.

He threatened your boys! Are you going to do nothing? Are you going to just stand there and let him take them?

Rattling and chains was all I could hear.

"NO!" I stomped my foot in rage. The impact was so strong that it boomed for many feet around me, shaking trees and houses and making the asphalt crack as if it had been hit by a bomb. A small crater formed where I had stomped.

My hair whipped around my face, overpowered by the fierce wind, and I tried hard to control my temper. I felt like a lightning bolt had just run through me. I was breathing heavily, but I couldn't stop to rest. I had to get back home. I had to get there before Nick. I had to get to my boys before he did ...

Chapter Twenty-One
Rattling Chains

"Come on, come on, come *ON*," I urged myself, speeding as fast as the car would take me.

Mr. Skittles tried to gain purchase on the passenger seat, looking slightly terrified as he bounced back and forth. My mind was completely focused on getting back home as fast as possible, but every now and then, for a fleeting heartbeat, my mind flashed with terrifying thoughts of Nick's furious jaws biting one of the boys. I tried to push the images to the back of my head.

Why couldn't I get a grip on these powers, already? Why were they so hard to tame? Every time something triggered them, they flooded out of me uncontrollably. It was like trying to stop water spilling from a broken dam, or fire from burning dry straw. When unleashed, the powers were too potent to be contained. How on earth did Vigil do it? I had almost blown up the entire block back there. If only I could have focused some of my angry energy on Nick instead of everything else surrounding me.

And what about now? If only I knew how to use Vigil's teletransportation powers to beam myself instantly into the house. Bam, problem solved! No need to worry about getting back in time, about being too late to save anyone, about being this useless, pathetic waste of space …

But I didn't know how to make light spells or protection wards. I didn't know how that glass ball worked. I didn't know a goddamned thing. If I hadn't been so conceited as to think I could handle everything on my own, I wouldn't have gotten myself into this mess in the first place. I screamed aloud in frustration, the thought of getting there too late tormenting me more and more every passing second.

As soon as I reached the house, I bolted to the door, jamming the key into the lock and then running inside. I looked around frantically, but there was no one there. *Please don't let it be too late.*

Then I heard chatter drifting from the backyard; I ran to the back door and my body sagged in relief when I saw the boys, Celeste and Vigil, all standing in the middle of the garden, safe and sound, talking like they were at a freaking party.

"What the hell, people?" I shouted, making everybody jump, startling them with my sudden arrival. "Everybody get inside, right now! What do you thinking you're doing? It's night-time, dark, and you're all hanging around, waiting to be eaten alive."

Everybody stared at me, alarmed, suddenly realizing what a big mistake it was to be out in the open like that, and they all mumbled their apologies before shuffling inside the house. Celeste ventured to my side, giving me an apologetic smile, just as Mr. Skittles appeared by my foot, meowing happily.

"Mr. Skittles! You got him!" Celeste exclaimed, picking him up in her arms and patting his head lovingly. Then she glanced at my shoulder and noticed my ripped shirt. "Oh God, did he do this to you? He can be … temperamental sometimes."

"Huh? Ah, no. That wasn't Mr. Skittles. That was Nick. He paid me a quick visit on the way here. Almost made me crash the car. Tried to rip my head off and then threatened to kidnap and slice the boys up piece by piece until I give him his things back. Charming, right?" I walked into the living room and stood facing the boys all gathered there. "Is everyone all right?"

They all looked at me sheepishly and nodded in unison. I let out a heavy sigh of relief and slumped down on the couch. I was so tired.

"Okay, now, listen up. Nobody leaves the house during night hours. That thing is serious about hurting you," I said, indicating my ripped shirt, which made them all flinch. "If you leave during the day and can't get back before dusk, it's best to stay away from here. Celeste, Vigil and I are trying to fix this as quickly as we can, but until then, leave all lights on in the house." I looked around and realized that the house was already all lit up.

"Where's Tristan?" I asked, suddenly feeling my heart pounding in my chest. The boys all went very quiet at the mention of Tristan's name. Seth came to sit beside me, placing a hand on my leg.

"I talked to Tristan this morning and he told me about you and him … breaking up. He didn't want to say what happened. I tried to talk to him, but he wasn't listening. He looked like hell. As soon as he got up he told me about you guys, then packed up a few things and left." Seth looked lost, like a little kid who'd just found out his parents were splitting up.

"He ... left?" I asked in a small voice. Of course he had. What did I expect? I was the one forcing him to do this in the first place. But hearing Seth saying those words ... it made my stomach drop. He was leaving me. No. He had already left. I felt like someone had just punched me flat in the chest.

"Yeah, I mean ... he said he needed to think things over, I don't know. I'm sure if you guys just talk ..." There was a hint of hope in his voice.

"Does this mean we're breaking up the band?" Harry asked.

"No, of course not! This has nothing to do with you guys or the band. The band is fine. This is between me and Tristan, all right? It's something Tristan and I need to work out," I said, raking my hand through my hair. It was hard to think as I was so exhausted. "Guys, I understand you are all upset. Tristan is your best friend; I know you care about him a lot."

"You are our best friend too," Seth said, putting his hand over mine and squeezing it reassuringly. "If you need us, we're here, okay? We want you to know that."

"Thanks, guys. I know," I said.

They all nodded and Josh and Sammy even came to give me a tight hug before they each drifted away to do something in the house, leaving me alone with Vigil on the couch. Celeste excused herself and went to the kitchen to make us a cup of tea.

"How are you, Joe?" Vigil asked with an intent stare.

"I'm fine."

"Are you really? You don't sound fine," he said, still looking deeply into my eyes. He also looked very tired, I noticed.

I sighed. "I-I don't know how I am, Vigil. Honestly. I haven't got time to stop and think about anything," I confessed, rubbing my face. "Everything is such a mess ..."

"Yes, I know what you mean," he said softly. "We will fix this soon, Joey. Keep holding on and stay calm and you'll be fine," he instructed, but his voice wavered with uncertainty, despite his attempt to show confidence.

Once Celeste returned, I left them drinking tea in the living room, and went to look for Harry. When I found him in his room he looked so crestfallen about my fight with Tristan that I wanted to reassure him everything was going to be fine and that he shouldn't worry.

He beckoned me inside and I sat down on his bed, watching him pick through the mess of scattered clothes around the room, a can of beer in his hand.

"Harry ... you shouldn't be drinking now," I said, perhaps a bit too harshly.

He frowned, glancing at the can. "It's just one can of beer, Joey," he mumbled uncomfortably.

"I know, Harry. But it's dangerous to let your guard down, with that thing out there waiting to get us." I thought about evil Nick and his sharp yellow teeth. An intoxicated boy wouldn't stand a chance against that creature.

"I know you're drinking because you're upset over my fight with Tristan." I looked closely at him and only then saw how much sadness his eyes held. I didn't even need my empathy-sight. Harry was suffering, and I had been so worried about my own problems that I hadn't stopped to see what was going on with my best friend. He was in pain and I was causing it with my careless actions. I was hurting Tristan; I was hurting everybody.

I was so ridden with guilt I could barely look him in the eye. "I'm so sorry, Harry. I promise I'll sort through all this mess and make things right again ... for everybody," I said quietly, trying to steady my heart. Seeing Harry suffering was one of the worst things in the world.

"Are you guys really breaking up?" he whispered, sitting down next to me, his eyes brimming a little. He must have noticed the pained look on my face.

"We just need to figure some things out, Harry," I said, leaning in and wrapping my arms tightly around him, hoping that I could pass him some comfort, some relief from his worries. "But everything will be all right. You don't need to worry; we'll work things out."

He rested his head on my shoulder and let out a deep sigh. "I'm sorry. I was supposed to be the one comforting you here. But your fight with Tristan made me think of my own messed-up life and my head just got all tangled up ..."

"What messed-up life, Harry?"

He smiled sadly. "It's been a little hard ... after my break-up with Jackie. I'm still bummed about it, I guess," he murmured.

"It's okay to be upset, Harry. But you will find someone good for you, you'll see. Jackie doesn't deserve you if she gave up on you that easily. You deserve someone better."

He made a face, like he didn't quite believe me.

I knelt in front of him and cupped his pale face, making him look at me. "Harry, you are an extraordinary guy. I'm telling you, you deserve someone truly amazing at your side, an extraordinary girl to measure up to *you*. And believe me when I say you *will* find this girl. I have the most absolute certainty in that. Anyone that spends five minutes with you can see how incredible you are," I said with total conviction.

"Not *anyone*," he mumbled, and I knew he was referring to Jackie.

"Jackie wouldn't know extraordinary if it slapped her in the face," I retorted, annoyed. "If Jackie can't see it, that's her narrow-minded, stupid fault. It's her problem, not yours. Don't ever let this be your issue. It's hers and hers alone," I said firmly.

"I know, *I know*," Harry said, looking at me.

I put my hand over his heart. "But you have to realize, Harry, that there are people in your life that will never leave you. Seth will never leave you. Josh, Sammy and Tristan. Your sister, your mom. *Me*. And you will find a girl who will love you more than anything in the world. You have to trust me on this. I'm a witch. I know these things," I said in an eerie voice.

He forced a laugh. "I totally believe you when you say things in that voice …"

"You better believe it, Harry. I'm being absolutely serious."

He nodded and stared at the floor. He didn't look as tired as he had a moment ago. It seemed like a weight had been lifted off his shoulders.

"Thank you for talking to me; you've really helped, Joey. You're the best." He gave me another hug. Then he stood up, grabbed my hands and pulled me up too. I pushed myself up at the same time and ended up stumbling forward, landing against his chest. He laughed at me and my clumsiness, his face really close to mine.

"You're always doing this," he mused. "I pull and you push at the same time. Do you remember that first party at Sagan? On my secret terrace? You did the exact same thing!" His face broke into a smile. He was still holding me tightly against him.

"I thought you were making a move on me that night," I said, chuckling.

"I wasn't. I was trying to move your chubby ass off the floor! But when you crashed into me like that ... I did really want to kiss you," he confessed.

My brows arched, surprised. "Why didn't you?"

He chuckled, but still didn't let go. "You looked so guilty, like you'd been caught cheating. I thought it was because you already had a boyfriend. I didn't know you and Tristan had a thing back then ..." he said, and smiled, like he had just heard an old familiar joke. He spun me around and tilted me backwards, with his arm cradled under my back for support. "It would have been an awesome kiss, though." He smirked and tilted me some more, teasingly, making me hold on to him firmly so I wouldn't fall back onto the floor. His face was really close. I closed the remaining inches and gave him a quick peck on the lips. When I pulled away, he was smiling softly at me.

"See? There you have it. It's just a kiss. Nothing much," I said, chuckling.

"Yeah. I guess so." He gave me a sideways smile.

We locked eyes then, and this eerie silence surrounded us, as if the world was watching for some really important moment to happen. This time he was the one who leaned in, deliberately slowly so I would have time to pull away if I wanted to.

My eyes were lost deep inside the emerald pools of his eyes. His lips brushed softly over mine, delicate and sweet.

And then he kissed me.

But it was nothing like the brotherly peck of a second ago. This was not a kiss of a brother. It stirred things I had buried deep down and forgotten about. Little jolts of electricity ran through me, making my pulse quicken. His tongue found mine and his taste was so sweet yet tinged with sadness. I wondered if he could taste my fear.

Fear that this could destroy us, destroy what we'd had for such a long time, break our friendship into pieces. Fear that I had nothing to offer him, because my heart belonged to someone else.

He deserved so much more. He deserved someone who could give him everything. He deserved a full heart of his own. But all I could give him was my friendship, my everlasting, undying friendship. That was all I could offer him. Nothing more.

I wondered if he could taste my sorrow.

Because I could taste his: bittersweet.

I could feel the truth. He tasted cool and dark, burning and bright. Cold and heat wavering in a passionate dance, forever moving, recoiling and striking, so much beauty in every movement. He kissed me without holding back. We had crossed the line we had previously been so careful not to tread. We'd never dared to give in to that dangerous first step, because we both knew how much pain that path could bring us.

His lips were demanding mine, claiming what his heart truly desired.

Harry stopped kissing me and leaned back a fraction of an inch, ragged breaths escaping from his lips. He remained so close that our noses still touched.

He gazed at me in silence, his eyes carrying so much

longing that they threatened to shatter through the force of it.

Suddenly, realization dawning, his expression shifted to a serious frown and he tilted me back upright and finally let me go. "Sorry. Shouldn't have done that. That was wrong of me." He stepped away from me quickly and stumbled back to his bed. His hands were closed in fists as he stared hard at the floor. I stood in the middle of the room, still trying to recover.

"Joey … can … can you please … just … forget about what happened?" he pleaded. We had broken the unspoken rule; we had gone beyond the line and he was regretting it now. He looked even more dejected than before.

I moved to his side and sat down, taking his hand into mine, opening his fist and interlacing our fingers. He relaxed considerably at this small gesture, understanding what I meant by it.

"Sure, Harry. I'll do whatever you want," I said softly.

He gave me a sad smile. "You belong with Tristan. Anyone can see that – except you two numbnuts." He squeezed my hand. "Things seem a little out of control right now, but you will always find each other. When all this is over, you'll be together again. You are meant to be. I don't want to be the one standing in the way.

"And I will always have your love as a friend and you will have mine. What more can I ask for? I'm happy being your friend. I don't want anything more. Do you understand, Joey?"

He knew the battle would be a lost one. My heart *was* in Tristan's hands, and there was nothing any of us could ever do to change that.

"Yeah, I do," I said, resting my head on his shoulder.

He wrapped an arm around me. "I don't know what I would do without you in my life."

"Hey, you're my best friend." I nudged him in the ribs. "I would never leave you."

"Never, huh?" he asked incredulously.

I cupped my hands around his jaw and made him turn to face me. "Harry Ledger, you listen to me now. I would never leave you, not even if you turn bald, fat, ugly ... Not if the band breaks up and everybody goes their different ways. I wouldn't leave if you screwed up, again and again. Even when you find an amazing girl that makes you truly happy, I still won't leave you and I will never stop loving you. You are my best friend for ever. I swear to you, on my heart," I said, staring steadily at him.

His eyes filled with tears and he buried his face in my neck, trying to hide it. "*God,* Joey! Could you please stop making me cry? It's like you're doing it on purpose! Soon I'll be menstruating, growing boobs and reading chick lit, and *I swear to God,* if I'm Team Edward, I'm going to kill myself."

I laughed out loud and rubbed his back, trying to comfort him. "Okay, Harry. I seriously doubt you could ever be Team Edward. You look more like Team Jacob to me." We both laughed and joked for a while, the tension and heartache melting away with the ring of Harry's happy laughter echoing in the room.

I left him soon afterwards and went to find some fresh clothes to change into.

"Oh. Dear. God." I gasped in shock as I opened my bedroom door and looked inside.

On top of my bed was something that looked like it had once been a bouquet of lilies, but was now shredded into many, many, pieces, the flowers rotten and torn apart. I stared in horror. There was a black lacy ribbon on top of the mess, and a note, with the same handwriting as before. Someone had been inside the house.

Inside. My. Room.

I opened the note with shaky hands.

My cold-hearted Gray,
This is what you are doing to my heart,
Trampling and stomping all over it and tossing it
*   away*
To dry and rot inside my chest.
You tear me up and leave me in pieces.
Can't you see what you're doing to me?
Because I don't know how much longer I can take
*   this.*
But I will make you see your wrong ways
So we can be together for ever.
Yours always,
Secret Admirer.

Chapter Twenty-Two

Slow Dancing

"Joey, calm down *now*!" Seth ordered, but I paid him no attention.

Everybody was talking at the same time. I wasn't listening. I was too mad. Someone had broken into my house. Into my room. I paced up and down the small space like a caged lion. Who could have gotten inside the house? Who had access? My mind couldn't stop throwing out these questions.

You should rip their head off when you find them, the alien voice whispered in my head. *No one should threaten you.* Chains rattled inside. *All you have to do is let it out, and this person will learn to never cross your path again.*

"Joe?" Vigil's hand brushed softly over my arm. "Calm yourself," he warned me, eyeing the rattling window panes with worried eyes beneath furrowed brows.

"Yeah. Okay. I'm calming down. Don't worry," I said in a strained voice. "Who's been in the house over the past couple days?"

"Uh ... just us. Oh, and Becca. She was here yesterday."

"Who else?" I asked, nervously scratching at the inside of my arms.

"No one else," Seth replied.

The memory of Jamie popped into my head. Jamie had access to the house. All he had to do was slip into my room when the boys weren't looking. "What about Jamie?"

"Oh, yeah. Jamie was here too. He wanted to drop off some edited footage of our last show." Seth frowned. "Come on, guys, it's only Jamie. He's harmless!"

Hmm. Jamie with his blank stare. I never could tell what was really going on inside that boy's head. Jamie's mind was always a mystery … Could it be him doing all this, leaving me creepy flowers and notes?

I didn't think I would ever look at lilies the same way again after today. They would always freak me out.

Great. This had totally ruined my favorite flowers for ever.

"Should we call the cops?" Harry asked, his body tensing as if ready for action.

"I've known Jamie since school; I can't believe he'd do anything like this," Josh protested with a frown.

"There was that loopy kid at the bookstore, too," Sam reminded us.

I buried my head in my hands while the boys argued about the best course of action. We'd never had a crazy stalker before and had no clue how to proceed.

I couldn't believe my bad luck. First an evil cat from another dimension; then the power switch; then the weird voices inside my head threatening to blow everything up all the frigging time; then Tristan leaving; and now a stalker. Seriously, I was really starting to lose it.

"Look, I called Tristan and told him about what

happened. He's coming over; we just need to wait for him to get here. He'll know what to do." Seth's voice rose above everyone else's.

"Wait, Seth, what did you just say?" I jumped up, startled.

"Huh … Tristan is coming over …?" Seth repeated hesitantly.

"Seth, NO! Why did you do that?" The only reason I hadn't freaked out more about Tristan leaving in the first place was because I knew he would be safer away from here. But now he was coming back. The sun had already set and it was pitch black outside. It was too dangerous for him. "It's not safe outside the house. Nick threatened to get one of you, and now Tristan is coming back," I explained, agitated.

"I-I'm sorry, I wasn't thinking about Nick when I called …" Seth apologized. "I'll go give Tristan a call, see if I can stop him from coming."

"Come on, switch all the outdoor lights on. I'll wait for him outside. You all stay in the house. As long as you stay inside, you'll be safe," I ordered and hurried outside.

I shifted my feet nervously on the doorstep, waiting for the one person I missed the most to arrive.

"Sorry, Joe, he's not picking up," Seth told me, following me outside.

"Don't worry, he'll be here soon," Vigil said reassuringly.

"It's getting late … why is he taking so long? Why isn't he picking up our calls?"

All my mind had the capacity to do at that moment was focus on the driveway as I waited.

Tristan was in so much danger, increasingly more as the evening slowly advanced.

If he ever gets here, I'm going to kill him for making me worry this much, I thought to myself. *God, why was he taking so long?*

Then his car appeared down the street and parked in front of the house. He walked out as if he were taking a stroll in the park.

"Hey, guys. Why's everybody outside?" he asked, frowning when I stormed over to him.

"Why? *Why?* What the hell is wrong with you? Why did you take so long to get here? It's night already, can't you see that? We were worried sick about you. You weren't picking up your calls, either!" I yelled, slapping his arms non-stop. I was completely losing it.

"*Ouch!* Wait." He flinched. "My battery's dead and I came as fast as I could."

Seth let out a big sigh of relief. "We were *all* really worried, man," he told him, giving me another apologetic, weak smile as we walked back inside the house.

"Why everybody is freaking out so much about *me*?" Tristan asked.

"It's dangerous to be outside after dark," Celeste explained. "Nick made another appearance tonight, and threatened Joey, saying he was coming after you boys."

"Oh ... I didn't know," Tristan mumbled.

I hunched in my seat and just glared grumpily at him, sniffing loudly from time to time. Everybody settled back on the couch and Tristan kept his distance, probably waiting until I'd cooled down a little.

I still wanted to punch him for making me worry this much, but everybody else had moved on from it and eventually I let go of my anger, listening to their chatter. But I could still feel the tension in my body. I was worried that something bad was going to happen. But it wasn't just the "Nick situation" that was making me rattled. I was also antsy about Tristan being in the same room as me. I couldn't help but feel nervous every time he glanced my way. Sometimes our eyes would meet for a second, leaving me a mess of conflicting emotions and wanting to call off this break we'd started. I wanted him back with me. I faltered whenever he smiled at me, his silver eyes glinting.

I could feel the pent-up energy crackling inside, making me edgy, and with Vigil's constant, ever-worried stare looming over me I was getting even more nervous. I tried to steady myself, taking deep, long breaths, and when that didn't work, I went to splash some cold water on my face to calm my nerves.

When I walked out of the restroom, I noticed that the sliding glass door to the backyard was open. I immediately froze, terror filling me with each pump of my heart. Was someone outside?

I ran through the open doorway and looked frantically around, panic starting to rise. But there was no one out there. It must have been me who had left the doors open earlier, in my haste to get everyone back inside.

"Is everything all right?" Tristan asked, appearing at my side and looking curiously around the garden.

"Yeah, yeah. I was just being paranoid and checking to see if there was someone out here," I muttered, embarrassed.

Tristan reached out and clicked the switch on the wall, turning on all the lights above us. "Don't worry, everybody is safe inside," he said calmly.

"I know but … I still worry," I mumbled, shifting a little on the spot, even more nervous as he got closer to me. Each step he took in my direction made my heart speed up a little.

"Are you all right, Joe?" he said quietly as he stopped in front of me.

"Y-yeah. I'm fine." *If by fine you mean a fine nervous wreck.*

"You sound ... odd," he said, choosing his words carefully. "Like you're not yourself. I'm worried about you ..."

"Don't worry, I'm *fine*, Tristan."

"Okay, if you say so." He shifted his eyes from me to the ground. "I've spent the whole day today trying to think of a way to fix things between us. I couldn't get you off my mind, not even for a second."

I savored every moment of hearing his voice, feeling the ring it had in my soul.

There was a long pause and we both just stood there in silence, listening to each other's breathing.

"Have you ... have you been thinking of me?" he whispered, his voice sounding a little choked up. "I really miss you, Joey."

How could I tell him I missed him so much that it was hard to keep going? That it felt like I was having a drug withdrawal, that the mere mention of his name, or the fleeting memory of his face, made me feel sick with longing? This need for him gnawed deep into my guts, making it almost impossible to breathe ...

"I miss you too, Tris. Every second of the day. I miss you even now," I told him. It was the truth. He was constantly in my thoughts, too.

He took my hands in his and pulled me closer.

"I was so worried, before you arrived ..." I said, staring down at our hands.

"You didn't have to. I can handle 'Nick' just fine," he said, slipping his fingers between mine and wrapping one arm around my waist. "Dance with me?" he asked, smiling, his eyes twinkling, close to tears, as we started to slow-dance in the silence.

Everywhere he touched left my skin burning. I had forgotten what his touch could do to me. It could obliterate all my senses. I smiled back, my eyes also filling up with emotions – too many to count.

I leaned my head against his chest and closed my eyes, breathing him in and listening to the strong beat of his heart. It was thumping fast, just like my own. His scent enveloped me, drowning any feeble thoughts of being apart from him. There was nowhere else in the world that I wanted to be right now other than here, in his arms.

"I love you," he whispered, making goosebumps rise on my skin. I shivered at the nearness of him, the blasting heat emanating from his body, the jolts of electricity that his raspy voice fired within me.

I wanted to tell him I loved him too, but I was tongue-tied. I held on to him tighter, for fear of crumbling down if he let go of me. I wished we could keep dancing like this for ever, all our problems forgotten, all worries and concerns lost while he held me in his arms.

He leaned back and tilted my chin up with one finger, still dancing. "Kiss me." His tone held so much emotion. It was both a quiet request and a resolute order; a desperate plea within a whispering wish; a despairing urge and unfaltering hope, all at once.

And then he dipped his head and claimed my lips.

He really was like a drug to me, because his lips meeting mine felt like the wildest rush. I was on the highest high and wanted to stay there for ever, to keep kissing him like that for all of time. Energy jolts flashed and burst out of me. I was losing control; I could feel it slipping out of my grasp, like steaming liquid lava, unstoppable and endlessly consuming. Too much longing and lust, love and joy rushing out of my core. It was too strong for me to contain it all.

The wind picked up speed around us, making the trees dance and slash their branches. A storm was mimicking the state of my mind. And then all the lights around the yard burst and shattered, one by one, until the whole garden was left in darkness.

I pushed Tristan harshly away from me, and he stumbled backwards with a look of surprise on his face. That's when I heard the deep, menacing, nerve-racking hiss that I'd been fearing all day long.

Chapter Twenty-Three

Rescue Me

As soon as my ears registered that threatening hiss, I ran towards Tristan to protect him. But Nick was faster than me and launched himself in my direction. He hit me like a sack of cement, making all the air rush out of my lungs as I landed on my back, sliding along the lawn with the impact. It was like a Sumo wrestler had just brick-pounded me in the chest.

"J-Joey? What's going on?" came Tristan's scared voice. He couldn't see Nick in the dark and didn't understand what the hell was happening.

I wheezed, trying to catch my breath so I could warn him, but Nick had bounced off of me and was already preparing to attack Tristan.

Panic filled my mind with such an intensity that it somehow caused lightning to strike above the backyard, cascading light over us. Nick hesitated in fear, giving me time enough to catch my breath and shout a warning: "Tristan, watch out! It's Nick!"

Nick turned his malign yellow eyes to me and hissed loudly, sickeningly sharp teeth revealed. He had come to take something of mine and wasn't going to leave before he was true to his word.

"Celeste, out here!" Tristan shouted as loudly as he could, his voice full of urgency.

Celeste was leaning against the sliding back door, concentrating on casting a powerful spell. A brilliant sharp light glowed intensely above our heads, making everybody freeze and look up. The bright light made Nick's camouflage fur flicker and malfunction. We could see the sneaky, evil thing now. But that didn't deter Nick from his evil purpose. He skipped fast as lightning towards Tristan, at the same time that Celeste threw a light ball at the spot where he had been standing, missing him by inches. The light burst on the grass, momentarily blinding me, and when my vision returned, I watched in astonishment as Tristan did the most unbelievable thing.

He faded out.

The last time he had been able to do that was when he still had his "ghost powers" – before I had made a deal with Death. After Sky brought him back, he told me he couldn't do it, his fading, any more. In the three years we'd been living together he hadn't done it even once.

He faded quick enough for Nick to pass right through him without a scratch. Nick pounded on the grass in anger at having missed his primary target, Tristan. His eyes flickered everywhere, trying to understand how he had missed his mark so badly. I stared in shock as a faded Tristan stood unscathed in the dark.

"T-Tristan? H-how …? How's that even possible?" I choked out in disbelief. "It can't be … You said you couldn't … after all these years … you've been *lying* to me?"

"Wait, Joey! Please, it's … I-I can explain," Tristan pleaded, when he saw the broken look on my face.

Nick's head snapped angrily towards Tristan's voice, his yellow eyes squinting in the dark. He couldn't see Tristan, but he had heard him. That was good enough to locate him and he jumped again, long sharp claws already stretching out of his paws. But Nick again passed right through as if he had jumped through a mirage. He couldn't catch Tristan when he was faded.

"Vigil! In the yard!" Celeste shouted from the door, already conjuring up another light spell. All I could do was stare at Tristan.

He had lied to me.

"All this time … you were lying?" I whispered again. My head felt too heavy; there was something wrong going on inside of me, but I couldn't make it stop. I couldn't make it go away. My legs felt too weak and finally they faltered, making me fall to my knees on the grass. *That's all he does to you. He lies; he lies all the time! He's a liar and a cheater. He doesn't deserve you! You need to make him pay for this,* something wicked whispered in my head. *Make him suffer. Make him pay!*

"Everybody stay inside! That's an order!" Vigil's sharp voice boomed near the sliding door.

He ran outside and then stopped abruptly, trying to assess the situation. Seeing Vigil arrive was enough to make the evil little creature give up on his attack. Nick hissed one last time before flattening himself against the grass and sliding quickly towards the wall, trying to escape.

Celeste tried to launch one more light spell at his scurrying back, but once again she missed him by inches.

Nick was just too fast for her aim. He was far away by the time the light ball burst over the grass.

The scorching ground and the blackening spot on the wall was all that was left in the yard. Tristan immediately faded back in, walking hurriedly in my direction. I had managed to stand up by the time he caught up to me.

"Joey, please ..."

I shook my head, trying to clear my thoughts. I was done with his begging.

He didn't deserve my forgiveness; he didn't deserve anything from me any more.

He deserves to fucking die! That's what liars and cheaters deserve. Make him pay. Make him suffer! You need to step on him like the filthy trash he is.

Chains were rattling too loudly; it was too much noise, too much betrayal to take in.

"Shut up!" I hissed, clutching at my ears, trying desperately to make these maddening voices go away.

"Joe, let me explain," Tristan urged, getting close to me. *Too close.* I couldn't let him get close. *Not again. Not ever again.* Something inside, vicious and uncontrollable, snarled at the thought of Tristan's touch. Shaking shackles, rattling chains; it pushed and pulled, yanking at its leash. It wanted out. *Something* powerful wanted out.

Tristan took one more step towards me and lightning struck once again, this time over our house, making the ground shake with its powerful fury. It shattered a piece of the roof, making it crack and tumble onto the power lines, snapping the wires and making the lights throughout the entire block blink and go dark. Sparks of electricity showered over us, but I didn't cower. I didn't care any more. *Nothing* could hurt me more than Tristan's betrayal.

"Stay away from me!" I shouted at Tristan, but he paid no attention and kept reaching out his hands, trying desperately to make me listen.

Vigil was also running in my direction. I could hear Celeste's voice in the background, urgent and full of fear. Everybody was panicking now. And I was losing my mind, energy crackling and bursting out of me, the wind lashing viciously against my body, making my hair fly out wildly in all directions. The rattling chains were too loud. They deafened all my thoughts, all my reason; they made my blood sizzle and boil inside.

You want to hurt him. I know I do. *You could hurt everybody.*

"Don't touch me," I growled angrily, and then I raised my eyes slowly, my voice coming out cold, hoarse and completely not my own. *"You don't get to touch me ever again."*

Inside a whisper lingered in my head: *I am free now. I don't need him any more. I can rule my own life. I don't need anyone.*

I closed my eyes and wished with all my will to be elsewhere, anywhere but here. I imagined every part of me away from Tristan, away from his web of lies and deceit that had grabbed me and held me for so long in its sickening prison. Not any more.

There is no one holding you back now; no one to make you weak and pathetic. You can do anything you want to. The world is yours for the taking.

When I opened my eyes again, everybody had disappeared. I wasn't even in my backyard any more. Where was I? I looked around, trying to recognize my location. I was still in my town. I knew this place, but I was too far gone to remember anything.

You have beamed yourself … just like Vigil used to do. I had used one of his powers.

You can use all of them now. You can do anything you want. Strike at your will!

Strike? I didn't want to strike anything … or anyone …

Of course you want to, can't you feel it? In your heart? The hurt, the anger, the hate?

"Shut up, shutupshutup!" I mumbled, clutching my head in despair. I wanted this alien voice out of my head. I wanted to make it stop saying all these horrible things. These were Vigil's powers taking up my mind, making me go insane.

But of course you know this isn't true. This isn't Vigil or anyone else; this is all you, Joe Gray. All your anger, all your thirst for revenge, your violence wanting to break out. You cannot make it go away! It is a part of you, and you know it.

"NO! It's not! Shut up!" I shouted at the empty air, completely lost in madness.

You cannot silence your own thoughts, or make your desires go away. This is what you truly want. You want payback. You want revenge. You want to make him pay for all the pain and hurt he has caused you. It's all his *fault. And the hate is* all *your own.*

I whimpered in despair, looking desperately around, trying to find an escape from this madness. The street was almost deserted. A storm was moving closer, thick black clouds rolling over one another, clashing with thunder and lightning in the inky sky.

I crouched on the pavement, my head still between my

hands. "I don't hate him," I whispered to myself, rocking back and forth. I was drowning. Suffocating.

You hate him now. Stop fighting your true emotions. Stop being so weak and pathetic, with this stupid co-dependence. Remember Jessica; remember how close her lips were to his; remember the look on his face when he faded out of sight: you saw it. He knew what he was doing; he knew of his lie. You know he betrayed your trust. He tossed your love away like it was nothing to him. How does that make you feel now?

Rattling, rattling …

You need to let it out. You know I'm right. You know you are right. Let it out. Let me *out.*

I stopped rocking and stood up slowly. Everything felt blurry and dark; the chains were too loud, my boiling blood too scalding. My whole body felt feverish, but strong at the same time. I'd never felt as strong as I did then.

Nothing can ever hurt me if I remain like this. Yes. Let it out.

I looked up and watched the sky, the storm reflecting what I was feeling inside: raging, uncontrollable, powerful. Anger leaked out of every pore of my skin, burning hot. So hot.

Cold rain started falling. It poured and drenched me in seconds, the water sizzling and steaming when it touched my burning skin. I wasn't aware exactly when I had started walking. I just knew I needed to keep walking and not stop. There was too much energy barreling up inside. *I could walk for ever.*

I didn't know where I was going, but at some point the entrance of a park loomed over my head. I headed inside, tossing my shoes away at the borders of the grass. I wanted to feel the soaking grass beneath my toes, all the energy rushing out of me, the grass, the earth, the water seeping through my skin.

I could control it all. They are there to do my will.

I don't know for how long I walked in that park, how many times I crossed those grass fields. Could be dozens, could be barely once. I had completely lost track of time. There wasn't anyone in sight; it was too dark, too late in the night and raining too much for anyone to dare go in there.

There was only me and the rain and the trees. Or so I thought.

Shouts in the distance disturbed my already deranged thoughts. I felt like I was dream-walking in a nightmare and that soon I was going to wake up. But the dream kept going, the rage kept flooding out of me, sizzling in the rain. *Would I ever wake up from this? Or would I stay in this nightmare for ever?*

The shouts were much closer now, making me look in their direction with a cold, curious detachment. It didn't matter who was doing the shouting. *Nothing could hurt me. Nothing mattered.*

Two dark silhouettes appeared in the distance. Two big, heavy men who let out excited, drunken howls. They spotted me and started heading my way. "Look what we've got here!" One of the men ran and halted right in front of me, blocking my way.

I stopped and regarded him coldly, as if he were a fly buzzing in front of me. He was massive, a huge, heavily muscled thug. The second man stopped by his side and sneered cruelly. He didn't look as strong, but that didn't mean he couldn't be just as harmful as his buddy. In fact, maybe even more so, because he seemed more intelligent, which made him more dangerous and manic.

It was clear they meant me harm; I could see it. It was written all over their faces, flashing through their crazy red eyes. They howled excitedly and clapped their hands, their dark clothes drenched and heavy with the rain, clinging to their bodies and showing their muscles. "What luck we have, mate. Look at this fine piece of ass here," the clever-looking one shouted. "And you said we shouldn't cut through the park. We could have missed this perky treat!"

"I was the one who spotted her, man. You should be thanking me and my blessed eyesight," burly, stupid-looking thug barked.

"I don't care, I'm the one who goes first. You can have her after," the friend said, taking a step closer to me.

Stupid thug regarded me for a second, starting to get edgy. He looked like he was dumb and slow, but apparently he had a better survival instinct than his "buddy". He knew something was off with me; something definitely looked wrong.

Maybe it was the fact that I hadn't moved since they'd arrived. Nor did I try to run or even cry out in fear.

Maybe it was the fact that although I was drenched and barefoot, walking alone in a park in the middle of the night, I didn't seem to care. *At all.*

Maybe it was the eerie storm lurching in the background, making everything seem scarier, as if we were all in a horror movie.

Or maybe it was the fact that I was grinning at them – and not a friendly grin. There was nothing friendly about my smile and he knew it.

"Uh … dude, I think maybe … it's best we let this one

go," he suggested with a smidgen of apprehension, his eyes never leaving mine. Alarms were sounding inside his thick skull – I could tell by his expression. He wasn't as stupid as he looked, after all.

My grin widened.

"What the hell are you talking about, you idiot? If you don't want it, stay the fuck away! She's all mine," sneering guy barked, and then pushed his friend away, making him stumble backwards. He turned his attention back to me and matched my wicked grin with one of his own. "So, sweet cheeks, we're going to have such a good time tonight." He grabbed my wrist.

We sure are, I hissed inside my head. I glanced down at his hand.

Something snarled in me, loud, vicious, merciless. *Strike them down*, it growled, rattling its chains. *Make them pay.*

"Shit! Your skin ... it's burning up!" the man exclaimed, puzzled, looking at my wrist and back up to my face. We locked eyes. His grin faded slowly and then his sloshed, drugged brain realized that something was seriously wrong. *Deadly wrong.*

"Y-your eyes ... They're all ... white! W-what's wrong with you?" He panicked and tried to move his hand away but I was faster and grabbed his wrist. I was the one holding him now. It was *my* time to sneer while I squeezed, slowly and painfully.

He cried out and hit me in the face with his free hand, trying to break free from my iron grip. I didn't move an inch. *I was made of stone; nothing could stop me.* I felt a tingling on my cheek that disappeared in less than a second.

He raised his hand slowly, looking at the blood staining the rings on his fingers. He had cut me when he slapped me.

And now you must kill him for striking at you.

"W-what the ...? H-how did y-you ...?" he stammered, looking wildly at my face.

I knew I had healed by now. And he had watched it happen. His weak mind was trying to process this, trying to understand what was happening.

I grabbed the arm he had slapped me with and constricted it until I heard the bones break. Then I let go. He was shouting and crying. *I didn't care. I barely listened.*

"Let go of him, demon!" his stupid friend yelled, running at me.

My eyes darted quickly to my second attacker, and I grabbed him by the arm, too.

He cannot stop me. I kicked him in the legs and heard bones cracking again. There was more shouting and crying. I still didn't care when I punched him hard in the chest, making him fly into the air and crash a few feet away, landing on the grass with a loud thud. He tried to stand up, but ended up slumping back down, clutching at his broken leg.

I turned my attention back to the man I was still holding by the wrist. He looked terrified out of his mind now.

Good. He should be scared. You need to strike him down. End his miserable, filthy, pathetic little life.

"You have done this many, many times before, haven't you?" I asked, my voice sounding raspy, like a soft growl.

"W-w-what?" he whimpered.

"Preying on other girls. How many others did you have a 'good time' with?"

He didn't answer and kept sobbing like a baby.

"How many girls have you hurt? How many have shouted and cried because of you?"

"Ah! P-please! Stop! STOP!" he shouted in abject horror as my grip tightened around his wrist.

"How many begged for you *to stop?"* I asked again. The fury in my voice burst out like steaming lava. Red and pure, blasting out of my core. I could feel my hands heating in rage and then I smelled skin burning. He started screaming and thrashing against me, trying to free his arm. I was burning him.

"HOW MANY?" I asked one more time.

"I DON'T KNOW! I don't, all right? Many, loads, I don't know! I lost count! Let me go!" he screamed at the top of his lungs, his mouth foaming. He was deranged with fear.

I was exploding in anger.

I tilted my head, observing him closely with cold, distant eyes. But inside I was burning. I should strike him now. I should kill him. *You should. That's what he deserves. Revenge. Make him pay.* But maybe he deserves a better punishment. He deserves to remember what he did. *Every day of his fucking disgusting life.*

"Let you go?" I said with a sneer. *"I cannot let you go like this. Like nothing ever happened. You have to remember this. For the rest of your life, you will remember me. Whenever you look in the mirror, you will remember,"* I said, and planted a hand flat against the right side of his face. The smell of burning flesh hit me again and the sound of his screams filled the night air. I could hear chains snapping off from their hold inside my head and I rested my hand over his entire face.

I let go of his unconscious form and he slumped to the grass like a bag of trash, blisters and raw flesh swelling up on his ugly face. I turned and walked slowly to his broken-legged friend. He had witnessed everything, his eyes darting manically in every direction. But he was still trying to survive, crawling across the grass, trying to get away from me.

I stopped next to him and knelt by his side. He stopped crawling, giving up his feeble attempt to escape. "I'm s-sorry!" he sobbed in despair. "I won't ever do it again! Please, I swear!"

I tilted my head again, watching him. The urge to crush him into a puddle of blood in the mud was almost irresistible, but I stopped myself at the last minute.

"I know you won't. You're smarter than your friend. You know that if you ever do this again, I'll come back for you, don't you?"

"Y-yes! I know!"

"Tell your friend this. He must know he will be punished too if he ever hurts someone else. And you ... you need to have something to remember as well. A slap on the face, a mark of your shame for ever etched on your cheek. Remember this," I said, planting my hand on the side of his face the same way I had done with his friend. He didn't cry as much and didn't faint, either. But I knew he would never, ever forget.

As I walked out of that park, a series of lightning bolts struck dozens of trees around me, scorching their trunks into black coal. I could feel the release of all the pent-up energy bursting out of me. As soon as my bare feet hit the pavement outside the park gates, I felt completely drained. I didn't have any strength left. No more rattling chains, no more anger, just complete exhaustion taking over my soul.

And it was so cold; my blood was freezing. I was

trembling uncontrollably, the rain still falling heavily, chilling my drenched clothes like ice pouring over my flesh and bones. My teeth chattered as I crossed the street and sat on a bus stop bench. The merciless wind slashed furiously, cutting through me.

The power I'd felt moments ago had abandoned me, and all the fog and haziness returned tenfold.

I was dream-walking again. Wasn't I? When would I wake up?

I didn't notice that I had my cell phone clutched in my hand. I remember thinking I needed to call someone to help me. Someone to calm me down and stop all this madness. I remember sticking my hand in my pocket and taking out a wet, smudged piece of paper. I could barely discern the numbers; the note was almost ruined. I dialed. It took two rings for him to pick up.

"Hello?"

"Hey," I whispered, shivering.

"Who is this?"

"It's me, Joey. I need help," I pleaded, my voice faltering, my teeth still chattering from the cold.

I think he asked for directions. I don't remember what I said. There was a street sign a few feet away and there was the park. I didn't know the name of the park. I didn't remember reading the signs, either. All I knew was that the phone line cut and I remained on the bench, too drained to move, too tired to do anything. I just sat there and trembled from the cold. Soon I couldn't feel my fingers any more, or my feet. I couldn't feel anything except the cold, and I was aware of nothing but the sound of rain falling down, thunder rolling above me and the yellow, sickening light flickering from the streetlamp.

Maybe this would be a good time to wake up. This dream wasn't fun any more.

And then a car stopped right in front of me, making me glance up. He walked out of the car, his face consumed by worry. He asked me things. I didn't understand him. I couldn't speak, I was shaking too violently, too far gone, barely seeing him, my mind a shambles.

He grabbed me by the arms and tried to walk me to the car. I managed only a couple of steps before crumbling to the ground. He scooped me up in his arms and carried me. I think I passed out, or just drifted in and out of consciousness for a while, like I was submerged in water, dreaming I was drowning. My body was too exhausted to fight back and to be awake. I thought he carried me up some stairs at some point. But I couldn't be sure.

I was aware of feeling dry and warm again, and being in a dark room. And then I was aware of nothing.

Chapter Twenty-Four

Search & Destroy

I woke up groggily, my eyelids heavy as lead. I felt like I had a hangover, but without the headache, just a heavy weariness inside. I couldn't quite identify what was wrong, but something definitely felt it.

I let out a ragged breath and only then became aware of the heavy arm draped around me. And the different bed and the strange room. This wasn't home. Where was I? And most importantly, *whom* was I with?

I turned around slowly and was trying to dislodge the stranger's arm from me when he shifted on the pillow.

Caleb woke up, blinking at me, looking a little startled.

"Hey. You're up," he said. He let go of me and yawned. "How are you feeling?"

I moved to the edge of the bed, while he came to sit next to me, ruffling his dirty-blond hair. He was wearing large sweatpants and an old Rolling Stones T-shirt. "You gave me quite the scare last night, Joey."

"I did?" I tested out my voice hesitantly, and breathed a sigh of relief when I found I sounded normal again. "What happened last night?"

"I don't know! You tell me," he said, raising an eyebrow.

"I-I don't remember ..." I rubbed my eyes, tiredly. "How did I end up here?"

Everything was a distant blur; I only remembered fractures of things, glimpses of scenes. It was like trying to recover a dream that was slipping away. The harder I tried to pinpoint it, the faster it drifted away from my memory.

"Don't you remember calling me?"

"No. I called you?" I asked, surprised. My head felt kind of numb.

"You don't remember me picking you up from the bus stop, close to dawn, completely soaked, freezing to death in that blasting storm, barefoot and looking quite ... out of it?" He glanced at me worriedly.

I blinked slowly, trying hard to recollect last night's events. "It's all hazy and jumbled," I said, rubbing my temples. "I think I was in the park ... walking ... for a while."

I remember screaming, men screaming, the rain, the wind, burning flesh, rattling chains ...

I shook my head. Something inside flashed in alarm – a warning. *Don't go there.* It was best to leave this memory buried wherever it was.

Caleb noticed my distress and put a hesitant arm around me, trying to be reassuring. "Hey, don't worry. It was probably some heavy shit someone gave you; you had a bad trip or whatever there. You should be careful with this stuff ... I had a friend once who tripped so bad he was never the same again ...

"Hell, I had my share of heavy stuff too, back in the party days. Took me a while to realize the shit isn't worth it. Take my advice, you're better off staying away from that."

"I didn't ..." I trailed off, unable to tell him that I had never done drugs in my life. But how else was I going to explain last night to him? "What happened when you picked me up? Did I say anything?" I asked instead.

He shook his head. "No, you were basically freezing to death and almost passed out. I got you here, dried you up, put you in some warm clothes and laid you in bed."

Only then did I notice I was wearing one of his T-shirts. It had a faded Foo Fighters logo on it and it was too large for me, covering me to the middle of my thighs. I knew I should feel embarrassed or something – he had taken my clothes off and all – but I wasn't. I didn't care. Inside there was no embarrassment or shame, just numbness.

"Then I went to change into something dry myself, and I came back to give you a blanket. You still looked like you were so cold ... But when I'd covered you up, you grabbed my wrist, and didn't want to let go. You've got quite the death grip on you!" he said, playfully rubbing his wrist. "The more I tried to pull, the more you tightened your hold. I gave up and lay by your side." He chuckled, but then changed his expression to serious again. "I hope you don't think I was taking advantage ... I was planning to crash on the couch, but you were dead set on not letting go."

I glanced at his arm and extended my fingers, touching his wrist lightly. There were faint purple bruises, little finger marks, wrapping around it. I must have grabbed him real hard. "I'm sorry," I whispered. "I don't remember doing *this*."

"That's okay. You were feeling scared, that's all," he said, rubbing the bruise. "Has something happened ... between you and Tristan?"

Another warning flashed inside: *don't go there. There*

is nothing there for you but pain. I felt light-headed, blood rushing through my brain; everything felt hazy again as I tried to force the memory out. There was something about Tristan, a flickering image of him in our backyard, but I couldn't remember exactly what had happened ...

The effort to remember versus the warning that I should forget was making me feel sick to my stomach.

"After you grabbed my arm, you whispered something ..." Caleb insisted on carrying on his probing. "You said, 'Tris, please, don't leave.'"

I stood up and started picking up my clothes off the floor, a sudden urge to leave taking over me. I needed to get away.

"I reckon I look a lot like him. You must have got me mixed up," he said, standing up as well.

I shook my head, in denial. "I'm sorry. I don't remember ..." *I don't want to remember.* I forced myself to feel numb, letting nothingness wash over me while I got dressed.

"Joey, tell me what's wrong," he insisted.

I turned to look at him, my eyes blank. "I don't know, Caleb. I think something is broken. I think ... *I'm* broken." I didn't feel sad; I just felt this overwhelming sense of loss. Something was missing inside of me. I didn't know what, but I knew it was something important.

"Hey," he murmured, putting a hand on my shoulder. He looked so worried ... like he truly cared.

I shook my head. "Caleb, listen. Thank you so much for everything, for helping me, for picking me up last night. But I have to go," I said, walking out of the room.

"Hey, wait!" he called out, running after me. "I'll make you something to eat before you leave, okay?" he said.

"Thanks, but I'm not hungry," I said, carrying on towards

the front door. Come to think of it, I hadn't felt hungry in a long time. I didn't recall the last time I had slept, either – proper sleep, that is, not just crashing out.

He sighed. That was definitely not the answer he was waiting for. "Okay. I'll drop you off wherever you need to—" he started to offer, but I interrupted him.

"No. You've done enough for me already. Don't worry," I said, walking out of the door.

"Hang on! I can't let you walk away like this. You don't even have shoes on!" he exclaimed, following me.

I stopped and glanced down at my bare feet. "It doesn't matter, Caleb."

"Let me at least call one of your boys to come pick you up, then. Not, you know, *him*, but one of the other guys … Bass player dude, he can pick you up, right?" Caleb suggested, his pale-blue eyes filled with concern. He looked so much like Tristan, even more so when he was worried.

"I'm going to meet them right now, Caleb," I said, dismissing his suggestion. "I really need to go."

He slumped his shoulders in defeat. "All right. There are taxis at the front of the building. And if you need me, you know where I am."

I turned away from him and headed down the hallway. I only stopped when he finally gave up the idea of helping me and I heard his front door clicking shut. I couldn't remember many things from the night before, but one thing was clear and bright, glowing in a burning way inside my head.

I remembered using Vigil's power.

I remembered the key to using it, the right way to channel it. It was like I finally understood the magical equation behind it, the switch to make it work, and how it worked.

I had finally solved the puzzle. Now I could do anything I wanted with this power. It was all in my hands.

I closed my eyes and visualized home. When I appeared in the middle of the living room, Vigil was the first person I saw. He had his elbows propped on his knees, his chin resting on his hands. He was staring intently at a rumpled map outstretched over the coffee table. I could feel the tension in his shoulders, the hardness of his eyes as he concentrated on the map. Celeste was slumped on the couch next to Vigil, fast asleep, her neck bent at a weird angle. She looked exhausted. The boys were nowhere to be seen, but Tristan was standing by the window with his back to us, guarding the street outside. He didn't notice me appearing.

Vigil did.

He lifted his head and stood up slowly, a cautiousness about his movements, a guarded look in his eyes.

"Are you all right?" was his first question.

"Yes. I am fine," I answered plainly as I walked towards him. "Vigil, I can help get Nick now. We don't need to wait for him to come to us any more. We'll go after him. I know how to do it now."

He narrowed his eyes, trying to read something in me.

"Joey?" Tristan called out.

I didn't turn around or acknowledge him. "Vigil, you said you were working on a tracking spell with Celeste. Can you locate Nick now? I can finally take care of him," I stated, looking at the map spread out over the table. What had Vigil been doing? Trying to locate Nick? Or me?

Celeste stirred when she heard her name. "Joey! You're back. Thank God!" she breathed in relief.

I didn't acknowledge her, either. "Vigil? The tracking

spell? Can you do it?" I asked again, getting impatient. I wanted to get out, away from these people.

"Yes, I can," he said, his eyes fixed unblinkingly on mine.

"Do you have the glass ball with you?"

"Yes, it is in my pocket here."

"Joey, we need to talk," Tristan called again, his tone urgent. I sensed his presence close to me. Too close. *You can't ever let him touch you.* A flash of the previous night passed through my mind. A memory of Nick surfaced as well – the backyard; Tristan ... *fading.*

And rattling chains.

I walked away from him, reaching for the map on the coffee table. *You need to get out of here and away from him.*

"I have nothing to say to you," I said coldly.

"Joe, it's important, please," Tristan insisted. "Can you please just look at me?" His voice wavered a little.

I grabbed the map and turned to look at him. He had dark shadows under his tired eyes. He was hurting. *I didn't care. He deserved it.*

I watched this person, this boy that had meant the world to me, looking back at me with those big gray eyes that once were so dear, and now all I could see were his lies, his deceitful intentions, his betrayal masking every beautiful aspect of his face. There was nothing connecting us any more. *He meant nothing to me.*

"I have bigger things to worry about," I said with a blank stare. The deep look of hurt on his face did not bother me. Any other time, it would have destroyed me, but today, it didn't. *Today I didn't care.*

Celeste put a hand over her mouth in shock. Tristan made an attempt to walk towards me, but Vigil stopped him.

"Wait. Don't," he warned Tristan. "Something's wrong. Do not come closer." Then he turned slowly to me. "Joey ... what happened last night, after you left?" he asked, visibly alarmed, searching for something in my eyes.

"It doesn't matter what happened. What matters is that I had an opportunity to better understand your powers. And I do understand them now. I know how they work. I can use them for my benefit. I can use them to hunt Nick down."

"Did you ... hurt anyone?" Vigil asked slowly, as if I was carrying a loaded gun and pointing it in his direction.

I shrugged. "Does it matter if I did? I told you, this is not important. We need to focus on Nick and stop wasting time with unimportant things."

"Unimportant? Vigil, what the hell is wrong with her?" Tristan asked abruptly.

"I-I think she has finally disconnected herself from her emotions, like I told her to do. But something went wrong ... I-I don't know why, but she is losing her humanity ... I can see it in her eyes. There is only a void and coldness; detachment from herself."

"You told her to disconnect herself from her *emotions*?" Tristan asked.

"There is *nothing* wrong with me," I retorted in a cold tone.

"So you're telling me that all this time she's been stuffing her feelings down her throat, burying them and pretending it didn't bother her instead of dealing with it?" Tristan raised his voice, making Harry, Josh, Sam and Seth come running into the room in alarm.

"Her emotions were only causing her to lose control!" Vigil countered, agitated. "I have been watching her carefully for signs. She lost control whenever she got in contact with her emotions. I was trying to find a way to make everyone safe around her while she has my powers. They are not meant for humankind to wield; they are not meant for *her.*"

"She can barely contain her feelings as it is, even when she's calm," Celeste said, jumping in to support Vigil's side.

"And you think telling her to *pretend* they're not there really helps?" Tristan asked. "News flash, Vigil: human beings need to express their emotions. When we stuff all our feelings inside, it doesn't make them go away; it only makes them boil and grow a thousand times stronger, until it all blows up in the end, in the worst possible way. I don't even know how she managed to make it *this* far; no wonder she's flipping out!"

Vigil flashed a panic-stricken look at Tristan. "I-I am sorry ... I-I did not know! B-but the truth is ... the longer she has my powers, the harder it is for her to keep her mind sane. Every time she loses control and lets my powers take over, she loses a piece of her humanity. I was desperately trying to keep that from happening. I was trying to protect her!" he stuttered, guiltily.

"This is *not* Vigil's fault. Don't make this about *him,* Tristan," I said sharply. "If there is anyone in this room who failed me, it is you. It's your presence that is upsetting me; it's your big pile of lies. Vigil has only been trying to help me since the beginning. And since the beginning, he has never lied to me. *You,* on the other hand ..." I was making the window panes rattle quite loudly as I spoke.

"... you broke everything we had, Tristan," I said darkly. *And crushed it all under my feet, like shattered glass. It hurt and cut deeply, but nothing can hurt me any more.*

I have healed. I am made of stone; nothing more can cut through me now.

"Joey, you have to let me explain—" Tristan began.

"I have to?" I cut in. "I don't *have* to do anything. And I don't want to hear any more of your lies. We're through, Tristan. And this conversation is over." There was an undeniable tone of finality in my voice.

The boys had watched the fight in silence, eyes wide and frightened. I didn't let anyone say anything. I was done talking. I didn't need anyone's permission; I could do anything I wanted. *I was invincible.*

"Vigil. We are taking care of Nick *now*," I said, grabbing him by the arm and taking the map in the other hand. And then I beamed us both out of there. One second we were in my living room, the next we were standing in the middle of some deserted road.

Vigil lurched forward, a hand clutched over his stomach like he was about to throw up. I guess this sort of transportation wasn't intended for humans. Vigil had never brought me along during his teletransportations, so we didn't know how it would affect me.

"Ugh ... that felt awful," he muttered, turning very pale in the face.

"Sorry. Didn't know it could have that effect on humans," I said, already walking towards the side of the road.

He glanced worriedly at me when I said "humans" but followed me close behind. "What are we doing here?" he asked, looking around suspiciously.

I stopped by the pavement and looked at him. "Where's the glass ball? Give it to me."

Hesitantly he took the ball out of his pocket and slowly handed it to me. I grabbed it and watched the ominous darkness glow inside before I tucked it safely in my own pocket. "What about that tracking spell?" I asked, turning around and handing him the map.

"You are really serious about going after Nick?"

"I just need to find him first. Can you help me with that?"

He eyed me quizzically for a moment before crossing his arms over his chest. "Only if you promise to take me with you. You have to give me your word you will not leave me here after I give you his precise location."

I shrugged. I didn't care whether he stayed or not. "Sure. You have my word. I'll take you with me."

He opened the map and stretched it over the road, then took a small granite arrowhead stone out of his pocket. The stone was wrapped in a thin string line. "It is a rather simple spell. We didn't use it before because we couldn't get to Nick even if we found out where he was. You were not able to use my powers back then," he said meaningfully, glancing at me.

He spun the arrow, holding it by the line, and closed his eyes, concentrating hard, while the arrow twirled and danced around the map until it landed heavily, as if something magnetic was tugging it to a very specific point.

"There." Vigil pointed at the spot on which the arrow had landed. "Nick is there."

I knew that place. It wasn't too far from our house; a little patch of wood bordering a wildlife reserve. I knew where that was.

"Come." I took Vigil by the hand. "Let's go take care of some vermin."

Chapter Twenty-Five

Nowhere Left to Run

Before our eyes a green forest stretched endlessly, filled with tall pine trees and old oaks, but with no living soul in sight.

"Do you think he's really there?" I asked, looking eagerly around.

"It is daylight. That old cabin looks like a good hiding place," Vigil said, pointing to an abandoned shed in the middle of the woods. "He is most likely inside."

Now that I could use his powers properly I made him explain to me how to form a light spell and then how to trap Nick inside it.

He had reasoned that the key to catching Nick was not trying to shoot the spell at him, like Celeste had attempted in our garden, but to form the light around him and enclose him firmly inside. Nick wouldn't be able to escape this perfect sphere of light. The tricky part was to make the evil thing stand still long enough for me to form its prison around him. I remembered how Celeste had missed all her shots. Sneaky Nick was deviously fast.

I watched Vigil as he explained things to me, his light

jeans smeared with dirt and the white T-shirt Seth had loaned him hanging close to his body. He looked so young, so normal, his face smooth and round, his rosy, soft lips and big, round, black eyes with long eyelashes forming an angelic face.

He watched me with attentive glances as he gave me the final instructions about the light prison spell.

"OKAY. I understand, Vigil. I will go alone from this point on," I stated, and began to make a move.

But he stopped me, protesting fiercely. "No! You promised you would take me with you. You gave me your word." He glowered, upset.

"All right. If you feel that strongly," I said, allowing him to follow as I walked quietly towards the cabin. It looked like a hunter's abandoned storage hut. I tried to make as little noise as possible as I sneaked close to a broken window and made to peek inside, but a creak at the front door caught my attention and I spun around in time to catch Vigil's hunched form hurrying into the cabin.

"Wait! No, Vigil," I hissed, but he was already inside and out of earshot. I cursed before running to catch up with him. "Vigil, you were supposed to wait outside," I said, exasperated, shutting the door firmly as I followed him inside. I was trying to block all escape routes; no way in hell was I going to let that sneaky bastard run away from me again.

Vigil turned to look at me, clearly confused.

"You could get hurt," I told him with a scowl.

He made a face, realization finally dawning on him. He glanced around in panic but a clanging noise behind us made us both snap our heads to attention. Something had woken up and was stirring in the dark.

I grunted, giving up on any attempt at an ambush now. We were just too loud and obvious. It was better to go for the wild and crazy tactic, then.

There weren't too many windows, so the cabin was in semi-darkness. Boxes, ragged sacks and rotten dusty objects were thrown everywhere. The place had been abandoned for a long time, by the looks of it.

"Come on, you little piece of trash! I've had enough of this. Let's get this over with," I shouted, walking to the center of the cabin.

Something heavy thumped on top of a crooked wooden table a few feet away from me. I could see Nick's little paws brushing through the thick layers of dust, leaving marks as he moved.

"Gotcha!" I muttered, forming a small ball of light around Nick, exactly the way Vigil had explained to me. But as soon as the thin line started shining around him, Nick hissed violently and skipped over it as fast as lightning. The light ball formed around nothing but thin air.

There was a heavy thumping noise on the floor and a scary, throaty growl followed. Nick launched himself at me. My mind flashed in warning and I covered my face with my arm, the palm of my hand outstretched to block Nick's attack. All I could think of was "shield", and then, astonishingly, something wavered in the dark, glistening brightly while Nick slammed against it – an invisible shimmering wall right in front of me.

He landed heavily on the floor and jumped away, shaking his head, disoriented, while his fur short-circuited again. I could see his deformed shape in the dark now.

I prepared myself to cast another light spell but once again Nick was faster in his recovery and he jumped in my direction, allowing no time for me to prepare another magic shield.

He landed on me, making me stumble backwards and fall straight into Vigil.

At that moment, a split second before we all hit the ground, I made a tactical battle decision.

I needed to get us out of that little hut. It was too crowded, too much junk piling up everywhere, all those boxes getting in the way with a very fragile Vigil in the middle of it all – also too many places for Nick to hide. But if Nick managed to break out of the cabin, we would have to chase him through the forest.

So I took advantage of the fact that we were already tangled around each other and pictured a place I had once seen in a photograph. It was the perfect place to handle Nick: a wide, vast and deserted place. I closed my eyes and imagined us there.

Everything felt rushed and out of focus and then we were landing on solid ground. It felt dry, hot and incredibly hard. It took me a second to adjust to the brightness of the place as I crouched next to Vigil.

I frowned at the intensity of the light and blinked rapidly, looking around to find myself in the middle of a desert. The reddish ground had millions of cracked and parched lines engraved in the scorched earth. There was dry land stretching as far as the eye could see, and nothing else. The sun burned mercilessly in a clear sky.

Vigil groaned loudly, once again feeling the disorientation and sickness from my teletransportation. I stood up fast and looked around urgently for Sneaky Nick. He had rolled a little further away from us and was looking quite sick and disoriented himself. He was trembling, too, the blazing sun too bright for him to bear, his camouflage fur completely gone.

Nick bristled and tensed up when he sensed me walking closer to him; he cast around for a way out of this hellish place. There was no way out; dead, dry land stretched out endlessly and the scolding sun reigned imperiously in the cloudless sky.

He darted his head to each side, then clawed at the dry earth in an attempt to hide underground, but the earth was so hard and solid that he could barely make a scratch on the surface.

Then I heard Vigil gasping a little behind me, biting back a soft sob. I snapped around and saw him clutching at his forearm, blood trickling in streams through his fingers. Nick had taken a big chunk out of Vigil's arm during our tangled struggle in the cabin. My eyes registered the wounded arm, the blood trickling down vivid red, the deepness of the cut, and then I met his eyes. That was what did it for me.

When I saw the look in Vigil's eyes – the terror and fear marking his face, the hopeless realization of his frail human condition, his mortality, all those emotions bursting out of him like an unstoppable avalanche – something inside me snapped and I finally let go of any illusion of control.

Vigil was hurt.

I felt the chains snapping, all of them breaking free, one by one, undeniably, irrevocably free.

He was scared. Terrified. Hurt.

Something inside me snarled viciously, and ferociously. I turned my face to Nick and he reeled back when he saw the murderous look in my eyes.

"*You hurt him*," I growled, my voice coming out all ragged. It was taking all my willpower to stay still, to contain this fury rising inside, this burning fire running through my veins. All I saw was red, all I felt was fire, and all I heard was my heart hammering inside my chest and my thoughts drowning in anger.

I wanted to destroy him. Destroy everything.

I watched as Nick prepared to bolt, even though there was nowhere left to run. He was desperate; his irrational fear had taken over his twisted brain, making him take drastic actions. He knew he was in serious danger. He didn't have time to make so much as a move, though, because I beamed close to him and grabbed him roughly by the scruff of the neck. He yelped and I heard Vigil shouting for me to stop, but it was too late.

No one could stop me. It was time for this filthy creature to get its deserved end. And I knew just the right place to do it.

I concentrated again, with Nick firmly under my grip.

He would not escape me again. Not this time. Not any more.

And especially not where I was planning to go. I left Vigil alone in the reddish deserted place, his urgent pleas quickly lost in time and space.

When I opened my eyes, the dark, moonless sky loomed over my head, and a glittery silver sand lay beneath my bare feet. It had been a long time since I'd visited here. Dunes and hills of warm sand spread like an ocean, and the inky sky bore down upon us like a velvety black cloak.

Sky's desert. Death's domain.

In the distance, sitting on top of a steep hill, was a small gothic-looking girl, watching over us with curious eyes. Sky didn't show any sign of wanting to approach us and just stood still, watching from her silvery mount far away.

I tossed Nick hard onto the sand and watched him tremble and squirm under my gaze.

"You will never hurt anyone I love again, you filthy thing," I said, deadly resolution ringing in my voice. *"Do you know where you are?"* I spat out.

He looked around, bewildered, trying to understand what was happening. He seemed genuinely at a loss.

"Do you know who she is?" I said, turning to gesture at Sky sitting on her silver sand hill.

Nick wasn't clueless any more. The moment he laid eyes on Sky, he flinched, the fur of his back rising, his yellow eyes wide in fear. He knew who she was.

He knew what was going to happen to him.

He tossed himself at my feet, trembling and crying out in despair. "Pleassse, please, graciouss witch! Sspare me! Take pity on me, pleasse!" he begged, rolling around in the sand. "I promissse I'll leave you be; I'll leave all your friendss in peace. Pleasse, don't kill me!"

"Oh, I am not worried about you any more. I don't even have to do anything. All I have to do is leave you here. There is no way out of this place; but you already know that." I growled menacingly. *"I will leave you here and soon there will be a sun rising right above those hills,"* I said, pointing behind him. *"And when the sun comes, it will burn more than anything you've ever felt in your life; it will turn the air into fire; it will scorch everything in its path, blazing and merciless. It will turn you into ashes, into silvery sand. There is no escape from the heat of this sun."*

As soon as I finished explaining, a light glow started to rise over the hills. *His doom was coming. The sun was rising.*

"You don't have much time," I told him. *I wanted to watch him burn. I wanted to see him suffer and die.*

He panicked and started scraping at the ground, trying to dig, to hide beneath the sand.

"NO!" I shouted, and stomped my foot on the sand. A blasting wave of heat exploded with the impact, and the energy unleashed made the sand crinkle and turn into smoldering glass, like a glittery, melting wave spreading for miles around.

The sand turned into glass all around him and Nick jumped in the air. When he landed again, his paws scrambled over the smooth, shiny surface.

"You cannot hide from this, creature. That sun will burn you; it will ignite you whole, flesh, bones and soul. There is no escape and I will not let you hide any more. I want to see you burn," I told him furiously.

"Pleasse, benevolent witch, pleasse, ssspare me! You can take me away from here! I'll do anything you want! I'll give you anything you need!"

I stopped and mused over his pathetic trembling form. I needed to know. I reached inside my pocket and extended the dark glass ball for him to see.

"Do you know what this is?" I asked. He cowered beneath his paws, dreading the mortal sunlight that threatened to rise in the distance. He glanced up and frowned at the ominous dark glass ball.

"Y-yess, it'ss the—" and then he stopped abruptly, understanding dawning on him.

"You sswitched! You sswitched with him! You have hiss

powerss! I knew no witch could be thiss powerful!" he exclaimed.

"How does it work?" I asked impatiently. *"How do I make it switch back?"*

He frowned again, trying to understand the question.

"Tick tock. You are running out of time."

He looked at the rising sun and back to me, panic filling his face as he shrank into a tiny ball just as the sun started peeking its first burning rays over the hills.

The sun rose and the blasting heat rolled off it in a hellish wave towards us, turning the air into molten lava.

"Y-you havess to repeat again, do the same thingss you did the firsst time when you triggered the magic ball. You have to do it again, the exact ssame way!" he shouted, terrified.

"I already have. It didn't work."

"It'ss the only way, I sswears! You have to do it again! You missed something. I wass there, I remember! You have to do it again, the lightss, the nightss, the blood on your handss, the rainss, the two of you together. That's the only way. I swearss! Pleassse, hag. Pleasse, have mercy!"

My eyes widened. *Nick was right.* We'd missed a lot of things. We hadn't repeated everything we needed to repeat. We'd missed the rain, the light, the night and especially the blood on my hands, the blood of my wounded leg. That was why the glass ball hadn't worked again. We did it all wrong.

"Please, ssave me now. You promised!" he bawled, as the sun rose fiercely in the sky. Nick heaved and choked as the heat burned his throat.

"I didn't promise you anything," I said in disgust.

A big part of me wanted to watch him die. But a small piece of me couldn't. I ignored the trashing and snarling inside my mind, urging me to strike down and destroy everything, and instead I lifted my hand and formed the light ball prison-lock spell around Nick, enclosing him safely inside. I waved my hand up and the ball floated into the air in front of me. The light sphere shrank to the size of a marble and I pocketed it in my jeans. Then I turned to watch as the blazing sun rose completely.

It was an alien sun, rays of red, orange and vivid bright yellow bursting around its blinding white center. It was mesmerizing: a destructive, merciless, unstoppable force. A thing of beauty and power, something to worship and respect.

I had never witnessed such a tremendous display of glory like this. I thought about all the extraordinary, unworldly things I could now witness with Vigil's powers, all the realities I could see, all the adventures I could experience. I had unlimited possibilities to live now. *Unlimited power.*

A sudden revelation struck me right there and then.

Vigil had always been in love with the idea of being "human". It was his unspoken dream, and now he could experience it just like he'd always wanted. He could stay human.

And I could stay like this. There was no one to say I could not. I could do whatever I wanted. And I wanted this power for myself.

"It is beautiful, isn't it?" Sky asked, suddenly by my side.

She stood like me, watching the sky, with a glint in her fathomless black eyes.

I nodded as I watched, still in awe. *I could be deadly and powerful, just like this sun. No one would ever hurt me again. No one would ever break my heart.*

"So, you're a Gray Hooded One now, eh?" she asked, and chuckled before I could answer. "Life really is never boring around you, Gray, I'll give you that," she said, turning away from the sun and looking at me. "You need to be going now, Gray One. He's beginning to panic down there without you. You'd better hurry."

I nodded again and, remembering the ritual Vigil used to do around Sky, I bowed slightly as a farewell gesture. She bowed back, chuckling gently at me, and before I disappeared I heard her say, "I'll see you soon, Joey."

And then I was back again in the desert place where I had left Vigil.

Chapter Twenty-Six

Let it All Burn

Vigil was crouched on the floor, hunched down and cradling his wounded arm close to his chest. He had his back to me so didn't notice that I had returned. He looked so frail and small, so filled with despair. I walked silently towards him and knelt down in front of him. "Vigil," I said, making him snap his head up.

"Y-you came back," he whispered. "I-I thought you were going to leave me here ..."

I watched as his eyes searched for something in mine. He looked so scared. Did he really think I would leave him to perish in this desert?

"How long have I been gone?" I asked. Time back at Sky's desert ran differently from here. It could have been hours or just a few seconds.

He shook his head. "No, you were gone for just a few minutes. I-I ... panicked. I-I was scared," he confessed.

"Don't be scared. You don't need to worry any more. I *took care* of Nick," I told him.

He held his breath in surprise. "D-did you kill him?"

I stood up and took a few steps around him, surveying the place. "Does it matter?"

"Of course it matters!" Vigil stood up as well. "The mission was to catch him, not kill him! And how can we find out the key to making the glass ball work if you've killed him? He was the only one who knew. Please tell me you did not kill him. You need him to switch us back to normal," he shouted, anguished, his wounded arm clutched tightly against his body, drenching his T-shirt with blotches of deep red.

"Why do we need to switch back?" I asked, turning to look at him.

"W-what?"

"We can stay like this, you know. Isn't it what you always wanted, Vigil? You can stay human, live a 'normal' life, like you always dreamed of doing. And I can keep your power. I don't mind staying this way."

"This power is my responsibility. It is my burden to bear, not yours," he said in a cautious tone.

"It is not a burden to me; I don't mind," I reassured him.

"It will be. Believe me, it will. Not only a burden, it will deform and destroy everything good in you; it will tear you apart inside. It is already doing it; can't you see how it is changing you?" he said, raising his voice. "It is not meant for humankind to bear, Joey. Your emotions are too strong; they render my power too unstable and volatile. You think you can control it? It is already controlling you!"

I shrugged and turned my back to him. *"You underestimate me, Vigil. This power ... it is strong, but I can control it. I'm not used to it, but I will be, just give me time and you will see."* His words stirred up trembles inside me, and my voice grew huskier.

"Joey, please, listen to me. I know what I am talking about; you cannot continue like this. This power is stronger than your will, and very soon it will corrupt you completely. And when it finally takes over, it will make you lose control of all your actions. How many times has it tried to do it already? How many times have you lost your grip on what is real? On what is right and wrong? As soon as it breaks loose, it will unleash all its force; it will destroy everyone you once held dear in your life. It will destroy everything. It will destroy you!" he said, urgency filling his voice. "You cannot keep this power!"

"I cannot?" I leered. *"I can do whatever I want, Vigil. With this power, no one can ever tell me what to do ever again. There is nothing you can do to stop me,"* I growled. *"Look at me! Look what I can do,"* I said, and spread my arms wide, letting all the pure, blasting energy pulse through my body, igniting my blood again. A rush of excitement and exhilaration sparked, making red flames burst through my skin; but the fire did not burn me. I was just like Sky's alien sun, deadly and powerful. Nothing could stand in my way. I could let it all burn if I wanted to. Something inside whispered soothingly, seductively …

Let it burn.

"Look what I can become. I can be a goddess, Vigil. There will be no limits to what I can do," I exclaimed, while the flames around me intensified.

"This is not you talking, Joey! This is my power taking over your mind, like I told you it would," he warned me, taking a step back, scared of the flames around me.

"Ah, but it is me, Vigil. This is all me. It has always been a part of me, hidden deep inside, but it is me. This voice whispering in my head has always been mine. This

power is only making it louder, stronger – but the voice is all my own," I said, and waved my hand, watching the fire dance over my skin. The scorched red earth crackled beneath me.

"No," Vigil said firmly, a deadly certainty in his words. "I know you, Joe Gray. I know who you are. You are losing yourself, but you have to remember. Remember your name, Joe Gray. Remember who you are," he repeated, his hard eyes fixed on me.

"This is a new Joey. A better Joey. More powerful, invincible, indestructible," I said, and let a wave of power erupt out of me, fierce flames bursting high up in the sky, the floor shaking and thundering beneath our feet.

Vigil stumbled back a few steps, gasping loudly, his eyes wide and scared as he witnessed – as a human – the huge force of this incredible power that once was his.

"This is not you, Joey. The real Joey is somewhere in there, fighting to be heard, struggling to surface! She is in there, trying to do what is right. Listen to what she is saying!" he shouted. "You are still in there, Joey. I know you are. I have faith in you to do the right thing."

"I don't care about right or wrong any more." I laughed maniacally. *I was above judgment now.*

"That is not true. You still know the difference between right and wrong. That is why you did not kill Nick, am I right? I know you didn't!" he shouted.

I paused, the flames diminishing with my hesitancy. *"I wanted to."*

"But you didn't. Joe Gray would never kill a living being. Joe Gray would never take a life. You do care. You still care. There is still hope. We can still fix this."

I hesitated for a second and something snarled inside my

mind. *He's tricking you; he wants the power for himself. Don't fall for his lies!*

Vigil never lied to me. I trust him.

You can't fool yourself, silly girl; you know what you really want, what your heart truly desires.

He was right: I would never kill anything. *But you wanted to, so badly. You know you did! You wanted to destroy it all.*

Yes. I did. I'd wanted to kill those men in that park. I'd wanted to kill Nick; I'd wanted to watch him burn in Sky's desert. *I'd wanted to so much.*

But I didn't do it. I couldn't.

I shook my head, trying to clear my mind. *"That only proves I'm capable of controlling this power. I have it under control."*

"No, you do not. You will eventually slip and then it will take you over. You cannot fight this force for much longer, Joey. You know how strong it is, how badly it wants to break free."

I remembered the rattling chains, the whispering in my mind, relentless and never-ending. I remembered how many times it had urged me to destroy it all. How badly it craved chaos and pain. For how long would I be able to drown and silence these cries inside my head? How long until I finally give in to those urges?

The flames around me lowered and smouldered softly.

Vigil continued speaking. "Think about everything you would lose if you choose to stay this way. You cannot have both worlds: you cannot be human, and have a human life, and still keep these powers. You would have to give up your family, your friends, everyone you love ..." He took a step closer to me. "You would have to give up your whole life and everyone in it. I know how happy they make you feel. Are you ready to lose all that, Joey?"

"They would understand. They would move on with their lives without me. It wouldn't matter; life will still go on," I said, my voice sounding unattached.

"What about Tristan? Can you give up on him too? Can you forget about your love? Or does that not matter, either? Can you accept never being with him again, Joey?" he asked. "All these fights you two have had, because you have my powers; it is messing with your head, with your connection. If you were your normal self, you would have listened to him. You would have understood and forgiven him. He is your soulmate. Will you still choose *this* over *him*?" His voice cracked as he finished.

I hesitated again but shook my head. *"I am tired of letting his chains imprison me. I have freed myself from his hold. I am free now."*

"You were never a prisoner. These are not chains, they are connections, can't you see? You are breaking them apart and rupturing the strings that interwined your souls. If you keep my powers, you will sever them all."

"Humanity only makes me weak. Pathetic. I am better this way."

"No, you are not. This way you will lose everything that makes you *you*. You think you are weak because you are human? You are too blinded by promises of power to see clearly. You conquered me with your humanity, Joe Gray. Like this, you are powerful … scary … but nothing more." He shook his head, holding in an anguished sob. "And if you really choose to stay this way … you will lose something you cannot replace. The very humanity that captured me – my loyalty, my friendship, my … love. And it would be my fault," he said in a frail voice, his knees buckling. He sank down to the ground.

"I would not be able to continue living knowing what I had done to you," Vigil said. "I would not. I will not," he said, tears streaming down his face. "So you'd better just kill me, then, Gray One. You might as well do it, right here, right now. If you want to keep these powers, you must be merciless, remember that." His head hung low; his eyes stared at his bloody arm, which lay across his lap.

I stared at him for a few seconds. *"I am sorry, Vigil,"* I said simply.

He looked at me despairingly, his eyes filling with tears. "You said you are ready to give up on your humanity. Kill me to prove you are right."

I stared at him, unblinkingly. When I spoke, my voice came out cold and filled with suspicion: *"Are you testing me? Is this a trick?"*

"Prove to me you are right, Gray One," he said. "Or I will do it myself."

"I can lock you somewhere safe, where you can't hurt yourself."

He shrugged lightly, not caring any more.

I opened my mouth to speak, but nothing came out. I would have to make him a prisoner. Or even worse, watch him take his own life. I knew if I refused to do it, he would do it himself. I couldn't stop him, just as he couldn't stop me right now. No matter how powerful I was, I couldn't change his decision. Those were the only options I had.

And they were all too horrible for me to bear.

The starkness of Vigil's ultimatum, of the choice I had to make, pierced through to the core of me. I felt the stirring of feeling I'd buried; I felt the burgeoning of my old self.

But still the voices swirled inside my head, tugging at me, tempting me with their promise of power.

I knelt down in front of Vigil, soft flames still burning through my skin, and I tilted his head up to make him look at me. "You are cornering me into surrender, forcing me to give up."

He blinked, trying to clear tears from his eyes. "I give you my word that I am not. I am telling you the truth. I can't keep living, not like this."

"You love being human."

"I do. But I can't be human, not after this. This is my responsibility and I will pay for it. Your humanity for my human life: it is a fair punishment. I don't blame you for anything that happens after this, Joey. This is not your fault. And I ... I am sorry ... for everything." He whispered the last part, his voice broken.

I cupped his face with one hand. "I am sorry, too, Vigil. I never meant to hurt you like this." Then I leaned in and gave him a soft kiss.

He wasn't expecting it; he froze in surprise. But then he kissed me back, a kiss filled with so much sorrow.

When I pulled away, he remained still, and then opened his eyes slowly. "Was that a goodbye kiss?" he asked quietly.

"It was a thank you kiss," I replied, and put my hands lightly over his. "Come on. Let's get this over with."

He nodded slowly and closed his eyes, waiting in resignation for his fate, which I now held in my hands.

Chapter Twenty-Seven

Night of the Hunter

When I felt the release of pressure around me, I knew we had arrived.

Vigil lurched forward and snapped his eyes open, gasping for air, trying to recover from his dizziness.

He looked around and then he realized where we were. He passed his hands softly over the grass, cherishing the feel of it beneath his fingers.

"I don't understand," he said, looking to me. "Why are we here?"

I smiled and grazed both of my hands over the grass, tenderly, just like he had.

I missed home. I missed the security and love I had here. I wanted my old life back, a life without rattling chains constantly in my mind, a life of creation, not destruction. I missed the love I felt from my friends and family. A life without my Lost Boys would have no purpose. It would be meaningless.

And Tristan … I missed the boy with silver eyes the most. How could I ever have thought it possible to live without him?

Vigil's challenge had shocked me into realizing everything I was about to lose, finally empowering me to slip through the grasp of those destructive voices that pulled at me, and kick my way back to the surface. Now that I had drowned out the voices inside my head and I couldn't hear any more angry whispers, I was able to hear myself again. The real Joey, my real voice, not the voice of that person who craved power, but the one who loved her friends. And loved Tristan. I loved him. He was real and made mistakes, but that was what made him human.

And so was I, full of flaws and mistakes, but still human.

I could never live for power. I could never kill another living being. No amount of power was worth that sacrifice. Not now, not ever.

"The key is to do exactly what we did the first time," I instructed. "We missed a lot of important parts to make it work right. It is quite silly, if you think about it ..."

Vigil's eyes widened, a look of surprise on his pale face. Then deep relief. I leaned closer to him and held his face. "Are you going to be okay, Vigil? I mean, once you get your powers back ... after everything you've been through, will you be okay handling your powers again? I know how tiresome it is to keep holding back ... to block everything out all the time. Will you be all right?" I asked, worried. "I don't want anything bad to happen to you."

He smiled and a stray tear slipped down his face. "I'll be all right," he whispered softly. "And so will you."

I nodded and stood up, surveying the backyard. I could still feel the flames burning on my skin, the heat coursing through my veins. But I held back once more and, for the last time, fought the urge to let it lash it out. The soft yellow glow from the flames cast a warm light in the garden, but the rest of the house remained dark.

I waved a hand and the wind started to pick up speed as clouds gathered in the sky. We needed a storm now; we needed rain to make the glass ball work. Vigil stood up, still clutching his wounded arm, and glanced at the sky. The wind whirled, making our hair dance.

I slid my hand inside my pocket, took out a small marble of brilliant light and made it float towards Vigil. "Nick's in there. Safe and sound," I said.

He nodded and tucked the marble safely back inside his pocket. Rain started to fall then, but it didn't extinguish the flames on my skin. The fire still burned softly – wavering, but never-ending.

Soon it will all be over. There will be no more dark whispers and rattling chains, no more snarling urges or cravings for destruction. It would all soon be washed away by the rain. As I let the flames slowly fade, I could still hear a lingering howl. *Let it burn.* But it was far too weak, and I was stronger now. I knew better than to listen. I now knew what was important. Vigil had helped me to see that.

I raised my hands, palms up, and let the rain fall through my fingers. There was no fire on me any more. Only the night, the wind, the rain, the grass under my feet and the cold water pouring down my face.

I waved another hand and a circle of light flashed next to us, just like the spotlights that had been there last time. Then I made a movement and slashed at my hand, making a deep cut which oozed momentarily before healing up before our eyes. Now we had the blood.

All that remained was the last piece of the puzzle. I took the glass ball out of my pocket and watched as its dark orb swirled with tiny specks of white stardust floating inside. I extended the glass ball towards Vigil and gave him one last smile. When his fingers wrapped around the ball, a fierce blast of piercing light shot out, making the specks of light inside the glass burst and take over the entire sphere. My whole body was enveloped by this implacable light and an excruciating pain washed over me. It was unbearable and, just like the first time, the intense agony made me black out completely.

When I woke again, the first thing I noticed was how much I hurt. It felt like I had been hit by a bus or something. My head, my arms, legs, stomach, even my hair felt like it was hurting. And I was exhausted, completely and utterly drained. Even moving my head was painstakingly hard.

"Are you okay?" I heard Vigil's soft voice calling out to me.

I blinked a few times and focused on his face, which loomed over me. He was holding me gently in his arms. I tried to answer but only a low whimper came out; pain shot through all my nerve endings whenever I tried to move.

"Do not try to speak … or move. Just rest for a while and you will be fine. I will carry you inside and dry you off, okay?"

I managed a small nod. Only then did I notice that I was cold and completely drenched. It wasn't raining any more; I could even catch a glimpse of the moon right above our heads.

He carried me inside the living room and laid me down on the couch. He gently smoothed some wet locks of hair from my face. All the lights were off and there was no one else in the house. For a moment I wondered where everybody could be, but the thought quickly vanished as I was taken over by pain.

"You did good, Joe Gray," Vigil said softly, adjusting a cushion under my head.

I nodded again and sighed deeply, closing my eyes in exhaustion. I wanted so badly to sleep.

"I will get you a towel and a blanket," he told me, but stayed seated by my side. My eyes were still closed when I felt something brushing against my lips, warm and soft. It was Vigil kissing me, a gentle, chaste kiss of gratitude.

I wanted to say how sorry I was about everything I had done, about all the suffering I had caused him; I wanted to thank him for not giving up on me, for saving me from myself.

But I was so tired I couldn't even open my eyes. I felt his fingers brush my cheek and then he stood up and left. The all too familiar stabbing pain shot through my wrist.

At least now I knew everything really was back to normal – even my weird, painful wrist connection with Vigil.

I must have dozed off for a minute because I was suddenly jerked awake. My hair was now dry and a warm blanket covered me.

"Joey, I have to go. Will you be all right?" he asked. "I have to take care of this now," he said, holding the small white marble that imprisoned Nick. "But I will return as soon as I have finished."

I mumbled something and closed my eyes, already drifting back to sleep.

"Joe! Joey!"

Someone was calling my name, but I couldn't open my eyes. Or move. I was too tired. My body had given up and

I just lay there, lifeless. There was someone talking to me, asking questions. The annoying voice insisted on calling my name over and over, but I couldn't reply. I was almost comatose.

I felt someone holding me by the arms and then I was carried somewhere. It was probably one of the boys carrying me upstairs to bed. My body shook and slumped against something. I was lying down, half-asleep still. It felt like I was in a car – a moving car. Everything was pitch black, or was it that I couldn't open my eyes? I could hear a motor running.

Maybe it was one of the boys taking me to a hospital, scared that I wasn't waking up. That was probably it. I was too tired to think of anything else.

The motion of the car lulled me back to sleep. My head rolled to the left and brushed over something soft and velvety, like the petals of a flower. Before I slipped out of consciousness completely, the thought came to me that it smelled a lot like lilies …

In the hazy mist of my slumber I recognized car horns and the muffled sound of rushing traffic. The air was stuffy and hot, and the smell of lilies was strong and putrid, suffocating me.

At some point my sluggish brain tried to get my attention, warning me of something, but I was too drowsy to focus my thoughts.

I tried to open my eyes but realized it was dark anyway. Wherever I was, it was too dark to see anything. When I tried to move, I couldn't; something tugged and was constricting my wrists. Something was holding me down, binding my hands and legs.

That's when I realized I should be paying attention to what my brain was so urgently trying to warn me. *Something was wrong.*

I moved my head and realized there was something around my mouth too, gagging me. I knew I should be panicking, but my mind was still slipping as if in mud. I heard the sound of a door opening and it dawned on me that I was in the trunk of a car. Light flared, blinding me.

"Oh, you're waking up. Good," I heard a man's voice say, and I blinked dizzily at his dark silhouette. Then, just as suddenly as he had appeared, he disappeared, and I was left there, alone, tied up and helpless. I glanced around, confused, as bits of information started to hammer into my aching brain. I was tied. Hands, feet and mouth bound. There were squashed lilies next to my head. White lilies with a black lacy ribbon.

A red alarm blasted inside my mind. *Move! You have to get out! You're in danger!*

My body still felt stiff and heavy, like I had been drugged, but I knew it was the after-effects of my power switch with Vigil. I remembered how worn out and exhausted he had been when our powers switched the first time. My brain fought hard against the lethargy that gripped me, but it was a useless battle. Nothing was responding like it should.

I saw the outline of someone approaching again. "Come on, let's get you out. I have everything prepared for you." Jarvis's face came into focus and he leaned in and lifted me out of the truck.

Jarvis.

I blinked furiously and tried to break free, but I couldn't even hold my head up. Jarvis – our bodyguard Jarvis, silent and observant security guard Jarvis – carried me bridal style in his arms. Where the hell was he taking me? And what the hell was he trying to do?

"I'm sorry for tying you up like this, Joey, but I had to be careful. No need to draw attention," he said, putting me down on the ground and walking away, still shouting to me. "I have to say, it was such a stroke of luck to find you passed out on your couch like that. First I thought you'd overdosed, but then I checked your pulse and breathing. You probably took a few too many sleeping pills there, huh? I knew then that this was the opportunity I'd been waiting for."

The ground was cold and hard but with my feet tied together, I couldn't stand up. I looked around wildly, trying to figure out how to escape. I was in a sort of old warehouse, or an abandoned hangar, with high metal walls and a few piles of crates lying around. Fluorescent lights blinked at me from the ceiling.

"And now here we are! You and me, alone at last." He walked back, holding some ropes. He knelt by my side and pulled my bound hands upwards, tying them above my head to a metal structure behind us. I searched his face, trying to make some sense out of this madness.

"And the best part is, your boys left me alone in the house to wait for you, can you believe that? They were practically begging me to take you!" He cackled loudly. "All I had to do was leave a few lilies at your front door again and they all went into hysterics. You had to see the panic on their faces ...

"Okay, I have to admit, the knife I put between the flowers could have been the reason they freaked out so much. But I was so happy when they called me and my idiot cousin. They all went to the police station and sent me alone to the house to protect you if you returned. I mean, talk about perfect timing!"

I listened to him, panic rising in my chest. No one knew I had been back in the house and that I didn't have Vigil's powers to protect me any more. No one knew Jarvis had taken me.

Where the hell was this place?

"You should have seen my stupid, ugly-mutt cousin, all worried about you. Haha! Big Johnson thinks he's so clever, the brainless git. He went running for the main house to check the security cameras to see if he could catch who put those lilies at your door. But I'd disabled the security system – I was the one who installed it in the first place!" he confessed, smiling wickedly at me.

Then he leaned in close and whispered, sickeningly sweet, in my ear, "They won't ever know it was me."

I was too horrified to do anything other than stare at him in complete terror. Then he stepped back and watched me, curiously.

"So, Joey, did you like the flowers and notes?" Madness swirled dangerously in his eyes. But unlike that crazy boy from the bookstore, whose thoughts ran in a jumbled chaotic mess, Jarvis's eyes reflected a focused kind of madness. I saw a sharpness that made me think of a predator: piercing, dangerous and deadly. My empathy-sight was back, I realized.

"You read all the notes I sent you? I've been writing them since the first day my eyes landed on you when I took this job as your security guard. I knew in that minute that you should be mine. I know everybody wants you, but I want you more!" As he stared at me, his eyes gleamed with excitement. "You know I'll do anything to have you, don't you, my sexy thing? I've been wanting for so long to have you, and now I have the courage to finally reach out and take it." He pressed his sick hands over my face, making me cringe in disgust.

Oh God. This was really bad. I looked around, trying to find help. This guy was completely out of his mind! And without Vigil's powers I was in serious danger. I was helpless: a useless rag doll all tied up and at his mercy.

He frowned as he watched me and his eyes darkened dangerously. "Joey, Joey …" He sighed deeply. "Why do you do this to me? Why do you act like this, like you don't like the way I touch you? You let all those dirty boys put their filthy hands on you all the time and now you act like mine disgust you? Hell! You've probably slept with all of them. Now you think you can act all prudish like a saint with me?" he asked, gripping my chin hard, digging his fingers in painfully, forcing my head up.

I let out a muffled cry but the gag drowned my voice. I tried pulling at the bonds on my wrist, but he intensified his grip on my face and I stopped moving.

"It makes me furious seeing how those boys look at you, baby. All of them: Josh, Sam, Harry and, good God, *Tristan.* Tristan is the worst, the hungry looks he gives you … It's disgusting! And now this freaky Vigil kid following you around, too! He is messed up in the head, Joey. He's not normal. He makes my blood chill just looking at him – how can you stand being so close to him?

"I warned you in my notes, Joey. I told you I was going to make you see your wrongdoing. You can't ever be with them again. You are mine now, only mine!"

One minute he was letting out violent outbursts of anger, the next he was all excited and manic. Completely insane.

"We will have a lot of fun tonight, babe." His voice held a dark promise. He squeezed my face again and leered at me, dangerously close. I could feel his hot breath on my face. I whimpered and tried to wriggle free from his grasp, but he gripped my face even harder.

He pressed his chest against me, a wicked smile on his filthy lips. I needed help. *Someone, anyone, help me!*

I twisted and writhed beneath him, crying out as I tried to break free.

He shouted at me to stop struggling, and punched me hard. My head snapped back and blood started to trickle out of my nose and down my throat, the coppery tang filling my mouth.

I wanted to spit but the gag stopped me from doing so. I started to choke. I struggled even more, turning my head to the side to see if that would help. I couldn't breathe through my nose. I was suffocating, slowly drowning in my own blood.

He grabbed the cloth covering my mouth and yanked it down to my neck, freeing my mouth. I sputtered and coughed, trying to catch my breath. He stood above me, looking calm, like the sickeningly deranged psychopath he was.

I cussed and started to shout at him, but that only egged him on, making him cackle maniacally, his arms raised high in victory.

"YES! Shout at me, Joe Gray. Call me names! This is even better than I imagined. Go on. Shout at me!" He laughed. "There is no one to hear you. It's just you and me, no one else for miles and miles around. Go on, shout again. Louder!"

That got me to shut up pretty fast. Fucking sicko. He

was enjoying hearing me scream. Before I could think of what to say he leaned close again, a sneer on his lips and a dangerous glint in his eyes. "I like it when girls get scared, when they shout, when they cry my name. Say my name, Joey."

"Fuck you," I said, and spat at his face.

He wiped the bloody spit with one hand and gripped my neck with the other, smiling warmly at me. "Ah, that's my little spitfire talking. But I will make you behave, Gray. I'll break down your wild heart." Then he whispered close to my ear. "I will tear you to pieces and rip you apart."

A shiver ran down my spine and I forced my tears back. I wouldn't give him the satisfaction. I wasn't going to cry. I wasn't going to show him I was scared.

"I'm not scared of you, Jarvis," I told him in the calmest voice I could muster. "You're so pathetic, really. It's pitiful to look at you. You know what the real torture here is? Listening to your crap. Can you just shut up already?"

That changed his mood, fast. He was seething now. And then he punched me again. Hard. I spit more blood on the floor but didn't cry out. I didn't make a sound. That made him even more pissed.

"Hit me all you want, it will only prove you're pathetic *and* a coward," I spat out, anger slowly taking the place of my fear.

He narrowed his eyes. "Let's see if you still say that after I'm finished with you, then," he snarled.

He stood up and walked back to the car, leaving me alone for a brief time. I looked around desperately, tugging frantically at my bound wrists, trying to break free from the damned ropes that burned and dug into my skin. There was no escape. They were bound too tight. Then I caught sight of my black tattoo. *Vigil*. He was my way out of this. I closed my eyes hard and chanted his name over and over in my head. *Please, please, please, Vigil, come back and save me. I need you now. Come back, wherever you are. Help me!*

I looked around, feeling panicky. There was no one there. Nobody. I was alone, in an abandoned dark room; alone with a monster.

Then Jarvis came back, holding a knife in his hand. This time, I couldn't hide the fear on my face. He saw it, and smiled gleefully.

One of the fluorescent lights gave one last sharp buzz and cut out, leaving the room even darker; shadows danced along the walls, wrapping their ominous shroud over Jarvis's evil form. He looked even more scary now in the half-light, like a monster straight out of a fairy tale.

This was just a nightmare, I told myself; a vivid, horrible, scary dream. I was going to wake up any moment now – right? I was still sleeping on the couch back home and this was just a really bad dream.

I watched as Jarvis straddled me and brushed the tip of the knife close to my chest. I shut my eyes hard and silently pleaded. *Vigil. Vigil. Vigil.* Why wasn't he listening to my pleas? Where was he? Why wasn't he here?

Please, please, Vigil, come back to me.

Jarvis grabbed my jaw and squeezed it painfully. "Stop mumbling some other man's name, Joey," he growled furiously. "Can't you see this is our special time alone? You're saying another man's name. You're breaking my fucking heart, Joey. Guess I'll have to break yours back," he threatened. "Tear it apart."

I felt a sharp, stabbing pain at my side and something warm and sticky started to drench my shirt. A loud gasp escaped my lips but I clenched my mouth shut, despite the pain I was feeling. I wasn't going to let him hear me cry.

But when he put the knife close to my face, I started to break down.

Vigil wasn't coming. No one was coming to help me. It was just me and this monster alone in this dark room. I was powerless, helpless, bound and hurt. There was nothing I could do to stop him. I had nothing. I was nothing. And I was going to die here, alone in this place, and no one would ever know.

If only I had paid attention. If only I had listened. I'd thought nothing could ever hurt me then ...

My eyes filled with tears, which began to run down the side of my face. I couldn't hold them in any longer. I was in too much despair, too broken down by fear.

I didn't want to die. Not like this.

I turned my face to one side, staring at the ground in the distance. I could see black heavy boots moving far away, not making a sound. I looked up to see Sky's face. Her beautiful face with sorrowful black eyes staring back at me. She stood still, watching in silence.

She was here for me.

Was this the way it would all end for me, then? Couldn't she do something to help me? Couldn't she intervene, one last time? Sky smiled sadly when she saw the look in my eyes, my silent pleas inside.

"Sky ..." I croaked through parched lips. My voice was coming out shaky and weak.

Jarvis's head shot up, searching for what I was staring at, but found nothing but darkness. It was like he could sense something was there, lurking in the shadows – something eerie, but he couldn't see what it was.

"Please ..." I called again, still looking in her direction.

Jarvis looked at me angrily. Despite the fact that he couldn't see what it was, he knew that my pleading was not to him, but to someone else. Or *something* else.

"Let's see if I can make you beg for me, Joey. Let's see if I can make you cry my name now," he hissed.

I turned to look at him and then my eyes widened in surprise. Stabbing needles shot through my wrist. I started laughing. It was low and quiet at first, but soon it rolled into a crescendo, growing louder, heavier.

Jarvis stared at me in puzzlement, trying to understand what was happening.

"I'm going ... to love seeing this ..." I told him between laughs, "... so much."

"GET OFF HER." Vigil's cold, hard voice boomed through the room, making the walls shake as if in fear. Vigil was here. He had finally come.

Jarvis's body lurched violently away from me and he was thrown up in the air by an invisible force. The knife he had been holding flew out of his hands and clattered loudly to the cement floor.

His body smacked against a metallic structure in the middle of the room a couple of times, and he cried out in pain. Then his body stopped and hung limply in the air like a floating rag doll.

I had stopped laughing and was crying now. Vigil knelt silently by my side, setting my hands and legs free with a swift wave of his fingers. He didn't help me get up, or ask me if I was okay. He didn't say anything.

He just stared hard at me, a deep frown painting his angelic face as his dark eyes swiftly morphed into complete white. His fists clenched and an unyielding fury broke out of him. It was like nothing I had ever seen before: cold hatred flaring out like a dying star transforming into a black hole deep within his eyes.

He wasn't in blazing flames like I had been when wielding his powers. He was cold – like space: unforgiving and without mercy.

The air in the warehouse began to freeze in front of me, making puffs of hot air steam out of my mouth.

Vigil stood up, staring at Jarvis's form hanging in the air a few feet away from us. Vigil's fists were clenching and unclenching at his sides as he struggled internally with something. Jarvis began to shout and try to break free from the invisible force that held him captive. Vigil watched in silence, and then turned to me.

"I am sorry," he said. "But I have made my decision. I will have to break some rules today. I do not care for the consequences," he stated, his voice cold and implacable. "That is one of the reasons why you were not meant to wield these powers. You could never do this and forgive yourself afterwards. But I can. It is built in me to have no mercy. And I shall have none with him. He is going to have to die."

Jarvis heard this verdict and started to thrash widly in the air, spit and foam escaping his mouth like a rabid dog. Vigil waved a hand and Jarvis slowly descended until he was hovering inches from the floor. Vigil stepped close to him. "Silence now, you poor excuse for a human being," he ordered. The look in his white eyes and the deadly tone of his voice were enough to make Jarvis go completely still.

"You are not only going to die, you despicable thing," Vigil spat out, leaning close to Jarvis's face. "I'm going to obliterate you out of existence. Not only will your body cease to exist, not only will your flesh and bones vanish, but your spirit and soul will also die. You will never be able to come back; you will not be able to return in any possible way. You will be completely and utterly gone. For ever. I am going to give you the ultimate death. You can never *be*. Ever again," he invoked, his voice sharp and cold like an ice blade.

Sky finally decided to let herself become visible. She walked ahead and stopped right next to Jarvis.

She had come for him.

Sometimes I wonder if I could have tried to persuade Vigil in that moment. I could have tried to change his mind, reason with him.

I knew all too well what it was like to let anger and hate take over your mind until there was nothing left but thoughts of destruction. I knew Vigil was angry – no – he was furious. I tried to imagine how loud the rattling chains were inside his mind.

But *I* also knew how to have compassion. I could vividly remember how I couldn't kill those men in the park, how I couldn't even hurt Nick in Sky's desert. Looking back, I should probably have tried to stop Vigil from killing Jarvis. I should have tried.

But I didn't. I sat there bleeding on the cold floor and watched as Jarvis burned in agony, his bones, flesh, blood – every cell in his body igniting from the inside. He completely disintegrated right before my eyes until there was nothing left of him, not even ashes or dust. He was gone. In the most complete and possible way.

I have never seen someone die before. I was shocked, but it wasn't the shock that got me so rattled. It was the fact that I didn't say anything. I just wanted to watch him burn. I wanted him dead and gone. For ever.

I was just as guilty as Vigil of Jarvis's death. I had silently witnessed this murder and done nothing to prevent it. I had been an executioner just as much as he. And I was going to have to live with that for the rest of my life.

It was only after the flames disappeared completely and the room was once again bathed in darkness that I realized I was freezing. I was still on the cement floor with a pool of my own blood surrounding me. I felt so cold. So very cold.

Vigil kneeled by my side and held me carefully in his arms. I couldn't feel my limbs any more, just this icy cold gripping my body, running slowly and relentlessly through my veins.

"You came for me," I let out on a ragged breath which I hadn't known I was holding. His eyes were still ice-tinted.

"I am so sorry, Joey. I was really far away. I had just delivered Nick to my colleagues when I felt your call. I came as fast as I could … I-I shouldn't have left you alone in your house … I wasn't thinking straight … I'm sorry."

"That's okay, V." I gave him a weak smile. "How could you know this was going to happen? It's not your fault." My voice was getting weaker and weaker by the second. I felt so tired and so cold. The pain in my stomach didn't seem to hurt as much any more. I wanted to go to sleep now and rest for a long time. I blinked slowly. Even that small action seemed monumentally hard, as if my eyelids were glued together.

Vigil shook me hard, making me focus. "Joey, I don't know what to do. I cannot heal you; my powers don't do that. There is too much blood. What should I do?"

I blinked again and managed to croak one word before I slipped into dark oblivion: "Hospital …"

Chapter Twenty-Eight

Into Dust

I jolted awake and found myself standing on a worn-out wooden platform. A thick mist surrounded me, making it impossible to see mere feet away. It floated eerily, bathing everything in a pale hue of gray.

After a few seconds' disorientation I stopped to check my stomach, where the wound had been. All the horrid memories came rushing back to me – the stabbing pain, the blood on the floor – but I didn't have any wounds now. Where was I? Was I dead?

I peered into the distance. It seemed there was a vague silhouette way ahead of me. Someone was out there, but the mist was too thick for me to see who it might be.

I headed over hesitantly, being careful not to step off the old platform. Each step I took made the mist dissolve a little more, making me increasingly confident. I seemed to be on a wooden pier, the sound of splashing a sign that there was water below.

When I reached the end of the pier I realized the shadowy silhouette was a ferryman, perched on top of a long, thin boat moored to the platform. He had his back to me and a long sandy cloak covered his body completely.

I stopped as I took in his view: it was an infinite silvery ocean. The mist had cleared considerably now, allowing me to see for miles. The water glittered oddly whenever waves crashed over one other, and that's when I realized that it was not, in fact, water, but sand. Silver, wavy, moving sand. The movement was beautiful, catching the glittery reflection from the big, white moon above us.

Was this a dream? Somehow I knew it wasn't. Something deep inside of me knew this was as real as it could get.

The ferryman's boat sank into the sand, wobbling a little just as it would have done had it been on water. I glanced to the ferryman, his long cloak billowing on the soft warm breeze. The air smelled of ancient parchments, of dust and sand. His hood covered his face and the bottom of his cloak merged into the sand.

Tiny specks of sand floated from the sea upwards into the dark sky. It was like the sand was so light that gravity could not hold it down, and it drifted towards the sky like tiny stars. It was the most beautiful thing I had ever seen.

The ferryman noticed my presence and turned slowly. A washed-out skull of dark wood, the same color as the boat, stared at me intensely from inside the hood. My eyes went as wide as they could get. It is not every day you see the empty eye sockets of a live wooden skull.

"S-Sky?" I risked. The long cloak and eerie skull were pretty good indicators that this could be Death in all its stereotypical glory. Was Sky portraying herself like this to me now?

The ferryman frowned slightly – if a skull could even do that – and bowed. "I am but the Ferryman. 'Sky' asked me to fetch you and bring you to her domain. She is waiting.

ow, we must leave." He waved a long, knotty, bony finger at me.

"Huh … right. But I've been to Sky's 'domain' before … This doesn't look like it. It does have a lot of sand, but no moon in the sky, and the sand doesn't move, not floating about like here."

The Ferryman stopped and rubbed his wooden chin. "That is her workplace, so to speak. This is her residence. Here you don't have to worry about the scorching sun. Here you have to worry about the dust sea." His voice was raspy and gritty. He waved his hand towards the sand that brushed against the boat.

As I stepped inside the boat, the subtlety of his threat reverberated in my head. *Here you have to worry about the dust sea.*

"Shouldn't I give you a coin or something?" I asked, remembering the old stories about Death's Ferryman. No coin, no ride.

He nodded as he began to row us away from the pier. "Ordinarily, yes. But you are a guest this time."

We drifted away quickly, swiftly gliding through silver waves of sand as if it were water. In the distance I could see dozens of other piers, which slowly disappeared one by one in the distance.

The boat rocked as the Ferryman continued rowing steadfastly forward. The action made his cloak float back, showing all that was inside. Instead of a skeleton made of wood I saw that the Ferryman was, in fact, part of the boat itself. His body fused with the boat below his waistline, his wooden bones and muscles protruding from the woodwork and his feet merged with the floorboards.

It was as if he had melted into the wood. It was creepy.

And the more I thought about it, the more creepy it got –
because I was sitting in the boat … and the boat was kind
of part of him. So I was kind of sitting on him as well! I
shuffled uncomfortably and decided to look at the ocean
rather than the Ferryman.

The silver sand never ceased floating to the sky. It moved
slowly and lightly all the way up to the unknown dark void
above our heads.

Then something started following the boat, something
incredibly big, swimming alongside us beneath the sand.
Soon others like this creature joined to accompany it. They,
whatever "they" were, seemed to be escorting us towards
Sky's home, gliding alongside the boat.

One of them passed really close to me, its cracked,
giant back surfacing above the sand only to quickly
disappear again, burying itself in the dust sea. I made to
reach my hand in its direction but the Ferryman warned
me not to.

"Beware of the dust sea and what lies beneath it," his
dry, raspy voice said.

In other words, *Do not touch the alien creatures in the
sand.*

I nodded and pulled my hand quickly inside the boat,
all the while observing the alien-looking whales swimming
close by.

A big wave of sand – boy, is that as weird to say as
I think it is? – splashed over us, rocking the boat, and I
turned to see what was causing the commotion. A mile or
so away a gigantic whale-creature surfaced. But not only
that, it also started rising completely out of the sea, floating
upwards in slow motion towards the sky, in the same way
as the glittery sand.

It was falling. Into the sky. Or flying up. Whatever. This was getting way too weird for my brain to comprehend.

My mouth gaped widely as the giant continued its ascension until there was nothing left but a tiny dot in the distance, too far away for me to discern its form any more.

I was about to ask the Ferryman what the hell that was all about, but he had stopped rowing and was now looking fixedly at something ahead. I followed his gaze and then gasped in even greater astonishment.

In front of us there was a steep glass staircase leading up to a huge glass mansion. The entire structure was translucent and transparent, shimmering and glinting in the moonlight, almost fusing with the black sky. It was like something out of a wild fairy-tale dream. It was as outlandish and beautiful as the strange sea of silver sand, and the alien creatures that swam beneath it. It was as scary as it was breathtaking.

A small, narrow, wooden plank rolled out from underneath the boat and parked itself, resting on one of the glass steps: my way out.

"Milady," the Ferryman called out to someone, bowing deeply and making the entire woodwork creak with the movement. "In accordance with your request, I bring your guest Joe Gray, Witch Sorcerer, Conjurer of the Underworld, Gray Hood Bearer and Fire Wielder."

I turned and looked behind me to see who the hell he was talking about, because that was certainly not me.

Sky's deep laugh caught my attention and made me turn in the direction of the glass staircase. "Thank you, Erwin!" she said, acknowledging the Ferryman, and then turned to look at me. "He can be so posh and formal sometimes, you know?" She beamed widely and winked, walking in my direction.

I skipped quickly out of the boat and stopped at the bottom of the glass steps. Sky's midnight hair covered her bare shoulders, and wristbands, necklaces and rings adorned her ankles, neck and fingers. She still wore the heavy make-up and black pants, tank-top and those black boots I had grown used to seeing on her at all times.

"Joey, I've been waiting for you," she said, giving me a tight hug which, as usual, sent cold shivers down my spine as if a cold bucket of ice had just been thrown over my head. I cringed and clenched my teeth, bearing the coldness of her embrace. It was not her fault that she had this effect on people. And everybody deserved a good hug now and then. Even Death.

"Hmm, you were?" I mumbled when she stepped away.

"Of course. I told you I'd see you later. Now is later!" she said, with a wise smile on her lips.

"Am I dying?" I blurted out. This question had been nagging at me from the moment I'd jolted awake on the pier. I remembered what I had been through in the warehouse, the sheer panic, the terror, the pain, the fear of dying. But since I had been in this place, all of that seemed like a distant dream, as if this had been the real thing all long. I wasn't afraid or scared; I wasn't in pain. And nothing from before mattered any more.

And that was freaking me out big time because deep down inside I knew that it should *all* matter. I should be scared. I should be sad that my life was ending. Was I really dying?

"Yes, you are," she answered me, still smiling. "But

you have been dying since the moment you were born, Joe Gray. I'm sure you knew that already."

I blinked stupidly at her. That was not what I meant! God, I forgot that speaking with Sky was just as philosophically challenging as speaking to Vigil.

"Come inside! I'd like you to see something, and it's almost time," she exclaimed excitedly, grabbing my hand and pulling me along with her into her glass mansion.

Goosebumps rose up my arm from her touch as I let myself be dragged inside.

"The place wasn't like this a few days ago, but I got the idea from you, from when you stomped your foot in the sand and turned it into glass. That was so clever of you! Heat and sand equals glass. So obvious! And since I have all this raw material available, I thought to myself, why not just do like Joey? So here it is! What do you think? Do you like it?" Sky asked, as she skipped quickly through the glass hallways.

As it turned out, the mansion really was made of glass, as in, *everything* was glass: the long floors, the high ceilings, the huge doors and the numerous chairs, tables, vases – even the flowers in the vases were sparkling like beautiful crystal.

"Y-yeah, it looks great! Really beautiful," I said. Not very practical, or safe, or even comfortable, but I guess that was just from a human perspective. Death didn't need to be safe *or* comfortable.

It was also a little bit of a death-trap, no pun intended – well, a little pun intended. But since the only source of light was the moon outside and its reflection in the sparkling floating sand, the house was the darkest glass at night-time. If you pictured it, you'd realize how hard it would be to walk around without seriously injuring yourself. I was glad I had Sky to guide me safely through the vast rooms.

We reached a curling staircase and Sky pulled me up the steps after her.

"Thanks! I think so too," she said happily as we emerged on the second floor and walked to what looked like a balcony. "I love to come up here to watch the view."

I stopped by the balcony railings and gazed at the view with wide eyes. Although it seemed like we had walked up just a few stairs, when we stepped onto the balcony it felt like we were a dozen storeys up. Scarily high.

"H-how ... how can it be this high?" I muttered in amazement, peering cautiously down below.

Sky shrugged as if this were a most normal thing. "Time and space runs differently here. Ten floors, two floors, it's all the same, and yet not the same at all. It is what we make of it. And right now we want high, so high we must be."

The view stretched as far as the eye could see. I watched the landscape, a never-ending ocean of silver sand, so beautiful and mesmerizing it was impossible to take your eyes off it. The glitter-sand still drifted upwards, in its everlasting reverse freefall, taking hundreds of giant alien creatures with it. It was a raging dream, unbelievably beautiful and frightening at the same time.

Sky turned to me, a soft smile dancing on her pale lips. "I'm so sorry you had to go through that, Joey. I'm sorry I had to watch you being tortured," she said, a little more serious now. "But I couldn't intervene; I've meddled too much. I'm sorry I couldn't answer your pleas. I was there to collect Jarvis. A complete annihilation is very rare; the ultimate death of a being doesn't happen very often, so I had to be there. But I thought I could make it up to you now by bringing you here.

"I remembered how much you liked watching the rising sun, how you thought it was beautiful. So you should like watching this," she said, gesturing to the horizon where the dark sky met the silver sea of sand.

An intense white line shone brightly on the horizon, casting a spellbinding glow of pink, orange and yellow rays over the inky black sky.

The sun was rising!

Soon the bright molten ball rose, spreading its colorful fingers over the sand, tinting it slowly with amazing hues of vivid yellow. The sand now sparkled vividly like fairy dust, endlessly shining. The entire ocean was now moving like liquid gold.

I didn't think I would ever see anything more beautiful than this. I felt my eyes streaming with tears of joy. It was just too beautiful, too magical, too perfect. It left me completely frozen in utter wonderment.

Then all the silvery sand that was floating towards the sky slowly stopped, lingering gently in the air, as if it were holding its breath, and then started falling back to the sea of sand, its silver hue transformed into tiny specks of gold. And after that the soft yellow rain never stopped falling. The giant gentle creatures started descending back to the sea again. Everything that had been floating up was now falling softly down.

That's when I realized something.

This world, this never-ending cycle of sand floating up and falling down … it was an hourglass. Sky's home, Death's domain, was an hourglass universe made of sand, in infinite motion, moving up or down, night and day, silver and gold falling and floating. It was so simple in its beauty yet so complex at the same time. It was perfect. I was speechless.

"I knew you would like it," she said, smiling softly by my side. "It is quite beautiful, if I may say so myself. The sunset is quite extraordinary as well, in its unique way. Maybe one day you'll get to see it too."

"Th-thank you, Sky," I whispered, finally snapping out of my dazed torpor. "I'll never forget it."

She chuckled lightly and shook her head. "You probably will. The human mind is not fully evolved to behold this type of sight. It will slowly fade from your memory until there is nothing but a lingering, blurry image. You'll get to dream about it, though," she said, staring at the view, as if to memorize it herself.

"Oh … that's a shame." I mumbled sadly. I wished I could remember this for ever.

"Well, that was fun!" Sky clapped her hands and turned to look at me. "It's always great having you around, Gray. Now you must go."

"W-what?"

"Here, let me help you," she said, and pushed me softly forward. I scrambled to grab both of her hands. I stumbled and realized the balcony railings had disappeared completely and we were now standing on just a glass platform. I lost my balance and almost fell from the platform, but my grip on Sky's hands held me in place, balancing precariously on the edge, my body angled in a tilt so I had my back to the sand ocean.

"What are you doing?" I held on to Sky for dear life, quite literally.

"It's been lovely, but now it is time for you to go, Joey," she directed me firmly, but still smiling. "Let go."

I shook my head fiercely. Did she really want me to let go of her hands and fall a dozen storeys down into a deadly sand ocean filled with weird – and probably deadly – creatures? What was she, insane?

"Joey, you have to trust me on this. *Let go*," she said, more firmly now.

I glanced down and gripped her even harder.

"Let go," she said once again. Her tone was strange, ancient and full of power. Something in her voice triggered an immediate response, like a button connected directly to my brain, and my hands instantly opened up, releasing Sky's.

And then I fell.

I could feel the air rushing past me. But I wasn't scared. Even when sand and darkness enveloped me and engulfed me whole, I still did not fear my fate ... because I could feel Tristan's scent taking over my senses, and I knew he was close by; he was near me, somehow, somewhere. *He was with me*. And that's all I needed to know. With him close to me I knew I would be always safe, and that somehow everything was going to be all right ...

Chapter Twenty-Nine

Thought of You

Long after I was engulfed by darkness I still registered Tristan's aroma, lingering softly around me like an invisible blanket. Everything was still pitch dark, but I realized that it was more because I had my eyes closed than as a result of the shroud of sand that had enveloped me after my fall. I slowly regained consciousness and tried to move, but a sharp, agonizing pain shot through my abdomen, making me stop immediately.

I blinked groggily at the white ceiling. Everything was bathed in semi-darkness and I couldn't see clearly. My thoughts were hazy, as if I had been drugged, and I had this strange sense of déjà vu which made my heart start pumping considerably faster.

The lurking images I thought I had put behind me were brought back to my mind. Memories I wished I could forget for ever – Jarvis's truck, a dark warehouse, the cold knife close to my face – they all flashed in my imagination, making my stomach clench.

I knew I shouldn't need to worry about Jarvis any more.

Or ever again. He was gone, for ever gone. I didn't need to be scared now. Right?

I felt something tugging at my hand and my heart rate sped up. With some effort I managed to shift my head a little, to get a better view of my surroundings. I was in a hospital room; there was no mistaking it: the hospital bed, the sterilized smell and blank walls.

The sensation of something tugging at my hand again made panic rise in my chest for a second time, but I tried to fight the fear. I was no longer bound. I was fine; I was safe. Vigil had saved me. I had nothing to be afraid of.

I looked down to see what it was. Tristan was sitting in a chair right beside my bed, his head bent low, his face buried between his arms. One of his hands was holding mine, firmly, as if in desperate need for something to anchor him, as if he were holding on for his own life. His shoulders were shaking a little. He was crying. Hard.

That made me want to cry too.

I squeezed his hand lightly while I fought to hold back tears. I didn't want to cry now; I needed to be strong for him, to be his anchor. I owed him that much after everything I'd made him go through these past few days of fighting and arguments. I had treated him so badly, so unfairly. I had let all those violent, jealous thoughts take control of my mind and I had unleashed them all on him. I had been a horrible, horrible person. And he didn't deserve any of it.

His head snapped up as soon as he felt my hand squeezing his, and he stared at me in surprise, his eyes squinting a little in the dark room. His eyes were red and swollen from crying and his hair was disheveled, flopping over his tired face. He was a mess. And I was the reason for it.

"I'm sorry …" I croaked in a low voice. "Please, don't cry."

He blinked a couple of times, staring intently at me in complete shock. Then he wiped his tear-stricken face quickly with the sleeve of his coat.

"You're awake … you're okay …" he whispered, more to himself than to me.

I tried to smile but it was weak and I knew it looked insincere. When I tried to lift myself up on the bed, another wave of searing hot pain took over the entire left side of my body. I winced and bit my lip to avoid cursing out loud.

"Don't!" Tristan cried, shooting up from his chair. "Don't try to move, or you'll open up your stitches. How do you feel?" he asked, breathless.

"I'm okay, I guess. It only hurts when I breathe," I joked, trying to lighten the mood. Although my joke was indeed true.

He didn't laugh, or even smile, though. He knew it was all forced: my smile, the joke, the chuckle. He frowned, worried.

"Do you want me to call the nurse? She can bring you some painkillers … They have given you some already, but we can ask …"

I shook my head slowly, deciding to give up on trying to be spritely. I didn't want any more drugs. I wanted my head clear. I wanted to be able to think clearly for the first time in a long time. "What happened? How did I end up here?"

He cupped my face tenderly, his touch as gentle and soft as a feather, like he was afraid I might break if he touched me too hard. It was the same gentleness as Vigil when he held me in his arms while I bled out in that abandoned warehouse …

An image of a glass house drifted into my head, eerie, beautiful and so hazy. It was slipping away from me, like a fleeting, waking dream.

Tristan's soft touch brought me back to reality, his thumb stroking my face carefully. "You're going to be just fine," he said, reassuringly, trying to calm me down. His stare was intense. It held a dark, dangerous glint inside, a hardness that didn't match the softness of his touch. He studied my face, his eyes flickering to my jawline. "Vigil told me ..." and he trailed off, unable to voice the rest of the sentence. "I'm glad he took care of him. *For good*."

My jaw tingled and the flesh underneath stung. That's when I understood why Tristan's eyes looked so murderous. Jarvis had punched me real bad a few times ... It must have left me bruised all over. That was probably why speaking or moving my head hurt so much. When Tristan glanced up, the hard look in his eyes softened almost instantly, changing quickly to sadness.

"Hey ..." I said shakily, holding his tired face in my hand. "I know I must look bad right now, but *you're* not one to talk about it. Have you seen yourself in a mirror lately, mister? You look way worse than I do!" I tried to joke again. Seeing him that sad was seriously killing me inside.

His eyes filled up fast and he moved his face away from my hand. He tried to cover up his tears by glancing down and wiping at the corners of his eyes. He nodded and chuckled lightly at me. "I know. I probably do."

"Tristan ..." I said seriously, holding his hand tightly to get his full attention. "Seeing you hurting and sad like this gives me more pain than anything that I ... I just, please ...

I can't bear ..." My voice broke and I was the one unable to finish the sentence this time.

I swallowed my tears. I knew if I started crying now, I wouldn't be able to stop. I would probably cry for days straight, if the amount of heartache I was feeling in my chest was any indication.

Tristan exhaled deeply and forced a weak smile. "I'm sorry, I should be the one trying to make *you* feel better, not the other way round," he said, sighing. "Do you ... do you want me to leave? I don't want to upset you. I can go. I'm not even supposed to be here. They wouldn't let anyone in – just family members are allowed, and ... well, I couldn't but I-I just snuck in," he said, glancing down to avoid my eyes.

He had used his fading powers to get into the room; that was the reason for all his guilt now.

And that brought the cat out of the bag, I suppose.

He risked looking up briefly before flickering his eyes away again, a distressed grimace carved on his worn-out face. He didn't want to upset me any more and he knew from previous experience that this was a sore point between us.

"I-I'm sorry. I just wanted to be sure you were really okay. Your mom couldn't find a flight for tonight, but she's getting one first thing in the morning. I'll let you rest now. I'll just ... leave," he stammered, and started to walk away.

He thought I was still mad at him. The last time we spoke I had told him he wasn't important to me any more. What a bloody mess I had made ...

I held on to his hand, hard. "No. Please, don't leave," I pleaded, pulling him back. "I don't care."

"W-what?" he said, confused.

"I don't care. About any of this. It doesn't matter if you can fade again; it doesn't matter about your reasons for not telling me. I know that I didn't even let you explain anything, but Vigil's powers were messing up my head. I didn't mean anything I said to you; all those horrible things, they were not true," I let out on a shaky breath.

"Who am I to yell at you for keeping things secret? I kept my empathy-sight from you for so long. I lied to you about my ability so many times. I don't have the right to be mad at you about yours," I said, pulling his hand to rest on my chest. "So, please, don't leave. I don't even need to know, Tris. I don't care about any explanation. If someone needs to be forgiven, here in this room, it's me."

And there was so much I still needed to tell him, so much for which I needed to ask for forgiveness. I had kissed Harry. Because we'd needed to know, to know for sure, that we could never be together, that I truly belong with Tristan. But it was something that could still destroy everybody, not only me, but Tristan, Harry and the whole band as well. And then I had kissed Vigil. It was a kiss of gratitude, but I had done it nonetheless. And now I had to tell Tristan everything: he deserved to know. He needed to forgive me for so much …

"I'm so sorry … for everything," I whispered.

Tristan leaned in, both hands cupping my cheeks softly as he rested his forehead against mine. "Vigil told me what happened and then he brought me here to see you. I've never been so scared in my life," he said quietly, closing his eyes to steady himself. "The doctors told me you had lost too much blood. They had to stop the bleeding and give you a blood transfusion straight away. And then after what seemed like for ever, they told me you were going to be fine, but I couldn't see you because I wasn't family ..." He opened his eyes and pleaded fiercely. "Please, don't ever scare me like that ever again."

"I'm sorry." It was all I could say to him.

He smiled weakly and closed the remaining inches between us, giving me a feathery kiss. "I'm sorry too, my love," he let out with a sigh.

Then he stood up and glanced quickly at the door of the room, and for an instant I thought he was getting ready to leave and I began to panic inside again.

"Ah, screw it," he muttered under his breath, and turned to me. "Scoot over," he ordered and climbed into the bed next to me. I bit back the stinging pain to let him lie down beside me. Any pain was worth it to have him here with me. He turned and wrapped an arm behind my head, bringing me warmth and comfort as he held me, sheltering me from all grief. I could almost visualize our auras intertwining as we lay there together, the connection deepening and shining as brightly as ever.

We stayed like that, in a comforting silence, just listening to each other's breathing in the semi-dark, sterilized room, until he risked speaking again.

"I know you said I don't have to ... but I'd like to explain," he said very quietly into my ear.

I let out a deep breath. "Tris ... I mean it, it's not import—"

"Just hear me out ... please?" His voice was soft, like a delicate caress.

I turned my face to look at him. His gray eyes had an eerie light glowing from within, giving him a ethereal radiance.

"You know how you always admire my gray eyes?" he began.

I nodded. I could never get tired of his sterling-silver eyes. Even if I lived a thousand years, those eyes would always be a wonder to behold.

"I never told you this, but ... I hate it when you do. Because I hate my eyes being gray. I think it's unnatural, and weird, and it makes me feel like a freak. I mean, what normal person has gray eyes like this? Every time I look in the mirror, it's a constant reminder of how I'm not supposed to be here; I'm not supposed to be alive. That I belong with the dead, with the ghosts. And that I may be living, but I'm not human, not entirely. I'm this freak of nature with weird gray eyes ...

"I even avoid dressing in white or black, because it makes it so evident ... I thought about getting contact lenses for a while, but I knew it would cause lots of arguments with you, so I didn't," he confessed. "And that's how I feel about the fading thing too, only ten times worse. If disappearing like that doesn't make me a certified freak, I don't know what does." He sighed heavily. "I realized I could still fade the first day I was brought back again, but I hated it so much ... I just thought I could, I don't know, pretend it wasn't there. That I couldn't do it any more. I wanted to feel normal, like any other normal human being, you know? So I lied. And I never ever used it again. Until that damned hell cat jumped on me. I faded by instinct then. Survival reflex, I suppose.

"I don't think I can get rid of it; it's something built inside me, since I was a ghost. I can't separate this from myself: the eyes, the fading, it's all part of the combo ... I can't make them go away. And I hate that I'm stuck like this. Don't get me wrong, I am grateful for the chance to live again. I know I'm the luckiest bastard in the world.

But ... I still hate these things about me. Every day it makes me remember that I am not supposed to be here ... with you.

"I wanted to tell you; so many times I almost did. But ... I didn't know what I would do if you started looking at me differently, like I'm a freak. I already do it myself and it's hard as it is," he said, looking down. "So that's why I lied ... and kept this a secret for so long. I hope you can understand, Joey." He grazed his fingers softly over my shoulder.

"I understand," I said, shifting a little on the bed so I could face him. "But understand this, Tristan. I would never look at you like you're a freak. Just like you have never looked at me that way for having my empathy-sight. So if you think of it this way, we are *both* freaks. Although I like to think that we are just different, not better or worse than anyone else," I said, pulling a lock of dark hair away from his gray eyes. I guess I knew now why he always wore his hair long, with his bangs falling over his face, to cover his eyes. "And as you can see, this fading deal can have its uses, especially when you need to sneak inside a hospital room when your girlfriend needs you," I said, giving him a goofy grin.

A small smile forced its way to the corner of his lips in response.

"But if you choose to never use it again, that's okay too, Tris. I will never mention the fading *or* your gray eyes, ever, if it makes you feel better. But I will always think they are beautiful and captivating, no matter what you say. And you can never make me think you're a freak, either, because, my dear Tristan ..." I said, grazing my fingers over his face, "... if you can't see how special you are, and how brightly your stunning gray eyes shine, how they make my heart skip a beat … You have to know that these things don't make you a 'freak'; they make you rare and unique, something to be valued and prized.

"They should be a constant reminder that you are a miracle. You're *my* miracle, Tristan, can't you see?" I asked softly. "You will always be my ghost boy … and I'll always be your witchy girl. How could *that* be a bad thing?"

A single tear ran down from the corner of his eye and landed on the pillow between us. "I'm sorry, I'm such a fool," he said quietly. "When did you become so unbelievably wise, anyway? Is that left over from Vigil's powers?" he asked, wiping at his eyes again.

"I have always been unbelievably wise. I'm an old soul," I joked, feigning smugness. "Vigil's powers actually made me more stupid, if we stop to think about it …" I mumbled, kind of embarrassed.

"I'm glad this mess is over," he murmured.

"Me too. I feel like I've been in a nightmare and I'm just waking up," I whispered, sighing quietly and resting my eyes. "I feel so tired …"

I think I dozed off then, because I don't remember anything else after that, just the warmth of Tristan's arms around me and his scent enveloping me completely. I must have been more tired than I had realised, to have fallen asleep mid-sentence like that …

I woke up at some point in the night with Tristan still holding me tight, his deep voice murmuring that I was safe now, that everything was going to be all right, and I realized I had been thrashing around and crying from a nightmare. I couldn't remember the dream, but I was shaking and trembling, drenched in cold sweat, the hospital gown stuck to my skin. Tristan tried to calm me, whispering soothing words in my ear, and I slowly drifted back to sleep.

When I awoke for the second time, Tristan was fast asleep behind me, his arm holding me safely and his face tucked into the crook of my neck. I could feel a sharp pain shooting in my tattooed wrist. I glanced up and saw Vigil sitting in a chair, right in front of me. His elbows were resting on his knees and his fingers were intertwined, making him look like he was praying. He was staring, a small smile on his lips. I pulled my free hand out of the bed, leaving the other safely enclosed beneath Tristan's, and reached out to Vigil. He scooted closer and took my hand in his. The prickling pain stopped immediately.

"I am glad you are okay," he said quietly, so as not to wake Tristan. "For a moment there, I was worried."

"I'm fine. Thank you for saving my life ... again. You've been doing that quite a lot lately," I mused. "But seriously, thank you, Vigil."

"You do not need to thank me. This whole ordeal was my fault. I am glad it is over and that I did not lose you," he said sorrowfully. "You have a lot of healing to do. You first need to concentrate on healing your body, then you can mend your soul. It will take a while before you are fully back to yourself again. But you are strong-willed; I am positive that you will prevail."

"Huh ... okay, I think," I muttered, still feeling uncertain. Here we were again with Vigil and his cryptic conversations.

"While we were kept waiting as the doctors tended to you, I told Tristan everything that has happened. He was very upset ... He wanted absolute assurance of that man's irredeemable state of inexistence. I can't say I blame him; I would want this certainty as well if I were in his place," he said, and shifted uncomfortably in his seat.

"Joey, I'm sorry if I ... disappointed you," he said after a moment's pause. "I know you do not approve of any type of extermination ..." And he trailed off, glancing at the floor to avoid my eyes.

"N-no, Vigil. You were right: I could never do that, but I'm glad you could. I'm in a safer world because you did," I told him honestly. "Thank you."

"It was my pleasure," he said, with an eerie glint in his angelic black eyes. I recognized the feeling; I had given in to it too many times before.

"Sometimes it gets too loud, doesn't it?" I murmured quietly. I still vividly remembered the sound of rattling chains.

He blinked a couple of times before exhaling deeply. "It is not as loud with me as it was with you. My race has the inborn ability to block emotions," he said, staring with glazed eyes at some point above my head. "It has become more ... *strenuous* dealing with it since I got afflicted by human feelings. I can partially understand what you had to go through. I am sorry for that. This was not for you to bear."

"Is there something I can do to help you?" I asked. "You told me you were going to be okay with your powers back ... Are you, Vigil?"

He squeezed my hand, reassuringly. "You need not worry about me, Joe Gray. I am going to be fine. You worry about getting better, all right?"

I stared at him with a deep frown.

"I promise I am okay, Joey," he said more softly.

"Okay, then ... if you say so," I mumbled.

"That is why I came here to talk to you," he said, leaning closer to me. "Well, that and also to check up on you. But since I see that you are faring well, I must tell you. Be safe and stay out of trouble, because I will be gone for a while. There is something really important I need to tend to. It might take some time for me to get back. We can talk more about … the 'noise' and everything you have experienced with my powers then, okay?" he said, giving me one last smile.

"Okay. You be safe and stay out of trouble too, you hear?"

"I hear you," he said matter-of-factly. "Listen to Tristan; he has a wise head on his shoulders and will take good care of you. I will be back … eventually," he said in a soft voice. "Until we meet again, this is goodbye, Joe Gray."

And then he let go of my hand, bowed a little, and was gone in the blink of an eye.

Chapter Thirty

Holding On

The next days at the hospital passed by with an unceasing stream of visitors, despite all the frowns of the nursing staff, the heated glares from Security and the doctors' constant reminders to let me rest in peace. People insisted on coming over, whether it was visiting hours or not.

My mother had been the first to arrive. If I had thought Tristan looked a mess, that was nothing compared to the state my mother was in. She must have stayed up the whole night and was a nervous, worried wreck.

She had apologized for, like, ten minutes straight before hugging me too tightly, crying all the while though trying hard not to. She was trying to show me she was strong and that she was there for me, but she failed miserably. I had patted her on the back, reassuring her I really was fine.

Becca was already being kept on her toes, working hard to keep the media out and the whole hospital emergency a secret. She promised me she would take care of everything; I didn't need to worry or think about anything at all.

Just like Tristan, Seth looked awful, like he had had no sleep whatsoever in the past few days. He didn't say a word, just ran to me and hugged me for a long time. When he finally let go of me, he began flustering around, worried that he had hurt me with his tight hug. I laughed weakly and told him I was all right before turning to look at the rest of the boys, who were huddled by the door.

They were all silent, eyes wide and faces worried. I guess the bruises on my face were making a bad impression.

Josh had clenched teeth, as if the sight of my face was actually hurting him. Harry's face was so drained of color, it looked like he was about to be sick; and Sam just tilted his head down, staring at the floor, unable to meet my eyes.

"Oh, come on, guys. It's not as bad as it looks!" I gave the best smile I could muster. It hurt when I smiled but I bore the pain. Anything not to see the scared looks on their faces.

Then I turned to Sam, who seemed the most scared of all, and raised my arms to him, asking for a hug. He shuffled to me slowly and sat by my side, giving me a soft hug that ended way too quickly. He was scared to hurt me, too. I forced another smile and ran my fingers through his messy brown locks.

I motioned for Josh to come over then. He stalked over, his face serious and jaw still clenched. He sat on the bed and looked down at his hands.

"I'm so sorry, Joey. If we hadn't left the house to go to the police, nothing would've happened to you. This is all our fault ..." he muttered.

"Josh, dude, you can't possibly be blaming yourself for this right now. Are you serious? There's only one person who should be blamed for this, and that person is no longer a problem, do you understand?" I asked him.

"Yeah ... I do." He nodded. "Tristan told us ... I would

have killed him myself if …" He trailed off, fists clenching at his side. I could tell he was scared.

"I know you would," I said, giving him a hug. He tensed up when I wrapped my arms around him and only relaxed after I rested my head on his large chest.

I turned to look for Harry. He was leaning against the wall close to the door, shuffling his feet and staring hard at the floor. He looked so small, like all the happiness had been sucked right out of him.

"*Harry Ledger,*" I said firmly. "What do you think you're doing? I forbid you to be sad like that! Get your ass right here and give me a hug now or I'll risk my health so I can get up just to whack you repeatedly for being so silly! What's this nonsense with everybody acting so damn grave anyway? It's not like anybody died here, sheesh. Harry, what are you doing still standing there? *Get your butt over here!*"

I was trying to shake everybody out of their shock. It seemed to have worked. Harry snapped his head up, a little embarrassed, and shuffled quickly to my bed. "I'm coming. You don't need to shout like that, woman," he mumbled. "You can get really cranky when you're injured, you know that?"

I chuckled at his reaction. "Can I have my hug now? You do know your hugs can make anyone feel so good – they should be prescribed as medicine," I said as I hugged him back tightly. "I promised I would never leave you, remember?" I whispered in his ear. "I never break my promises."

And that made him start crying.

"Aw, Harry …" I patted his back soothingly.

"I told you, you are always making me cry. It's like you do it on purpose!"

"I know, I'm really sorry, sweat pea," I said, ruffling his hair a bit.

My mom came back in the room and almost had a fit when she saw the amount of people inside. She ordered that everybody say their goodbyes and leave: I needed to rest and sleep and they could all see me again later.

Everybody got up and left grudgingly, promising to be back tomorrow with Tiffany and Amanda, with treats and pampering things to cheer me up. The only people left behind were Tristan and my mother.

She tried to tell Tristan to go home too but he refused, vehemently. When she pointed out there was only one bed in the room he said he didn't mind, he would be fine staying in the chair. She started arguing again but he stopped her, insisting he was going to stay no matter what, even if he had to be on his feet all night long. The adamant steeliness of his voice made her see there was no point in arguing. She caved and agreed that Tristan could stay with me for the night.

After my mother had gone, the nurse brought in a tray of food and asked if she could check on me. She took my temperature, measured my blood pressure, checked my bandaged stomach and looked at my wrists. Only then did I register the deep, gnawing rope burns on both of my wrists, where Jarvis had tied me up. My skin was torn and red where the ropes had dug in.

Tristan's eyes had that sharp, dark look in them again, as he watched the nurse tending to my wounds. After she had left, I moved around the bed and tried to stand up. Tristan shot to my side, sneaking his arm around me for support.

"I need to go to the bathroom," I told him, wriggling out of his hold.

"I'll call the nurse to help y—"

"There's no need. I can go by myself, Tristan," I dismissed him, taking a few wobbly steps. My stomach was throbbing, but I could manage walking.

Tristan hovered around me until I reached the door of the bathroom.

"I think I can take it from here, Tris. Don't worry, I'm fine. Get out of here." I shooed him out.

I had forgotten to prepare myself for the view in the mirror. The girl staring back at me was pretty beat-up: purple bruises marked the length of her jawline and neck, there was a red scratch on top of one cheek, a busted lip, but the worst thing for me was the look in her eyes. They were so sad and hollow, like a spark had gone out.

I didn't know how long I stood there staring at myself, wondering how I was supposed to move on from this. I had survived twice: Vigil's maddening powers and mad Jarvis. I had survived the noise of rattling chains and the urging whispers inside my head. I had survived bonds, ropes and a steel knife. I had survived it all, with just a few bruises and a stomach wound.

For a moment I had thought I'd escaped fairly unscathed from this nightmare, but I couldn't have been more wrong. Vigil's powers had messed me up so badly and left me living in a broken shell of a mind. Now I had to deal with the wreckage that was left: the overload of guilt, sadness, fear and helplessness taking up my soul, just like the burning fire once did my veins.

I had to learn to be me again, to be human again in this broken body. And I didn't know how. I had lost myself in the midst of all my struggles for survival; gone was that little part of me that used to spark with life and make my eyes gleam with courage and confidence. Now I needed to get that light back and start over. How was I supposed to do that? I didn't even know where to begin.

The door of the bathroom opened and Tristan peered inside. "Joe? I've been knocking on the door for some time and you didn't respond ..." He peeked a glance at me through the reflection in the mirror. "You've been in here for a while now; I was getting worried. Is everything ... okay?" he asked hesitantly as I looked back at him. We could both see that I'd been crying. I wiped the tears away quickly with the back of my hand.

"Ah, Joey ... come here," he said, stepping inside and pulling me into his embrace. His arms wrapped around my battered body, his chin resting on top of my head.

"I'm sorry, I'm okay now," I apologized, burying my face in his chest.

"Stop apologizing for this and stop saying you are okay. Anyone can see you're not," he said. The harshness of his tone made me cringe. I was afraid of his anger.

"I'm sorry, please don't be mad."

He let out a long breath of frustration before pulling me away from him, so he could look me in the eyes. "My love, I'm not mad at you." Then he wiped the rest of my tears away, sat on a little plastic bench in the corner and pulled me to sit on his lap, cradling me softly in his arms. "I'm mad at a lot of things right now, but not at you, Joey. I'm mad for not being in the house when you switched your powers back with Vigil. I'm mad at that psychopath who hurt you ... I'm mad for not getting my hands on that sick bastard Jarvis and killing him myself. I'm mad at me for being this useless, this helpless."

"I'm so sorry, Tris," I said, gripping on to his neck.

"I'm the one who's sorry. I'm sorry you had to go through all that, Joey. But you don't have to pretend everything is all right. I saw how hard you were trying to be fine for everybody today. You don't need to do that. It's okay to be sad, to cry. You've been through a lot," he said, pulling me closer to him. "But you don't have to go through this alone. *I am here*. You have *me*. Please, let me be here for you. Let me help you."

I wanted to cry, but I couldn't. It was as if the moment I saw Tristan looking at me in the mirror, something had frozen all of my tears inside. Maybe it was because I couldn't handle the pain that flashed in his eyes whenever he saw that I was in pain. I didn't want to make him suffer. I had done plenty of that already.

I snuggled into his chest and he rocked me slowly back and forth. My hand brushed across his jaw, and the scuff of his stubble scratched at my skin. He had been in the hospital for a long time and hadn't shaved. He looked less of a boy now, more of a man. But it wasn't just his appearance on the outside. The glow in his eyes was more mature, too. He had grown up in the past few days ...

"I can't stand seeing everybody so worried and sad because of me," I confessed quietly.

"They worry because they want you to be okay. They are sad because you're hurting, and they don't want to see you hurt. They love you very much. I love you very much."

"I love you too." I sighed deeply. "I'm so tired ... Can I sleep now?"

He smiled softly and kissed me on the forehead. "Yes, you can, sweetheart."

And then he carried me back to my bed. I was asleep before my head hit the pillow.

Chapter Thirty-One

Letting Go

After I was discharged from the hospital, Tristan had called Big Johnson to talk about Jarvis – his cousin. I made sure I was there so I could use my empathy-sight to note if he told us the truth or not, and if he'd had any part in Jarvis's plans.

Tristan had changed a few parts of the story to cover all the supernatural stuff. Big Johnson had been in complete shock at it all. I could see the disgust in his eyes as well as the shame and guilt at having been deceived by his cousin, and for not being able to protect me.

Yet even after I had confirmed his innocence, I still had to let him go. He was sad that he wouldn't be working for us any longer, but he understood why. The memory of his cousin would always be with me, and I couldn't bear to relive it every time I looked at his face and saw the resemblance to his cousin.

Tiffany, Amanda and Becca came to visit every day, and sometimes other close friends, including the Harker sisters, who were eager to know how everything had worked out with Vigil and Sneaky Nick – Celeste particularly asked about Vigil. But I didn't want to see any of them. I was tired of explaining the bruises on my face and on my wrists, having to cover up the horrid story behind them. I was tired of it all. I kept myself locked in my room whether there were visitors or not, to be honest. My room was my sanctuary, my fortress, the only place I felt safe.

Tristan and the boys kept hovering round me, checking to see if I needed anything. I knew they meant well and that they were only worried, but their constant attention only irritated me and stressed me out. I had to keep forcing myself to put on a brave face around them, and it was exhausting. I began to feel so incredibly tired all the time.

I tried to look happy on the outside, but inside I was breaking down. Depression filled me to my very core. I felt so weak, vulnerable and powerless, and every little thing seemed too big to face. Everything scared me.

Everybody had sort of put their lives on hold because of me and that made me even more upset. They shouldn't have to stop their lives for me, and it only made me feel like a burden.

I was done being a cause of grievance in everyone's lives. So after the second week of bed rest and motherly pampering, I told my mom she should get back to her life and her work; I was going to be just fine with the boys. She agreed to go home, reluctantly, and left soon after my stitches were out.

I knew Sam, Harry and Josh had travel plans for the summer break with Jamie and his friends, and that Seth and Tiffany had booked an awesome trip to the Worthingtons' summer cottage too. I had already taken up too much of their vacation time with my problems, and now that everything was back to normal they should get out and enjoy themselves. They had been waiting for me to get better before they could enjoy their time off. It took some time and a few tantrums before I managed to get them all to agree to start packing.

I was going to stay in the house with Tristan, who didn't even let me suggest that he should go and have some fun and enjoy his vacation too. We had been sleeping in different rooms since returning from the hospital. I had decided to have my mom stay in my room with me, so she could take care of me, and after she left I just stayed there. Tristan didn't press me to move back to his room, but I knew it was something he constantly thought about.

He didn't understand why I kept putting this distance between us; he didn't know where we stood. I could see the confusion in his eyes. Were we together? Were we not? Why was I avoiding being alone with him? At the hospital I'd told him that we were good, yet I wasn't acting like it. I didn't know why. I didn't understand what was going on inside me. All I knew was that I wouldn't let anyone get too close. I kept pushing everyone out – even him – locking myself away in this tight shell.

He had been struggling to find a middle ground between smothering me and giving me space. He didn't know if he needed to force himself to be more present, or to just leave me alone. It was turning Tristan into this anxious, conflicted, neurotic person. And again, it was all my fault.

We were both lost, not knowing what to do next. Maybe he couldn't do anything for me at all; he couldn't help me with this. This was something I had to do by myself. I had to heal on my own.

The day after the boys had left for their holidays, we received a surprise visit.

I was resting on my bed when I heard the doorbell ring, and a couple of minutes later Tristan entered the room, his face looking slightly flustered.

"Uh, Joey ... Caleb Jones is here to see you."

I looked at Tristan and snorted loudly, as if he had just told me the most amusing joke.

"No, I'm serious. He's really here. He's asking to see you." He hesitated, clearly at a loss for words. "I think someone told him you were sick ... I dunno ..."

"You're not joking," I said, raising an eyebrow.

"No, I'm really serious. Caleb Jones from The Accidentals is downstairs, in our living room."

"Who told him where I lived? Or that I was sick?"

"I don't know. What should I do?"

"Well, I'll go downstairs and talk to him, then ..."

I tried to move too quickly on the bed, making my stomach sting a little. I grimaced. I guessed I wasn't a hundred per cent healed like I had forced myself to believe.

"Stop! You stay put, I'll bring him up," Tristan said, frowning at me.

I was about to protest but he had already left the room. He returned a few minutes later with a beaming Beanie Boy right behind him.

"Hey, Gray! Heard you had some hospital problems and were feeling a little down, so I thought I'd stop by and pay you a visit, help raise your spirits," he said, smiling. But he faltered when he saw my face. There were still a few bruises lingering; the nasty darker ones were gone, but a few light spots still remained here and there. I hadn't been expecting any more visitors, so I hadn't bothered trying to cover them with make-up.

"Whoa, what happened to you? Becca told me you'd

had a little accident, and you were recovering, but that looks nasty," he said bluntly, walking from behind Tristan towards my bed. "I may have insisted she hand me your address so I could visit. Hope you don't mind ..." He was wearing his gray beanie again, a few blond locks poking out in disarray.

"Huh. Yeah, you could say I had a 'little accident'," I said, embarrassed. "But I'm all right now."

"There were rumors that you were having your tonsils removed, but I get the feeling it was something more than that ..."

"Yeah ..." I said, and trailed off. I didn't really want to get back onto that topic again.

Caleb noticed I wasn't in the mood to discuss it and dropped the subject. "So, Tristan, do you think you can get me a drink or something?" he asked, not fazed by Tristan's intense stare.

"Oh. Okay, yeah. So, huh ... I'll go get you a drink, Caleb," Tristan said, clearly reluctant but being polite. He hesitated by the door for a second and sighed, then walked outside, giving us some privacy – even though he was clearly not comfortable leaving me alone with Caleb.

Caleb watched Tristan depart, with a mixture of curiosity and amusement, and then sat down on the bed, chuckling lightly. "Well, *that* was painful to watch. He really doesn't want you to be alone with me. Don't get me wrong, I'm not saying it was a bad judgment call ... I wouldn't leave me in a room alone with a girl, either," he said, giving me a wink.

I rolled my eyes. That was Caleb Jones: an annoying, conceited womanizer. "Don't make me throw a boot at your face, Jones," I warned him.

Both of his eyebrows shot up in surprise. "Ah! That's

my girl. My Snappy is back! Thank God," he said, putting a hand over his heart, dramatically. "I'm really not a fan of you with the chilling manner and blank stares, you know? Last time I saw you ..."

I fumbled awkwardly with the hem of my shirt. "Yeah, sorry about that. I was ... going through some stuff. But I'm okay now. I think ..." I mumbled, embarrassed that Caleb had seen me at my worst, flipped-out on Vigil's powers.

"I'm glad you're good, Snappy. I brought you some get-well flowers, but your boyfriend over there almost had a seizure when he saw them. He said you're allergic to flowers and tossed them in the trash, which I know is bull, cos I read somewhere you love flowers ..."

"You brought me white lilies, didn't you?" I asked, guessing why Tristan had freaked out.

"Yeah! How did you know?"

"Had a hunch. I kind of had a little ... traumatic experience, recently ... with lilies," I said. "It's a long story, but let's just say I'm not much of a fan of lilies now. But you didn't know that, so, thank you. It's the thought that counts."

"Oh. Sorry. Guess I'm all about embarrassing faux pas today," he said, leaning back and resting his hands behind him on the bed. "Next time I'll bring you some chocolate, then. Is chocolate clear around here?"

"Chocolate is good. Always a safe bet," I said, giving him a smile.

"So, how are you, really? This little 'I'm sooo okay' act of yours is really not convincing, you know?" he said with a side-smirk.

I sighed. "I *am* okay, Caleb. I wish people would stop asking me that every five minutes ..."

His expression softened. "People are allowed to be worried. And I'm not talking about the bruises. You look all ... sad ... and tired ... and depressed."

"Gee, thank you so much. You look amazing, too," I scoffed, glaring at him. "If this is you trying to console someone, I don't want to be around you when you're trying to be mean."

He raised both hands in an appeasing gesture. "I'm sorry, I'll try to be nice, Snappy. It's really painful to me, but I'll try." He really knew how to be annoying, the rascal. "But seriously, how are you?" he insisted.

I sighed again. So much for trying to divert attention from talking about what had happened. "I don't know, it's ... complicated," I muttered.

Caleb gave me a weird look, turned to face the wall and suddenly slumped back, lying on the bed and tapping the mattress by his side, indicating that I should lie next to him. I scooted closer and slumped by his side.

"What is the one thing you want to do right now? Don't think, don't over-analyze it, just answer me, honestly. What do you wish you were doing right this second?" he asked, the question totally out of left field.

"Ah ... Uh, I ..."

"Just say it, what do you want?" he pressed.

"I-I don't know. That's part of the problem, I think. I don't know what to do ..."

"Sure you do. I'm asking what you want to do, not what you think you should do, what people expect you to do. Don't think of anyone else; forget about your boyfriend, your friends, just think about you. Tell me, what do *you* want?"

I stopped to think, biting my lip.

"Joey, don't over-think it!"

"Okay, okay, geesh! I don't know, I suppose the one thing I really want is … to go away. Escape from everything, from everybody, you know. I just want to be left alone, I guess."

He turned his face to me and smiled. "There you go. Was that so hard?" He poked me, teasingly. "So, that's it. That's what you gotta do. Just pack up and leave, Gray. Get some time for yourself, get your thoughts back together. Go be alone. Find your way. Soul-searching; it does you good from time to time," he said.

"You … you really think I should do this?" I asked, hesitantly.

He shrugged lightly. "If that's what you really want, why not? You need to stop worrying about everybody else all the time. Be a little selfish. It's allowed, you know."

"Right," I said, and we stared up at the ceiling some more in silence.

I know I shouldn't have considered it seriously, but there was something in Caleb's words that rang true. And even though I'd only met him a few times, I had this feeling that I'd known him my whole life, and that I could trust him. I'd never considered talking about these kinds of private, serious things with anyone other than Tristan or the boys, and here I was, spilling my guts to this famous rock star I barely knew. But he had been there for me that night at the park, and he had always treated me right … Well, he sometimes acted like a douche, but he meant well …

"You know, this is really weird, because we kinda just met and all, but I feel like I've known you for, like … for ever."

"Get the fuck outta here! I was just thinking that," he exclaimed, excitedly.

I let out my first genuine laugh-out-loud laugh in a long time then. Not forced, not fake. Just honest, truthful laughter.

There was something liberating about Caleb cursing so freely like that. It made me feel like I was able to let all my demons out, instead of locking them inside. "Thanks, Caleb. That was some good advice you just gave me," I said gratefully.

"You think I'm just this incredible sexy, gorgeous guy, but I happen to have a good brain inside this pretty blond head, you know." He sniffed indignantly, still loving the exaggerated theatrics.

"I'm really sorry for thinking you were *just* incredibly sexy and gorgeous," I joked.

He turned to me and grinned. "That's all right. I guess you can be a little skeptical about it. I mean, what are the odds of one guy alone having these looks, brains, amazing talent *and* the genius all at once."

"You forget the unbelievable humility as well," I remarked.

"Yes, that as well. I know it's hard to believe, but hey, here I am!"

"God's gift to humanity."

"Exactly."

"You do realize I'm making fun of you now?"

"No, you were just stating the obvious," he said with a smirk. "And since you are so keen on taking advice from me today, may I suggest some that involves you getting single and agreeing to go out with me now?" he asked, raising one mischievous eyebrow at me.

I grabbed a pillow and whacked his face with it.

"Is that a no, then?" he asked, his laughter muffled beneath the pillow.

After Caleb left, I stayed in my room, mulling over his advice while pretending to read a book. Tristan came in, leaning on the doorframe and watching me in silence. I glanced over the top of my book to look at him. "Is everything all right?"

He gave me a weak smile, just like the ones I'd been mastering over the past few days. "No, I was just going to ask you the same thing," he said.

"I'm okay, Tris," I said, closing the book and marking the page with my finger. "You're not mad because Caleb came to see me, are you?" I asked, seeing the weary resignation on his face.

I really didn't want to fight with him because of jealousy again. I didn't want him to be mad at me. And I still hadn't told him about kissing Harry or Vigil. I didn't have the guts to tell him. I was too afraid, too scared. It was like I'd been living on fear and guilt alone, and his anger scared me the most.

He shook his head. "No, I'm not mad. I'm glad he got you to laugh again, even ..." He trailed off, looking sadly out of the window.

Even though I couldn't. That was the rest of his sentence. *I'm glad he got you to laugh again, even though I couldn't.*

"Anyway, it doesn't matter. I'm just glad," he finished, turning to look back at me.

"Tris ..." My voice faltered.

"No, it's all right, Joe. I mean it," he cut in. "I'm happy to hear your laughter again. I don't care about the reason, or who it is making you laugh. I'm only glad to hear it. It has been a long time," he said, smiling softly at me. "I'm going to go out, get us some food, okay? I'll be right back." He left the room before I could say anything.

I watched the empty doorway for a long time, guilt corroding my insides. What was I doing to that boy? I kept crushing his feelings over and over again. I couldn't continue doing this to him.

It was in that moment that I decided to take Caleb's advice. I needed to leave, to stop hurting him like this, stop hurting him every time he asked me if I was okay and I lied to his face. Every time I forced a smile, he saw right through it; every time he tried to help, I pushed him away.

I needed to be alone right now, so I could stop trying to hide the pain, all the time, wishing I was all right instead of actually doing something about it. I needed to act. I needed to figure out what was wrong with me, to fix what was broken.

I needed to get away to start healing. And I needed to do it now.

I gave Tiffany a quick phone call to see if she had a place where I could stay for a while, and asked for her word that she couldn't tell anyone, not even Seth. Then I threw a few clothes in a bag and wrote Tristan a letter. I left the note on my bed, knowing that it would be the first place he would look in the morning.

That night, after we had finished our supper and he had retreated to his room to sleep, I read the letter one more time then grabbed my bags and silently left the house.

My dearest Tristan,

I'm writing you because I know that if I was standing right in front of you and had to say this looking into your eyes, I would never be able to do it. I would give up at the first sign of pain I see in you . . . So I decided to tell you in a letter instead.

I hope you can forgive me for being this cowardly.

Sometimes I think I can only feel tired, and guilty and afraid, these days. That is all that I am, all that is left of me. A weak, scared, broken person. I hate myself for being all those things, and I hate that you have to see me like that, too.

You have asked me plenty of times, in the hope that I would give you an honest answer, and all those times I haven't been truthful when I answered you. I keep lying to you, to everybody, even to myself, every single time.

And the truth is that I am not all right. Sometimes I fear I'll never feel all right again. I think I will, I hope I will, but I don't know for sure. I can't tell the future. I wish I could say I am strong and will prevail, but I can't see myself being strong right now.

And that is why I need to leave. I need some time for myself, some time to heal on my own, and I know that I need to walk this path alone. No one can help me find my strength again. This is something I need to do by myself.

I hope you can understand. I know you worry and that you love me. I worry about you too, and I don't want to keep hurting you all the time like I've been doing. I'm sorry about all the pain I've caused you. Please know that I love you more than anything in the world. Thank you for never giving up on me, and for being there for me, always.

I'll understand if you get mad at me for what I'm

doing right now. You have every right to. I know I have put you through so much pain already, and here I am, doing it again.

I promise you if I need help, you'll be the first person I will turn to. If something happens, you'll be the first to know. And when I'm back on my feet, and truly okay, you'll be the first I'll call.

There is so much I need to tell you, so many things I want to talk about and share with you … and I will tell you everything, I promise. But first I need to find myself again.

Please, please, don't be mad. Please, try to understand.

I've never stopped loving you since the first day we met, and I'll never stop loving even after the day I die. That has been the only certainty in my life and that will never, ever change.

I will love you always, no matter what.

Until the end and from the start.

Yours,

Joey.

Chapter Thirty-Two

Walking in the Sun

I was on a ferry that was taking me to a small island a few miles into the Mediterranean Sea.

Tiffany had told me her family's villa was at my disposal for as long as I needed it. It was on a small, remote island with only a few local Italian villagers – a very secluded and private place. That was all I wanted: privacy and solitude.

I grabbed my bags and was preparing to climb off the ferry, my black hoodie hiding my face and earbuds in my ears, when I felt my phone vibrate in my pocket. I took it out to check. It was a text message from Tristan.

I understand.
Be well. Be safe.
I'm here if you need me.
Love you.
T.

I smiled softly at the message, feeling as if a heavy load had been taken off my shoulders.

Obviously, the Worthingtons' place was the biggest

house on the highest part of the island. I didn't stop to sight-see or even to acknowledge anyone on the way up there. I just wanted to get to the house and lock myself in my room.

When I got there I didn't even pause to appreciate the vastness of the house, or admire the huge swimming pool outside, or even the sea view from the balcony. I just wanted to be alone.

I closed the doors, shut the curtains and slumped down on my bed. And that was where I stayed for the next few days. I turned my phone off, intending to keep it that way, disconnected from the world.

I mostly slept. My body was accumulating some much needed rest to compensate for all the battles it had been put through.

I could feel the heavy flow of depression settling in. I cried a lot. I had been holding in these tears for so long, and only now was I able to let them all out. I cried without worrying if anyone could hear me; I cried without feeling guilty that someone might get sad for seeing me sad. I let the tears flow freely. As weird as it might sound, it felt good just to be able to feel sad and nothing more.

It was like my body needed to get into this state first, before it could get out of it. I cried until there were no more tears left to shed. And when I was done, all that was left was relief.

One night, I had the strangest dream. I found myself in a field with mist sweeping lazily around me.

This wasn't Sky's home or her desert workplace. There was no scorching sun, moonless night, or silvery sand, only a grassy field with white, wild country flowers blooming everywhere. The silence was eerie, but not threateningly so. And Vigil was standing a few feet away from me.

"Am I dreaming?" I said, turning to look at him. "This feels like a dream."

"Yes, I am in your dream. But I am also very far away. I thought I might try to reach you in here. It is a faster and easier way to connect with you. I have done this many times before – in the first year we met, remember?" he said, walking closer.

"Oh, yeah. I remember." I reminisced, chuckling a little. "This is so weird; it feels so real."

He frowned, just like Sky used to do whenever I said something she didn't understand. "This is very real. Just because it is a dream does not make it less real," he stated. "Are you all right? I can feel the sadness through our bond; your distress has been very intense lately."

"W-what do you mean?" I asked, and realization dawned on me when I looked at my wrist and watched the black lines of my tattoo closely, the magical mark that bonded me to Vigil.

He took my hand lightly, stroking his thumb softly over my tattoo. His touch tingled a little. "I know when you are hurting. This mark binds us. I can sense it, when the feeling is too strong, like it has been for the past few days," he explained.

"Oh. Sorry," I apologized, embarrassed at disturbing him with all my sadness, even if I'd done it unintentionally.

"The power switch we performed leaves a scar of sorts. Healing the soul is the hardest part. But you are almost there, Joey. I did not doubt for a second that you would get out of this stronger than you ever were before." A sort of melancholy flickered briefly inside his deep black eyes.

"You look ... *different*."

His eyes seemed different somehow, more grown up. He didn't look skinny and frail any more; he looked like a man.

"You look *different* as well," he said, staring at me intently. "You have not yet realized how much this has changed you, but you will soon enough."

"What do you mean?" I said. "I don't want any more supernatural surprises, Vigil!"

He paused and regarded me in silence for a moment, his head tilted while he watched me. "I mean, you will be able to handle your own powers a lot better now. They are stronger than you know, but you can control them, the same way you controlled my powers. The key is the same. You have already learned this lesson."

"I don't want stronger powers. I don't want any kind of power. I don't even want to remember the time when I had yours!" I said, recalling all the horrible things I had done when I had all that power, how horrible I had become with it.

"Too much power in avid hands is the most dangerous thing. The best hands to wield it are the ones who do not wish for it. That is why you have survived this; you walked past its alluring whisperings and conquered them. You have already won this battle, Joe Gray; you do not have to fear the downfall of power any longer," he said. "You should embrace your own powers, because they are part of you. You can never be fully yourself if you deny who you are."

"I just want to forget all this ever happened," I said.

"Do not forget your struggle. Do not bury those memories inside. Remember, always. Remember the noise, the whispering, the fire burning inside of you, Gray. Because then you will always remember how you conquered it. And you will not have to fear power ever again. It does not control you. You control yourself," he said, and extended his hand, as if he was touching something invisible in the air. Little ice crystals formed around his hands and fell softly onto the grass, so beautiful and magical.

"You have walked through fire, as I have plunged into burning ice. And we remained ourselves, despite it all," he said, and millions of snowflakes started falling around us, filling up the air. "Remember that, Joe Gray."

I reached out, letting a snowflake fall into the palm of my hand. Vigil reached his hand slowly towards mine and when he touched it, I felt a current of energy unleash and the burning heat ignite my veins once again.

Let it burn.

I heard his voice inside my head, my eyes never leaving his deep black orbs. He nodded reassuringly, and I let the energy surge through me. Fierce red flames flashed into life, enveloping me whole. Vigil's eyes sparked brightly with an emotion I couldn't quite discern as he smiled at me.

Make it stop. His voice once again echoed inside my head.

We stared at each other unblinkingly, and then it was my turn to nod. The flames subdued and died away, taking all the snowflakes Vigil had created with them. All that was left was a heavy fog and the grass beneath our feet.

"You are stronger when you remember your weakness. So do not forget, *Gray Hood Bearer*," he said. "I have to go now, Joey. I have important things to answer for. I just wanted to make sure you were okay."

"Answer for? Are you in trouble, Vigil?" I asked, worried.

He smiled softly, moved by my concern. "Yes and no," was his short reply.

I rolled my eyes. "You know, the paradoxical answers are really, *really* annoying," I chided. "Are you going to be okay with your problem, Vigil?"

"Do not worry; I've got it covered. I am manoeuvering things to my benefit. But I really need to go. Take care of yourself. Until we meet again ..." he said, giving me one last bow before disappearing into the fog.

And then I woke up.

I blinked a couple of times in the dark room, trying to recall and memorize the conversation I had just had, Vigil's wise words echoing in my head.

And then I realized I was done crying. That unbearable sadness no longer ruled me; that crushing weight over my chest had left. Was that what Vigil had meant by being almost there?

The next day I decided it was time to leave my room. Maria, the Worthingtons' caretaker, was surprised to see me out and about, and hurriedly bustled around to attend to my every wish. She was a very sweet old lady, with warm, twinkling eyes and a caring, motherly smile. Her Italian accent was thick, ringing vibrantly whenever she tried to say my name: *Joanna Grei*. It sounded oddly cool, though, so I never really corrected her.

I went out for short walks around the island almost every day. The view was outstanding from the top of the hill, the sea so bright and clear, sparkling vividly in the sunlight, the same amazing emerald green as Harry's eyes. Every time I looked at the sea I thought of Harry.

I tried to avoid people as much as I could while walking along the shoreline, wandering mostly on the deserted parts of the beach. It felt really good just to walk alone, my feet digging into the warm sand, the bright sun caressing my skin with its golden heat, and the rushing sea whooshing soothingly at my side.

I thought of Tristan constantly during those walks. But those thoughts no longer had that addictive edge to them. I didn't feel like I couldn't breathe without him, or that I couldn't go on if he wasn't by my side. Something had changed inside me; something about the way I perceived him. It wasn't need, now; I just missed him – pure missing, without guilt, pain or anguish.

When I wasn't walking, I would sit on the beach and just watch the sea. I would sit there for hours and hours without ever getting tired. The sight and sound of the waves dancing endlessly back and forth brought me so much peace, a steadiness and calm to my heart.

It was during one of those times when I had been sitting by the beach, surveying the sea, that I met Robin.

"They won't quit tossing that ball over here, you know," I heard a girl say, an infectious chuckle in her voice. She gestured to where a few kids were playing with a ball nearby, having discovered the same secluded patch of sand. The kids had been throwing the ball my way quite often but I hadn't really noticed. I turned back to look at the owner of the voice.

It was a very beautiful girl about my age. She beamed widely at me. She had a sun-kissed glow, her skin like caramel in the sunlight, her hair wild and dyed with all the colors of the sun: streaks of yellow, orange and red mixed with one another. She had a thin, small body and a delicate face with hazel golden eyes that made her look like a fairy.

"I overheard them talking," she told me. "They are trying to start a conversation with you. Hence tossing the ball over here all the time. They are all quite smitten with you," she said, chuckling again.

"Oh, I see." I averted my gaze. I still felt self-conscious, as if people could tell what had happened to me if they looked hard enough. I also didn't want anyone recognizing me here. My piece of paradise would be ruined if anyone did.

With this in mind, I decided it was time to leave.

The girl stood up as well, watching me with amused, golden eyes. "I can show you another private beach where there's no pesky kids around, if you want?" she offered kindly.

I stared at her eyes, hard, trying to read her intentions. The offer and the risk of being alone with a stranger rang suspiciously in my ears. Jarvis had made me paranoid, and I was now wary of any stranger's kindness.

She didn't seem to have any dangerous plans in her head, though. Or even have a clue who I really was. She looked genuinely honest and trustworthy. But I was still wary.

"That's okay. I can find someplace else," I said in a tense voice.

"Come on, I know this awesome spot. I've been coming to this island since I was a baby; I know this place inside out," she insisted. "Let me show you."

I eyed her suspiciously, but her honest smile won me over. "Okay, let's see this place, then," I conceded reluctantly.

"Yay! Follow me," she said, giggling and skipping joyfully over the sand.

"I'm Robin, by the way," she introduced herself, giving me a quick wink.

"Nice to meet you, Robin. I'm Joe."

She turned to look at me with the widest grin. "Really?

That's so cool! You have a boy's name too, just like me!" She looked genuinely pleased with that odd coincidence.

Robin directed me out of the sand and into a maze of narrow alleys until we ended up on another small patch of beach, hidden from view by a sheer cliff with rocky boulders at each side. It was very small and beautiful – and private.

"See? What did I tell you? Amazing, right? I can show you a lot of secret little patches of shore like this one," she said proudly. "There's all sorts of cool things on the island for you to see. I can give you a tour later."

"This is really beautiful. Thanks, I'd love to do that," I exclaimed, and she beamed happily at me. "You've been coming to this island often, then?" I asked curiously.

"Yeah, almost once a year. My parents' house is that orange one up there, the second at the top of the hill, you see?" she said, pointing to a huge house which neighbored mine.

"I'm staying at the one at the top, right next to yours," I told her.

"Oh, you're with the Worthingtons, then?"

"Yeah. They were kind enough to lend me their home for a while."

"I know Tiffany. She used to come here a lot, too. We used to play on the beach when we were little. She hardly ever comes these days. I guess it's because she has that boyfriend now. I saw them in the house together once. I think he's a rock star or something. Never thought Tiff would be the type to go for one of those sorts," she mused.

"Those *sorts*?" I tried to suppress a smile.

"Yeah, you know, rocker dudes. I feel sorry for her. She

deserves a good guy, and musicians are very … you know," she said, giving me a significant shrug.

"Very …?"

"You know, volatile, unstable, egotistical, self-centered, spoiled brats …"

"Geesh. That's kinda harsh," I said, still trying hard not to smile. "I know Tiff's boyfriend. He's a good guy. And not *all* rocker dudes are like that. Believe you me."

"If you say so. He's too pretty, though. No one is *that* pretty without being a conceited brat. But I'll shut up. I'm here bad-mouthing him and he's your friend," she said, chuckling. "I guess I'm just a tad jealous. Oh, look! A starfish! I'll go check it out," she said, running to the sea.

She forgot about me the entire time she was entertaining herself with that starfish. Then she switched her attention to some glittery shells, then a butterfly which flew past us. Her attention span wasn't very long, I noticed.

Over the next few days that I shared her company, I learned a lot of interesting things about Robin. I learned that she was a bit random and eccentric.. She had the attention span of a toddler and the brain activity of a hummingbird: incredibly fast and in constant movement, always bursting with energy.

She never pressed you to talk about things you didn't feel comfortable with; she never smothered you and she knew when to give you space. She was bluntly honest and often said exactly what was on her mind. She was true, kind and loved life intensely. And she was a tad crazy.

She would come and hang out with me for hours and then disappear for long periods of time, doing God knew what. She always came back with a novelty of sorts, whether it was an interesting tale or a curious souvenir she'd discovered in the market. She was always full of surprises.

One day she convinced me to go out and buy new clothes to celebrate our newfound friendship. I had a haircut, too, because she had inspired me to do things that I really wanted to do.

I'd always wanted short hair, yet I'd never taken the plunge because Tristan liked my hair long. I didn't think twice now about chopping it all off. It was time to make some changes – be bold, be wild, do what my heart desired.

I stopped caring about the people who stared, and I didn't try to turn my face away any more, either. I was done trying to hide who I was, trying to hide myself. I was proud of every part of me, every bruise, mark and scar. I was *a brand new Joe Gray.*

I had finally found my self-confidence. I was finally standing on my own two feet, without any emotional crutches, without leaning on anybody. I was fully healed. It finally hit me: I felt mended, whole again. That's when I decided to call Tristan. I was finally ready to see him. To be with him again. To love him completely again.

When I turned my phone on, it instantly flooded with messages and missed calls from the boys, Tiffany, even a few from Becca and my mother, but none from Tristan.

What did I expect? I had told him to leave me alone. He was doing what I'd asked him to. I tried calling him a couple times, but he never picked up any of my calls. I tried calling him on the phone at home, but there was no answer there, either. Was he avoiding me now? Was he mad at me? I had been away and unreachable for a long time. Despite his note, he could still be feeling hurt by my silence and my running away ... I couldn't blame him if he was.

But I was going to try to make things right with him, no matter what. We knew we loved each other; we could work through any problems.

I was pondering this in my room when Robin knocked on the door. She had been waiting for me to get ready. We were going for a walk on the beach.

"Yeah, Robin, sorry. I'm ready to leave," I said, startled by her arrival.

"Good, but ... there's a guy down there to see you," she said, and only then did I notice how wide her eyes were. She was in awe. "And he's, like, *oh-my-God-that's-a-mother-loving-good-looking-dude*, if you know what I mean. He's asking for you."

I turned abruptly towards the open door. "He's down in the living room? Right now?"

"Huh ... yeah? Have I mentioned he's drop-dead gorgeous, too? Who is he? Is *he* the mysterious boyfriend?" she asked with raised eyebrows.

I ran past her and down the stairs as fast as I could, my heart beating hard in my chest.

Chapter Thirty-Three

To Win Over a Princess

I halted at the top of the stairs, my smile faltering for a second. Then I tugged it back upwards again as I took in the sight of Harry standing anxiously in the middle of the living room.

He turned and gave me the most heartwarming smile. His shorts hung low on his hips and he wore a light-blue T-shirt that made his usual evergreen eyes take on a bluish hue. He opened his arms wide for me, his wristbands jiggling with the movement.

"Harry Bear!" I shouted, and ran to him, jumping into his arms, my legs wrapped around his waist and my arms around his neck. "What are you doing here?" I asked, after giving him a peck on the lips.

For a second I had been disappointed that it wasn't Tristan standing there, but you just couldn't stay sad around Harry Ledger for long. Harry could brighten up any day.

He huffed and buckled a little, staggering backwards under my weight. He grabbed my butt for support so he wouldn't drop me straight to the floor. "Hey, you know me. I bugged the hell outta Tiff until she caved and told me your whereabouts. But geez Louise, you've gained some weight there, eh, chubby cheeks," he teased. I let go of him and punched him hard on the arm.

"Shut up. I know. The ice cream here is insanely good. I can't stop eating it." I beamed, rubbing my belly. I had gained a few extra pounds and was showing a few more curves ever since I'd started being catered for by the lovely Maria, as well as discovering this amazing little ice cream shop near the beach.

"No, please, keep at it! You were too skinny before and if it makes you this happy, I say gobble down as much of that magical ice cream as you can!" he encouraged, eyeing me approvingly. "So … you're not mad that I came?" he asked, sprawling on the couch. Harry never sat anywhere; he always sprawled or slouched around.

"Of course not," I said, sitting happily by his side. "I just needed some time alone to get better, but I'm better now."

"You know, you got us all worried when you weren't picking up your phone … If it wasn't for Tiff, we'd be freaking out about your disappearance."

"I'm sorry, Harry. I didn't mean to worry you—"

"So, is this the mysterious boyfriend I *haven't* heard so much about?" Robin interrupted, making herself known.

"Oh yeah, Robin, this is Mr. Harry Ledger, my best friend in the whole wide world!" I said, presenting Harry with a flourish of my hands. Harry gave her a shy smile and a nod. "Harry, this is the awesome Robin, the best and craziest tour guide you'll ever find." I made her giggle at my goofiness.

"Best friend? Really? Cos I could've sworn … You guys act like girlfriend and boyfriend," she said, eyeing us curiously.

"I'm *not* her boyfriend," Harry said politely, and then turned to me. "Speaking of which, is he around? I thought he'd be here for sure ..."

"No, he's not here. In fact, I've been trying to get hold of him, but he's not taking any of my calls ... Have you spoken to him lately?"

"Now that you mention it, it's been a while since we last spoke. Let's see, here ..." Harry said, pulling out his phone and pushing some buttons. "Hmm. He's not answering for me, either." He eyed the screen for some time.

"How was he? I mean, last time you spoke with him?"

"He was a bit grumpy and, you know, he wasn't talking much. But then again, Tristan has never been the talkative type."

"Do you think something's happened to him?" I asked, a little worried now. What if something bad had happened? What if he was hurt and needed me while I'd been unreachable all this time?

Harry waved a hand to dismiss my worries. "Chill, Joey. I'm sure nothing bad's happened. We'd be the first to know if it had. The media would be all over it; we'd be hearing it from TV, radio, phone messages, paparazzi, you name it. We'll try calling him back again in a while, all right? I'm sure he'll pick up later."

"Why would the paparazzi be all over it?" Robin asked, baffled. "Is he famous?"

Harry gave Robin a curious look, trying to figure out why she'd ask such a weird question. I hadn't told her yet that I was in a famous band.

Robin was quite clueless about celebrities and wasn't into music much, either. I'd been thankful for her obliviousness. It felt kind of refreshing to be around someone who didn't know about my fame, or my band, or anything about me at all. I guess Harry's arrival and his big mouth was going to put a stop to that.

"Hum, yeah, about *that*, Robin … I've been meaning to tell you. I guess now is as good a time as any," I said apologetically "You know when we've talked about Tiffany's boyfriend who has a rock band and all?"

"Yeah. Rocker blondie dude. What about him?"

"I'm in his band too. So's my boyfriend. And Harry here as well."

"Bass player," he said, raising his hand.

"Whaaat? Get outta here! You're not … Are you serious?" she asked, surprised. "Why haven't you told me this before?"

"Well, it was kinda nice that you weren't all flustered about it … Plus, you went on and on about how rocker dudes are all self-centered, spoiled brats. Which, by the way, is not true at all. Because, as you can obviously see, I'm awesome. Wait … that kinda sounded a bit conceited." I laughed, scratching the back of my head.

"I can't believe you didn't tell me you are famous. And in a band!"

"I'm really sorry. I just didn't want you to freak out about it!"

"Well, I'm freaking out about you not telling me, then," she said, pouting.

I sighed. "Fine. How long are you going to be like this? Because I want to take Harry to taste some of that ice cream down at the beach, and if you come with us, you can get anything you want there. I'm buying," I said, thinking that bribing her with some ice cream deliciousness would help.

"Ooh, I want the tangerine and lemon cup," she said cheerfully, sulk completely forgotten. That was Robin. So easily distracted.

"Okay, then. Let's go, people! Ice cream heaven is waiting." I chuckled, pulling Harry up as I stood.

The best thing about Robin was that she couldn't hold a grudge for more than five minutes.

"Where did you find that one?" Harry asked, amused as Robin skipped happily in front of us as we walked to the beach.

"Hey, she's awesome," I said.

"Sure. Didn't say she wasn't. She's a bit weird, though."

"*You're* a bit weird. *I'm* a lot weird. Our whole band is frigging weird. She'll fit right in," I said smartly. "Plus, give her one hour and you'll fall in love with her. She has her enchantments. And I think she's part-fairy somewhere down the family line," I mumbled as an afterthought.

"Really?" Harry asked, impressed.

I chuckled and gave him a mysterious shrug. "Who knows? Anything is possible, right?" I almost believed it myself.

Robin twirled around the corner, her wild hair flowing magically in the wind.

"Your new hair looks great, by the way. You look so … different." He gave me a sideways glance.

Automatically I touched my newly short hair, cut in a pixie style. "It's just a different hairstyle, Harry." I laughed.

"No, I mean … I know, but you look really different. It's not just the hair. I was worried for a while after we left you in the house, but I can see now you're better," he said, smiling softly.

"Oh, it's the ice cream, Harry. The ice cream here makes

you feel loads better! You'll see!" I said, grabbing his face and giving him a hard kiss on the cheek.

His laughter rang with happiness. "All right. Bring on the gelato!" he cheered, grabbing my arm and running past Robin, who gave us a surprised look before following us, laughing as loud as Harry.

"Is he *always* like this?" Robin asked, watching Harry as he sat on his surf board in the middle of the sea, far away from us, "woohooing" all the while. For the past few days he had been accompanying me on my daily walks along the beach, but at the end he would always stop to surf a little. It was becoming his favorite hobby. Even though he had left Sam, Josh, and other friends to come look for me, I could see that he was having the time of his life surfing here every day.

"He has his moments, but then he also has quiet moments. You just have to learn to cherish all of his moods as they come," I explained, smiling softly in his direction.

"You sound like you're totally in love with him," she pointed out.

"Oh, but I am. I love Harry with all my heart. But he is my best friend. Our friendship is a bit different. Most people don't understand. We don't care what anyone else thinks, though. His ex-girlfriend could never understand," I said.

"I think I get it. You're kindred spirits," she said, smiling at me. "It's lovely to watch your connection. Doesn't your boyfriend mind, though? Most guys would freak over this."

"No, he understands. He loves Harry very much too; they're best pals," I said, averting my gaze from Harry in the distance.

I still hadn't told Tristan about our kiss. Would he be as

understanding about Harry then? This doubt kept clutching at my heart, and since Harry had arrived on the island, it had intensified its grip.

We still hadn't heard from Tristan and he was still not taking my calls, which made me increasingly worried with each passing day, but Harry promised he would get hold of him somehow. He'd also got Seth, Josh and Sammy to help try to track him down.

"He's really weird, though," Robin said, giving Harry a quick glance. "And that coming from me is something, because I'm well versed on weird."

"I thought you said he was 'out-of-this-world-gorgeous' when you first met him?" I teased her, splashing some water at her face.

"He's the weird, gorgeous type," she mumbled, blushing a little.

"Those are the best types." I chuckled.

Since Harry had arrived, I'd been watching the development of their interaction curiously. They were both such free spirits. I was intrigued by what would happen when all their wired energy and craziness clashed. It would either be a huge disaster or an epic combination of forces.

At first, as was customary, Harry was overly polite and extremely quiet around Robin, as he always was around new people. He was like a skittish baby deer. But after he had grown used to her presence, Harry entered that bizarre stage which I liked to call his flirting stance, where he would stand shyly in a corner and stare silently at the girl he was interested in. Harry was truly awful at flirting. Girls didn't care about his awkwardness, though. He had his good looks and now his rock star fame to rely on.

Robin became skittish then. Apparently Harry's silent stares were freaking her out. It was like trying to catch a bird. Any time he got too close, she would skitter quickly away. I swear, with those two it was like watching some peculiar mating show on the Animal Planet channel. And for Harry Ledger, it was the first time this had happened. He had never had to fight for a girl's attention before. But now he had a weird, wild, fairy girl he couldn't charm right away. He was baffled. He didn't know what the hell he was supposed to do to get her attention. So, in the mysterious way a male brain works, he decided – God knew why – to go for a five-year-old's tactic. Which meant bugging the hell out of her in the most annoying way possible.

"Says *you*!"

"Pfft. Please, tell me *one* famous musician who isn't a conceited spoiled brat," Robin said, countering another of Harry's jibes yet again.

They had been going at it for quite some time now. I mostly tried to stay out of it. If I remembered correctly, this was how Seth had got Tiffany as well: he never stopped fighting her back when they'd first started dating. I guess that still gave Harry hope.

"I happen to know loads. Starting with moi as well as my entire band," Harry scoffed, swinging his legs lazily off the beach chair.

"I haven't met your band yet, but if they are the tiniest bit like you, then my argument is still pretty damned valid. They must all be spoiled rotten!" she jeered, pulling her hat over her head to cover it from the bright sun.

"Says the rich girl staying at her daddy's mansion beach house in the Meditteranean …"

"It's not *my* fault my parents are rich," she said, flustered.

"It's not *my* fault I play in a famous band," he snapped back. "You just can't admit you're being prejudiced. You're a musician-hater; that's why you don't like me."

"I don't hate ALL musicians, just the conceited ones," she cried indignantly. "And I never said I didn't like you," she let slip in the midst of her angry outburst.

They both stopped talking and stared at each other, wondering what had just come out of her mouth. She had just admitted out loud that she liked him.

Harry perked right up on his chair, his eyes flaring the brightest sea-green ever. "Why don't you prove you don't hate musicians, then?" he asked. "Go out with me."

Robin's gold eyes flickered briefly to Harry's naked rippling chest, sweeping quickly over his green and red tattoo before she lifted her gaze to his face, which was looking smug. Her face glowed red like a tomato then.

"You're impossible!" she cried out.

I rolled my eyes at the both of them and turned to Robin. "He's not going to stop bugging you until you agree to go out with him, Robin. Why don't you just say yes?" I suggested in a hopeful voice.

"Fine, you win. Come on, Joey. You're helping me pick my clothes," she said, and started dragging me back to her house.

Harry's face exploded with joy. He was finally going to have his chance with Robin. "See you in one hour, then, princess!" he yelled after us, smiling like he had never smiled before.

I shook my head, amused, as Robin stomped along at my side, mumbling the word "impossible" quietly to herself.

*

It took her an hour and a half to try on dresses for her date. For someone who wasn't eager to go on this "forced" date, as she put it, she sure was trying hard to look her best.

The sun was about to set and the air was warm, the clouds tinted with soft oranges and pinks.

Harry was already waiting, leaning against the wall outside the Worthingtons' house, which he'd made his home from home for the last few days. He was wearing his usual baggy olive shorts, his salmon-colored T-shirt that hung nicely over his body, and beads and wristbands twined loosely about his wrist. His emerald eyes twinkled with excitement and mischief as he waited for his date to arrive.

"At last, the princess arrives!" he greeted her, smiling broadly, making Robin roll her eyes at him as we approached. "You look beautiful, by the way," he added, and shyly looked her up and down. She blushed hard, caught off guard by his sudden chivalry.

"Okay. You two kids have fun now. Go on, get out of here," I said, shooing them away while trying hard not to giggle at their cuteness.

"Okay, let's go, then, princess. I don't have a carriage waiting, so it's going to be walking for us today," he teased, bowing with a dramatic flourish.

Robin rolled her eyes again, faking a snobbish sneer. "Oi, gods. Is this what I get for dating a plebeian? I mean, walking? The *horror* ..." she mocked, flipping her hair theatrically, making Harry laugh.

"Don't wait up for me," he called out, strolling to where Robin was waiting on the cobbled street.

Then he stopped and turned to me, a mischievous glint flashing in his green eyes. "Ah, Joey. I left something for you on the balcony by the pool. Go have a look, will ya?"

"What is it?" I asked, but he just raised a hand up in the air and walked away with Robin.

I gave an exaggerated sigh and headed back to the house. I hoped Harry hadn't brought a turtle back. He was always bringing weird animals back with him. He loved pets. I took my sandals off, leaving them next to the sliding doors, and walked distractedly to the balcony outside, my head too full of turtles and other odd animals.

My breath caught in my throat as I lifted my head to see Tristan leaning against the iron railing, his back turned to me as he watched the deep-blue sea.

I hesitated for a second. My pulse quickened. He hadn't noticed my presence yet. I wanted him to turn and look at me; I wanted so badly to see his face and look at his beautiful eyes again, but I was afraid. The fact that he hadn't taken any of my calls the past few days was indication enough that he was angry with me. It didn't matter, though. I should walk on, head held high ready to face whatever, with courage and determination. I would make him forgive me. I would make him love me again. I would do whatever it took to have him again.

"Tristan."

His back tensed and he turned slowly. A strong wind brushed past him in my direction, bringing me a soft scent of carnations mixed with his scent, making my hair flow back and my dress twirl in waves in the air, as we stared silently at each other.

Chapter Thirty-Four

One and Only

His sterling-silver eyes glowed with a light of their own. He didn't smile or show any expression; he just stood still and stared fixedly at me.

He looked incredibly beautiful, his raven hair framing his pale, flawless face. But he looked taller somehow now and ... stronger. He had cut his hair very short too, clipped sharply at the base of the neck and at the sides, his long locks completely gone, giving a clear view of his amazing gray eyes. He wasn't hiding them under his hair any more. They were completely unveiled for the world to see, piercing and bold, holding a strength that I hadn't seen before.

He had changed. A lot.

But it wasn't just the physical appearance that made him look so changed, although that was quite a noticeable sight to behold. He also looked so ... *grown up*; he had this older, wiser look about him, a perfect picture of masculinity. I realized it wasn't just me that had been going through a life-changing experience of self-discovery. He had gone through a lot as well. I had *made* him go through a lot ... I was the reason he looked so different, so changed.

This guy in front of me wasn't the same Tristan I had left back home. He wasn't the same boy I had left behind. This was no boy. The guy staring back at me with steady, piercing gray eyes was a man. When I looked into his eyes this maturity reverberated in his soul; it showed clearly in his whole stance, in the air all around him.

It was kind of intimidating.

The Joey of a few weeks ago would have crumbled at the feet of this glorious man. She would have buckled in insecurity and guilt. She would have thought she was beneath him, that she didn't deserve him, that he was clearly so much better than her.

But the new Joey knew better. She knew nothing could ever stand between her and the man she loved. Even if he had changed so much that he no longer wanted her and was here to tell her that, she was still going to fight the hardest she could to win back his heart.

"Wow. Look at *you*," I whispered, more to myself than anything. "You look so ... different."

I was about to take a step closer to him; all I wanted right now was to hug him. It didn't matter that he held a guarded look, or that he might be mad at me. All I wanted was to feel him in my arms one more time. But before I could make a move he broke eye contact and turned to look at the view.

"This place is beautiful," he said quietly.

The moment had passed. I stood still, not daring to walk closer. It was clear he didn't want me in his proximity; his posture, his voice, said it all.

"Yes, it is," I answered, and I was surprised at the steadiness of my voice. I was ready for whatever he had to say to me. I was ready for his anger, his disappointment and even his rejection. I knew that, no matter what, we would always be connected. No matter the outcome of this conversation, he would always have my heart, even if I didn't have his any more. We could never be completely apart for that reason alone.

He looked at me again and his eyes flickered with an emotion, but I didn't want to know what the emotion was. I didn't want to rob him of his privacy.

Vigil's words came back to me: I could control this. I had already done it once.

Then something shifted and I remembered that moment of insight I had of how to control Vigil's powers. I used the same principle on my empathy-sight now. I simply turned it off, like an internal flick of a switch. The emotions immediately stopped flashing in Tristan's eyes.

"I can control it now." I breathed out in relief. "My sight. I can turn it off. You don't have to worry about it. I will never peek at your feelings ever again," I said calmly.

He seemed taken aback. "Is that so?" he asked, surprised.

"Yeah. At least I got something out of all this mess. It feels good to be able to finally control it."

He nodded but didn't reply.

I walked slowly to the railing and leaned over it, surveying the view. "I've been trying to call you," I said, looking at the sea.

He had turned around and was leaning over the railing as well, right next to me. "I know. Harry told me. I had a little ... *accident* with my old cell phone. I spoke to Seth yesterday and he told me you'd been trying to reach me. He gave me this address. So I came. I promised you I would," he said matter-of-factly.

"I tried calling you at the house, too."

"Yeah, I wasn't home," he said, staring ahead. "I was doing some soul-searching myself. Did a little traveling, too."

"Oh. Okay." I noticed he didn't elaborate on his travels. It was only fair, since I hadn't told him where I was going when I left the house ... when I left him.

"You look very ... different," I said, peeking at him.

"I suppose I do," he said, a quiet smile tugging at his lips, but his eyes never left the sea view in front of us. "I feel different."

"I'm sorry I left the way I did," I apologized. "I should've talked to you in person, but I would have just given up if I had and ... I really needed to be alone."

He leaned his arms on the railing and looked down. "I understand. I probably wouldn't have let you leave anyway if we'd talked about it ... I was really mad, though ... When I read your letter. I felt powerless – I couldn't control your impulsive actions. Then I got worried that something would happen to you on this trip. In the end I calmed down, after I'd read the letter ten times over, and I understood what you were trying to tell me. That's when I wrote you that text message."

"Thank you for sending it. You don't know how much it meant to me," I said.

He watched the sea in silence for a while before speaking again. "I've come to realize that, regarding you, Joey, it's better to let you go free, to let you do what you have to do, than to keep trying to hold you still. The more I try to hold you, the harder you fight to slip through. So I packed some clothes, went for a trip myself and decided to just ... let you go," he said calmly.

I pursed my lips. "You're still mad at me." He sounded

so distant; a quiet, calm tone hid stormy waters beneath.

It took him a few seconds to register what I'd said, and he blinked a couple of times before turning his head to look at me.

"Actually, no, I'm not," he said, and his eyes lingered on mine, studying something inside. "You really have no idea what I'm feeling right now, do you?" he asked curiously.

I shook my head, feeling completely at a loss. His eyes and expression gave nothing away, and he had put such strong walls around himself I could barely even read his body language. I had no clue whatsoever what he was feeling. I was in the dark, begging for him to give me a sign.

He let out a deep breath and turned to look at the view again. "I *was* mad at you for some time, though. Mad that you didn't let me in to help you get through this, that you needed to do this by yourself. I even smashed my phone against the wall one night."

Ah, so that had been his little accident, then.

"After a while I realized that, deep down, I was really mad because you'd left me. I have always had this irrational fear that you would eventually leave. In my head it was only a matter of time before you did, and then it finally happened," he said, brushing his hand over his now-short black hair. "And then I was stuck with this anguished pain and weight in my chest. And I hated you for making me feel that way."

He turned and looked me directly in the eyes. "That's when it finally hit me, and I understood what you'd been trying to tell me back then in our room ... about how we were being crippled because we couldn't stand on our own feet, because we couldn't stand being apart. I was hurting because I was away from you. I was alone ... and the pain was so strong that it even made me start hating you for it."

I cringed a little as he used that word a second time. The thought of Tristan hating me pierced through me like a stab to my heart. Hearing him say it out loud was devastating. What had I done? I had made him hate me ...

"But that's just insane, isn't it?" he continued. "Because you didn't leave me, you'd just gone away. I get it now, what you mean about being addicted. It sure felt like an addiction. The withdrawal was painful, but without that pain I would have never understood. You were right about us ... What we had, it wasn't right. For any of us. I get it now. I was fighting so hard, throwing tantrums, trying to keep us together, that I never stopped to think about what you were trying to show me. That this was for the best, for the both of us. We both needed this change.

"When I finally let go of that old notion of us, all the anger, the hate, the pain faded away. Being alone no longer hurt me. It took a while, but now I can honestly say to you that I can stand on my own; I can walk alone and be complete without you," he said, nodding to himself. "I don't need you any more."

I held my head high as I stared back at him. The old Joey would have cried, would have wished to be dead instead of hearing those words coming out of his mouth. But I was stronger now. I had walked through fire and endured such pain, but remained true to myself, despite it all. Tristan's words would not make me lose sight of who I was. And they would not make me give up on him. I would fight for him until the end.

"And *you* don't need *me*," he said, brushing his thumb softly over my cheek. "I can see you have also learned to walk on your own now. You stand alone, right here, strong and proud. Look at you. Stronger than you ever were. Fierce and beautiful ..." His eyes flared with admiration. All of his words turned around in my mind as I watched him in awe. I saw him with the same eyes. He was also standing alone, in front of me, strong and proud, a real man, beautiful and magical. A true miracle. *My* miracle.

"And now that we have learned to walk alone, learned that we don't need each other in that desperate, dependent way any more ... *now* we can be together. I don't need you any more, like you don't need me, not in that addictive way. Now I can have you by my side, as a companion, not as a crutch," he said, giving me his first smile since he'd arrived. He held my hands softly in his. "So, will you have me, Joey?"

I slid one of my hands out of his grasp and cupped his face. "Tristan ... you never need to ask me that. I will always love you, no matter what. The real question is, *will you have me*?" I asked with a sad smile. "Before you answer me, though, I need to tell you something."

I stared into his eyes for a long time, and he held my gaze anxiously. Then I turned and leaned over the railing again, trying to gather the courage I needed to confess. This could destroy everything we had, but I *had to* tell him. No matter what, he deserved to know the truth. Then, he could decide if he still wanted me by his side.

I took a deep breath. "I kissed Harry."

I felt Tristan grab the railing right next to me.

"It was different, though. It wasn't like how we always kiss as friends. It was a *real* kiss. We've crossed a line. It was just once, but it happened. And we regretted it as soon as it was over. We're just friends. Nothing more could've happened because my heart belongs to you. I can't give him anything more than my friendship. And he wants nothing more from me than that. He told me so," I said in one breath. "It happened while I had Vigil's powers, and I wish I could blame it all on that, say that it was those powers messing with my head, but it wasn't, really. I knew what was happening ... and what we were doing. And I think you deserve to know, despite it being a gigantic mistake, and it will never happen again."

Even though I was staring hard at the sea, I could still see Tristan in my peripheral vision glancing down where his hands gripped the railing. I couldn't fathom what he might be thinking. So I decided to continue. Might as well go all the way.

"And I kissed Vigil, too. It was a kiss of gratitude, a way to thank him for saving me from my own insanity. I was losing my mind at the time; his powers were twisting me inside so much I could barely distinguish reality from anything else. But Vigil dragged me out of that madness and saved me from myself. I wanted to thank him for everything he had done for me, and I kissed him. It meant nothing but gratitude for me, but I think it meant more for him ... and I know how you feel about me and Vigil ... so ... I thought you should know about that, too," I finished, and we both stared straight ahead in silence for a long time.

"I wanted to tell you before ... in the hospital, and after I got out of the hospital, but ... I couldn't," I said after a while, breaking the silence.

"Why didn't you?" he asked quietly.

"I guess I was too scared of how you would react. I felt like anything could crush me, like I would fall apart over the smallest of things. I felt scared of everything, and the thought of what you might do when you found out ... I was terrified."

"What did you think I would do?"

"Leave me. Give up on me," I said plainly. "Even though you have every right to ... At the time, I just couldn't bear the thought."

"And now you can bear it?" he asked.

I let out a big sigh. "Yes. If that's what you decide, I will have to bear it. It won't be too hard, though ..." I said, leaning on one elbow and turning to face him. He mirrored my move, his face impassive and guarded again.

"Really? You'd take it that well, me leaving you?" he asked quietly.

I shrugged and his eyes flashed with something I couldn't read. "It wouldn't be too hard because you'd never leave me completely. We have this connection; it goes deeper than any hurt, any rejection, any storm; it's a feeling larger than life. No matter what we go through, we will always be connected. Even if you leave, even if you find someone else, even if we go through different paths in life, something will always link us together, and pull us to each other again. So I'm not really worried, because we wouldn't really be fully apart. Plus, you have my heart. So I will always revolve around you somehow. I can't be too far away from my heart – it's a commonly known fact. It would majorly suck if you have to be with someone else, though," I said, smiling at him. "But like I said, we will always gravitate towards one another, no matter what. And I have to tell you that I have no intention of letting you go without a good fight. And let me tell you something else: I fight really hard for the things I love."

I watched as he tried to fight the smile that was breaking

onto his lips. "That speech was so good I'm tempted to leave just to see what you would do next," he teased.

I grinned widely at that. "Does that mean you're staying? You forgive me, then?"

"I'm tired of being angry, Joey, and of fighting over things that don't matter," he said, tilting his head up to look at the sky. "I got mad at you for all the wrong reasons, and now that I have something valid to be mad about ... I just don't feel like going there again. I'm tired of being upset all the time.

"I always knew you and Harry would eventually have to go through that. It took you guys long enough ... but I knew you'd come to the same conclusion I did, when I first watched you together at Sagan. I knew you wouldn't ever stop being friends. Now we can finally get past the what-ifs and move on. And I can't really hold anything against Vigil. He saved you from that monster; I'll be for ever in debt to him for that. Even though I know he loves you – very much – he doesn't have your heart. I do. And that is that," he said with finality. "Plus, how can I leave if you have my heart? I can't go very far away from my heart, it's a commonly known fact, didn't you know?" he said, with a grin.

I smiled and moved closer to him. I had this one thing I needed to do which I'd been meaning to do since I first saw him standing on the balcony. I closed the space between us, stood on the tips of my toes and pulled him close to me in a deep embrace.

"I love you so much," I whispered as I buried my face in his neck, feeling the warmth of his body, his pulsing heart pushing strongly against his chest. He snaked his arms around me and tightened his grip.

"I love you too," he whispered back. He held me in

silence, just reveling in our embrace. Then he leaned back a little and tucked a stray lock of hair behind my ear. "Can I kiss you now?" he asked with a soft smile, his voice slightly hesitant.

"Why are you even asking me? You never needed to ask before." I chuckled at his sudden weird formality.

His eyes twinkled, glowing with a new fire inside. "I know, but you look like a goddess now, it's a bit intimidating," he mumbled.

That made me laugh even harder. I mean, *really*? The man standing in front of me making my knees turn to jelly was surely joking at my expense now. "What on earth are you talking about, Tristan?" I asked, chuckling hard.

"Have you looked at yourself in the mirror lately? I came here to find the amazing girl I fell in love with, and I found this breathtaking, mind-blowing, beautiful woman instead. You look … God, I don't even have words to describe it!" he said.

We locked eyes, his burning silver orbs ablaze in the sunset. And then he leaned in and took my lips, kissing me so deeply and with so much emotion that it left me reeling at the amount of love his lips bared to me. I matched his kiss with the same love he was giving me, and my body trembled, reacting to his every touch and the taste of him.

Soon we were tangled in each other, trying to pull closer and closer until our bodies were mashed into one. He grabbed me and pulled me up, and I wrapped my legs around his waist. We managed to stumble on to the mattress on the deck, swiftly discarding pieces of clothing along the way.

I needed to have him; I needed to release some of this excruciating heat which burned through my veins. My head was filled with pleasure and my body with a fire that pulsed stronger each time his hands touched me, each time his body rocked and pressed hard against me and his lips claimed mine hungrily. A fire that pounded along with my heartbeat, along with the strokes of his fingers, this inhuman heat consuming my very core, until there was nothing left but the feel of our climaxes exploding in unison.

The last thing I heard was a faint whisper in my mind:

Let it burn ...

"Joey!" Tristan's sharp voice called my attention as I was still dazed and breathless. But the hint of panic in his tone made me snap my eyes open and look at him with a start.

His eyes were wide and fixed on my hands, hands that were grabbing his arms tightly. They were burning with light-yellow flames. I gasped in surprise, but a memory instinctively came back to me. Vigil's faint words in a distant dream. I knew what to do.

Make it stop.

And the flames extinguished immediately. I looked at Tristan, my eyes as wide as his; then I glanced at his arm, where my hands were still holding on to him.

"D-did I burn you?" I asked, a little shocked myself.

He shook his head. "No. It didn't burn ... It felt a little warmer than normal, but ... It was a nice feeling. Kinda hot. But good. Is there something you forgot to mention to me?" he asked, raising an eyebrow.

"Uh ... well, apparently – and mind you, this is as new to me as it is to you – I have uncovered this other new treat after the 'incident'," I said, sounding baffled even to my own ears.

"New 'treat'," he repeated in awe.

"I-I shouldn't have let it go this far. I could feel it taking over me but it felt so good and I was distracted by ... *you know* …" I explained, giving him an embarrassed smile. "But don't worry, I can control it. And apparently it doesn't hurt you, so … I'm sorry I scared you."

"Has this ever happened before?" he asked.

"I did something like it once, but that's when I had Vigil's powers. This is the first time since we switched back. I guess the fire isn't as much about Vigil's powers as it is about mine." He didn't move, still hovering half on top of me, hands planted either side of me, supporting his weight. He stared at me, a smug smile showing in the corner of his mouth.

"So, you're saying it only happened because of *me*?" he asked with a smirk.

I rolled my eyes. *Men.* "Yeah, Tristan, you made me so hot I burst into flames," I said, feeling a blush tinting my cheeks. Might as well say it. It was a sort of truth anyway.

"You know … I could feel it too. The heat, taking over, under my skin wherever you touched me. It was kind of an intense feeling. Remarkably good, though. Would you mind trying it again to see how it goes?" he asked, a mischievous smile playing seductively on his lips.

"You mean, have another go at it?" I asked.

"For purely experimental purposes, of course," he added, still smirking.

"Well, we do need to learn more about it," I agreed.

He leaned in closer, biting his lips in such a sexy way that I couldn't help but stare. "It's kinda dangerous, though. I could set the whole house on fire," I whispered, my eyes still fixed on his swollen lips.

"We're right beside the pool; it's the perfect place to test it out," he countered, closing in slowly and planting kisses all over my neck. "So … let's see if I can give you enough pleasure to make you spontaneously combust again." His hoarse voice vibrated against my neck. "I always knew we were amazing together, but this puts it into a whole new level of amazing."

"God, you'll be forever bragging about this, won't you?" I whimpered, trying to suppress a moan as he skilfully nibbled.

"Oh, yeah," he murmured, homing in for another hungry kiss.

I must proudly say that I managed to not burn down the house the second time around, but fire still sprouted from my hands at the end of round two. We discovered then that my flames couldn't really hurt Tristan, which was a huge relief.

And he was quite ecstatic with this newly discovered ability of mine. He said the sensation was better than anything he had ever experienced before.

I had to admit I had never felt like this, either. It was quite a rush, letting the energy out like that. And I guess we were both really comfortable with the supernatural part of us being so present in our lives now; we had both learned to accept it instead of freaking out all the time.

Then Tristan carried me to my room to test it again. He was quite keen on experimenting with fire. And I wasn't posing any objections, either. Eventually, when the night rolled in, we decided enough was enough and we took a break from experimenting for the night. I rested my head on his chest, listening to his strong heartbeat, our bodies wrapped in the white sheets. We weren't talking, but lost in our own private thoughts as he grazed his fingers up and down my back in soft, gentle strokes.

A silver chain glinted around his neck, catching my eye.

"What's this?" I asked curiously, touching the thin silver chain between my fingers. Tristan was never much a jewelry type of guy, unlike Harry, who was always jingling with, like, a thousand necklaces and wristbands. Tristan glanced down and when he realized what I was asking he blushed a little, clearly very embarrassed.

"Oh, hmm … it's, uh, nothing. I forgot I had it on me. I've been wearing it for some time now and … you know, I was supposed to take it off before getting here, but it must have slipped my mind …" He trailed off.

I pulled at the chain and it tugged back. Something was weighing it down. A pendant of sorts. He leaned on his elbows, pushing me away from his chest and preventing me from investigating any further.

I sat on the bed, clutching the sheets close to my body, and gave him a baffled, hurt look. He sighed, giving up and reaching to unlock the chain. Then he pulled it from his neck to show two silver rings swinging gently. I raised a very curious and surprised eyebrow.

"I'm sorry. I know how you freak out about the wedding subject. I'd asked for these to be made after we had agreed to go public. They were finished a few weeks ago and I've been wearing them since then …" he said, sighing loudly and handing me the chain. "Please, don't freak out."

I slid one of the rings off the chain and examined it. It didn't look like a traditional wedding ring. For starters, it was silver instead of gold, flat in shape instead of rounded, and had two engraved lines running parallel on its surface. It looked custom-made, very beautiful, clearly made by a talented craftsman.

"It's beautiful," I said honestly, and that encouraged him to keep going.

"I know you don't like golden stuff, so I asked for it to be made in white gold instead. The two lines running alongside each other represent us, together on the same path. And I got it engraved. Look inside."

I squinted, peering inside. It was kind of hard to read in the semi-darkness of the room, but I could still faintly discern the words engraved in beautiful cursive letters:

T. J. Until the End & From the Start.

The other ring was smaller and bore the same inscription inside, and at the end of the text there was a small diamond incrusted in the metal.

"There is a diamond in your ring. I put it inside because I know you don't like wearing things that glint on the outside," he said, chuckling a little, but then he switched quickly to an apologetic expression. "But you were not supposed to see them. I know how strongly you are against marriage."

I handed him back the rings and chain. "I'm not *against* it, Tristan, it's just … I think the whole concept is fake: the white dress, the church, the nonsense rituals. I don't believe in anything a priest can say to me … It won't mean anything, the whole thing is just too … pointless. I'm sorry."

"You're talking about the ceremony. Marriage has nothing to do with dresses or priests or traditions. Or even about what gods you believe in. It's about believing in each other and committing. It's about the vows we take, the promises we make. It's about giving up my heart and being worthy enough to hold yours. About pledging to be together and always being true to our love, no matter what.

The rest is just ... for show. I don't care about the show," he said, closing his hand firmly around the two rings.

"So are you saying that all that matters is love and commitment, and there's no need for anything else? The ceremony doesn't really matter?" I asked, uncertain.

"Yes. If the love is true, and we vow to it with all our hearts, then yes. That's all it takes to be married. At least to me."

"That sure makes sense. *That* kind of marriage I can understand." I glanced down to where his hand clutched mine and then back to his face. "That I can do," I said, smiling. "Ask me again."

He blinked, suddenly awestruck. "W-what?"

"Ask me again," I said, grinning.

He looked absolutely baffled, surely never expecting this sudden turn of events.

"Ask ...? Y-you mean ...? Really?" He bolted upright on the bed so frantically that the sheets fell to his waist.

"If you don't, I will," I warned him playfully.

He opened and closed his mouth like a fish, gray eyes glinting in surprise.

"Tristan, I would gladly ask, but I know you are sort of a traditional guy, and I know you'd be upset if I did it for you, so ..."

He snapped out of his stupor and gulped a couple of times before looking down at the rings on his palm. "Right. Okay. No, I can do this." Then he picked the smallest ring and held my hands in his, trembling a little. "Joe Gray ... w-will you marry me?"

I smiled and squeezed his hand reassuringly. "Yes, I will. With all my heart." He slid the ring onto my finger, still trembling with emotion. "I promise I will honor you and love you always," I said, my eyes locked with his. "And now, my turn. Tristan Halloway, will you marry me?" I asked, and he smiled, elated.

"I will. With all my heart. Until the end and after," he said, and I pushed the bigger ring onto his finger.

"This means we're married now?" I asked, light-headed all of a sudden.

"I-I suppose we are," he said, smiling like a fool in love.

"Huh," I said, and extended my hand to appreciate my beautiful white gold ring. "I guess we'll have to sign legal papers to make it official, of course, when we get back home. But we're pretty much married, aren't we?" I felt like giggling, but I stopped myself just in time. "No hospital will ever block you from seeing me ever again, sir. You'll be my husband."

The look on his face was indescribable. "Can I kiss my fiancée now? Even though you hate traditions, it is said to be customary."

My heart fluttered and butterflies erupted in my stomach in anticipation. It felt like this would be the first time he'd kissed me in my whole life. I tried to steady myself and still my beating heart.

Why does this feel so much like a first kiss?

"Maybe it's because it will be your first kiss as my future wife," he answered, his grin wide, his eyes glistening with emotion.

"Oh, oops. Did I say that out loud?" I blushed, embarrassed. My heart was still pounding like crazy in my chest. What was going on with me?

You're in love. You'll be married to the man of your dreams, your one and only, the love of your life. Your soulmate. Your miracle ghost boy.

You'll finally be his wife. You'll be Mrs. Halloway. That's what's going on, a tiny voice in my head told me.

Oh. So that's what's happening.

I'm happy.

Undeniably, incredibly, breathtakingly happy.

My eyes met his, which shone with an unmeasurable happiness as well. And then he closed the remaining inches between us and gave his future wife her first kiss.

Chapter Thirty-Five

Honeymooning

I woke up early the next morning and stared at the white ceiling above me in blissful joy.

I had the oddest of illnesses. I had a permanent smile plastered on my face and it wouldn't go away, no matter how hard I tried to make it. The cause: extreme happiness. It was a most vexing condition. A silly smile was stuck to my lips as if glued there. I must have looked like a loony. A very, *very* happy loony.

I yawned and stretched, looking at the breathtakingly gorgeous man sleeping peacefully by my side, belly down on the mattress, one arm sneaking under his pillow. A hint of a smile was creeping to the corners of his lips even though he was deep in sleep. His smooth back was laid bare for me to admire, the sheets only covering a small part of him. I would never get used to how beautiful this man was.

Not man, *my husband*. I have a *husband* now.

In the eyes of the world there were some papers still to be signed, but in our hearts we were already husband and wife. I extended my hand and surveyed my wedding ring in the light of the day. The white gold ring looked even more beautiful in daylight.

God, I was a *wife* now. The word made me feel strange inside, but so excited at the same time.

I shuffled slowly out of bed and went to stand by the window, surveying the view outside. Even though I had only slept for a few hours, I had woken up filled with energy. I grabbed a light-yellow summer dress that was tossed over one chair and pulled it on, deciding to go downstairs for an early breakfast. I could prepare a tray of food and bring Tristan his breakfast in bed.

I'll bring breakfast in bed to my *husband*, I thought, smiling to myself.

I was gathering a breakfast tray when Harry and Robin bustled inside, all merry and chirpy, with identical goofy grins on their faces.

"Hey, guys! You are up pretty early," I exclaimed, and noticed their hands clasped together as they headed for the table.

"Up? We're just getting back from our date, dude!" Harry said, sitting on a stool at my side and taking a piece of toast from my tray.

"You're *still* on your date?" I asked, surprised.

"She's like that energized bunny rabbit advert," Harry said, resting his head sleepily on the table. "You won't believe half of the stuff we've done since we left yesterday … She never gets tired!" he whined, but there was a smile in his voice.

"I told you to drink that coffee in the middle of the night," she jeered at him.

"I'm never making that mistake again. Next date I'll gulp down as much coffee as I possibly can," he promised, yawning, his blond hair falling over his face in disarray.

"Next date, huh?" I teased, wiggling my eyebrows suggestively at Robin, who giggled a little and nodded, smiling happily at the news.

"I might need some time to recover from this first date, though," Harry mumbled, crossing his arms over the table and resting his head on them. He looked like he was ready to sleep right there and then. "Just wake me up in a couple of days and we can go on our second date," he grumbled sleepily, and closed his eyes.

Robin chuckled and silently mouthed "best date of my life" to me. I beamed, happy for her. They deserved this awesome date. They deserved to be happy.

"Oh, hey, speaking of happy, Robin. I need to ask you this big favor," I began. "I need you to let Harry stay at your house for a couple of days."

"Sure, he can stay. There are a lot of empty guest rooms there," Robin said, and looked quizzically at me, not understanding why I would toss Harry out in such an outrageous way.

"I want to have some privacy in the house with Tristan," I explained.

Harry's head snapped up and he stared at me with wide eyes. "Oh, *right*! Tristan. I forgot all about him. You and lover boy want the house all to themselves, you naughty thing you," he sniggered teasingly. "I take it you two finally worked things out, then?"

"I guess you might say that," I hinted mischeviously, twirling my wedding ring underneath the table. "But you have to ask him about it." I didn't want to drop the bomb yet; I was waiting for Tristan to wake up before breaking the news.

"Where is he?" Harry asked, bouncing on his seat, all sleepiness forgotten now.

"Sleeping upstairs."

"I'll wake him up; I need to hear this from him!" Harry exclaimed, already darting out of the kitchen and running upstairs, shouting as loud and obnoxiously as he possibly could. If I knew Harry's tactics well – and I'm positively sure that I did – he was probably going to bounce on the bed until Tristan gave in and woke up.

"Oh, so do I finally get to meet the famous and mysterious boyfriend after all?" Robin teased, wiggling her eyebrows at me.

"He's not my boyfriend any more," I mumbled, glancing down at my toast with my best poker face. She frowned, not understanding what was happening.

After a couple of minutes, during which Robin tried desperately to catch my eye so she could read what was going on, we heard Tristan's and Harry's voices coming from the living room, chatting happily about something. Then they wandered into the kitchen. Tristan was wearing sweatpants, but he was shirtless and barefoot. His hair was a bit of a mess, but not as much as usual as it was really short now.

"Oh, hey." Tristan halted, a little surprised by Robin's presence in the kitchen. "Sorry, Harry didn't tell me we had company ..." he apologized, passing a hand through his hair, embarrassed at his lack of clothing and general state of dishevelment.

"It's ... fine," Robin squeaked, wriggling on her seat, her eyes bugging out of her sockets as she stared at Tristan's bare chest. I couldn't blame her for staring; a half-naked Tristan had that effect on most people.

I chuckled and turned to Tristan. His attention was fixed only on me as he leaned in to give me a light peck on the lips.

"Morning, sweetheart," he murmured in a low, raspy morning voice. "Did you tell Harry?"

I shook my head, giggling. "I didn't. I thought you'd want us to do it together."

Harry was watching us with a curious frown, and was about to ask what that was all about, when I chipped in, grinning like a mad woman. "So, Tristan, this is Robin. She's an old friend of Tiffany's and we've been hanging out these past weeks. Robin, this is Tristan," I introduced. "My fiancé."

Both Harry's and Robin's eyebrows shot up.

"Are you saying …" Harry began, stunned.

"Yep," I replied, wiggling my ringed finger.

"You did not!" He gasped in awe.

"We sure did," Tristan said, sitting on my stool and putting me on his lap, wrapping his arms around me. Harry's eyes wandered to Tristan's ringed finger as he searched for confirmation. "We still need to sign the legal papers, but it's official in our hearts. And we have the rings on already to prove we're very serious about it."

"Wow, I can't believe it. This is epic news!" Harry exclaimed. "From getting back together to getting married … You guys are fast!" he said, and then rushed over to us. "*Ohmygod.* Congratulations to the soon to be officially married couple, then," he said, giving us both a big squeezing hug.

"Thanks, Harry," I said, grinning happily.

"How did you trick her into doing this, man?" Harry asked, bewildered. He knew of my aversion to marriage and how I used to fight against it.

"Actually, she was the one who asked me." Tristan chuckled behind me.

"Hey!" I scoffed, smiling, jabbing him lightly in the ribs. "You sold me the idea, mister. Don't come complaining to me now!"

"That's true." He smiled, leaning his chin on my shoulder. "It turns out she was really against the ceremony, but not marriage per se, so we skipped the festivities and got the vows and rings exchanged last night, just the two of us. Pretty swell, isn't it?" Tristan tended to slip into his old-fashioned slang when he got too excited about something.

I laughed and leaned against his broad chest. "So, Harry, you have to pack up and leave so we can start honeymooning in here," I told him.

Harry looked at us, startled. "What? Leave? But aren't we telling people about your engagement? I wanna hear what you guys are going to say to everyone!" he whined.

"Harry, we'll tell people later ... like, when we get back home. I don't want to deal with people right now. In about five minutes I'll be locking the front doors and will be jumping his bones. So you have five minutes to pack," I warned him, as Tristan started laying light kisses on my neck, tightening his arms around me.

Harry widened his eyes. "Oh, dear God! They are not kidding. I really have only five minutes. Gah!" he shouted, and ran out of the kitchen in a hurry to get his things from his room.

Tristan stopped kissing my neck and watched as Harry ran, a chuckle rumbling in his throat.

"Is it really okay for you to take Harry in for a couple days, Robin?" I asked.

"It's fine." She shrugged. "You two can honeymoon freely, don't worry. I'll keep him busy."

"I'll bet you will," I teased, raising my eyebrows at her.

She blushed vividly, clearly not meaning what I had implied. "Shut up, your mind is too full of naughty thoughts right now!" she admonished.

Harry burst into the kitchen precisely seven minutes later, a little out of breath and holding a backpack over his shoulder. "Done! We can go now." Robin giggled at his flustering and waved us goodbye before darting out with Harry tugging at her arm. Then we heard Harry's muffled voice coming from the living room, asking if he could sleep in her room, followed by the sound of a smack, then Harry's low voice piping, "I'll take that as a maybe, then . . ." before they disappeared out of earshot.

I laughed then hopped off Tristan's lap. "So, *hubby*" – and I shamelessly giggled at that – "get back to the bedroom now. I was planning on bringing you this awesome breakfast in bed, and I'm sticking to my plan. It is romantic as hell," I told him. "You'll act all surprised and stare lovingly at me in appreciation when I get there, okay? Now, go."

"Such a bossy wife I have . . ." He shook his head, but looked pleased. "All right, *wifey*," he said, and that made me giggle again. "You don't know how amazing it is to be able to call you that." A wide grin spread over his handsome face as he crossed the kitchen and leaned against the doorframe.

"I know." I grinned back. "It's friggin' swell!"

He laughed at my teasing and wandered off to our room. "So I'll wait for you to jump my bones after breakfast, then?" he shouted from the stairs.

"Fine by me, hubby!" I shouted back.

"I'll be waiting, my darling wife!" came his distant reply.

That made me giggle some more.

Tristan and I spent the next few days in my room. Sometimes we would slip downstairs to the kitchen to grab something quick to eat, but we mostly spent all of our time upstairs. Life had never been sweeter and I cherished every single minute of it. It almost felt like this was the happiest I would ever be in my whole life. But as I watched Tristan I knew that thought was just silly, because many more happy days would certainly come.

I tried to memorize all the little details of those days, even the most insignificant parts, like the way the sun hit Tristan's skin as he lay in bed, the beautiful ring of his laughter in my ears, or when his smile reached his gray eyes and made them shine for a fleeting second.

I would always remember the smell of sand and salt that the sea breeze carried inside our room and onto our skin. Even after these times were long gone for us, I would always remember what it felt like to be with Tristan then, the intimacy and the love we had.

I retold Tristan about my experience with Vigil's powers, and everything I had learned from them. I told him what I had gone through: everything I'd felt, all the pain and anger, the heartache and the struggle to come out alive and sane. He held me in his arms and cradled me, wiping away my tears when I told him what had happened in that dark warehouse. It felt like it had been so long ago, almost in another lifetime. I shared everything I could with him and he did the same, telling me of moments when I hadn't been there with him.

Sometimes I felt content just watching him walk around the room; I was always in awe of his beauty and his strength. Other times I woke up in the middle of the night and just watched him sleeping peacefully in my arms. And I knew life couldn't get any better than this.

I kissed him endlessly, until my lips felt raw and swollen. I loved him with a passion bigger than myself and I let him love me back as strongly as I did him. Again and again.

I have never been the type of person who believed in happy endings or the whole "lived happily ever after" deal. Life isn't a fairy tale, and eventually things would go back to normal; this happiness I was feeling would gradually fade away and bad things would happen again.

I also knew I had to fight for my marriage to work, because that's how you keep the good things in life, through hard work and love. I knew Tristan and I would still argue and struggle in the future; things were bound to get rough some time or another, but we would work through any storms that came. Of that, I was certain.

But for now we didn't worry about the future; we focused on enjoying the happiness of the present while we were on this island. We talked for hours, sang together, laughed, loved, cheered and teased each other. Sometimes we would just lie in bed, wrapped only in the soft white sheets, and talk about life and dreams and things that made us happy and passionate.

And then, as all good things in life must surely come to an end, our happy honeymoon was over.

One very early morning, I had this most strange, eerie feeling, as if someone had been watching over me in my sleep, which made me jolt awake with a start.

I peeked through half-open eyelids and saw a blurry

face only a few inches from mine. As my eyes focused, my mind registered the scariest grin I had ever seen, and I jumped back, instantly wide awake in complete shock and horror.

Chapter Thirty-Six

Vows of Love

"Oh God!" I gasped in fear. "M-mother? Is that really you?" I sat straight up and stared at her grinning face.

"Of course, Joey dear. Who else did you think it was?" she said, still with that creepy grin fixed on her face. Then she retreated a few inches and sat calmly on the bed next to me.

"Uh ... what's with the wake-up call from creeper's land?" I asked, dragging the sheets protectively against my chest. The fact that I was kind of naked under there made the situation even more awkward.

"Oh. *You know*."

I watched her smiling crazily and suddenly realized. I mentally cursed Harry and his big, fat, blabbering mouth. She knew about the engagement. "You've come to kill me, haven't you?" I asked weakly.

"Don't be silly, Joey." She tsked me. "I came to congratulate you and my dearest future son-in-law. Now come here and give your old mother a hug," she ordered, opening her arms.

I scooted closer to her and gave her an awkward pat,

still holding the sheets firmly around me. Leaning back, I eyed her with suspicion, ready to flee in case she was about to scalp me for wanting to elope. But she just kept smiling like a lunatic, which, in all frankness, was starting to freak me the hell out.

"So, how about you wake your fiancé so I can give him a hug, too?" she asked, and gave a pointed look beside me towards a still-sleeping Tristan. Maybe she was waiting for him to wake up so she could kill us both at the same time for getting engaged without telling anyone. That sounded like a plan she would make … I gulped hard, my throat suddenly very dry, then turned to poke Tristan in the ribs.

"Tris, you need to wake up now. Like, right frigging now!" I whispered in a strangled voice.

"Humph?" was his muffled reply in the pillow.

"I'm serious, Tris. My mother's here!" I said, poking him more urgently.

"Hmm? She's here in the house?" he asked in a sleepy voice, his eyes still closed as he gradually woke from his slumber.

"No, she is *right here*, in this freaking room, sitting on our bed. In our room. Right at this moment." I gave her a forced smile for appearance's sake.

"What?" he asked, suddenly very alert. He turned to us and when his eyes registered my mother he had almost the same reaction as me. First he gasped a little, frozen in shock, and then he pulled the sheets up to his chest protectively, gulping hard as if he was also waiting for a horrible death at the hands of a raging, disappointed mother.

My mom stood up and calmly walked to his side of the bed, sitting down next to him and extending her arms wide open. "Tristan, dear! Come give me a hug!"

He glanced quickly at me, asking for some reassurance that this wasn't a trick, but I was as clueless as he was. I shrugged at him while he let my mother hug-smother him. The fact that he was also naked under the sheets made the whole thing as awkward as it could be. Number One on the Top Ten Awkward Moments of my life for sure.

"I can't believe this day has finally come!" she said, clasping both hands over his face, her eyes filling up with tears. Then she stood up and patted her clothes, getting very serious. "So, my lovelies ..."

Uh, oh. Here it comes. The part where she murders us. I knew it would come sooner or later. Well, at least we got to have an amazing honeymoon ... I could die a happy woman.

"You two have ten minutes to get dressed and head downstairs; there's *a lot* to be discussed. And I am not joking about the ten minutes; you will regret it dearly if you don't hurry up. I'll be waiting," she said, and walked out of the room.

"Crap," Tristan muttered after a minute of shocked silence. The fact that he was cursing meant we really were royally screwed; Tristan never swore.

"Well, at least it was good while it lasted, right?" I asked, a little uncertainly.

"The clock is ticking, dearies!" Mom shouted from the stairs, making us jump. We scrambled out of bed as fast as lightning, looking for our clothes in complete panic. In about two minutes we were running to the living room to face my mother – or, as I also liked to call her, the Head of the House of Executioners.

We halted when we saw that the living room was crowded with disgruntled Lost Boys, who were shooting us angry death glares.

Seth, Josh and Sammy were huddled together on the couch, arms crossed over their chests and frowns etched on their faces. Harry (the sneaky little squeaking traitor) was sitting on the arm of the couch, dangling his feet and smiling happily. But the most scary thing in the room was the Worthington the Third standing furiously in front of the boys, her eyes shooting bloody daggers at us.

They all had one thing in common. They all looked *very* pissed.

"Ugh. Heeey … guys … and Tiffany …" I squeaked lamely, stepping back and bumping into Tristan, who had already cleverly positioned himself behind me for cover. The coward! Using his own fiancée as a human shield.

"Hello, there, *Gray*," Tiffany greeted me coldly, making me cringe. She only called me Gray when she was really mad at me. She was so going to kill me today. I was genuinely scared, even more so than I had been with my mother, who, I noticed, wasn't anywhere in the room. I guessed that had been her plan all along: to let my friends do the dirty work. She was diabolical, that woman … and a bit lazy, if I may say so.

"So, I hear congratulations are in order." Tiffany broke the cold silence in the room.

"Erm … thanks?" I mumbled in a terrified voice. Yep. Definitely going to die today.

"You know, I knew something was afoot the minute I called Harry, a few days ago. He had a very suspicious, shifty voice. You know the voice he uses when he's trying hard to hide something very, very, important?" Tiffany said, her hands resting defiantly on her hips. "It didn't take long to get him to spill the beans. And what lovely beans those were, let me tell you."

I glanced quickly at Harry, who was still smiling happily at no one in particular. I slumped my shoulders in defeat. I couldn't even be mad at him. I knew how merciless Tiffany's interrogatory tactics were; anyone would have folded to her.

"So let's get down to the business, shall we?" she snapped, making me glance back at her in dread. Tristan's grip on my arms tightened ever so slightly. "This is how this negotiation is going to go. In exchange for *all* our forgiveness, you two are going to agree to do something. There won't be any 'it depends' or 'maybes'. You will agree fully to do what I tell you to," she stated with a steely coldness.

That sounded pretty much like making a deal with the devil – the type you sell your soul to – and there's no turning back after that. I gulped.

"It's a fair request, Gray, to make us forgive you two for leaving us *all* out of this engagement deal. This is your chance to rectify things with your band-mates and best friends, who've stood by you for so long, and were there for you always," she said, motioning to the boys sitting on the couch, who nodded righteously back at us. "Just this one small thing to set things right with them and with me, your faithful, loyal, best friend, and with your poor old mother, who had to hear the news that her only daughter had gotten engaged without telling her."

"All right, Tiff! Fine, we agree. You can quit the guilt trip!" I threw my hands in the air. "What is it? You want us to be your slaves, is that it? To go shopping with you every single time you call? I'll do anything you want, okay?" I shivered at the thought of all the shopping I was doomed to do from now on. Oh, dear Lord, have mercy on my poor soul.

Tiffany smiled triumphantly and turned to the boys, who were all grinning from ear to ear. "Told you I was going to make her do this," she said smugly.

They all cheered and high-fived each other, upset frowns all gone from their faces. Tiffany watched Tristan and me with a weird glint in her eyes.

"What? *What?* What's going on?" I asked, confused by all the cheer. I had turned my empathy-sight off since I had learned how to. Apparently I was quite clueless and stupid without it ...

"Okay! All right people, settle down. There's a lot to be done before sundown, so I need you all to be at your best so we can pull this off," Tiffany bellowed to the rumpus in the room.

"Pull what off? What's happening at sundown?" I asked in a strangled voice.

"We are all going to be celebrating your engagement at sunset, that's what's happening!" she explained with a grin. "I hear you will sign the legal papers when you get back home to make this marriage official without having a proper ceremony, so this can be your wedding celebration, too! I'm giving you a party today to commemorate the moment with your best friends and family, like a decent, civilized couple should do. That's what I want. And you have agreed. *Ta-da!*" she finished with a theatrical flourish of hands.

I gaped at her like a fish. I mean, *seriously?* Had she just guilt-tripped me into getting married here? I waved my hands frantically in the air. I didn't want any priests and traditional, lame ceremonies. We had exchanged vows, rings, and as soon as we got back home, we were heading for the courthouse and that was it! "Oh, no! I'm sorry, Tiff, but I'm not doing this!"

"I'm sorry, Joey, but it's not up to you any more. You have agreed. It's a done deal. You can quit your whining and just be there at sunset. You don't even need to do anything; leave it all to me and your mother; we have it all covered," she said matter-of-factly, already dialing on her phone.

"What? My mother was in on this all along? And what do you mean you've got it all covered? How could you know I'd agree to all of this?" I asked, bewildered, as the boys bustled around Tristan to congratulate him.

"Seriously, Joey, when don't I ever have things the way I want? It's like you don't know me at all ..." She tsked disapprovingly. "I have been planning your wedding since the day you brought Tristan back to life – the second time around, anyway – remember? I knew it was only a matter of time before you tied the knot ... You took an awfully long time alas, but the time has finally come. You won't leave me out of the most amazing moment of your life, you hear? And now I have a wedding to plan, so if you don't mind, go help your mother with the luggage," she ordered, at the same time as my mother entered through the front doors with a group of people trailing after her: Amanda, Robin, Jamie and Becca.

Flabbergasted, I turned to Tristan, who raised his hands in surrender. "Don't look at me like that, I didn't know about any of this! I'll do anything you want me to, Buttons. It's your decision," he said, and turned to my mother. "Rose, let me help you with that." He ran to help with the suitcases she was carrying.

She patted his cheeks lovingly and gave him another hug. Seth, Sam and Josh came to huddle around me then, giving me a rib-crushing group hug, and then Harry ran and jumped on top of us all, starting a pile-on celebration huddle. My mother was ordering a bunch of people I'd never met to put endless streams of bags and boxes inside the house, and Tiffany was on her phone giving instructions about the festivities in her customary bossy tone. I was so stunned by the hurricane of congratulations and the striking turn of events that I couldn't even think properly.

The room was in uproar.

It was insane.

I felt Tristan grabbing my hand and pulling me softly to the side. "Hey, are you okay?" he asked, clasping his hands tenderly around my face. "Look, you don't have to do anything you don't want to, Joey, but …" – he held up a finger to make me wait for him to complete his thought – "these are our closest friends and family, and they want to celebrate our union, that's all. They are happy for us, and they want to share this moment with us, to make it memorable, to make it even more special. It's not a ceremony, it's a celebration. You have nothing to worry about."

"Okay. I guess you're right."

Tristan smiled warmly and leaned in, giving me a soft kiss. "All right, let's do this!"

"No."

"You don't like it?" Tiffany asked, a hint of disbelief in her voice as she looked at the dress she had designed for me a long time ago, having kept it a secret all this time.

"No. I don't like it," I said firmly, which made her pout in disappointment. "I simply *adore* it! It is the most magnificent dress I have ever seen in my whole life."

"Really?" she squealed, her voice hitting an ultra-high pitch in excitement.

I looked at the dress I was wearing. It was truly the most amazing thing I'd ever seen. How could I refuse to wear this? Only if I were brain-impaired or plain crazy.

All that was left for Tiffany to do was to fix my dress. I had gained a few extra pounds so Tiffany was making a couple of adjustments.

It was so beautiful I almost cried, and the ceremony hadn't even started yet. I was going to be a mess by the end of the day!

The fabric of the dress was a gorgeous, soft, creamy satin with white lace at the top and part of the back. It was designed in the Fifties fashion in homage to Tristan and the time he grew up in. He was going to adore this! It had a vintage look: the lace was extraordinary and the satin and gauze of the skirt made it look ethereal and magical. It was a thing of beauty. Tiffany was right, it was impossible not to love it!

I glanced at my reflection one last time.

My hair was also styled in a Fifties hairdo, and I was wearing stunning teardrop pearl earrings. The only make-up I had on was a very dark ruby lipstick and a light, pearly cream eyeshadow. Robin, Amanda and Becca were watching me with huge grins on their faces. They were already dressed in their bridesmaids gowns and looked absolutely lovely.

I had forbidden my mom to be in the room because I knew that the waterworks would be relentless, so I asked her to stay with Tristan and calm his jittery nerves. She caved after I'd told her she was like a mother to him as well. A low blow, I knew, but I needed her away for the dress fitting. If I saw even a glimpse of her tears I'd lose all my cool and bawl like a baby, which I was trying to avoid at all costs.

"Let's go, Joey. Your handsome groom awaits. He's so gorgeous in his suit, you'll want to cry at the sight of him!" Tiffany squealed with a giggle.

Tiffany had arranged to close a private plaza on the island for the wedding. It was only a couple of blocks away from her house. The small plaza was by a steep cliff which had an extraordinary view of the sea. Tiffany had had the whole place decorated with paper ball lanterns, and thousands of origami silver stars and twinking lights were hanging in lines over the walkways surrounding the plaza. The stars had been made for a festival on the island a few months ago, and Tiffany had borrowed them as an improvised decoration. The place looked beautiful, with a hint of magic glinting off each silver paper star.

"I still can't believe you took care of all this in just one day, Tiff!" I exclaimed, truly amazed as we walked out.

"I know. I rock." She beamed proudly at me. "Anything for my best girl friend!"

She had been busy all day long, taking care of things, with my mother and the girls helping out. The decorations had been quickly arranged, food and drinks were set, the flowers, the suits and dresses, everything had been taken care of insanely fast.

I walked all the way to the front of the house with my girls dutifully escorting me by my side. My mom was waiting by the front doors, hoping to get a first look at me before everybody else did. She turned when she noticed us approach and gasped out loud, her hand flying to cover her beating heart. "Oh, my goodness . . ." she whispered, shell-shocked. "You look like an angel," she said, tears falling quickly down her face. "I can't believe my baby girl is getting married!"

"MOM!" I admonished, my eyes already filling up as well. I knew I wouldn't be able to hold it in if I saw her crying. Damn it! "It's not even the real thing; we're making it official when we get back home! Stop making me cry; I'm going to be all puffy and red-eyed now!" I complained, sniffing loudly.

"I'm sorry! *I'm sorry!*" She chuckled, giving me a tight hug. "Come on, your man is getting anxious. It's so cute seeing him so flustered and handsome waiting for you up there!"

I shook my head in dismay. Although, I had to confess, I was also feeling really anxious myself, my stomach filling up with a horde of overexcited butterflies.

We walked quickly through cobblestoned streets until we entered an open area that was encircled by a stone railing, with the sea view in the distance. There were white flowers wound all through the railing, giving an air of festivity to the place. Everybody was already there, talking animatedly, dressed up in suits and lovely dresses.

Tiffany knew of my aversion to traditional ceremonies, so she had agreed to cut out the priest from the proceedings and arrange something more modern, with my Lost Boys in charge of the vows exchange, and I was about to rule out the walking down the aisle routine.

I swept my gaze through the small gathering of friends, searching for my Lost Boys. I knew Tristan was going to be amongst them, for sure. Soon I spotted Josh, Sammy and Harry talking in a small circle with Seth in front of them.

And then I saw Tristan right next to Seth, at the same time he saw me. All the others had stopped talking and turned to watch me arrive.

Tristan was wearing a light-gray suit over a gray vest and tie which matched the suit perfectly. But my eyes didn't linger so much on his clothes; my eyes were drawn irrevocably towards his handsome face. He looked breathtakingly beautiful. I should have listened to Tiffany's warning; the sight of him was indeed enough to make me want to cry.

But what made my heart speed up the most was the smoldering look in his mercury eyes. They flared with shocking intensity, boring into me and making me feel like there was nobody else in the entire world he thought was worth looking at but me.

Tristan looked like he was shellshocked as well. He lost his balance for a second at my arrival, and Seth caught him quickly by the arm, laughing softly. I guess he was as stunned by the sight of me as I was by him.

A smile spread over my lips and I ran towards him, not even bothering to stop and greet anyone in my rush to get to him. He remained stock still as I wrapped my arms around his neck and stood on tiptoe to kiss him. It took him a few seconds to recover and envelop me in his arms, kissing me softly back. It was just a sweet, quick kiss, but filled with so many unspoken emotions.

I leaned away and smiled, watching his dazed expression. "You look so handsome!" I murmured in awe.

"I-I-I ..." he stammered, at a loss for words.

Seth chuckled by our side. "He means to tell you that you are the most beautiful thing he has ever seen in his entire life, but you need to give him some time to recover so he can form coherent thoughts and be able to properly speak again."

Tristan just nodded, confirming Seth's statement.

I laughed and turned around to watch a sea of staring eyes looking expectantly at us. "Oh, sorry, guys! We're not doing the lame, traditional walk-up-the-aisle thing. This is my new way to do this," I exclaimed. "My boys! Come give me a hug!" I ordered, turning to face Sam, Josh, Harry and Seth happily. They huddled around, giving me a massive group hug. "Come on, let's greet our friends," I told Tristan, grabbing his hand and heading for the guests.

We greeted everyone, hugging and thanking them for being here to share the day with us. Sometimes I'd catch Tristan giving me sly, timid glances, as if he was still a little overwhelmed by the way I looked.

The ceremony was unique, very untraditional and truly beautiful. I wouldn't have changed a thing. It was perfect in every word, every tear, every heart-touching confession. The boys had taken the priest's position, standing between me and Tristan, and each of them took turns with a beautiful speech prepared especially for us. They retold stories, moments and memories they had lived with us.

Sam remembered our times at boarding school, the egg-smashing prank that brought the band together for the first time, our pile-up celebrations and late-night band practices. Seth took our hands in his and made a speech about how they were proud to see that our love always remained strong, no matter how difficult our struggles were. And that we truly were his brother and sister in his heart. That made me cry unbelievably hard, and Tristan got a bit teary as well.

At Harrys's turn he confessed he had never believed in true love and "all that soulmates jazz" until he got to see

Tristan and I together. Josh talked about all our amazing times together: our moments shared in the tour bus, at concerts and onstage, the birthday parties, Christmases, New Years and all the celebrations we'd shared, and how lucky he was to have our friendship.

Tristan turned and took my hands in his after the boys had finished their speeches.

He told me in a shaky voice how much he loved me. That I was right when I said our love was stronger than anything. It was stronger than life, and death, he had told me with watery eyes.

That I'd made him feel alive since the first moment he laid eyes on me, so long ago.

That I was the only one who was able to see his soul when no one else could.

That he had been waiting for me his whole life.

I started crying all over again as he continued with his vows.

He told me that I was the only one who could see him for who he truly was, and accept him fully.

That I made him stronger, brighter, happier than ever before.

That I was the joy in his heart; his rising star.

That he would always be by my side, and that he would always love me. No matter what.

Until the very end and from the start.

I was sobbing so hard I could barely speak. I couldn't think of a single word to say to him; too many emotions churned inside, making me tongue-tied.

So I did the same thing I had done a long time ago, when we were still at school and he confessed he loved me, truly loved me, right in Sagan's backyard, beneath a silver moon.

I put my hand over his chest and tried to imprint into his heart all that I was feeling. His eyes widened in surprise as he took it all in, and he nodded quietly, holding his hand over mine, overwhelmed. He had felt everything. I could see all the emotions in his teary eyes.

He held my shaking hands so he could put the ring (once again) on my finger. It comforted me slightly to see he was shaking as much as I was.

Everybody cheered loudly when we kissed, and then they all screamed *'Jostan!'* at the top of their lungs, making me laugh. It was their nickname for me and Tristan; our honorary couple title.

It was time for some happy celebration then, and hopefully, there would be no more tears for me.

Chapter Thirty-Seven

Never-Ending Love

"Joey!" Robin called, skipping in my direction.

The party had been going for a couple of hours now, and everybody seemed to be having a lot of fun. I'd never seen Tristan so happy in his life. It warmed my heart seeing him like that.

"You just missed your friend. She asked me to deliver this to you," Robin said, showing me two boxes wrapped in parched black papers. "She was running late for an appointment and had to leave."

"A friend?" I asked, picking up the boxes.

"She said her name was Sky."

I glanced down at the two packages in surprise. The wrapping looked old. No. *More* than old, it looked ancient. For Sky, this might well literally be the case.

One of the boxes was rectangular and had Tristan's name scribbled on it in silver ink, and the other was really small and had my name on it.

"Thanks, Robin. Could you do me a huge favor and get Tristan to come over?" I asked, my eyes never leaving the gifts in my hands. They felt heavy, and filled with an air of importance. It was not every day you got presents from Death herself.

I sat on a stone bench, a little away from the commotion of the party, and unwrapped mine. A small box of corroded metal glinted eerily as I opened it to see a big coin made of hollow glass nestled neatly inside on a velvety black cushion.

I took the coin carefully and twirled it around my fingers. There was golden sand filling the interior. The sand sparkled and floated like it was weightless. It was beautiful and so delicate.

On a piece of yellowed paper stuck at the top of the box a note was written in beautiful cursive calligraphy:

A free pass to my home, so you can visit me any time you want. Sky.

Tristan sat down by my side, making me jump. "Robin said you wanted to talk to me?" he asked,.

"Yeah … Sky just left us these gifts," I said, showing him my glass coin. "This is yours." I handed him the larger box.

He eyed it curiously and opened the wrapping. Inside was a very ancient wooden box, and when he opened the lid, we saw a beautiful crystal hourglass laid inside, but in his the sand was translucent and transparent at the bottom.

"This feels really valuable. As in, *priceless*," he murmured in a low voice "Do you know what it is for?"

"Look at your note." I pointed at the yellow parchment stuck to the top of the box, just like mine had been.

He took it and read out loud:

For a moment with your loved ones long gone.
Spend them wisely. Sky.

And then he whispered, "Wow." This is ... *amazing*." He gaped and then turned to look at me. "What does yours do?"

"Free pass to her home," I explained, twirling the coin slowly between my fingers.

He frowned, looking puzzled. "She has a *home*?"

"I suppose she does," I said, scrunching up my nose in deep thought. A fleeting memory of a glass palace flashed in my mind. Had I dreamed about this? It felt like such a blurry, unreal vision, but also all too familiar somehow ...

"Well, I think we should put these in a very safe place," Tristan said, closing his box carefully.

"Agreed. I'll put them both in the safe in our room," I said, and took his box.

"Do you want me to go with you ...?" Tristan asked.

"Nah, go ahead and party with the boys. I'll put them in the safe and be right back," I said, giving him a quick kiss and walking back towards the house.

After I had locked up our unworldly gifts safely, I wandered outside to the balcony to survey the party which was happening a little further down the hill.

I leaned over the railing and glanced down; my eyes glanced at the black marking on my wrist. I instantly thought of Vigil.

It would be amazing if he could be here today. I had my boys present, all my friends, my mom; even Sky had surprisingly showed up for the event. I wondered if Vigil was still too far away; or if I dared to call him, would he be able to come right away?

I pressed my fingers over my tattoo and thought of him.

It couldn't hurt to try, right? It'd really mean a lot to me if he could be here, even if it was for only a brief moment.

A smile spread over my lips when my wrist started to throb with pain. I turned around to see Vigil standing a few feet away, dressed as usual in his formal gray clothes. He still looked older, just like he had in the last dream, his shoulders larger, his chest stronger. He looked a little distressed, but still managed to smile affectionately at me.

"Vigil! I can't believe you came," I exclaimed, running to give him a big hug. "I'm so happy you're here!"

"Of course I came. When have I not?" he said with a chuckle.

"I thought you wouldn't because you'd be so busy dealing with the rest of the Gray Hooded Ones," I explained. I was particularly jittery as I knew he had broken some serious rules because of me. "Is everything okay?"

He gave a strained smile. "Work problems are resolved."

"Are you all right?" I asked, cupping his face in my hands.

"Y-yes. Everything is fine," he said, slightly uncomfortable at my closeness and my affectionate gesture.

"What happened, Vigil? Did you explain to them what happened? Did everything work out fine?"

He surveyed the view in silence for a while, and when he spoke again, his voice was nervous. "I sort of ... *retired* from work," he finally confessed.

"Did they force you to do it? Because of the power switch accident and the warehouse ..." I trailed off, unable to dwell too much on that last memory.

"No. It was not forced. I had to discuss what happened at the warehouse. Complete annihilation is something of a big deal for us, so I had no other choice but to report it.

And I knew the outcome would be severe punishment," he told me, and I flinched with guilt. I'd known he would be in trouble because of me, but it stung me to hear it confirmed.

"Oh, God, Vigil. I'm so sorry! It's all my fault—" I began, but he interrupted.

"It was *not* your fault. It was entirely my decision and I do not regret a second of it," he said firmly, his tone harsh. "Normally, I would take whatever punishment they think fair, but I have had this idea brewing inside my mind for a while." His voice softened as he continued, "I did not know how I was going to make them all agree to this, though. It had been only possible to put it into motion after this latest incident."

"What idea did you have? What did you want them to agree to?"

"I wanted out. That brief time I spent as a human in our power switch was a mind-opening experience for me. When I got my powers back, I no longer wished to bear the Gray Hood. I no longer wanted the title and the responsibilities it held," he stated. "But how could I make them release me from my duties as a Gray Hood Bearer? None of us has ever wished for this before."

"What did you do to make them agree?" I asked with wide eyes.

"When the punishment was being discussed, I subtly implied that it should be exactly what I wanted, for them to dismiss me from my duty and strip me of my cloak. I tricked them, made them think that taking my job away would be a fair punishment. There has never been anyone who ever wanted to 'quit' before."

"And they agreed?" I asked, surprised.

"Not at first. They thought it was too drastic a

punishment, to take away my purpose in life like that. They did not know I've already found a new purpose. I had to steer them in the direction I wanted, make them think I was being honorable for taking this decision and that it was a fair result of my actions. I made them agree.

"I manipulated them and lied. I am no longer one of them. I wasn't even before they agreed," he said in a low voice, his tone mixed with shame, excitement, fear and a hint of vulnerability as well.

"Does that mean you're human now?"

"No, it does not. But close enough … the closest I could ever get, I suppose," he explained with a soft smile. "I do not have the Gray Hood powers, but I am still of their race, and we have a magic of our own. And I still have Death's gift bestowed on me, which makes me far from powerless. But I am, however, officially and fully excused from my duties as a Gray Hooded One from now on."

"And let me guess, you've decided to spend your retirement days on this lovely little planet called Earth, am I correct?" I asked, grinning widely and squeezing his hand eagerly.

"Indeed I have." He smiled back. "So, are you going to tell me why you are dressed like this?" Vigil asked, changing the subject.

"Oh, today is my wedding day!" I exclaimed happily. "And this is my wedding dress," I added, beaming proudly.

"Wedding? Is it a celebration of sorts?" he asked, puzzled.

"Oh, Jeez, Vig. You still have so much to catch up on about human habits!" I huffed at his clueless face. "Yes, it's a ceremony we humans have to celebrate the union of two people who love each other and want to spend their lives together," I explained. "So we have this party and call all our friends to commemorate the moment with us. That's why I called. You are a special friend and I wanted you to be here with us."

"Oh, I see. It makes sense. Tristan is your soulmate, after all. It is inevitable that you want to be with him," he stated matter-of-factly.

People had often spoken that line during the years I'd known Tristan, and sure, it sounded romantic, but to be honest, I wasn't much into this fairy-tale nonsense. Soulmates and happily-ever-afters and things like that just didn't exist.

"Come on, you say it as if you really believe in this, like it's a real thing." I laughed at him.

"It is very real. How could you not believe in it?" he said, puzzled.

"Are you saying that Tristan is the other half of me? The piece that is missing to make me whole?" I said, playfully.

He shook his head. "Actually no. That is not how it works. To explain about soulmates, I first need to explain about auras," he said, thoughtfully. "Every person has a unique aura, like a signature code built in each soul. And each aura 'vibrates' on different frequencies. So, sometimes there are auras that connect with your own wave signals. That happens when you find true friends or kindred spirits. Your auras vibrate in similar ways. Your boys all have connecting auras, as do you," he explained.

Okay. That actually made a lot of sense and explained quite a bit.

"But soulmates are not complementary or co-dependent, as you have put it. Your auras are fully functional and complete on their own; there is no missing piece at all. They work completely fine alone. But when you are together, when you find a soulmate, you will have the highest points of connection ever made, and your auras connect in a way that they normally don't with others. It is a deeper connection, with a far more finely balanced tune. The frequency then amplifies, intensifies. In other words, the connection makes them both better, stronger, brighter. You become more when you are with your soulmate; you are a better version of all the things that you already are."

He paused and watched my awed expression. "A-and Tristan is really ..." I trailed off.

He watched me intently before answering me. "It is blindingly bright when you two are together. Like your souls are exploding in continuous blasts of pure energy." Then he leaned over and grazed his fingers lightly over my cheek. "You are greater when he is at your side, and so is he when you are at his.

"Your human wedding tradition is probably a celebration of that," he mused. "Then I am very honored to be present on your wedding day, Joe Gray." He bowed respectfully, one of his hands still holding mine so I wouldn't feel any pain.

"Thank you for coming, Vigil," I said in a shaky voice, giving him another tight hug.

"It is my pleasure. Congratulations on your wedding, Joey," he said, before stepping aside. "I must leave now, there are some things I still need to do for my transition to your world to be complete, but we will see each other again soon."

He nodded gratefully again and bowed one last time before disappearing into thin air.

*

"You look so handsome in your fancy suits," I exclaimed, walking towards Harry, Sam, Seth and Josh, a hand fluttering over my chest appreciatively after I left the balcony where I'd met Vigil and went back to the party. The boys were all wearing dark-gray suits with gray shirts underneath, and a different color tie each. I hadn't had the opportunity to properly gush over how beautiful they all were until now.

A slow song started playing and Josh extended his hand to me. "Okay, so, I'll take this dance with her, if you all don't mind," he informed the boys as he took my hand, directing us firmly to the center of the plaza.

"You look like a fairy-tale princess," he complimented. "I've never danced with a princess-looking girl before … it's a bit thrilling," he reflected, mostly to himself, with a goofy smile.

"Stop being silly. I ain't no princess, boy," I teased him in a mocking tone.

"Twirl?" he suggested, already stepping away and twirling me to the rhythm of the music. He wrapped his arm around my waist again as we continued dancing across the stone floor.

I was glad I had discarded the high heels. My dress was very long and covered my feet, and no one could see I had no shoes on. Tiffany would never find them under my bed, which meant I got to walk around barefoot, unworried and pain-free the whole day.

Sam suddenly cut in on our dance. "*Excuse me*, but it's my turn to dance with her now. Scoot away." Josh made a funny face at him and walked away shaking his head in amusement. Sam could be so silly.

He grinned like the daft fool that he was, and twirled me around. "So, you are aware that you need to have a little *talk* with Amanda and tell her to drop the nagging about wanting to get married too, right?" he asked in a slightly worried tone.

I laughed loudly at his scared face. "All girls go into marriage-nagging mode at weddings, Sammy. Suck it up and take it like a man. It will be over by the end of the day, don't worry."

"Oh, really? I didn't know that. Huh," he mused thought-fully. "You and Amanda look really gorgeous today," I remarked.

"It's easy for Amanda. She's beautiful in everything. I, on the other hand, actually had to put a lot of effort in looking this awesometastic today!" he said, giving me a cheesy grin, and then Harry was tapping him on the shoulder, jumping up and down to get our attention.

"Hey, let's trade!" Harry suggested, handing a cheerful Robin to Sam while he swiftly manoeuvered in between us to have his turn dancing with me. "I never got to thank you for introducing Robin to me, by the way. She is truly amazing, Joey."

I smiled and he leaned closer, resting his chin on my shoulder and sighing quietly while we danced. "You're welcome, Harry. I knew you'd like her."

"Maybe some day I'll love her as much as I love you," he said, quietly into my ear.

I almost skipped a step. "Harry ..." I hesitated, slowing down our dance.

He leaned back to look me in the eyes. "What?" he asked, blinking curiously at me.

"I-I thought ... we talked about this ..." I tried to find the right words so I wouldn't make him feel bad, but I didn't know where to begin.

His face softened when he recognized my worried

hesitance, and he smiled a little. "I know," he said. "But I really do love you, Joe. You're my best friend. You don't know how happy I am for you and Tristan. Seeing you two so happy like this makes *me* so happy," he confessed, with genuine honesty flashing in his green eyes.

"Really?" I said quietly.

He paused and looked intently at me, brushing his hand softly against my face. "Really, Joey." He spoke firmly. "I was so ecstatic when you told me the news; I've always known you two belonged together. And I wanted you two to celebrate this moment with us, you know? Why do you think I ratted you out to Tiffany in the first place?"

I glanced at him, grateful for his honesty and for speaking what was truly in his heart. Along with Vigil, Harry was the only person that had never, ever lied to me. Even if the truth was painful or embarrassing for him, he'd always speak his mind. I was so lucky to have him in my life, to have him as my true friend.

I hugged him tightly, burying my face in his neck. He hugged me back as tightly as I had him, and we stood like that, hugging each other in silence while the music played in the background.

"Thank you for making this day happen," I said quietly. "This is the most perfect day of my life."

"You're welcome. You deserve it, Joey," he said, with a smile in his voice.

Tristan walked up to us then and it was his turn now to interrupt the dance. "May I have a dance with my wife?" he asked, with a glint in his silver eyes.

"Why of course, dear sir." Harry faked graveness. "Mrs. Halloway, 'twas a pleasure!" He took a step back and tilted his imaginary hat before leaving us to dance alone.

Tristan turned to me with a gentle smile, his gray eyes twinkling as he looked down at me. "Have I told you already how beautiful you look today?" he asked softly, as he put one hand on my waist and pulled me closer to him, his amazing scent enveloping me as I pressed against him. Then he dipped his head and gave me a soft kiss on the lips.

"This dress makes you look even more magical than you already are," he said, and leaned close to whisper softly in my ear, "But I have to confess that although it is really a lovely dress, I can't wait to take it off you tonight."

Okay. Blushing like a blooming ripe tomato now. I was so glad he couldn't see my face. Just to be sure, I rested my head on his chest to avoid making eye contact, and continued dancing, but he knew what I was trying to hide and I could feel him shaking a little with laughter. He passed his fingers softly over my hair in gentle strokes as we swayed to the slow music.

"I wish we could stay dancing like this for ever." I sighed in his arms, content to listen the amazing sound of his heart beating. "I wish you could feel how happy I am right now."

"I can," he murmured, his voice wavering with emotion as he tightened his grip around me. "I'll remember this day always."

I smiled and snuggled against his chest, while everyone around the plaza looked at the two of us dancing in the middle. My mom was wiping a few tears from the corners of her eyes, and I saw the smiling faces of my boys, and Tiffany, Amanda, Becca and all of our friends as they watched us as we danced.

I will always remember the overwhelming happiness I felt that day. For as long as I live and even after that. A love larger than life to remember.

I closed my eyes and everybody faded out, leaving only Tristan's warm presence pressed against me, his arms enveloping me in a treasured embrace. It was only him and me dancing now, and that was all that mattered. A lovely ghost boy dancing with his witchy girl.

Who was to say it wouldn't last for ever?

It had been a really extraordinary, memorable day, a real-life fairy-tale moment for me – for all of us. It almost felt like we were all under a love spell. It felt surreal and intoxicating, like we were all immersed in a summer dream's haze.

I watched the smiling faces of everybody I loved the most celebrating. The sun was casting its last rays of vibrant, warm colors over the horizon and the night sky descended quickly with a bright moon in its wake.

As the party continued on, I knew people were talking to me, and part of me listened and even responded somehow, but another part of me never stopped searching the plaza for the sterling-gray eyes that I knew shone with the brightest light of them all.

I would find him somewhere, talking, smiling kindly or merely listening to a group of friends chatting, but his eyes would also drift away from time to time, searching for mine. Our gazes would dance endlessly across the square, always longing for the awareness of each other's presence, and then when our gaze finally met, his eyes would shine for a brief second with an emotion so strong it took my breath away, each and every single time.

And I knew my eyes reflected the same emotion I witnessed in his, the same force, and the same undeniable truth.

Never ending love.

Acknowledgements

I dedicate this book first and foremost to the fans and to all the lost girls and lost boys out there.

I dedicate it also to my husband for sharing with me the good moments of my life, for helping me in the hard times and for being by my side always.

I'm brighter, stronger and happier when I'm at his side.

I dedicate this book to my two amazing editors Gillian Green and Emily Yau and I thank them immensely for all their help, encouragement and support.

Keep rocking always.

Lily.